Literary Criticism and Cultural Theory

Edited by
William E. Cain
Wellesley College

A Routledge Series

Literary Criticism and Cultural Theory

William E. Cain, General Editor

The Other Orpheus
A Poetics of Modern Homosexuality
Merrill Cole

The Other Empire
British Romantic Writings about the Ottoman Empire
Filiz Turhan

The "Dangerous" Potential of Reading
Readers and the Negotiation of Power in Nineteenth-Century Narratives
Ana-Isabel Aliaga-Buchenau

Intimate and Authentic Economies
The American Self-Made Man from Douglass to Chaplin
Thomas Nissley

Revised Lives
Walt Whitman and Nineteenth-Century Authorship
William Pannapacker

The *Real* Negro
The Question of Authenticity in Twentieth-Century African American Literature
Shelly Eversley

Labor Pains
Emerson, Hawthorne, and Alcott on Work and the Woman Question
Carolyn R. Maibor

Narrative in the Professional Age
Transatlantic Readings of Harriet Beecher Stowe, George Eliot, and Elizabeth Stuart Phelps
Jennifer Cognard-Black

Fictional Feminism
How American Bestsellers Affect the Movement for Women's Equality
Kim Loudermilk

The Colonizer Abroad
Island Representations in American Prose from Melville to London
Christopher McBride

The Metanarrative of Suspicion in Late Twentieth Century America
Sandra Baringer

Protest and the Body in Melville, Dos Passos, and Hurston
Tom McGlamery

The Architecture of Address
The Monument and Public Speech in American Poetry
Jake Adam York

The Slave in the Swamp
Disrupting the Plantation Narrative
William Tynes Cowan

Reading the Text That Isn't There
Paranoia in the Nineteenth-Century American Novel
Mike Davis

Racial Blasphemies
Religious Irreverence and Race in American Literature
Michael L. Cobb

Ethical Diversions
The Post-Holocaust Narratives of Pynchon, Abish, DeLillo, and Spiegelman
Katalin Orbán

Postmodern Counternarratives
Irony and Audience in the Novels of Paul Auster, Don DeLillo, Charles Johnson, and Tim O'Brien
Christopher Donovan

Postmodern Counternarratives
Irony and Audience in the Novels of Paul Auster, Don DeLillo, Charles Johnson, and Tim O'Brien

Christopher Donovan

Routledge
New York & London

Published in 2005 by
Routledge
270 Madison Ave,
New York NY 10016

Published in Great Britain by
Routledge
2 Park Square,
Milton Park, Abingdon,
Oxon, OX14 4RN

Routledge is an imprint of the Taylor & Francis Group.

Transferred to Digital Printing 2009

Library of Congress Cataloging-in-Publication Data.

Donovan, Christopher, 1971–
Postmodern counternarratives : irony and audience in the novels of Paul Auster, Don DeLillo, Charles Johnson, and Tim O'Brien / by Christopher Donovan.
p. cm. -- (Literary criticism and cultural theory)
Includes bibliographical references and index.
ISBN 0-415-97127-6 (alk. paper)
1. American fiction--20th century--History and criticism. 2. Postmodernism (Literature)--United States. 3. Experimental fiction, American--History and criticism. 4. Johnson, Charles Richard, 1948---Technique. 5. Authors and readers--United States. 6. Auster, Paul, 1947---Technique. 7.O'Brien, Tim, 1946---Technique. 8. DeLillo, Don--Technique. 9. Reader-response criticism. 10. Irony in literature. I. Title. II. Series.

PS374.P64D66 2005
813'.5409113--dc22 2005016636

ISBN10: 0-415-97127-6 (hbk)
ISBN10: 0-415-80344-6 (pbk)

ISBN13: 978-0-415-97127-0 (hbk)
ISBN13: 978-0-415-80344-1 (pbk)

Publisher's Note
The publisher has gone to great lengths to ensure the quality of this reprint but points out that some imperfections in the original may be apparent.

Contents

Preface

This book, which began as a doctoral dissertation submitted in early 1999, attempts to answer the deceptively simple question asked by Paul Auster in the title of one of his essays, "Why Write?" Serious novelists, despite a climate of decentralizing theory, exhausted literary experimentation, and the prospect of a marginal role, at best, in popular consciousness, continue to enter the fray in hopes of carving out their own niche. In the process, some of our most intriguing writers have manifested similarities in their work that suggest a new strain of postmodern fiction (to rely on an overused and under-specific term) clearly distinct from the blueprint drawn up by celebrated forebears like Thomas Pynchon, William Gaddis and John Barth. Of course, the real motivating question in exploring this work was, as in many studies of contemporary fiction, "why read?" and for me the novels of Paul Auster, Don DeLillo, Charles Johnson and Tim O'Brien provide some of the most convincing answers.

The past five years have seen a steady growth in the academic industry around these novelists, especially DeLillo in the wake of *Underworld,* his most significant critical and commercial success to date. There have also been comprehensive, career-spanning studies of Johnson (by William Nash) and O'Brien (by Mark Heberle). I have been careful to indicate where such insightful works examine in depth ideas that I only touch upon in passing.

The novelists have not been idle themselves, of course, and have continued to explore new creative frontiers. O'Brien's *Tomcat in Love* and *July, July* both include Vietnam veterans in their cast of characters, but their wider range of social exploration thwarts the war novelist categorization that has long dogged their author. Johnson's *Soulcatcher and Other Stories,* originally commissioned as a companion piece to the television series *Africans in America,* suggests a refined social role, a conflation of novelist and documentarian. Auster has shown himself a media jack-of-all-trades, directing another film (*Lulu on the Bridge*), writing other scripts (including, controversially, *The Center of the World*), and undertaking a number of projects with National

Public Radio, among them the collection of listener stories ultimately published as *I Thought My Father Was God,* as well as several programs pondering and memorializing the World Trade Center tragedy.

The horrific events on and following 9/11/2001 obviously represent the most decisive change in our national fabric since 1999. Returning to this work, I winced at my portrait of the social climate in the nineties, an irony cushioned by a widespread perception of national security. Certainly the ironic age I discuss herein has given way to a more tempered irony in the public sphere. Our novelists found their perspective on the terror and its aftermath in great demand, hardly surprising given their celebrated analysis of the psychology of terrorism and their habitual itemization of the ideological cargo we ship overseas in our entertainment and rhetoric. Richard Rorty, whose philosophies lend structure to this study, has been notably and passionately vocal as well. Of these responses, DeLillo's article "In the Ruins of the Future" is of the most interest here because it not only mourns and probes our national trauma but also stands as his most definitive statement on his interests and approaches as a writer. Accordingly, I have woven some discussion of this piece, a decisively postmodern document that implicitly argues against postmodern abstraction, into my final chapters as well as a new afterword addressing writings since 1999.

I must thank Professor Frederick Karl, my dissertation director at New York University, for his unflagging support for my project even when his appraisal of literary value differed sharply from mine. Thanks also to my students, who have contributed much to my understanding of the novelist's role in the modern age by asking their own deceptively simple questions.

Acknowledgments

Excerpts from "The Transmission," "Confession," "Poetry & Politics," "A Soldier for the Crown," "Martha's Dilemma," "The Plague," "The People Speak," and "Murderous Thoughts" in *Africans in America, America's Journey Through Slavery,* copyright © 1998 by Charles Johnson, reprinted by permission of Harcourt, Inc.

From *Americana* by Don DeLillo, copyright © 1971 by Don DeLillo. Used by permission of Viking Penguin, a division of Penguin Group (USA) Inc., and the Wallace Literary Agency, Inc.

Reprinted with permission of Scribner, an imprint of Simon & Schuster Adult Publishing Group, from *The Body Artist* by Don DeLillo. Copyright © by Don DeLillo.

Excerpts from *Contingency, Irony, and Solidarity* by Richard Rorty. Reprinted with the permission of Cambridge University Press.

Reprinted with the permission of Scribner, an imprint of Simon & Schuster Adult Publishing Group, from *Cosmopolis* by Don DeLillo. Copyright @ 2003 by Don DeLillo.

Reprinted with permission of Scribner, an imprint of Simon & Schuster Adult Publishing from *Dreamer* by Charles Johnson. Copyright © 1988 by Charles Johnson.

From *End Zone* by Don DeLillo, copyright © 1972 by Don DeLillo. Used by permission of Viking Penguin, a division of Penguin Group (USA) Inc., and the Wallace Literary Agency, Inc.

Faith and the Good Thing © 1974 by Charles Johnson.

From *Going after Cacciato* by Tim O'Brien, copyright © 1975, 1976, 1977, 1978 by Tim O'Brien. Used by permission of Dell publishing, a division of Random House, Inc.

Excerpts from *Great Jones Street* by Don DeLillo. Copyright © 1973 by Don DeLillo. Used by permission of the Wallace Literary Agency, Inc.

From *If I Die in a Combat Zone* by Tim O'Brien, copyright © 1973 by Tim O'Brien. Used by Permission of Dell Publishing, a division of Random House, Inc.

From *In the Country of Last Things* by Paul Auster, copyright © 1987 by Paul Auster. Used by permission of Viking Penguin, a division of Penguin Group (USA) Inc.

Excerpts from *In the Lake of the Woods* by Tim O'Brien. Copyright © 1994 by Tim O'Brien. Reprinted by permission of Houghton Mifflin Company. All rights reserved.

Excerpts from *July, July* by Tim O'Brien. Copyright © 2002 by Tim O'Brien. Reprinted by permission of Houghton Mifflin Company. All rights reserved.

From *Leviathan* by Paul Auster, copyright © 1992 by Paul Auster. Used by permission of Viking Penguin, a division of Penguin Group (USA) Inc.

From *Libra* by Don DeLillo, copyright © 1988 by Don DeLillo. Used by permission of Viking Penguin, a division of Penguin Group (USA) Inc., and the Wallace Literary Agency, Inc.

From *Mao II* by Don DeLillo, copyright © 1991 by Don DeLillo. Used by permission of Viking Penguin, a division of Penguin Group (USA) Inc., and the Wallace Literary Agency, Inc.

From *Moon Palace* by Paul Auster, copyright © 1989 by Paul Auster. Used by permission of Viking Penguin, a division of Penguin Group (USA) Inc.

From *Mr. Vertigo* by Paul Auster, copyright © 1994 by Paul Auster. Used by permission of Viking Penguin, a division of Penguin Group (USA) Inc.

From *The Music of Chance* by Paul Auster, copyright © 1990 by Paul Auster. Used by permission of Viking Penguin, a division of Penguin Group (USA) Inc.

From *The Names* by Don DeLillo, copyright @ 1982 by Do n DeLillo. Used by permission of Alfred A. Knopf, a division of Random House, Inc.

The New York Trilogy © Sun & Moon Press.

From *Northern Lights* by Tim O'Brien, copyright © 1975 by Tim O'Brien. Used by permission of Dell Publishing, a division of Random House, Inc.

Oxherding Tale © 1982 by Charles Johnson.

From *Players* by Don DeLillo, copyright @ 1977 by Don DeLillo. Used by permission of Alfred A. Knopf, a division of Random House, Inc.

From *Ratner's Star* by Don DeLillo, copyright @ 1976 by Don DeLillo. Used by permission of Alfred A. Knopf, a division of Random House, Inc.

From *Running Dog* by Don DeLillo, copyright @ 1978 by Don DeLillo. Used by permission of Alfred A. Knopf, a division of Random House, Inc.

The Sorcerer's Apprentice © 1977, 1979, 1981, 1982, 1983, 1984, 1985, 1986 by Charles Johnson. Reprinted by permission of Georges Borchardt, Inc. For the author.

Excerpts from "Preface" in *Soulcatcher and other Stories*, copyright © 2001 by Charles Johnson, reprinted by permission of Harcourt, Inc.

Excerpts from *The Things They Carried* by Tim O'Brien. Copyright © 1990 by Tim O'Brien. Reprinted by permission of Houghton Mifflin Company. All rights reserved.

Reprinted with the permission of Scribner, an imprint of Simon & Schuster Adult Publishing Group, from *Underworld* by Don DeLillo. Copyright © 1997 by Don DeLillo.

From *White Noise* by Don DeLillo, copyright © 1984, 1985 by Don DeLillo. Used by permission of Viking Penguin, a division of Penguin Group (USA) Inc., and the Wallace Literary Agency, Inc.

Chapter One

Postmodernism, Liberal Ironism, and Contemporary Storytelling

In *Contingency, Irony and Solidarity,* Richard Rorty observes that "poetic, artistic, philosophical, scientific, or political progress results from the accidental coincidence of private obsession with public need."[1] In the process, he nimbly equates all fields of intellectual study and all avenues of creative pursuit, regardless of any pretensions of objective fact, isolated aesthetic craftsmanship, or national teleology, as nothing more or less than fertile sources of imaginative narratives, narratives hierarchical on the basis of imaginative potency rather than truth or accuracy. The absolutist tenets we habitually rely on—scientific principles, religious systems, versions of the past we cherish as true history—are transient constructs, shifting with the times, with the moods of the populace, with the whim of chance. Accordingly, Rorty celebrates a most romantic vision of iconoclastic genius, in which grandness of inspiration is what counts, ultimately, in our most potent philosophers, scientists, and novelists (poets all, to his eye); he is particularly drawn to those thinkers, those poets, who "try to get to the point where we no longer worship *anything,* where we treat *nothing* as quasi-divinity, where we treat *everything*—our language, our conscience, our community—as a product of time and chance."[2]

To many thinkers, such a relativist outlook might seem destined to result in a moral vacuum, but even as he posits these theories Rorty dedicates his own narrative to the fervent encouragement of those thinkers who "include among [their] ungroundable desires their own hope that suffering will be diminished, that the humiliation of human beings by other human beings may cease."[3] Although by his own philosophy liberalism's program in which "cruelty is the worst thing we do" can be nothing more than one in a spectrum of compelling and competing narratives, he is adamant that it nevertheless is or should be an inarguable tenet of civilized life. Pain and causality, he insists, are non-linguistic truths, a statement denying virtually every sentiment of modern critical theory, including, especially, his own.

Rorty is well aware that in this he seems to be committing himself to a grievous contradiction in terms, but he remains unruffled by charges of schizophrenia. Indeed, an embrace of contradiction is at the heart of his philosophy; simultaneously elitist and populist, theoretic and pragmatic, ironic and sincere, poetic and political, he represents a middle space, an unique equipoise, built upon his Quixotic desire to prove that in a world in which contingency and irony rule, the advocating of solidarity remains feasible and viable. Dedicated to substantiating his claim through art, specifically literature, he practices dexterous evasions and subterfuges in his readings designed to uncover conscience even where only aestheticism and isolationism seem apparent. The moral onus lies, finally, on the reader, to the point that it hardly seems to matter whether the strong poet in question writes solely for himself, toward some personal theory of art, or whether he aspires to galvanize readers by addressing those contemporary social issues and structures that concern him most deeply. Thus it is that Rorty's paradigmatic authors, Nabokov and Orwell, fulfill his ideal but represent polar oppositions, Nabokov's work suggesting self-absorption and Orwell's, certainly, social-absorption, even didacticism. Rorty does not examine, however, the poet who occupies the precarious position in which many of our most vital and conscientious novelists find themselves, both extolling ironism like Nabokov *and* encouraging solidarity like Orwell; Rorty serves as an illuminating model for these writers, though, because he himself fills this role, because the embrace of paradox he labels *liberal ironism* is the challenge increasingly taken up by writers like Paul Auster, Don DeLillo, Charles Johnson, and Tim O'Brien.

Like Rorty, the contemporary novelist faces a new world of contingency and irony, inheriting a medium decisively wrenched from its realistic or pragmatic mooring by the exploratory literature of the sixties and seventies and the influx of much European thought on linguistics, semiotics, and ideology (both comprising the entrenchment of what is generally labeled postmodern fiction and postmodern theory, though Rorty dismisses that identifier as "rendered almost meaningless by being used to mean so many different things"[4]). Novelists like Pynchon, Barth, Barthelme, Coover, Gaddis, Gass, Burroughs, Vonnegut and Reed have fostered upon us the realization that the novel is the blandest of conventions, laying bare the malleability of the human mind in its easy mastery of the reader, its capacity to infiltrate our dreams and craft our attitudes. In their terms, our celebration of "realistic" writers like Updike, McGuane, Stone, Tyler, Carver, Irving, Bellow, Ford and Malamud represents a mute acceptance of the logocentric authority against which Rorty cautions. But postmodern indulgences of form, plot, and self-consciousness threaten an irreconcilable schism in contemporary fiction between non-ambitious mainstream writing that remains largely traditional or mimetic in form and more profoundly observant work that is nevertheless self-absorbed, elitist, and erudite to distraction. Where Rorty's liberal ironist reader must establish a middle ground in his interpretations between values of genius and values of social utility, the liberal ironist *novelist* must maintain a middle ground in his writings between realism and antirealism, edification and esoterica.

For more than three decades, theorists retaining traditionalist or moralist leanings have attempted to identify writers who mediate in this fashion between "conventional" and postmodern values of the novel. Alan Wilde's *Middle Grounds,* perhaps the representative example, asserts the increasing prominence of "mid-fiction," referring to the work of Stanley Elkin, Thomas Berger, Donald Barthelme, Grace Paley and Pynchon (*The Crying Of Lot 49* only) which rejects both "the oppositional extremes of realism on the one hand and a world-denying reflexivity on the other, and that invites us instead to perceive the moral, as well as the epistemological perplexities of inhabiting and coming to terms with a world that is itself ontologically contingent and problematic."[5] Dissatisfied with the "moral catatonia" found in much-acclaimed minimalist fiction by Raymond Carver and Joan Didion, Wilde labors to find in his authors parabolic examples of "how to deal with the world," a successful equipoise, like Rorty's, amid the flux of perception, a willingness to "live with and in the untidiness of existence."[6] Wilde's plea is for humanist fiction, defined as featuring not only an eternally inquisitive mind but a valuing of the individual and an insistence on tolerance; yet in practice he often seems to be grafting moral significance onto texts which lack the wherewithal to maintain it. Thomas Berger's *Who Is Teddy Villanova?,* for example, is, like Auster's early "City Of Glass," a satire of the language and structure of the hard-boiled detective novel, gleefully rooting out convention until the effects on the reader parallel those wrought on its hero by villain Washburn: "to remove the sense of wonder is often tantamount to emasculation."[7]

Most of the other works Wilde describes do not move beyond a philosophic or linguistic understanding of contingency to address its frequent eruptions into political, social, and religious issues. Instead, there is a very self-absorbed whimsy in many of these works; though Wilde bases his reading of Barthelme on the "background of daily life"[8] found in his writing, there is little in the seminal *The Dead Father,* or the somewhat misleadingly titled collection *City Life,* akin to the wide-reaching depiction of such life in Tom

Wolfe's realist-throwback *The Bonfire Of The Vanities,* or, on the postmodern end, in the roving thematic exploration of the far more textually challenging *Gravity's Rainbow.*

Unlike Wilde's authors, Auster, DeLillo, Johnson and O'Brien clearly evolve away from the extremes of authorship represented by Pynchon and Wolfe. DeLillo and Auster are initially much nearer the postmodern end, DeLillo especially, as he is drawn to the benchmarks of postmodern writing—excess, play, and a Derridean exposure of the unreliability of language. Auster, more influenced by French poetry and existentialist writing than by postmodernists like Pynchon or Coover, gravitates toward "white spaces" (what Roland Barthes calls "writing degree zero"), in which what is unsaid is more important than what is. Even more than DeLillo, he is interested in the way language functions (or hardly functions), and, correspondingly, in the mechanics of literary expression, specifically the question of what transpires in the gray area between the writing and the final interpretation of the text by the audience. While this last interest would seem to represent a stronger awareness of the reader's role than is present in DeLillo's early approach, which expressly admits its disdain for the audience, Auster's defamiliarization of the story process in his early novels is so complete that narrative *as* narrative, as opposed to the *idea* of narrative, is enervated to the point that it can no longer "move" his readers. Yet Auster's 1999 novel *Mr. Vertigo* is, while fantastic in nature, a far more conventional narrative than his earlier and very self-reflexive *New York Trilogy* (1985–1987), just as DeLillo's 1997 masterpiece *Underworld,* though a long and challenging text, is nowhere near as dauntingly self-conscious as his earlier metanovel *Ratner's Star.*

Johnson and O'Brien, on the other hand, are public-oriented from the start. Johnson posits an ethnic voice to counter the hegemonic (white) voice of American fiction, a gesture that could be seen as mischievous, as disruption, as play, but he is determined to make comprehensible and constructive statements about racial consciousness in this country, aspiring to a "philosophic fiction" with specific lessons to be learned, specific values to be uncovered, a systematic broadening of the mind of his readers. O'Brien firmly grounds himself in the war narrative tradition, his voice an amalgam of the straightforward style of Hemingway and an adamantly moral tone increasingly rare in the modern novel. In his first book, the autobiographical *If I Die in a Combat Zone, Box Me Up and Ship Me Home,* he declares his intention to "expose the brutality and injustice and stupidity and annoyance of wars and those who fight them . . . when I was released, I would find other wars; I would work to discover if they were just and necessary, and if I found they were not, I would have another crusade."[9] O'Brien stresses that this is the immaturity of a young soldier speaking, but nevertheless such sentiment is vastly different from any expressed in Auster's and DeLillo's early work—and the fire and conviction, if not necessarily the idealism, still persist in the older, battle-scarred O'Brien. But both writers find, according to pattern, that the novel is a more contingent entity than they had foreseen, that they cannot easily re-center what the postmodernists have de-centered, and thus in the spirit of Rortyian compromise they engage this contingency to tell their stories more effectively.

In this they are joined by DeLillo and Auster, overcoming their reluctance to address the audience, overcoming a maxim much taken to heart by contemporary novelists: only the misunderstood work survives. H.R. Jauss, using the initially controversial but unpopular *Madame Bovary* as an example, believes that the greatest works confound the assumptions of their initial audience, their lasting value resting in an "aesthetic distance" he defines as "the disparity between the given layer of expectations and the appearance of a new work, whose reception can result in a 'change of horizons' through negation of familiar experiences or through raising newly articulated experiences to the level of consciousness."[10] Jauss implicitly suggests a writer's mandate: write for the future; write the novel that will stultify the masses; take comfort in the fact that later in history such works will be cherished for their innovation. As Peter Aaron, the narrator of Auster's *Leviathan,* explains: "books are born out of ignorance, and if they go on living after they're written, it's only to the degree that they cannot be understood."[11]

Yet a sense of responsibility toward contemporary readers continues to haunt these writers, as epitomized by the fact that they all, as we will see, share a very prominent motif in the storyteller's journey, in which the storyteller enacts the circle more customarily carried out by his hero: a self-banishment from the tribe; an accumulation by trial of knowledge and experience; an eventual return bearing power and insight. A typical example can be found in DeLillo's *Mao II,* in which the work of noted and reclusive writer Bill Gray reflects, in the eyes of his assistant Scott, "people's need to make mysteries and legends." His novels "made Scott think of the great leaders who regenerate their power by dropping out of sight and staging messianic returns."[12] Such a conflation of modern artist, ancient storyteller, and mythic hero is nothing new; of the tribal storyteller, Freud writes: "he goes and relates to the group his hero's deeds which he has invented. At the bottom this hero is no one but himself."[13] John Gardner describes how the Romantics "took upon themselves" various mythic roles including both the "heroic mode" and "the singer of the hero's deeds."[14] But the contemporary manifestation of this mythic alter ego is as doubt-wracked as he is powerful, either repulsed by images of primitive tribesman cowering in caves or menaced by images of brutish

Neanderthals huddled ominously around a fire, a poet-priest trepidaciously debating the cost of his journey, the worth of story, even as the fate of his tribe hangs in the balance.

Modern texts that repeatedly reference the primeval storyteller are referencing our primal need for narrative and our primal capacity to understand it; as such, they focus on rudiments of narrative such as plot progression and character development, building blocks of the novel that have often seemed opposed to the style and self-awareness that is also essential to its art. The novelist has always struggled with this primacy of story; it was only with great reluctance that E.M. Forster admitted that "the novel tells a story. That is its fundamental aspect without which it could not exist . . . and I wish that it were not so, that it could be something different—melody, or perception of the truth, not this low atavistic form."[15] John Barth suggests, though, that we have finally evolved beyond this low form. Unlike Joseph Campbell, who asserts that myth is alive wherever the reader of fiction can find in art constants relating to the human condition—"what, then, is both grave and constant, irreducible and inevitable, in this scene of conflict and death?"[16]—Barth insists that our ties to the world of myth have been severed and can be re-experienced only through ironic recapitulation, imitation, or satire; the culprits are an era of diffuse literary experimentation and the infringement of advanced technology on the modern consciousness. Barth "deplores" those who ignore "the whole modernist enterprise" and the influence of "Freud and Einstein and two world wars and the Russian and sexual revolutions . . . and now nuclear weaponry and television and microchip technology. . . . There's no going back to Tolstoy and Dickens and company except on nostalgia trips."[17] Such shallow readers, he argues, are clinging to "middle class realism."

Realism has long been the central precept of the Novel's unique variety of myth-making, according to Ian Watt, who matter-of-factly identifies a form "under an obligation to satisfy its readers with such details of the story as the individuality of the actors concerned [and] the particulars of times and places of their actions, details which are presented through a more largely referential use of language than is common in other literary forms."[18] But this precept, in the eyes of writers like Barth, cannot conceal the "fact" that, as Tzvetan Todorov observes, the novel is "sheer distortion. What exists first and foremost is the text itself, and nothing but the text. . . . Novels do not imitate reality, they create it."[19]

Such writers are unbothered by the fact that the ultimate distancing from readers is a dismissal of the world, their world, its realistic core. Even Rorty, flamboyant subjectivist that he is, feels it is necessary to remind his reader that there is an objective reality, a world "out there," even if there is no truth "out there:" "to say that the world is out there, that it is not our creation, is to say, with common sense, that most things in space or time are the effects of causes which do not include human mental states."[20] Brian McHale, on the other hand, wants little to do with "common sense," rejoicing in the post-modern "plurality of universes," in which ontological exploration "is not necessary to seek some grounding for *our* universe; it might just as appropriately involve describing *other* universes, including 'possible' or even 'impossible' universes."[21] William Burroughs, in accordance with McHale's theories, does not conceal the world as much as eliminate it altogether. According to Ihab Hassan, the postmodernists emulate Burroughs's trailblazing, his "complex desire to dissolve the world—or at least to recognize its dissolution—and to remake it as absurd or decaying or parodic or private."[22]

Burroughs's approach in *Naked Lunch* is to unleash a stream-of-consciousness barrage of grotesqueries, horrors, and sexual abuses, all presumably reflective of the "copulating rhythm of the universe."[23] Frank Kermode, insisting that "there is still a need to speak humanly of a life's importance in relation to [the world],"[24] finds no such "human" structure—no structure, moral or otherwise—in Burroughs's "avante garde" novel, which to his eyes is "unified only by the persistence in its satirical fantasies of outrage and obscenity."[25] Yet theorists like Sontag discover in it instead a pattern and a harmony, a cohesion found not in theme but in "the principles of (and balance between) variety and redundancy."[26] We recall Forster's ambivalent wish that melody could be the ideal of the novel instead of story; here the ideal is indeed, according to Philip Stevick, to "extend the idea of form beyond . . . linear progression . . . toward something more mosaic, concentrated, or circular."[27] Unlike Forster or Campbell, Sontag has argued that art has changed drastically from the "magical-religious operation" of primeval times, and is of value now only to stimulate the conscious with sensual pleasures; this needs be the writer's imperative given that the nation's tendency to excess has produced "a steady loss in sharpness of our sensory experience."[28]

But Rorty remains insistent about the role of narrative. He explains how the most powerful narratives bring about a new world view, a new self-image, grand examples being Galileo repositioning Earth in the universe, Darwin repositioning Man in the biological order, and (of most interest to Rorty) the founders of democracy repositioning the common man in the political and social arena.[29] The role of the novelist in this process is often to make sense of the transition, to reconcile the triumphant world view with the lost one, providing the comprehensible storyline required by the masses. Pinpointing another modern upheaval (if less grand) in our descent into irony, deconstruction and extreme self-consciousness, Rorty himself rewrites the history of philosophy so that it seems our greatest thinkers, even pragmatists like John Dewey, have always been drawing us toward an accepting acknowledgment of contingency. He may be misrepresenting their work, as many claim, but he hopes that as a result we will be better able to accept the moral possibilities he finds in contingency instead of letting an all-too-likely paralysis set in. In their mature work, our novelists supply similar explanatory narratives, alternative histories, only far more utilitarian than Rorty's in that they are more accessible to a non-academic audience. While they do not shy away from postmodern obfuscation, they explore the origins of postmodern confusion, presenting narratives of the birth of the postmodern age. In other words, they supply narratives exploring the end of narrative, a gesture of the most hopeful paradox. Jameson stresses that the postmodern freedom to toy with the past is emblematic of an irremovable barrier between the contemporary artist and his or her sense of history: "the symptom of social and historical impotence, of the blocking of possibilities that leaves little option but the imaginary."[30] Yet realizing that the excesses of the postmodern world (and the postmodern novel) are less threatening if their genesis is explained, our authors reengage this past, offering various myth-speculations, varied scapegoats for the unleashing of these confusions: for DeLillo, the JFK assassination; for O'Brien, the Vietnam war; for Johnson, the King assassination, compounding the process begun with American slavery. Such history lessons approximate Eliade's "myth of origins," which both unifies and renews the community: "in most cases, it is not enough to *know* the origin myth, we must *recite* it." Yet historical "fact" is often mangled in the configuring of these narratives, stimulating controversy; DeLillo especially faced criticism from conservative writers like George Will, for whom tampering with the sanctity of U.S. official history is dangerous business indeed. How limited, then, is the audience for their type of narrative?

Rorty stratifies the reading public between elitist readers and non-elitist readers, a distinction coinciding with his wider-ranging one between ironists and "commonsensically nominalist and historicist"[31] non-ironists. Rorty purports to defend both, yet his sympathies seem to lie firmly, and on occasion alarmingly, with the ironist camp; since only intellectuals of a certain type can process irony and accept contingency, he argues, they should minimize, however possible, the saturation of irony, *their* irony, into the masses. David L. Hall is ironic himself when describing Rorty's elitist program: "there must be the presence of a hope that cruelty may in fact be overcome. It is in order to protect this, often fragile, hope that Rorty wishes to ban irony from the public sphere."[32]

But Rorty's utopia is not diverse enough to reflect the pulse of contemporary America. While it is true that there are many conservatives like Will, and that, as Charles Hartshorne insists, "the skepticism of academics and intellectuals is balanced by waves of popular religiosity and superstition,"[33] there is clearly also a deep cynicism about all facets of modern life, including religion, that extends well beyond intellectuals and academicians. Such media-friendly flights from cynicism as visitations from UFOs and angels constitute a postmortem response to an irony that has dug deep into the American psyche; one would not struggle to recapture the religious sublime if it had not been lost. Irony of Rorty's type has been widespread for a long time; in 1956, Saul Bellow's Tommy Wilhelm observed that "cynicism was bread and meat to everyone. And irony, too. Maybe it couldn't be helped."[34] Hendin pinpoints the entrenchment of irony into the fabric of life during the fifties, when economic bounty bloomed under the cast of atomic war, the "consolidation of power and the promise of affluence."[35] In the current age, neither the national self-definition supplied by the cold war nor the optimism of economic bounty remains; filmmakers mourn the lack of easy villains, a problem compounded, not simplified, by 9/11, and the overriding perception is of an unforgiving job market tainted by the cold-hearted ethic employed by continually accumulating and merging mega-corporations (tellingly, this perception was in full force even during the healthy economy of the Clinton years). As a result, irony has become cultural currency; by the mid-nineties, musicians shrilly evoked it like a mantra in popular music, and journalists endlessly mulled over its pervasiveness and its contribution to contemporary directionlessness, despondency, and insensibility. The majority of the minority of citizens who vote remain decidedly non-idealistic, disillusioned even with their own candidate (the controversy around the Bush/Gore fiasco only aggravated a pre-existing jaundice). Relativism is commonplace, as Philip Roth sums up in *Operation Shylock:* "even the gullible now have contempt for objectivity; the latest theory they've swallowed whole is that it's impossible to repeat anything faithfully other than one's own temperature."[36] This irony epidemic does not antiquate Rorty's program, however, as much as prioritize it, necessitating the promulgation of liberal ironism on a far grander scale than he envisioned.

These ironists, more numerous than Rorty assumes, approach art in different ways. Some carry their ironism into their reading, insisting on the self-acknowledgement of contingency, but others turn to art for precisely the opposite reason, to suspend their irony, perhaps on some level to exonerate themselves of it. These readers are fully able to experience the primal story despite their entrenched awareness of its artificiality. Peter J. Rabinowitz explains that there are two types of roles we assume when reading, and to which the writer caters. The first is the role of the *authorial* audience, in which a self-conscious approach to the art "will generally intrude on the illusion of reality, and limit our involvement in the world of the work before us."[37] The second is the role of *narrative* audience, which "takes the work before it as real." The ironist majority is quite capable of the first role, much encouraged in postmodernism, but far more inclined to the second. This does not mean that they are disinclined to the kind of manipulation DeLillo utilizes in *Libra;* in fact, Rorty's idea that history is just a collection of narratives is a widespread one, as cinematic choices reflect. Despite the fervent debate in the media over the historical merits of Oliver Stone's *JFK,* most moviegoers accepted the film as a political thriller, a paranoid thriller, with a ring of truth but not factual accuracy; the potent message was to be skeptical of governmental claims, not to implicate LBJ in the conspiracy. The most presumably "adult" of nineties blockbusters, *Forrest Gump,* was inherently supportive of the status quo in most ways, yet "played" with touchstones of the last several decades both on the level of narrative and through Oscar-winning computer effects used to manipulate footage of presidents and celebrities—a technique that presents a light-hearted flipside of the scene in *JFK* in which conspirators doctor the infamous photograph of Oswald with his rifle. Immensely popular television programs like *The X-Files* (1993–2002), far more negative about the state of the Union than *Gump,* presented an alternative mythos, a darkly fabulistic and fatalistic counter-story to the surface national teleology; few viewers bought into the show's claims of alien abduction as fact, of course, but were instead invested in the dark narrative of governmental corruption, known by devotees as "the mythology." The narrative audience, the narrative ironist, is willing to embrace relativism so long as the story is accessibly told, credible within its circle of logic; so long as the story remains a story, undeconstructed. While Auster, DeLillo, Johnson and O'Brien supply no truth, only versions of the truth, their impulse is to approximate, if only for the space of a novel, the enabling *surety* of truth, an impulse toward the reader that goes against many prevailing notions of the modern Novel in which they themselves have often believed and against which Rorty often writes: first, that art that serves a social function is not true art; second, that the audience, the reader, is unworthy of such catering; third, that art and morality remain ever separate.

Chapter Two

Social Realism in the Postmodern Age

In the study of American literature, the term "realism" has come to signify more than Watts's standards of characterization, time and place. It has come to be associated with a particular movement of writers in the so-called Gilded Age, William Dean Howells and his often more talented cohorts, a loosely cohering school who in their rejection of commercially dominant novels of sentimentalism and romance and their avowed adherence to the mundane truths of day-to-day life often served to expose social injustices sorely in need of remedy. In the postmodern view, though, these texts ultimately *supported* the status quo. Brook Thomas summarizes this argument: "[the realistic novel's] final sense of cohesion offers implicit reassurances that contradictions can be contained within a significantly ordered structure inherent in society."[1] Such reasoning fastens on an inherent sense of order, order not as much in the story, in which violence and upheaval are common, but in the form, its relative confidence in the mimetic properties of language and the stability of perspective.

As a case in point, postmodern defender Lee Lemon, although purporting to stress the readability of Barth's work, his use of the "significant, thematic values" that "regularly win popular rather than critical support,"[2] criticizes Barth's accessible first two novels on the grounds that they employ "the common tricks that seduce the common reader." Lemon prefers instead "more difficult and more rewarding"[3] novels like Barth's *LETTERS*, a vast work requiring not only undo patience but a wide-ranging familiarity with Barth's entire oeuvre, without which the text is unrewarding and largely incomprehensible. Frederick Karl does not resort to Lemon's questionable rhetoric; he freely admits that *LETTERS* is "very difficult to read and in many aspects a display of authorial self-indulgence," and celebrates it for that very reason; as an antithesis of popularly acclaimed and more "traditional" work like John Irving's *The World According to Garp*, it does "what literature is supposed to do, which is probe new modes of perception, however tedious the process."[4] Karl categorizes this mode of writing as "literature," whereas more accessible works such as *Garp, One Flew over the Cuckoo's Nest, The Fixer,* and *Lie Down In Darkness* are simply "novels." Tom LeClair, in line with Karl, favors those writers derided by Tom Wolfe as a school of "puppet masters" who are "in love with the theory that the novel [is], first and foremost, a literary game, words on a page being manipulated by an author."[5] He argues that it is only the mega- or meta-novel, the work most reliant on theory and most likely to stifle the audience's expectations, that can combat the ever-present inflation or obesity of contemporary life: "only extraordinarily knowledgeable and skilled works of literature—masterworks—have the kind of power that asserts the efficacy of literature and leads readers to contest and possibly reformulate the mastery systems they live within."[6] In other words, he asserts a social function, a social role, for this disruptive urge.

In truth, the early, seminal postmodernists often shared the same social views as their realist forebears. Realist patriarchs like Howells exposed the detritus of a young and impudent American capitalism reliant upon spastic undulations of the market that were as likely to dash men's lives to pieces as to elevate them to prosperity, and that calcified the souls of even those who most prospered by them. Postmodernists like Thomas Pynchon and William Gaddis display in monumental texts like *Gravity's Rainbow* and *JR* a dreadful apprehension over the increasingly chaotic turns of modern economics, the explosion of data and multitudinous perspective brought about in part by the mass media (what Jean Baudrillard describes as "the obesity of meaning systems and information banks"[7]), the swelling of multinational corporations, and the encroachment of the artificial upon the human facilitated by scientific research often funded by those corporations. The recurring subject of their fiction is the apoplectic despair of any individual aware of these vast forces and futilely attempting to establish a sense of place and identity among them, a semblance of coherence, whether internal or external. It is on these grounds that Jacques Derrida has defended the *realistic* core of deconstruction in terms applicable to the postmodern novel that is its most self-conscious embodiment, insisting that his approach is not limited to theory, but is instead representative of "what is happening today in what they call society, politics, diplomacy, economics, historical reality, and so on and so forth."[8]

But even if the seminal postmodernists framed the challenges of their bulky texts—their indistinguishable characters, inscrutable plots, and erudite conceptual systems—in order to represent or embody the moribund conditions of society, they chose to do so to such an exaggerated degree that their work ultimately constitutes an affront to the reader, adding insult to injury, so to speak, the storyteller mangling his story, depriving it of its replenishing effects. Writing of the *roman a these,* Wolfgang Iser defines the limitations faced by all writers with Something To Say: "the problem is merely to ensure the reliable communication of the thesis, which means that the expectations and dispositions of the reading public must be linked as smoothly as possible to the contents. In other words, the strategies of the text must ensure a *good continuation* that will extend into the reader's store of experience."[9] When postmodern texts sunder this continuation, their social message, the potentially melioristic exposure, in LeClair's terms, of forces including "monopolistic capitalism, consensus politics, industrial growth, and an alienated consumerism of objects, entertainment, and information,"[10] comes to seem less important than their philosophic or linguistic methods of deflation, the deconstructionist principles uprooting, again in LeClair's terms, "the concept of transcendental or absolute truth; the primacy of origin, cause and end; the priority of substance, identity, unity, and homogeneity." Thus it is not surprising that, having deconstructed their own social program, these postmodern metatexts inspired not only imitators of their inflated yet socially conscious style but also such "playful" and largely irrelevant works as Barth's *Chimera,* Barthelme's *Snow White,* Gilbert Sorrentino's *Mulligan Stew,* and Ronald Sukenick's "The Death of the Novel," literature about literature, the writer uninterested in his world.

Umberto Eco defines the novel that not only admits its own contingency but elevates it to its main theme as the "open text:" "what matters is not the various issues in themselves but the maze-like structure of the text.... You cannot use the text as you want, but only as the text wants you to use it."[11] In practice, then, the open text proves to be closed; Eco prefers the freedoms inherent in the more conventional reading process, the give and take between text and reader, as opposed to Roland Barthes, for example, who favors the self-aware text, the "text of bliss" (*jouissance*) that "discomforts (perhaps to the state of a certain boredom), unsettles the reader's historical, cultural, and psychological assumptions . . . [and] brings to crisis his relation to language."[12] Rorty observes that many philosophers who share his ideas of contingency often limit their work *to* contingency, much as many postmodern authors limit their work to a discussion of the futility of our compulsion to interpret. Such endeavors, he suggests, offer only the most radically unfeasible ideas of human progress: "Philosophers who specialize in antifoundationalism . . . often see themselves as revolutionaries rather than rubbish-sweepers or visionaries. Then, alas, they become avant-gardist."[13]

Postmodern theorists like Robert Scholes stress the ludic impulse of postmodern fiction, "a more subtle faith in the humanizing value of laughter,"[14] as not only a replacement but a remedy for the idea of the novel as a "reforming instrument." Of course, even if this value were to be adequate compensation, one must question Scholes's confidence that this laughter is not at the reader's expense; in actuality, the ludic impulse epitomizes just what it would seem to, an insouciant regression into childhood, as our authors eventually conclude. Their evolving use of a Lewis Carrol motif demonstrates; Carrol is a cherished father figure of the postmodern movement, of postmodern theory, as the introduction to "Contemporary Approaches to Literature" in *The Bloomsbury Guide To English Literature* shows: "The implied mirror at first appears to reflect passively and accurately Alice's own drawing room, just as words seem to have fixed and true meanings. But the world behind the glass, like a literary text, destabilizes that certainty, for the language of *Through the Looking-Glass* constructs our world, rather than reflecting it."[15] Here again is Todorov's sense of the novel as construct. In the relentlessly self-conscious "City of Glass," Auster seems to find artistic imperative in the reaction of mad genius Stillman to the Humpty Dumpty declaration that "When *I* use a word, it means just what I choose it to mean, neither more nor less." As Stillman explains: "In his little speech to Alice, Humpty Dumpty sketches the future of human hopes and gives the clue to our salvation: to become masters of the words we speak, to make language answer our needs. Humpty Dumpty was a prophet, a man who spoke truths the world was not ready for."[16] Similarly, DeLillo relies on numerous *Alice in Wonderland* correspondences in his early metanovel *Ratner's Star;* Douglas Keesey claims that they "help lighten the burden, creating the potential for comedy and a happy ending,"[17] but the true program of the novel is to burden and baffle the reader, as DeLillo freely admits.

Conversely, Tim O'Brien recognizes from the start that Stillman's imperative, in which there need be no sense of restraint, responsibility, or realism, is a constant threat, and attempts, though with only partial success, to defend his *Going After Cacciatio* against the assertions of many critical readers who have seen it as a postmodern text blurring the distinctions between reality and fantasy: "Our imaginative capabilities determine, in large part, the shape and direction of our lives. [But] we often look at imagination as weird fantasy—a bunch of Hobbits running around, Alice in Wonderland stuff."[18] It is Johnson's 1998 *Dreamer,* however, that reflects the more mature understanding of these four writers, in which the audacity of Stillman's (Humpty's) declaration excuses the most alarming social and political irresponsibility. When a black militant claims that "you can't be a racist unless you have power. . . . Black folks don't have power, so they can't be racist," Johnson's narrator, Matthew Bishop, recognizes "the logic of Humpty Dumpty" at work: "and there in the Black People's Liberation Library, I felt as if I'd fallen down a rabbit hole where all the world's meanings were reversed."[19]

Tom Wolfe has argued stridently for a more conventional realism opposed to such potentially irresponsible avant-gardism. For a modern author, he argues, making sense of "the people" is both the greatest liberation and the most impactive flourish of the imagination. His contemporaries have fallen far from Howells's famous New York ambition: "I hope to use some of its vast, gray, shapeless life in my fiction."[20] In an essay clearing the way for his throwback *Bonfire of the Vanities,* Wolfe recreates the pivotal years of the sixties, the turning point when the publishing world could have maintained its vigor had novelists looked to the people for subject matter: "the publishers along Madison Avenue . . . had their noses pressed against their thermopane glass walls scanning the billion-footed city for the approach of the young novelists who, surely, would bring them the big novels of the hippie movement, the new left, the Wall Street boom, the sexual revolution, the war in Vietnam."[21] Of course, Wolfe was strategically whetting his audience's appetite for his own work, but the concordance of critical and popular attention accorded his novel may have proved his point.

Much of the realism of the realist movement was based upon the accurate imitation of society's many contrasting voices, for, as Janet McKay observes, "it is only through the representation of many voices and many perspectives that an objective reality emerges."[22] In addition, she continues, an interest in a wide spectrum of perspectives emphasized an egalitarian message. In *Bonfire,* Wolfe explores a cross-spectrum of New York life, the voices of urban America, rich and poor and multiracial, without surrendering his sense, or more importantly the reader's sense, of control. In contrast, heteroglossia as manifested in the postmodern novel is not, according to Brian McHale, "held in check by a unifying monological perspective," [23] as it had been in earlier attempts to address the life of the people such as John Dos Passos's *U.S.A.* The author's control is independent of the reader's; the multitude of voices that make up Gaddis's *JR,* for instance, are virtually indistinguishable, undifferentiated by punctuation or notation, so that the reader must always labor to determine who is speaking, let alone what their opinions might be. In addition, Gaddis unleashes a barrage of a communicative channels into the muddle—television, radio, advertising, music—that further derail one's scrutiny. Wolfe's novel, if not necessarily an aesthetically brilliant work of art, seems to capture the randomness and moral vacuum of modern life far more resonantly than *JR;* in light of the national trauma of circus-like events like the Simpson trial, it continues to touch a common chord. The egalitarian impulse of postmodernism, Pynchon's favoring of the preterit over the elect, is always undercut by a lack of investment in people, whether preterit or elect, in favor of voices severed from origin and context, spun around and against one another.

We have discussed how Sontag finds melody in this dissonance. While taking care to placate "outraged humanists," she clearly does not favor the ideal of "morally committed, human scale art."[24] She supports her position through such examples as Leni Riefenstahl's Nazi propagandist film *The Triumph of the Will;* while we must condemn its morals, she insists, we must also cherish its genius.[25] An antithetical work of art would be a film like Steven Spielberg's *Schindler's List,* which, while stylistically assured and masterful in most formal cinematic aspects, has achieved much of its public renown on the basis of its moral function as a testament to the Holocaust experience (Spielberg's similarly intentioned *Amistad* draws from much of the same source material as Johnson's *Middle Passage*). In such a work as *Schindler's List* it ultimately proves impossible to determine where the technician's craft ends and where the moralist's begins, both being facets of the same sensibility, that sensibility which Sontag attempts to divide according to the distinction "between the moral and the 'merely' aesthetic" that Rorty finds most vexing, as it is often used to "relegate 'literature' to a subordinate position within culture and to suggest that novels and poems are irrelevant to moral reflection."[26] Instead, he shares Gerald Graff's certainty that "literary thinking is inseparable from moral and social thinking."[27]

Rorty has himself come under attack for his negligence of underlying reality; Frank Farrel suggests that Rorty's support for creative narrative tends to belie the fact that the best approach for a writer who wishes to grant a particular social view ascendancy is "to attend to the world, and to discover something about how it works, rather than attend to strategies of sociological manipulation."[28] But more critics attack Rorty for the moral impositions of his utopian conjecturing; Honi Fern Haber, for example, characterizes Rorty's assertion that "only one form of political discourse, the liberal and democratic one, is valid," with "a form of terror."[29] The ironic writer in Rorty's mode, then, finds himself navigating between Scylla and Charybdis. It is clear, though, that Wolfe's "people" are an integral part of the mix; the modern author equates "the masses" with his literary audience.

Chapter Three

"Middle Class Realism" and the Acceptance of the Reader

Barth decries those readers, "the lobotomized masses," who cling to "middle class realism." His impulse is nothing new; Mircea Eliade, writing of the reader of *Finnegan's Wake* and other challenging modernist classics, recognizes that the central precept of the literary elitist, writer or reader, is revulsion for the bulk of humanity. The true appeal of difficult works, she states, is that they represent "closed worlds, hermetic universes that cannot be entered except through overcoming immense difficulties like the initiatory ordeals of the archaic or traditional societies." The ultimate aim is "to proclaim to the 'others' (i.e. the 'mass') that one belongs to a select minority," the latter opposed to "both official values and the traditional churches."[1] But if the impulse is nothing new, shifts in the status of both novel and novelist over recent decades have widened the divisions.

The Novel is no longer the primary form of American art, and there may be resentment as a result. J. Hillis Miller sees the end of the American intellectual in the new culture created by film and the full spectrum of recent technological innovations, the "popular visual and aural culture of radio, television, cinema, videos, CDs, CD-Roms, and The World Wide Web, which has replaced print culture as the crucible of public opinion."[2] Accordingly, the media often laments the grim prospects of the Novel, and it has a multitude of supporting evidence from which to draw, as attested by a 1997 column in the *Philadelphia Inquirer* describing the severe competition for our leisure time: "on the average, we watch more than four hours of TV a day, listen to three full hours of radio, and spend nearly fifty minutes reading;" the final category breaking down as "twenty-six minutes a day with a newspaper, ten minutes with a book, and fourteen with a magazine."[3] In *Dreamer*, published the following year, Johnson exemplifies how aware our novelists are of such accounting: "by the time most of you are sixty-five years old, you will have looked at 102,000 hours of television, heard 25,000 hours of radio, seen 300,000 comic pages and 3,599 movies . . . and never devoted one hour to meditating on the truth."[4] Although Charles Newman observes that the industry has underwent an inflationary surge in which "in the last thirty years, more novels have been published than in any other comparable period of history,"[5] the demand is for easy-to-read, unassuming crowd-pleasers, the "literary" novel retaining its place only due to its expendability, as George Garret observes: "the literary book is, almost always, more economical. Doesn't call for an enormous advance. If good things develop, good and dandy. If bad things accrue, why the publishers can quickly dump it, cutting losses."[6] As novelist William Gass observes: "Fame is not a whore we can ring up. The public spends its money at the movies. . . . While the books die quietly, and more rapidly than their authors. Mammon has no interest in our service."[7]

In "City Of Glass," Auster epitomizes the Catch-22 offered by the modern literary market through his characterization of fledgling detective Daniel Quinn, a moderately successful writer of pulpy, pseudonymous detective stories. Despite his secure livelihood, Quinn's concessions to the market have cost him his artistic integrity, his writer's soul, there being no middle ground between popular and imaginative/artistic writing: "as a young man he had published several books of poetry, had written plays, critical essays, and had worked on a number of translations. But quite abruptly he had given up on all of that. A part of him had died."[8] Such a state is what Auster obviously feared for himself while struggling to stay financially afloat as a young writer, producing his own generic detective stories, doing, in his words, "everything in my power to prostitute myself, offering up my words for rock bottom prices, but no one would have me."[9] Auster equates popular fiction with prostitution; DeLillo equates it to pornography. It is a wonder, given this environment, that writers continue to write at all.

Given the years of financial struggle recounted by our four novelists, it is no surprise that the homeless derelict is a recurring character in their fiction. Nor is it unexpected that they imbue this figure with simultaneous yet contrasting significances, the extremes between which their literary purpose swings: the first is a realist criticism of economic systems institutionalized to callousness, the chaff left to stumble the streets in forlornness and despair; the second is a celebration of the deprived life as the means to a pristine state in which true art, art without an audience, can be generated. Tom Wolfe is much attuned to the predominance of the second attitude, in which an absorption in text and language has seemingly necessitated a self-punishment through starvation and isolation, a wan cherishing of despair that has not been so much the vogue in print since the "celebration" of melancholy in Thomas Gray's era. Wolfe depicts the ideal home of the literary ascetic: "You can envision her apartment immediately. There is a mattress on top of a flush door supported by bricks. There's a window curtained in monk's cloth." [10] Wolfe pictures this young artist figure on a crowded subway train, disdaining the crowd, the masses, by blotting out the rush hour crush by focusing on the (inevitably challenging) book in her lap.

In his tumultuous formative years, Auster, taking part in forays that had "everything to do with James Joyce and *Ulysses,*"[11] walked the streets of Dublin in true Bloomian style, with "an insatiable urge to prowl." But drifting "like a ghost among strangers," he had no investment in the people around him—"after two weeks the streets were transformed into something wholly personal for me"[12]—very much out of sync with Joyce's own ideal of admitting, in Werner's words, "the full range of human life into the work of art."[13] Bloom's reflective sojourns become for our four authors an emblem of the dream of reconciliation, the thinker walking the busy streets, always apart from the robust life of the people yet always a part of it. The opposite, resentful impulse, a common pitfall for our writers, is summed up by Wolfe's subway rider, more a Stephen Dedalus than a Leopold Bloom: "I may be forced into this rat race, this squalid human stew, but I don't have to be *of* it. I reject all this."

Recent bearings in critical theory have inflamed this resentment by giving readers the upper hand; the advent of reader-response theory has inverted the relationship between author and reader. An author, according to George Poulet, provides a framework that can alter a reader's perception, but has little choice but to offer up his text, and in a sense himself, to the reader's intrusions, the reader's whim. Poulet describes this experience from the reader's perspective: "I am aware of a rational being, of a consciousness of another, no different from the one I automatically assume in every human being I encounter, except that in this case the consciousness is open to me, welcomes me, lets me look deep inside itself, and even allows me, with unheard of license, to think what it thinks and feel what it feels."[14] This description hardly takes into account the artistic persona still so cherished by the writer, that of the exile, the misfit, the terrorist, everything opposed to such intimacy; in *Players,* DeLillo suggests an aversion to any connection shared with the uncouth, undiscerning masses, the reading public. On separate occasions, protagonists Pammy and Lyle Wynant notice to their horror that they are being watched by a man masturbating in his car; Pammy recoils, but it is too late, she has shared his experience, in terms that recall Poulet's, only twisted, loathsome: "to see the offer was to accept, automatically. . . . He'd taught her his way of speaking, his beliefs and customs, the name of his father and mother. Having done this, he no longer needed to put his hands upon her. They were part of each other now."[15]

Of course, no writer can write without any reader in mind; there must be an ideal reader, as defined by Gerald Prince: "a certain type of reader whom he bestows with certain qualities, faculties, and inclinations according to the obligations he feels should be respected."[16] Jonathan Culler describes the importance of the properly equipped reader, claiming, commonsensically, that "works remain opaque to those who have not assimilated the appropriate conventions." Yet while Culler stresses socially formed and ratified conventions of reading in his observation that "someone who has read a lot of literature is better equipped to understand a work than someone who has read none,"[17] he suggests that in the end this equipped reader will not be the lover of literature at large but one whose techniques are those "explicitly manifested in literary journals, critical discussion, and literary education." Roland Barthes, waving off humanism entirely, believes that the audience for his "literature of bliss" is made up of "aristocratic readers,"[18] who are not averse to re-reading, who are not bent upon uncovering some easily packageable meaning. Gass constructs an ideal reader who is "a lover of lists, a twiddler of lines," and who forgives "the author's self-indulgence"[19] (DeLillo may have been thinking of this or similar Gass assertions when creating Scott, Gray's obsessive disciple in *Mao II,* who insists that "there was pleasure in the lists, faint and clear"[20]). Lemon, still under the pretense of asserting Barth's accessibility, admits that his most likely reader is nevertheless "the eager professional, the reader who reads less for enjoyment then for the unsolved problem or an unanswered question that can be converted into a publishable paper."[21] Rorty for his part laments the rise of the *theory-oriented* reader who resorts to "Foucault, Eagleton, Jameson, Lyotard, and Zizek" instead of "the stacks that contain Shakespeare, Sterne, Wordsworth, Dickens, Emerson, etc." [22] But Rorty remains sensitive to the needs of the elitist artist; he posits Freud as another example of a perspective embodying the seemingly fragile yet utilitarian middle-ground between the author's isolationist impulses and the needs of the common, not theory-oriented, reader: "Freud stands in awe before the poet, but describes him as infantile. He is bored by the merely mortal man, but describes him as mature. He does not enthuse over either, nor does he ask us to choose between them."[23]

In attempting to build stability on this blurred horizon, our writers find themselves, somewhat unexpectedly, following in the wake of paradigmatic naturalist Steinbeck. In *East Of Eden,* Steinbeck, committed to asserting the individual over the group, believes that even conceiving of people as "the masses" facilitates their exploitation by business interests, the pleasing realization that "two men can lift a bigger stone than one man" leading directly to the implementation of crass industrial policy: "a group can build automobiles quicker and better than one man." Yet at times Steinbeck's celebration of the individual seems to suggest a very contemporary elevation of the lone artist-figure over Barth's lobotomized masses: "once the miracle of creation has taken place, the group can build and extend it, but the group can never invent anything. The preciousness lies in the lonely mind of a man."[24] But his novel draws back from the precipice of self-indulgence; in the end, the pragmatists who make up the gray shape of humanity are as compelling as the isolated artist-figure, if not more so. The most admirable character, Irish immigrant Samuel Hamilton, has himself more than a trace of genius, but has turned his back on greatness to aspire to mediocrity, valuing, in Freud's terms, the mature over the infantile: "on one side you have warmth and companionship and sweet understanding, and on the other hand—cold, lonely greatness. There you make your choice. I'm glad I chose mediocrity, but how am I to say what reward might have come with the other?"[25]

For a novelist, the pursuit of this "mediocrity" involves a certain degree of realism, a certain degree of support for the status quo, and a certain amount of pandering to the audience. Accordingly, the works of the core writers in this study *do* come to cling, if precariously, to domestic ideals, the "official values" against which Eliade's elitist community defines itself, the "middle-class realism" that Barth decries. In particular, marriage and the family unit retain their value, cases in point including DeLillo's imperiled yet still vital Gladney clan in *White Noise,* Auster's glowing rendition of "the Auster family" in "City of Glass," O'Brien's family focus in *Northern Lights, The Nuclear Age,* and *The Things They Carried,* and Johnson's quite old-fashioned technique of concluding his novels with marriages, emphasizing stability in the social order (if possibly a more fluid social order than that which preceded them). This proposition runs counter to an idea of marriage in place in literature since the seventies, as described by Hendin: "the rise of the work ethic of sex correlates with the development of marriage as a literary symbol for every kind of political, psychological, and economic bankruptcy."[26] Our political climate has been much marked by the rhetoric of family values, of course, but clearly these authors are not passively echoing "hot button" issues but instead asserting a value despite their awareness of how that value has been manipulated by political agents whose social agendas do not coincide with their own. It is with his usual playfulness that Johnson chooses the figure of Karl Marx, of all people, to represent an approach that embraces "official values," and that casts off any trace of resentment toward the reader. In *Oxherding Tale,* Marx pays a visit to the Polkinghorne plantation, where, conversing with Andrew Hawkins's tutor, Ezekiel, he displays a remarkable sanguinity toward the disinterest of the populace to his work. He realizes that the people for whom he writes will probably never read him, yet nevertheless resolves to write *Pre-Capitalist Economic Formations* for a pretty, oblivious young woman spotted on his stagecoach. Hearing this, Ezekiel, an elitist intellectual himself, is affronted, and sullenly reminds Marx that "she'll never read your goddamn book." Marx replies that loving someone is more important than being loved, leading Ezekiel to reveal the deep wound, or fear of wounding, that motivates so many of these writers: "denying *me* love, they would, strictly speaking, deny me life."[27]

But accepting the fact that one's work will not be read is not sufficient; one must tailor his work to fit the audience's desires. This is the terrible realization with which DeLillo grapples in *Players.* Pammy Wynant, having just returned from a disastrous affair in the arms of a troubled, eventually suicidal homosexual, loses herself in vapid TV, a fifties movie in which a family faces dire, and melodramatic, straits: "Pammy couldn't stop watching. The cheapness was magnetic. She experienced a near obliteration of self-awareness."[28] DeLillo is fully aware of the tawdry nature of such art, its lack of aesthetic value, its crass manipulation of the audience with, as he calls it, "serial grief." But though Pammy shares DeLillo's awareness and deep-rooted cynicism, she cannot resist the onslaught on her emotions, even though she knows it is "tainted by the artificiality of the movie, its plain awfulness." She observes, somewhat bitterly: "Movies did that to people, awful or not."

Yet the insipid art that inspires her revulsion, the generic movie of domestic crisis, also inspires a genuine catharsis: Pammy finally collapses into tears over her *personal* crisis, the nightmare she has put herself through, and continues to put herself through, for no better reason than boredom or anomie. She experiences guilt, grief, and a newfound sadness over the absence of her husband, who is on an equally calamitous course, for similarly shallow reasons. Empathy for the human condition, the experience of joy or sorrow, love or heartbreak, is supposedly the aim of the "popular" novelist and the lowest common denominator novel, yet her long-overdue breakdown is, as the most human note in *Players,* a moment of extreme revelation, if not enough—too little, too late—to fully humanize Pammy.

Although DeLillo shares Pammy's repugnance of the Crowd in all its raucous permutations, he also shares her respect for the potency of the art by which it has chosen to be represented, even if he suspects he can never embrace it himself, as an inheritor of that school of literary thought best defined by Henry Miller: "An artist is always alone—if he *is* an artist. No, what the artist needs is *loneliness.*"[29] In his short story "Moving Pictures,"

Johnson suggests that the accessibility so fundamental to popular film may be one and the same in literature:

> You'd seen it as a miracle, an act of God when the director, having read your novel, called, offering you the project—a historical romance—then walked you patiently through the first eight drafts, suspicious of you at first (there was real money in this, it wasn't poetry), of your dreary, novelistic pretensions, and you equally suspicious of him, his background in sitcoms, obsession with "keeping it sexy," and love of Laurel and Hardy films. For this you wrote a dissertation on Derrida? Yet you'd listened. He was right in the end.[30]

The novelist is pretentious, theory-ridden; the purveyor of pop wares is puerile yet skilled, shrewd, a storyteller. It is clear that the former has much to learn from the latter; it is this type of admission, this type of growing process, that allows the ironist writer to dispel the pervasive negativity of the postmodern masterwork in favor of Rorty's more positivistic questioning, in which it has become "steadily easier to substitute Deweyan questions such as What communities' purposes shall I share? and What sort of person would I prefer to be? for the Kantian questions, What Should I Do? What May I Hope? What Is Man?"[31]

Chapter Four

Morality and Solidarity in the Ironic Novel

When Ihab Hassan asks the question, "What does it mean for humanists to dream?,"[1] the answer seems less important than the question, which implies that humanism is deep in slumber, or that it has entered the realm of fantasy. For many novelists, and for many readers, this is clearly the case; Harold Bloom believes, for example, that the durability of literature over time is attributable to factors *opposed* to those of social or moral advocacy, factors of genius and of *strangeness,* the latter being that visionary spin a true artist puts on the mundane world, "reading deeply into the Canon will not make one a better or even a worse person, a more useful or a more harmful citizen."[2] Arthur Saltzman concurs, scorning the sanctimonious conception of literature that permeates the mainstream: "books—that is, the correct books—are depicted as bristling like cut oranges with righteous guidance; their messages are to be plucked, polished, and transported across the ages."[3] Accordingly, Gass, rereading James's *Portrait Of A Lady,* focuses on "the very turn and tumble of the sentences themselves," relieved, apparently, that "there is . . . no suggestion that one should choose up sides or take to heart his criticism of a certain society nor any invitation to discuss the moral motivations of his characters."[4]

Rorty, in his celebration of romantic genius and his dismissal of any absolutist belief, would seem very much of the same mindset, did he not insist on singling out those among the nexus of viable narratives that stress "our chances of *being kind,* of avoiding the humiliation of others."[5] Understandably, many critics charge that Rorty's idea of morality is unfeasible, that there can be no adherence to solidarity without an adherence to fundamental concepts such as God or the soul. Jean Bethke Elshtain asserts that throughout history the aversion to cruelty so fundamental to Rorty has been primarily inspired by absolutist belief, non-ironist belief; the Italians who sheltered Jews during World War II, for example, often asserted that they were obeying, almost unthinkingly, their Catholic duty. She challenges him "to rewrite the Declaration of Human Rights so that it retains its power to condemn, separate, and define yet abandons the basis on which it now does so."[6] Rorty counters Elshtain's assertions by insisting that endless bloodletting, perhaps the majority of historical bloodshed from the crusades to the present day, has been based on such fundamental beliefs as the soul.[7] But Elshtain's deepest reservations remain trenchant; she questions Rorty's belief that thinkers can rely exclusively on contingency, on the idea that on some fundamental level even their identities are contingent, "because when they think of themselves they see concrete fears, pains, hopes, and joys embodied in concrete others—say a grandchild—and it is impossible for them to construe that grandchild . . . in the way Rorty says we must."[8]

Her true fear, of course, is that such a mindset *may* indeed be possible. Stanley Fish dismisses the threat of relativism on the grounds that it is a position "one can entertain" but can never truly occupy: "No one can be a relativist, because no one can achieve the distance from his own beliefs and assumptions which would result in their being no more authoritative for him than the beliefs and assumptions of others."[9] But Fish may be oblivious to very real modern dangers; in an apprehensive article in *The Chronicle of Higher Education,* Kay Haugaard convincingly suggests that the ironic age has lead to an incapacity to make even the most obvious moral assumptions. Haugaard, a creative writing instructor, describes the reaction of her class to a reading of Shirley Jackson's "The Lottery," with its famously brutal conclusion in which an innocent villager is stoned to death for no better reason but tradition, an atavistic belief in human sacrifice as the insurer of the earth's fertility. Haugaard is appalled when her students remain disinterested, without a trace of moral outrage; her frustrated insistence that Jackson is "pointing out the dangers of being totally accepting followers, too cowardly to rebel against obvious cruelties and injustices,"[10] falls on deaf ears. There are numerous factors contributing to her students' attitude. Weaned on relativism in the guise of multiplicity, they believe that a cultural practice is to be accorded an impartial respect, that our instinctual judgments, reflective as they are of a dominant or white or democratic or American ideology, cannot be brought to bear on different traditions and social mores. They have also assimilated new scientific theories minimizing our potential for moral freedom; we are, as DeLillo's Jack Gladney bemoans, "the sum of our chemical impulses . . . it's unbearable to think about."[11] Compounding the problem is the fact that there appears to be an innate distance between them and the literary medium that hobbles any possibility of an emotional reaction, a distance that postmodern obfuscation can only widen, as the assertions of Frank F. Madden, a professor at Westchester Community College taking part in a PMLA forum, would seem to suggest: "Most of us who love to read and to feel our way through a work we've never read before are confident that we'll make sense of it, but [today's students] don't have that confidence."[12]

It is clear that relativism threatens to obscure morality. It is clear, too, that for the individual who takes ironism to heart as Rorty does—including, ultimately, our four novelists—relativism can be still more dangerous. The apparition Elhstain fears, the thinker capable of stripping the Other down to the level of sign and flux, is the phantom that haunts these novels; a central motif is the isolated male observer/interpreter, envisioning himself at a high, secure vantage, "creating" the female stranger, selecting any woman at will and fashioning her in terms of his desires. David Bell, the protagonist of DeLillo's *Americana,* provides a case in point when he focuses his attentions on a passerby woman spotted during a Manhattan stroll: "There was a sense of the tropics, of voluptuous and plucked fruit, and also of the sea. . . . She stood by the window, not quite facing me, shapely and fair. . . . That was all there was and it was everything."[13] As is often the case, the female represents bounty and poeticism, though granted no voice, no expression of her own. The frequent recurrence of this sort of extra-personal fiction-weaving represents subjectivity given full reign, carried from literary reading into life; Frank Farrel suggests some of the hubris, some of the potential dangers involved, and fears them in Rorty: "In the modern period the finite human thinker takes over some of God's functions as subject. The qualities that things once were taken to have on their own migrate across the subject/object divide and are seen to be determinations imposed by the self."[14] When the "object" in this equation is the sexual, racial, or economic Other, the potential cruelty is clear to see.

DeLillo's *The Names* presents a notable example of this cruelty in action. The storyline revolves around a similar sacrificial rite as in "The Lottery;" an esoteric cult, obsessed with language, carries out brutal yet supposedly "aesthetic" kills, selecting victims on the basis of their initials and then pounding them to death with hammers. DeLillo makes no apparent moral commentary on the cult, and as a result the most obvious reading of his novel is as itself an example of intellectual and aesthetic indulgence, encouraging the reader to focus on the linguistic aspect of the killing alone, desensitizing him, in a sense, to killing. Yet Rorty would defend the novel on the grounds that it is a self-critical *condemnation* of the aesthetic response carried too far, the theoretical mind amplified to murder.

This is the manner of reading in which Rorty attempts to reconcile his moralism with his appetite for strangeness. He does not devalue the straightforward, didactic approach disdained by Bloom; after all, one of his paradigmatic authors is Orwell, who in novels like *1984* or *Animal Farm* imposes a most overt social program, as Irving Howe observes: "It does not take us away from, or beyond, our obsession with immediate social reality. . . . The world of *1984* is 'more real' than our own."[15] Rorty respects Orwell's appeal to the non-ironist audience, yet he realizes too that what Howe characterizes as Orwell's "linguistic clumsiness" would likely not sit well with the ironic aesthete, and nor would the common impression of Orwell as "a defender of common sense against its cultural, ironist despisers."[16] Milan Kundera, as a case in point, dismisses Orwell's artistry outright: "What Orwell tells us could have been said as well (or even much better) in an essay or pamphlet."[17] For such readers, including himself, Rorty tries to prove that there is a layer of artistic sophistication in Orwell, that his work belongs to Bloom's aesthetic order of reading and is "not usefully thought of as a matter of stripping away appearance and revealing reality."[18]

To this end he focuses on villainous bureaucrat O'Brien as an exemplar of ironist cruelty. O'Brien is an ironist without a sense of moral bearing, fully aware of the contingency of putatively fundamental knowledge and preying on non-ironists like the hapless Wilson, who remains desperately attached to the idea of a stable, inherited order of being, even if in it two plus two now equals five. O'Brien epitomizes the often smug superiority of the deconstructionist, the academically versed theorist, reader, or writer, translated into the political arena. In the process, Rorty imagines that Orwell is an ironic aesthete recognizing himself in O'Brien, and thus so may the reader. Such a reading seems far more vital when applied to writers like Nabokov who, unlike Orwell, openly challenge Rorty's idea of humanism. Nabokov unequivocally ridicules moralist fiction; his is a private world of beauty and black humor. Rorty, however, reads Nabokov's pivotal characters, a Kinbote or a Humbert Humbert, as manifestations of that same private impulse wreaking both public and moral havoc; the obstinately private novelist and aesthete is, in effect, writing of the menace posed to society by the private and aesthetic consciousness. Thus Rorty helps the ironist recognize his own negative potential and helps the moralist find social utility and worth where none is apparent: "we are more likely to notice the joys or the sufferings of one person if our attention is directed to it by the surprising indifference of another person. Just as the misery of the peasantry is made visible by the conspicuous consumption of the nobles."[19]

The fact that Nabokov may have intended no such self-criticism is irrelevant to Rorty's liberal ironist thinker. Yet the liberal ironist *writer*, torn between the extremes of Nabokov and Orwell, *consciously* incorporates these alternative possibilities into his texts. DeLillo's early *Americana,* for example, is largely a cold and relativist work, a harbinger of his early movement away from conventional realism. Yet, as we will see, DeLillo uses protagonist Bell to illustrate the moral shortcomings of that very approach, *his* approach. Similarly, just as Rorty tries to interpret Orwell as an aesthete in order to extend his message to an ironist audience, O'Brien conceals in *The Nuclear Age,* which is full of overt political expostulations, the subversive suggestion that what is really at issue is not nuclear fear after all but the artist's desire for creative authority, the sweep of the masterwork.

Yet subtexts and evasions may distract us from Rorty's belief that "there is such a thing as moral progress, and that this progress is indeed in the direction of greater human solidarity."[20] Thus it is that our novelists come to more openly clamor for solidarity while refusing to relinquish their postmodern liberties. We will discuss this new voice (including notable responses to the events of 9/11) at length in chapters nine and ten, but it is important to note here that these particular novelists are not isolated cases; in fact, even Pynchon has underwent substantive change in this direction, highlighted by the rift between 1973's *Gravity's Rainbow* and 1990's *Vineland.* The latter, much more devoted to exploring a particular time in history (the sixties activism whose omission in fiction Wolfe bewails) and its residue in the modern psyche, made vital points about the curtailment of private liberties and the threat of our increasing dependence on television; according to Pynchon, these factors, compounded by the stifling, idealizing influence of conservative government during the Reagan 1980's, rendered us a nation of living dead, of death-in-life. As Terrence Rafferty observes, Pynchon had never before been so clear in his purposes: "the most remarkable thing about it is the purity of its desire to get through to us."[21] Yet the novel was considered a failure by many critical readers because in its relatively straightforward approach it could not meet Bloom's standard of *strangeness,* of *misunderstanding.* However, *Mason & Dixon,* his latest novel, is long and chaotic, spotted with any number of creative digressions, and written in an often frustrating ersatz eighteenth century dialect; it is a mega-text with more surface similarities to *Gravity's Rainbow* than *Vineland.* Yet unlike his earlier novels it never truly ventures into incomprehensibility; the plot, though frequently absurd, is easily digestible and surprisingly linear. Although Rorty decried *Vineland* for its "rueful acquiescence in the end of America's hopes,"[22] the moral of *Mason and Dixon*—and it *is* a moral—coincides exactly with Rorty's: in the midst of unpredictable action and wild flights of fantasy, we must remember that cruelty is the worst thing we do. Rorty writes of our capacity to empathize with the victims of cruelty;

Pynchon places the likable Quaker Dixon in the path of a slaver in Baltimore. The scene stands out among the plethora of stories that constitute the novel, probably because an act of unqualified heroism is so unexpected in Pynchon: "Dixon, moving directly, seizes the whip,-the owner comes after it,-Dixon places his Fist in the way of the upcoming Face,-the Driver cries out and stumbles away. Dixon follows, raising the whip. 'Turn around. I'll guess you've never felt this.'"[23] In case his readers mistake his earnestness for more mischievousness, Pynchon has Dixon reiterate the point with one of Rorty's central questions: "What's a man of Conscience to do?"[24]

Pynchon has no qualms about promoting Rorty's sense of solidarity through the brotherhood of his characters. For this it is imperative that they *be* realistic characters, not postmodern figments, and indeed they are: they do not fragment and dissolve into the Zone, like Tyrone Slothrop, and they are not determined by conspiracies, although there are a number of them afoot, most revolving around the Royal Society. The early critical response to the novel noted that Pynchon had presented well-developed human beings for the first time; T. Coraghessan Boyle observes: "one feels for Herbert Stencil or Slothrop or even Benny Profane, but Charles Mason and Jeremiah Dixon are another sort of character altogether . . . more substantial, more inspired with the breadth of life."[25] Indeed, their well-tried friendship has resonance precisely because it remains intact despite the novel's wonderful strangeness. In *The Crying Of Lot 49,* Pynchon stressed the impossibility of a rewarding commingling of individuals; the most affecting moment in the novel comes when Oedipa Maas, after covering herself in layers and layers of clothing to delay the amorous advances of seedy lawyer Metzger, gives in to his ardor in a typically absurd scene and then unexpectedly bursts into tears—a surprising admission of genuine, not abstracted, human pain. In *Mason & Dixon,* on the other hand, union, respectful union, is possible, and it is highly significant that Pynchon closes the novel not with the pair's imagined journey into what passes for the Zone—the frontier beyond the edge of the Native American Warrior Path, where Pynchon's fancy has them voyage even inside the hollow earth—but with the aging of the pair both apart and more significantly together *after* this frontier dreaming has spent its course. Instead of leaving us with a sense of his absolute imaginative freedom, an exclusively literary gesture, Pynchon closes instead with two fireside sleepers, dreaming, perhaps, their equivalent of Hassan's humanist dreaming, "dozing together by Dixon's hearth. . . . Each is dreaming about the other."[26]

In our first chapter, we emphasized Rorty's belief that an impactive conflation of the private and the public can only be brought about by accident. O'Brien comes to realize, however, that this reliance on accident only enhances the vibrancy of the storytelling process: "The thing about a story is that you dream it as you tell it, hoping that others might then dream along with you, and in this way memory and imagination and language cohere to make spirits in the head. This is the illusion of aliveness."[27] In telling their stories, these writers make three gestures of reconciliation: to society, in holding their own cruelty up to public scrutiny; to the literary audience, in presenting an accessible fictional narrative; and to themselves, in exploring their own genesis as writers in light of their fictional exploration and rewriting of history. If one might be tempted to argue that the third impulse is sometimes more important to them than the first two, one must also remember how well aware they are that their novels will be read differently than they are written. The reader will re-stack the hierarchy. This too is an illusion of aliveness.

Chapter Five

"Evil is the Movement toward Void": Self-Absorption, Play, and the Ambiguous Gift of Genre in the Early Novels of Don DeLillo

To assert this sometimes subtle, sometimes tumultuous evolution in the work of our authors we must first accept the seemingly obvious proposition that all writers change during the course of their careers, that except in very rare instances an author does not plan out his entire career as if it were a single grandiose work of art. Systems theorist Tom LeClair, however, describes DeLillo's career as a strategic "loop" epitomizing the potentialities of an open, multifarious living system opposed to the closed, binary systems that define capitalism and much of Western thought—patriarchy, industrialization, statistical analysis, monotheism. This loop limits the possibility of true evolution, assuming, for instance, that plot lines discarded or inadequately addressed in one book are left so by design, to be addressed in subsequent novels, just as in Pynchon's *Gravity's Rainbow* seemingly minor statements, characters, plot elements, symbols, mantras, and theories of occult or scientific nature continually resurface in moments of presumably pivotal import. LeClair's approach to DeLillo is to analyze his entire body of work as if it were a single, massive novel, the literary career as metanovel.

For LeClair, therefore, *Americana,* though DeLillo's first novel, cannot be an immature work, only a pivotal, calculated opening salvo. What many see as the weaknesses of a literary tyro—"its length, a style run wild, amateurish plot construction, and DeLillo's failure to integrate his disparate materials"[1]—must be evidence of a mastery that can convey "the illusion of reciprocal simultaneity, growth to complexity, an ecosystemic plenitude."[2]

Douglas Keesey concurs, insisting that its "unorthodox structure and characterization," are "the result of fully conscious choices and not the accidental errors of an inexperienced craftsman."[3] In truth, however, *Americana* is, if extremely promising, a hesitant, unstable novel, a work of middle-of-the-road realism inclined toward excess, self-consciousness and metafiction—the urge to communicate giving way to the urge to obfuscate—yet besotted with reservations; unsurprisingly, Rortyian *self* irony, a self-acknowledging exploration of cruelty, is very much on its surface.

Americana is a kind of *bildungsroman,* except it is about a character who *never* really comes of age; the narrator is ex-television executive David Bell, residing in meditative solitude on a deserted island, revisiting, but not learning from, an arrogant youth in which he deserted his network to indulge not only in an adventuresome cross-country trek but also in a masturbatory film recreating pivotal events and emotions of his childhood, mostly concerning his father, an influential figure in the establishment of big-business advertising, and his mother, a slightly unstable and elusive figure (tellingly described at one point as "a question mark curled on the bed"[4]), a cancer victim whose flightiness and sickness define everything banished to the margins by her husband's consumer-oriented instincts: "She was not an advertising campaign and he did not know what to do about her."[5]

The successes of both male Bells span and exemplify the redefinition of labor linked to the economic boom that rose, like Clifton Bell's career, from the impetus of victory in World War II and would later culminate in the crass commercialism of the Eighties, a revolution in the nature of work that separated men from the visible fruits of their labor, basing itself on marketed images rather than craft, on vast amounts of always-unseen money, money planned, transferred, accumulated, and invested, impacting life not in tangible ways but continually exerting an amorphous influence on the psyche like an indifferent pantheon ruling from a distant mountaintop. A nostalgia for an idealized past, this lost ideal of Work, reveals itself when David, looking out an office window during a meeting, sees Mohawk workers, who carry with them an aura of forgotten times and ways of life, working now on skyscraper construction, standing out among all the metropolitan sprawl; he views them not in pity, as people of the Land now condemned to the twisted industrial world of looming buildings, but with a kind of special, attuned sight, seeing them "framed in girders, men and sky, for what seemed an impossible second,"[6] a moment of glory much like the glorified image of the plow in Willa Cather's *My Antonia,* symbolic of the bucolic labor upon which the nation was built.

To explore this material, DeLillo has crafted a largely realistic novel, with a conventional hero of sixties and seventies literary fiction. Bell's closest literary contemporaries are Heller's Bill Slocum in *Something Happened* and Updike's Harry "Rabbit" Angstrom. As with Slocum, Bell's defining characteristic is, in keeping with the tedious dictates of Freudian motif, stunted sexual puerility: "Then I unzipped my pants and took out my cock. I walked around the office like that for a while. It felt good."[7] Unsurprisingly, he is incapable of sincere intimacy in his sexual relationships, including his marriage; his affairs are tinged with violence, and even when on his best behavior he cannot abide any moments of human contact that might lead to sincere emotional attachment: "I wanted to wake up alone; it was a characteristic of mine, which many women learned to despise down through the years. . . . Solitude asks no pledges of anyone."[8] Updike's Rabbit is perhaps the defining character of post-World War Two American fiction, the man fleeing from everything though pursued by nothing more threatening than the relatively prosaic demands of domestic life. Just as *Rabbit, Run* begins with Rabbit, still in work attire, recapturing past basketball glory by dominating young children on the court, Bell spends his office time, also confined to business garb, shooting baskets, absorbed in himself absolutely: "I played quite seriously, my tie bellying out at each jump shot, sweat blossoming under my arms. . . . I had been my team's leading scorer in prep school; first in scoring, last in assists."[9]

Given the novel's familiar elements, LeClair's equation of the disruption wrought by David's mother Ann with *literary* disruption proves misguided. He is correct in observing that in her unsettling nature she is representative of all those suppressed by the American ideological apparatus, like those denizens of our urban slumlands who rise up from their poverty to pelt Clifton Bell's commuter train with rocks; but he is unconvincing in his insistence that DeLillo uses her to in effect set a trap for unsuspecting readers, promising them a traditional Oedipal complex, a traditional fiction ("good company," as he calls it) and then defusing its anticipated payoffs in order to jar readers out of their sturdiest ways of thinking and hopefully into an alternative world view in which, again, "relativity could become saving mutation and deconstruction might become reconstruction."[10] In actuality, the Oedipal material plays out exactly as expected, almost by rote, conventional to the point of being wearisome; at one point the sexual intimacy of mother and child actually seems impending until the sound of footsteps, the footsteps of David's father, ends the moment prematurely. DeLillo is not breaking ground, but instead resorting to one of the most common fail-safes of the mainstream literary novel. Like Jay McInerney in the far more streamlined *Bright Lights, Big City,* he severely weakens the impact of his work by unconvincingly rationalizing the self-destructive motives of his young protagonist, motives that promise to be emblematic of the American condition on a grand scale, as manifestations of confused grief over the death of a cancer-stricken mother.

LeClair's assertion is weakened further by the fact that the most seditious literary challenges of *Americana* constitute middling distractions and inconveniences rather than any major derangement of form and genre. But it is true that anti-realistic influences are beginning to exert a contrary drift. We can gauge the disparate echoes of both the Beats and Pynchon, for example, in the moment in which David perceives, with a sensation comparable to the decompression of a plummeting elevator, all of New York as a wedding cake: "something of this kind seems necessary to translate you from the image to what is actually impaled on that dainty fork."[11] This moment of clarity, which strips away all subterfuge, all residue of affluent, elite society to reveal the core of perception, is a very overt reference to the work of William Burroughs, a diluted restatement of the harrowing epiphany in the title of *Naked Lunch,* the "frozen moment when everyone sees what is on the end of every fork."[12] We have already discussed how Burroughs translated such revelation into disruptive form and practice. At the same time, the scene recalls Pynchon's Oedipa Maas, looking down on the city of San Narcisco laid out before her like a circuit board, about to undergo the temptation to very consciously take all perception into her own hands, to tap from the realization that all perception is subjective the paranoiac's empowering prerogative to create her own world: "there were to both outward patterns a hieroglyphic sense of concealed meaning, of an intent to communicate . . . in her first minute in San Narcisco, a revelation also trembled just past the threshold of her understanding."[13] Pynchon's revelation leads to similar liberties as Burroughs's, but lacks Burroughs's lusts, rages, and social context; it is linguistic intellectualization, epistemological pondering, and *Americana* is accordingly replete with tentative delvings into the general nature of language, enough that a so-inclined reader could easily (and accurately) project DeLillo's early path away from character, mimesis, and human issues. Bell explains the chaos at the network, where no jobs seem secure and all quality projects seem destined for cancellation, in terms of language loss and language flux, the kind of passage predestined to be seized on by academics with a deconstructionist eye: "Words and meanings were at odds. Words did not say what was being said nor even its reverse. I learned to speak a new language and soon mastered the special elements of that tongue."[14] Thus it is too that DeLillo admits his temptation toward LeClair's mastery, his desire to adopt the same dynamic of author to reader that Oh, David's Zen instructor in college, exploits between instructor and student: "It was Oh's practice to reveal some deep Zen principle, carefully planting evidence of its undeniable truth, and then to confront us with a totally different theory of equally undeniable truth. He seemed to enjoy trying to break our minds. . . . How will you ever know what to believe, you poor white gullible bastards?"[15]

But DeLillo admits not only that this appetite for disruption is his own but that it is a flaw. This is where the differences between Bell and counterparts Slocum and Rabbit become significant; both Heller and Updike maintain a strict sensation of difference between themselves and their protagonists. Slocum is clearly a satire of the corporate mind, Heller always above and outside him, while Rabbit clearly lacks Updike's sophistication to the point that the reader is always aware of a curbing of Updike's expressive nature in Rabbit's communicative and intellectual limitations. The line between DeLillo and the imaginative, literate, and arrogant Bell is not so clear; Bell's film obsession provides a notable example.

DeLillo and Bell share the same taste in film, an appreciation for those auteurs of foreign cinema who "seem to fracture reality [and] find mystery in commonplace moments."[16] Film is the key to Bell's soul, providing him a fleeting sense of control, but only by stripping content from image, as when he records a hawk in flight, processing one of the defining glories of nature as a filmic commodity: "a hawk glanced off the sun and I plucked it out of space and placed it in the new era, free of history and death."[17] This "freedom" is in truth static and sterile; most readers do not need to be reminded of the hunting bird's treasure-trove of accumulated symbolic significance, all that is denied in Bell's gesture: unpredictability, unconquerable energy, raw youth, the American ideal, the elements embodied, for example, in the ill-fated hunting eagle Caligula, initially reviled but ultimately empathized with by the wandering protagonist of Saul Bellow's *The Adventures of Augie March:* "I really felt dazed in all my nerves when I saw with what we would have to deal. . . . The bird looked to be close kin to the one that lit on Prometheus once a day."[18]

One of the defining metaphors of our time is that of the individual or institution in power reducing men and women (let alone birds) into filmed images. The medium of film, in this view, has changed our conceptualizing apparatus, and not as McLuhan promised; it enables and perhaps even provokes us to take a more detached view of humanity, robbing people of depth, soul, and character. The most common of DeLillo's character types is the "living schizogram,"[19] the seemingly random accumulation of individual elements that never add up to a convenient whole; we are inherently malleable, he argues, even on the level of identity, and we cannot defend ourselves. This idea of identity as mere fancy empowers the younger Bell to consume the novice actors in his film, replacing them with his own subjective whims: "I did not want to understand them too well. They were mixed things to me, living people qualified (perhaps enlarged) by my own past, by my fantasies, mirror-seeking, honors, shames, and by those I loved or failed to love."[20] He has fallen into the trap that Rorty admits is lying in wait for many of those thinkers bold enough to recognize the contingency of their lives: irony without direction or utilitarian purpose, irony cherished merely for the pleasure of discombobulating others and discrediting solidarity: "there can be sensitive killers, cruel aesthetes, pitiless poets, monsters of imagery who are content to turn the lives of other human beings into images *on a screen,* while simply not noticing that these other people are suffering [italics mine]."[21]

Accordingly, Bell's college film instructor, Simmons St. Jean, levels any number of animadversions against him. Bell, St. Jean argues, is missing the true point of film as an art form, that it must, like the novel, "leave an emotional residue."[22] Furthermore, he continues: "You crave bad news, defeat, punishment. Defeat is always glorious on film." DeLillo also acknowledges, then, that he shares Bell's predilection for mordancy: "I wanted to free myself from that montage of speed, guns, torture, rape, orgy and consumer packaging which constitutes the vision of sex in America."[23] This predilection is what leads so many critics to align themselves against DeLillo on the basis of defeatism.

The older, reclusive David Bell epitomizes not as much ironist cruelty as ironist ineffectuality. Swept away beyond recovery in a sea of references, he embodies Barth's "exhaustion;" he has reduced all the events of his younger life, whether traumatic or revelatory, to pre-packaged allusions. Memories of his privileged summers fall into imitation Fitzgerald, a portrait of the rich elite whose hypocrisy cannot entirely dispel their appeal: "I can remember that night well, a perfect August night with a warm wind raking the tops of the big oaks, with lawn sprinklers hissing and the silver couples standing near the trees, the men in white dinner jackets and their girls in chiffon and silk . . ."[24] Similarly, his flight from the network seems to be in Stephen Dedalus's terms, not his own: "I took off on the first stage of the second journey, the great seeking leap into the depths of America, wilderness dream of all poets and scoutmasters . . . westward to match the shadows of my image and my self."[25] But Dedalus at least aspires to be the artist of his people, the conscience of his race, whereas Bell is to be the artist of himself only. Accordingly, the elder Bell can only epitomize his current meditative existence with his most explicit literary echo: "The sound of the ocean seems lost in its own exploding passion. I am wearing white flannel trousers."[26] In the elder Bell, DeLillo depicts a soul long-stultified by overrationalization, literariness, and literary play; the metafictional aspects of the novel viewed by LeClair or Keesey as fortuitous harbingers of DeLillo's future writing are indications of a debilitating aestheticism/asceticism. The frigid grumblings of this weary thinker are those of the self-interested author who has abandoned the need for coherency, accessibility: "I look beyond the white lace of the surf of my own unassembled past and I decide to let others stitch together the systems." [27] For him, the prospect of providing a comprehensible narrative would be as unfathomably heroic as a seafaring voyage out of Old English verse: "The surf is massing and rolling, uneven now, page after page of terrible, wild words."

Even as he takes his fledgling steps in LeClair's direction, then, DeLillo senses where they might ultimately lead him. Instead, he attempts to provide St. Jean's "emotional residue" through the character of Sullivan, a sculptress whose abstract work reflects creeping industrialization and mechanization. As a character, she is very compromised, as are many of DeLillo's women; an ironist thinker very much in Bell's mode, she represents a feminine (feminist) strength, "a menacing bitchy hermaphroditic divinity,"[28] but she ultimately surrenders it to David along with her body in order to fulfill the maternal role in his tiresome Oedipal film. Although one could argue that DeLillo seems as confused and intimidated by her feminine authority as his male players, DeLillo allows her to convert stifled energy into story-telling, retaining in the process some measure of dignity and autonomy. Her first story is of Black Knife, a hundred-year-old Sioux, who fears the nation's ever-increasing appetite for urbanization, its continual devouring of our national resources in "the cause of efficiency."[29] Black Knife's rantings have a hopeful end; he believes that if Man continues to pursue his current course, the effects will be calamitous enough to inevitably inspire a return to a "natural" lifestyle, "living off roots and berries but no symbols, shedding the ascetic curse, letting the buffalo run free."[30] Such a childlike vision of rebirth might have seemed in place in a Richard Brautigan novel, but not in a narrative like *Americana;* the ironist reader's response is likely to be Bell's, a stream of snide remarks.

But Sully's second story frees the reader to accept the first. It concerns Sully's "hated and feared and bloody Ulsterman of an uncle," who renounces "church, state, family, and the adulterous shade of Parnell," to flee to Belfast, and later to Maine; he sunders ties to his family, especially to Sully's father, and years later Sully intends to confront him about an inheritance of Scottish land she feels he has stolen from her, depriving her of her birthright. Though her adroit retelling of their fishing trip together is, like Bell's memories, a distinctively literary construction, echoing Joyce, Faulkner, O'Neil, and Melville, Sully rebuffs David's immature whining not with her grasp of technique or her self-consciousness but with the inevitably of the story's moral: "you must permit me at least a fraction of the self-indulgence you reserve for your own tired ends. . . . Larger issues will begin to manifest themselves out of the dull set of pieties I'm constructing here." Her story culminates with the not-unanticipated possibility that her uncle may actually be her father; what is more important to Sully, though, is that her uncle became aware of his own guilt, his own complicity in whom he had become: "the war is not between North and South, black and white, young and old, rich and poor, crusader and heathen. . . . The war is between Uncle Malcolm and Uncle Malcolm."[31]

Malcolm's conflict is with his own self-enclosure, his self-obsession, as is Bell's; it is essential, DeLillo claims, that one assess his own personal flaws, in this case shallow generalizing, unbridled causticity, intellectual arrogance and constant sly banter, the very whims much-indulged in *End Zone,* DeLillo's first attempt at the truly postmodern novel predicated on play.

The subject of *End Zone,* addressed in a more jocular tone than is DeLillo's usual wont, is college football, mainly the logocentric views that permeate each level of its hierarchy of fanaticism: the coach with his passion for winning, the players with their blind devotion to the coach, the audience with its craving for violent catharsis and an illusion of potency. Names like *Logos* College and coach Emmitt *Creed* suggest that the novel functions as a sort of *Pilgrim's Progress,* an allegory in which the most seductive temptation is not to vanity or wickedness but to the utopian mirage offered by sport: "It's a form of society that is rat-free and without harm to the unborn, that is engaged so that everyone follows precisely the same rules; that is electronically controllable thus reducing error and benefiting industry; that routs out the inefficient and penalizes the guilty; that tends always to move toward perfection."[32] In allegorical terms, the pilgrim for whom salvation is achievable is the ideal spectator, DeLillo's ideal reader: "the exemplary spectator is one who realizes that sport is a benign illusion, the illusion that order is possible."[33]

This allegorical approach is necessarily at odds with realism, and also proves to be at odds with "emotional residue." LeClair has very appropriately described "a fable-like quality" to DeLillo's approach here, in which "bared concepts displace realistic surfaces."[34] To Bruce Bawer, always the counterpart to LeClair's system of reading, this constitutes a novel of "stunning implausibility,"[35] in which "it's hard to accept most of his characters as living, breathing human beings."[36] Character dialogue supports his assertions; Harkness's teammates speak, to a man, in a hypertalk very similar to his own, referencing any number of philosophic and scientific theories. DeLillo will later claim that his dialogue is, despite appearances, realistic: "I listen carefully to the way people actually speak. I feel that the closer a writer comes to portraying actual speech, the more stylized it seems on the page, so that the reader may well conclude that this is a formal experiment in dialogue instead of a simple rendition, which it is."[37] Yet this is clearly not the case in *End Zone;* his football players debate, for instance, whether Edward Gibbon or Archimedes was the greater man, and affirm that "the scarab has been a symbol of immortality since the ancient Egyptians."[38]

Their realism is lost, and so to is even the *concept* of "identity." Buddy Shock, during one of the team's intellectually catholic discussions, defines the term in a way that denies it could ever be an ideal, a human value, to be defined, developed, expressed, and defended; instead, it is "an equality satisfied by all possible values of the variables for which the standardized expressions involved in the equality are quantitatively determined."[39] Is DeLillo suggesting that to surrender to logocentric authority is to surrender identity, or is he merely imposing his postmodern imperative? William Gass has emphasized the true nature of literary artifice, in which characters are creations, constructs, tools, and nothing more; when readers respond to them emotionally, confidently, they do so as "gullible and superstitious clods."[40] With a finesse appropriate to Gass's semi-celebratory definition of writers as gods, "a little tinny sometimes, but omnipotent no matter what,"[41] DeLillo has created characters who have "a made up nature. They are pieces of jargon. They engage in wars of jargon with each other. There is a mechanical element, a kind of fragmented self-consciousness. . . . The characters are words on paper."[42]

In similar terms, the social exploration implied by DeLillo's comments on the "benign illusion" of sport prove misleading; certainly the oft-corrupted institution of college football is a target ripe for satire extending well beyond the domain of athletics, and indeed the novel begins with an investigation of the racial issues surrounding sport, centered on Taft Robinson, Logos's sole black player: "In time he might have turned up on television screens across the land, endorsing eight-thousand-dollar automobiles or avocado-flavored instant shave." [43] At such moments, our allegory would seem to be one of racial equality and inequality; school president Mrs. Tom (the allusion is obvious) is a mock hero in the history of the America's racial strife, "the only woman I had ever seen who might actually be described as Lincolnesque. Beyond appearance I had no firm idea of her reality; she was tall, black-browed, stark as a rail-road spike." [44] When Taft first steps out on the field, a more realistic depiction of racial stereotyping comes to the fore; Cecil Rector, Taft's teammate, buys into all the usual categorizations: "Coloreds can run and leap but they can't concentrate. A colored is a runner and leaper. You're making a big mistake if you ask him to concentrate."[45] But the racial question begins to fade, unanswered and half-spoken, just as swiftly as it became prominent in the text; Taft's ethnicity becomes merely a symbol of exile, a cousin to the emotional distance of Gary Harkness, our white ironist protagonist. Instead the focus will be on language, and, on cue, Harkness's own language becomes more obtuse, if arguably more poetic, to mark the transition: "But this doesn't happen to be it. There were other intonations to that year, for me at least, the phenomenon of anti-applause—words broken into brute sound, a consequent silence of metallic texture."[46]

This enigmatic phrasing counteracts the buttressing clichés of Harkness's father, who, stung by the fact that he never achieved athletic success himself, attempts to brainwash his son with a dose of handy American aphorisms on the order of "when the going gets tough, the tough get going." But to escape the ideological impositions of language may also be to escape social responsibility; when Harkness strips away the veil of illusions, he comes up against the void only glimpsed by David Bell in his profoundest realizations, a void conveyed through the image of a vast wasteland, if a far more concrete one than Eliot's: the blank slate of the blazing Western Texas desert. DeLillo's sere landscape, unlike Eliot's, sparks no associations in the mind, completely ahistorical, "the state of being separated from whatever is left of the center of one's own history." Inspired by the dead space of the desert, Harkness devises a spatial theory in which the determinant of human behavior is not learning, experience, or even random choice but simply geometry and location: "words move the body into position. In time the position itself dictates events." His roommate Anatole Bloomburg, a massive offensive lineman who has himself long struggled to escape his own past, his Jewishness, realizes that "history is guilt."[47] Harkness's suppression of history coincides with the familiar embrace of subjectivity and meaninglessness in which there is only the mind of the intellectual cynic facing a contingent world of shapes and locations: "in some form of void, freed from consciousness, the mind remakes itself."[48]

Like David Bell, then, Harkness represents the Rortyian nightmare of theory unbolstered by empathy. Unlike Pynchon's Oedipa Maas, who retains a sense of arguably redeeming social compassion even after "projecting her world," Harkness finds himself incapable of feeling the pain of others; in fact, he exploits it. When the team is struck by a series of freak deaths—the ill-named Norgene Azamanian dying in a car wreck, assistant coach Tom Cook Clark in a suicide, and Mrs. Tom in a plane crash ("coincidences" that further heighten that improbability described by Bawer)—Harkness desires to possess these victims by way of the imagination, filling in the mysteries of death and life with his own subjective configurations. The epitome of this unwholesome tendency is his fetishizing of an unidentified female passenger in Norgene's car, identifiable only as "passenger, female, white."[49] Although he first wonders "who she was,"[50] he eventually is content to invent her based only on the fine set of legs protruding from the wreck. He possesses her, she is his: "I wanted to dream that I put my hand between the dead girl's legs."[51] This is the equivalent, perhaps, to what DeLillo has done to his readers; as Rorty observes: "most people do not want to be redescribed. . . . The ironist tells them that the language they speak is up for grabs for her and her kind. . . . The best way to cause people long-lasting pain is to humiliate them by making the things important to them seem futile, obsolete, powerless."[52]

Yet DeLillo once again uses his female characters to work against the masculine tendency to reduce character to cipher; shortly after Harkness's "possession" of the woman in the car wreck, Myna, Harkness's lover, escapes the bounds of *her* role. For Harkness, Myna is wholeness: "it was refreshing to seek in these women a perfect circle whose reality overpowered the examiner's talent for reducing in size and meaning whatever value of experience he was currently engaged in sampling."[53] Such an idealization of women is nothing new, of course, as Campbell tells us: "Woman, in the picture language of mythology, represents the totality of what can be known."[54] Myna, overweight, seems to represent in her bulk the fullness and fertility of life, as did the voluptuousness of Faulkner's Eula Varner, or the heft of Ruth, Rabbit's prostitute-mistress in *Rabbit, Run;* the language of Rabbit's lovemaking with Ruth, as a case in point, is notably absorbed with weight: "He kisses this expanse," "but he does see; a quick glimmer of tipped weight," "her body is a pond of shadow deepening to a black eclipsed by the inner swell of her thighs."[55] Ruth's sensuality is easily compromised, however, based as it is on the sexual submission integral to the prostitute-client relationship; similarly, Harkness's passion for Myna, based on her maintenance of this physical symbolism, fades after she decides to lose her excess pounds. Myna's final appearance in the text represents an attempt to emerge as a person unconstrained by the mold fitted for her by men, and the mold to which DeLillo tends to confine his female characters: "You can't expect to just come searching for me for comfort. I want other things now. I'm ready to find out if I really exist or whether I'm something that's just been put together as a market for junk mail."[56]

But Harkness's potential for cruelty is not limited to the individual; he conjures up a scenario of nuclear holocaust, a destruction of a Milwaukee so abstracted that its devastation produces no human response: "But I could not imagine Milwaukee in flames. I had never been in Milwaukee. I had never even seen a photograph of the place. I had no idea what the city looked like and I could not imagine it in flames."[57] The children of the nuclear age are desensitized by recurring images of violence, but Harkness's detachment is self-created, a choice; any power he may have gained by recognizing and steeling himself against the military language swelling up in his Adirondacks town, the persistent sight of "-ize words" like "militarize," is counteracted by a fondness for jargon, a kind of joy in its subterfuges, its efficient denial of human implications: "I became fascinated by words and phrases like thermal hurricane, overkill, circular error probability, post-attack environment, stark deterrence, dose-rate contours, kill-ratio, spasm war. Pleasure in these words."[58] The "renaming" policies implemented by Nazi Germany stand as the most callous use of such phraseology, and Robinson's parallel fascination with the holocaust implies a link between Nazi policies and our own nuclear agenda.

In O'Brien's *Nuclear Age,* such terms will inspire the rage of Will Cowlings, who is painfully aware of all that they conceal. DeLillo is as well; his Harkness represents the dangers of the nuclear age psyche. Yet DeLillo's detached depiction of violence leaves open for debate the suggestion that, given his linguistic interests and his frequent dangling and withdrawing of social commentary, he is himself correspondingly inclined. Commentators such as Michael Oriard have suggested that physical play, equated here with postmodern play, can represent a kind of salvation inaccessible to those "without," whether spectators or conventional readers, "who see clearly neither their purpose in life nor the obstacles to achieving it, who are individually subject to forces over which they have no control in a society that is moved toward unknown ends by unknown agents."[59] On the field, on the other hand, there is the possibility of a kind of constructive, "positive violence," that can be used to "recreate language and thus a new perception of life." The game which inspires Oriard to this conclusion, an impromptu match in the snow, is the most cold-hearted athletic contest in the novel: "On the next play I cross-blocked, going after Deering . . . standing him up with two shoulder-blows to the chest, getting shoved from behind and going down with three of four others. The cold was painful now; it hurt more than the blocking and tackling. I got up, one shoe missing. . . . I went over and picked it up. It felt like a dead animal."[60] DeLillo's vagueness throughout *End Zone* has encouraged readings such as Oriard's skewed apotheosis. That said, his efficient, pared-down depiction of this bloody match parallels his no-nonsense itemization of the war games waged by Gary and Major Stanley, in which each seemingly simplistic move represents another horrific escalation in the march toward the annihilation of the human race. There is little of Gary's fascination with the instruments of death here, only a sense of rising action, momentum, the "flow of the game" that only heightens the significance of where the "game" is headed: "AMAC ICBMs, B-52's and B-58's strike at air bases, dams, bridges, railroads and missile sites deep inside the COMRUS territory. The tallin missile defense system is hit and partially destroyed. The antimissile complexes on the western outskirts of Moscow are badly damaged. AMAC orders almost total evacuation of major cities."[61]

DeLillo is clearly haunted by the prospect of a more straightforward approach to his subject (war, not football), one that could avoid such misreadings as Oriard's. Major Stanley, an instructor at Logos, insists that the public needs to be told about the realities of the cold war standoff in clear language: "Somebody has to get it before the public regardless of language. It has to be aired in public debate, clinically, the whole thing, no punches pulled, no matter how terrible the subject is and regardless of language. It has to be discussed."[62] Yet DeLillo remains devoted to his isolation, his disruptions, unwilling to experience the pathos for his reader that Stanley has for the public. The abstraction of *Ratner's Star* looms on the horizon; in fact, the dense scientific fact and science fiction that surface late in *End Zone* suggest that the seeds of his future metanovel may have already taken root in DeLillo's mind. When Harkness tries to ride out his ever-mounting anxiety by writing erudite letters, he testifies to DeLillo's dawning awareness—part arrogance, part compunction—that he verges on being the type of writer *necessarily* without an audience: "I wrote a long hysterical letter on the subject of space-time. Even though I knew nothing about space-time, the letter was fairly easy to write. . . . When I was finished I tried to decide to whom it had been written. This itself seemed the most important thing about the letter. To whom was it going. . . . I thought of a dozen people and concluded that none was worthy."[63]

Stanley is haunted by the idea of a paralyzed "tribe" that worships what it fears: "We have too many bombs. . . . There's a kind of theology of fear that comes out of this. We begin to capitulate to the overwhelming presence. It's so powerful. It dwarfs us so much. We say let the god have its way. He's so much more powerful than we are."[64] He supplies us with another image of the masses as primitive, totemic, and clearly in need of a heroic figure to deliver them from their fear; the mass audience DeLillo wants to stifle but cannot bring himself to do so unequivocally. DeLillo's next novel, *Great Jones Street,* centers on this missing heroic figure, his responsibilities and his likely failure; tellingly, DeLillo crafts him directly out of the stuff of Gary Harkness, the stuff of the seemingly unrepentant ironist.

Accordingly, an archetypal story lies beneath the typically ironic tone of *Great Jones Street:* the story of the immature young hero who shirks responsibility and must undergo a grueling and redemptive process of rebirth to regain his voice and guide his people. Campbell has spelled out the prototype: "This is in myth a perpetual theme, in the voices of the prophets a familiar cry: the people yearn for some personality who, in a world of twisted bodies and souls, will represent again the lives of the incarnate image."[65] DeLillo's structure, like his plot, keeps to "fundamentals;" his presentation is largely realistic, his characters are sharply defined, and he never releases his grip on the narrative, taking care that it does not disintegrate entirely into digressions, disruptions. Predictably, many critics have either attacked or neglected *Great Jones Street* for its failure to suit their criteria of disruption and challenge; Oriard labels *Great Jones Street* "the least interesting and most plotted of DeLillo's novels,"[66] although in the final analysis its plot is very comprehensible in comparison to DeLillo's other early work and certainly to the postmodern mean. What we likely have in Oriard is a categorical depreciation of plot as an essential value of fiction. On the other side of the divide, Hal Crowther extols a new sense of detail in DeLillo's characterizations that communicates his predominant themes with new vigor: "a representative novel like *Great Jones Street* or *Players* creates empathy with a recognizably human protagonist menaced by irrational forces."[67]

Before his transformation, rock superstar Bucky Wunderlick is of the mindset that to inflict a song on the airwaves is an act of pornography, an idea buttressed by unsuccessful writer Fenig, who resides above Bucky in a dilapidated building on Great Jones Street and schemes of striking it rich by appealing to society's most sensationalistic cravings, shock-genres like pornographic children's literature: "Serious stuff. Filthy, obscene and brutal sex among little kids."[68] In 1973, DeLillo was, like Fenig, writing in obscurity, but was creeping closer and closer here to accessibility, and to the equivalent, to his elitist eye, of Fenig's porn. It is no surprise that he was attracted to Bucky's minimalist philosophy; like the majority of DeLillo's characters, Wunderlick longs for a pristine state of language, and to this end he endeavors to strip away all the most frivolous aspects of our modern tongue in order to reach an elemental core, equivalent to the state of a baby at the moment of birth (described in one of his songs: "I was born with all the languages in my mouth. . . . Nothing-maker/ but to blurt/ But to sing/ Baby god and goo"[69]). The desired end result of such an artistic program would be awash in any number of paradoxes, a near-complete silence that yet expresses all the meanings incommunicable in the wanton excess of our contemporary tongue. There are numerous symbols in the text for this wordless or near-wordless state, such as "the package," a much-coveted, silence-inducing drug stolen from government labs which "has no trade name,"[70] or the Micklewhite boy in the apartment downstairs from Bucky, a horribly malformed mute who represents, by visage alone, "the beauty and terror of wordless things."[71] Thus we have the mantra to which Bucky's musical investigations have inexorably led him: "The Beast is loose/ Least is best."[72]

Yet Bucky's lover Opel recognizes that such theories of "no-language" signify only self-indulgence, and instead of "least is best" she insists that "Evil is the movement toward void."[73] Young Bucky, who sets fire to stewardesses, who has displayed no outward sign of compunction for his puerile acts, represents the DeLillo that Bawer sees, the shrewd and perceptive mind that has chosen mordancy. But as in Sully's story, DeLillo, through Opel, urges us to look inside before looking outside: "Ever since I've known you, you've been surrounded by money-grubbing and talk of money and people dealing and operating but that's the last thing you'll ever be corrupted by, money, even if you were literally starving. It's yourself you have to watch out for, that little touch of the antichrist."[74]

All of DeLillo's early protagonists abdicate positions of authority; Bell squanders his network position to pursue his pretentious avant-garde film experiments, and Harkness turns to asceticism immediately after being named team captain. Bucky's position is far more influential, however; he is the prophet-figure, the poet. He can hardly be faulted for wanting to step down from his authoritative position, though, for in the world in which he moves, authority and influence are always linked with brute force. This fact is recognized and manipulated by the militant group known as Happy Valley Commune, a perversion of both Thoreau's encomium to privacy and the sixties dream of communion, whose leader is Bohack, described by his compatriot Chess as the brains of the operation: "He doesn't have any special magnetism. His ideas just miss being interesting ideas. For a long time I couldn't figure out what made him so indispensable. It's because he's so big."[75] To emphasize that this environment has squelched the concept of artistic epiphany, DeLillo goes so far as to supply a character *named* Epiphany, who exemplifies the failure of all cultured ambitions: "She used to sing, she used to model, she used to act. Now she's doing security."[76]

Bucky's greatest artistic impediment, though, is his palpable scorn for the audience to whom he would be offering his work. He insists, as Bloom might, that aesthetic concerns completely overwhelm "the basic question of human values, human concerns." To a panel debating human values in art, Bucky states: "People dying from the effects of all this beauty and power. That's art, sweetheart."[77] He can rationalize this approach because his is an audience of grotesques in the grand American style, Anderson through West through O'Connor. The only difference is that where the "ordinary" men and women in Anderson and West turn on obvious grotesques like Wing Biddlebaum and Homer Simpson because they represent something they fear and despise in themselves, a falling short of the American ideal of perfection and civilized behavior, here the obvious grotesques *are* "ordinary" men and women; Bucky, reified in economic and media terms, represents the only other gradient on the social scale, and he feels nothing but disgust for the audience that has enabled his divinity: "the man who spotted me drew gradually closer, pretending to read the labels along the way, finally sidling in next to me at the counter, the living effigy of a cost accountant or tax lawyer, radiating his special grotesquerie, that of sane men leading normal lives."[78]

Corporations have now won out, putting a damper on whatever will to violence these grotesques might possess. The normals in West's *Day of the Locust* pilgrimage to Hollywood to claim some of its illusions for themselves, as if a proximity to movie stars might allow them to conquer death and fate by becoming like glitzy filmed images themselves. When they are inevitably disillusioned, the result is a simmering violence, a potential riot release. The music industry of DeLillo's world represents a far more savvy public relations approach, in which the innate negativity of the audience is neither ignored nor stifled to the danger-point but rather incorporated into the realm of "art." Instead of denying the death instinct with professionally-rendered glamour and beauty, it aggrandizes it, promising violence, loveless sex, and destruction; in the end, the effect is to intensify self-loathing but blunt the will to action. Bucky has played this part himself, harnessing social rage to no constructive purpose: "the country's blood was up, this or that atrocity, home or abroad, and even before we hit stage the whole place was shaking. We were the one group that people depended on to validate their emotions."[79]

Thus Bucky faces the extremes of the artist: superiority, misanthropy, paranoia, isolationism, pandering concession. To complicate matters further, his aspirations to prophet-hood are continually derailed by Globke, the most elusive character in the novel. Globke is Bucky's agent, manager, and handler, and therefore a fitting symbol for all the forces of the market. He steals away Bucky's hidden tapes, all for the money, of course: "We needed product, see. You were failing to deliver product. Product is something that matters deeply. You owed us product."[80] He represents impediments that are nothing new for the mythic hero, as Campbell observes: "the problem of making known the way of illumination to people wrapped in economic problems may seem too great to solve."[81] But Globke is himself a victim of media-minded society, representing, like Bell's mother, much that is glossed over in the capitalist view, the figure cut out of the ads: "See, oldness and fatness. They make me a bad person."[82] He is also an embodiment of Nietzsche's slave mentality, his bourgeois values and cushioning religion binding him to a life of servitude without possibility of exodus, martyrdom, resurrection, deliverance: "Globke was accustomed to being propelled, ballistically, to and from distant points of commerce, and so there was something agreeably serene, even biblical, in his rudimentary journey down those stairs . . . haunches rocking in that firm eternal way of beasts of burden."[83] Globke's shackles are no different from those worn by the parade of passerby workers, "bearers of a weight that went beyond simple pounds and ounces," whose own "moral obligations of . . . Saturday night"[84] seem absurd in light of the homeless who mill about Great Jones Street. Bucky, in his reified state, can be holy only because he is free of such a lifestyle; but his freedom has made him weak in character: "I became a half-saint, practiced in visions, informed by a sense of bodily economy, but deficient in true pain."[85]

Globke does recognize, with the kind of insight lacked by most of the music audience, the throng, that Bucky's angst and causticity have had nothing to offer him, nothing to use: "You attack even the things I hold dearest, Bucky." He craves music that stresses human relationships and, again, emotional residue; music that can depict meaning: "I wish you'd go back to writing lyrics, real lyrics, the way you used to write them. That would amaze and delight the whole world."[86]

In several beautifully wrought passages, DeLillo describes the media looming over the downtrodden working masses like the greedy bosses and newfangled skyscrapers of a twenties or thirties novel of social realism; in the courts, the newspapers seem to be the final arbitrators, a reference reaching back to *Bleak House,* only with the *Daily News* replacing the obscuring Chancellery fog: "Behind his counter the blind newsdealer loomed as justice does, something of a self-parody, appearing to sense every nuance in the hall. . . . Short purposeful men crossed the lobby on their way to and from duty, each slightly overweight and carrying the *Daily News* folded under one arm."[87] DeLillo is marking a transition point here, the giving way of the traditional novelistic approach, exemplified by these precise, beautiful passages, to the postmodern age of media saturation, which he will later convey in *White Noise* through his incorporation of the ambient babble of advertising jingles, the slight hissing of machines working their way into the subconscious. In *Great Jones Street,* though, he seems to be working his way back, an act of defiant nostalgia, a refusal to concede that the media has changed the medium.

Correspondingly, the novel has its share of Dickensian children abandoned to the streets. Although DeLillo insists that his New York is not much different from the Texas desert in *End Zone*—"these places are deserts too, just as beautiful and scary and as a matter of fact"[88]—New York is present for us here as much more than a symbol of epistemological meltdown. We are reminded not of *End Zone* or even *The Waste Land* but of the Manhattan of John Dos Passos's *Manhattan Transfer,* a city in chaos, in which fires burst into life without warning and raze blocks of homes, and in which men and women seem caught in cycles of success and impoverishment always beyond their control: "two feeble men wrestled quietly, humming wordless curses at each other, and an old woman limped into view, bundled in pounds of rags. . . . The fire engine went speeding down Broadway, pure sound now, shrill wind, a voice from the evilist dreams."[89]

It is when speaking of the city in his interviews that DeLillo seems most socially active and aware: "I think we need to invent beauty, to seek out some resisting force. A writer may describe the ugliness and pain in graphic terms but he can also try to find a dignity and significance in the ruined parts of the city, and the people he sees there."[90] Thus it is that a homeless man becomes a true prophet of the visionary sort, his message not only to elucidate economic issues—a beggar-like apple vendor holds up a sign that reads "YOU'RE BUYING I'M SELLING"[91]—but to force readers to acknowledge their complicity in his suffering, a complicity not attributable to our lack of public service but to our failure to even imagine another world, another order of things: "His seemed to be the type of accusation aimed at those too constricted in spirit to see the earth as a place for gods to grow, a theater of furious encounters between prophets of calamity and simple pedestrians trying to make the light."[92]

Before members of the Happy Valley Commune inject him with "the package," submerging him in a silence in which no speech is possible, Bucky admits to his persecutors Chess and Bohack how callow he has been: "I've done things without understanding them fully. . . . You can't kill yourself when you're half-rotten with plague. Only the innocent are received."[93] His time under the influence of the drug functions on symbolic terms as the descent of the hero into the darkness of the underworld, even if it is a peculiarly linguistic Hades; again, in Campbell's terms: "once having traversed the threshold, the hero moves in a dream landscape of curiously fluid, ambiguous forms; where he must survive a succession of trials."[94] His is the usual postmodern dichotomy: "How translate into terms of "yes" or "no" revelations that shatter into meaninglessness every attempt to define the pairs of opposites?" [95] Yet, as Bucky's admission to Chess and Bohack suggests, his transformation is personal as well; he has come to downgrade his more abstract intellectualization in favor of the human implications. The deformed Micklewhite boy is, as we have noted, the perfect "symbol" of some sort of language beyond words, or of an absolute detachment and solitude; too misshapen to move, perhaps not intelligent enough to think, he is the emblem of all that Bucky, pre-transformation, covets for himself, as Mark Osteen observes: "he has managed to achieve what Bucky has futilely sought in withdrawal: to remove himself from the failed economy."[96] But though Bucky is attuned to the boy's symbolic significance, he insists on always making connections to the boy's humanity, certainly not an easy step considering the extent of his deformity, let alone his literariness: "It would have been better (and even cheering) to think of him as some kind of super-crustacean or diabolic boiled vegetable. But he was too human for that."[97] After his experiences under the drug, Bucky will put these inclinations into action, becoming a father figure of sorts to street urchin Skippy, a more palpable sign of enhanced social involvement.

Bucky's loss of language is a purification that allows him to re-experience innocence, but this innocence is not the end-all nullity he has tried to approximate in his music. The true key to his growth is the regaining, not the loss, of speech, the renewal of his voice. He will not, we think, retreat into isolation like Bell on his island. The narrative voice, Bucky's newfound voice, suggests a markedly different level of maturity than that of the impudent young ironist it depicts. Leonard Wilcox believes that the novel marks "the demise of notions of a 'heroic' search for alternative, creative forms of consciousness, and the idea of art as specially endowed revelation."[98] Bucky's final narrative, however, may be such a form; at the very least, what it does make clear is that the worst postmodern nightmares are not the only postmodern possibilities.

This foundation of character and mimesis in *Great Jones Street* gives way to mathematics in DeLillo's next novel, the vast science/science fiction opus *Ratner's Star,* which depicts the efforts of the mathematicians and scientists of "Field Experiment Number One" to decipher extraterrestrial signals emanating from the vicinity of the titular star. DeLillo not only adopts their language but also composes his novel as if devising an equation; the implications of this decision on his structure dovetail perfectly with LeClair's ideas: "I wanted the book to become what it was about. Abstract structures and connective patterns. A piece of mathematics, in short. To do this, I felt I had to reduce the importance of people. The people had to play a role subservient to pattern, form, and so on. I believed I was doing something new and was willing to take the risk."[99] Steffen Hantke very pragmatically recognizes, however, that for all but the most obsessive readers the effect of the novel will not be any new perception but the same conceptual miasma that stultifies its characters: "there are too many characters for even the most attentive reader to remember; scientific discussion goes back to prehistory, and even crosses over into parascience."[100]

DeLillo is certainly aware of this effect; Viverrine Gentian, one in his flood of largely undifferentiated characters, describes a book she is reading, entitled *Somnium,* as "an experimental novel, an allegory, a lunar geography, an artful autobiography, a cryptic scientific tract, a work of science fiction."[101]

Somnium is an accurate characterization of *Ratner's Star*, of course, and the title suggests a sleep-inducing tome, DeLillo toying with Susan Sontag's assertion that in great literature there is no such thing as boredom.

Many of the text's challenges lie in the "scientific" prose voice, as exemplified by protagonist Billy Terwilliger's esoteric ruminations, in which he sees modern mathematics "crowding its boundaries. Coordinates numbering *n*. Nature's space and his. To increase in size by the addition of material through assimilation. To become extended or intensified."[102] DeLillo defends such prose as valid for artistic pursuit: "science in general has given us a new language to draw from. Some writers shrink from this. . . . To me, science is the source of new names, new connections between people and the world."[103] Yet in truth he may be drawn to mathematics more because it is "the only avante garde remaining in the whole province of art," as Endor, a renowned scientist living now in a hole dug in the earth, explains.[104]

There are moments in the book, however, in which DeLillo's intricate and over-determined scientific language does successfully describe and define human relationships in the modern age; one such example begins the novel's second half, which deals with a splinter group of scientists residing beneath Field Experiment Number One and attempting to construct Logicon, that postmodern holy grail of a perfected language. The frenzied pace of new character introduction slows in this section, finally allowing us to discern a handful of individual personalities; the passage in question portrays the post-lovemaking actions of Softly, once Billy's mentor, and writer-in-the-making Jean Sweet Venable: "Everywhere dense the space between them seemed a series of incremental frames that defined their passion's dark encompassment, man ostensibly engrossed in dressing, woman nude and on her side (a horizontal dune anagrammatized), neither failing to be aware of the sediment of recent links and distances . . ." The dulled writing effectively captures not only the spent quality of post-coital awareness but also, given that their shallow relationship seems based only on sex, the enervation of lovelessness. The scientific abstraction functions as a counterpoint to all the vitality that should be involved in this interpersonal dynamic but is clearly lacking: "sweat and re-echoing flesh serving to confirm the urgent nature of their act, the industry involved, the reconnoitering for fit and placement, the fundamental motion, the pursuit of equable rhythm." DeLillo is often compared to an anthropologist; here his scientific remove and observation of human interaction is astounding in detail and deliberately and effectively stagnant. The passage closes with a suggestion of feeling on Jean's part, a feeling that Softly, lost in abstraction, is not privileged to uncover or understand: "He spoke a moment longer (about terms, formulas, sentences and proofs), then he got up and hurried out of the room. . . . Had he happened to turn . . . for a final word or sweet and simple farewell nod he might have found himself a trifle mystified by the wry smile on his lover's face."[105] This is precisely the emotional residue that the novelist grasps and the mathematician cannot. Yet DeLillo has taken too great a risk; by this point in the narrative the reader may have been weaned off looking for such a thing, much like LeClair, who, though stressing the improved humanism of the novel's final sections, sees in this passage only the circular pattern necessary to back up his systems theory: "the single long sentence accumulates through a series of floating non-clauses and participles, shifting quickly between the two persons described, looping backward and forward to the act of intercourse, when the two bodies are continuous." [106]

LeClair's way of reading may actually be the easier approach, the easier choice. DeLillo forces a choice by insinuating quizzes into the narrative that question our style of reading, our own interests, as in the series of either/or statements in the "Space Brain Computer Quiz" (the Space Brain is a vast computer system that marks the pinnacle of abstraction in its "void core storage") which present Oedipa Maas's crisis all over again. The statement is: "faced with temptingly equivocal data, the annotator immediately begins to . . ." The choices the reader must choose between are "validate" and "salivate."[107] The urge to "validate," the bane of postmodern thought, suggests foundationalism, logocentricism, and nostalgia for conventional narrative. The contrary urge to "salivate" over inconsistency, paradox, and play re-introduces us to the scope of postmodern contingency, here defined courtesy of Orang Mohol, a scientist and dealer in drugs and porn who has won the fabled Cheop Feeley prize for "discovering" (inventing?) the mohole, a hypothetical coagulation of all that mass stipulated by the Big Bang theory that has remained undiscovered by science—and a scientific embodiment of contingency: "the essence of my brand of relativity—that in a mohole the laws of physics vary from one observer to another—is at odds with every notion of the universe that displays faith in nature."[108] Belief in the mohole, "part of a theoretical dimension lacking spatial extent and devoid of true value . . . value-dark in other words,"[109] is a belief in nothing, all belief systems becoming frivolous in retrospect. To accept the Mohole is to accept that all human action is, in the final analysis, meaningless, interchangeable, as summed up by Lester, one of the scientists working on the Logicon android: "If we are mohole-intense, it doesn't really matter, does it?"[110]

Jean, recruited by Softly not for her writing skill but for her talents in bed, steadily gains importance as a postmodern author-figure as the novel nears its conclusion. Like a New Critic poet, Jean first attempts to build an altar to form, sealing her work off from the outside world by way of an elaborate, precise structure: "Reading my book will be a game with specific rules that need to be followed. I'm free to make whatever rules I want as long as there's an inner firmness and cohesion, right? Just like mathematics, excuse the comparison."[111] Of course, all such illusions of order meet with ridicule throughout the book, the most glaring example being Schwartz's quixotic attempt to map out a comprehensive portrait of the galaxy via computer: "what we need at this stage of our perceptual development is an overarching symmetry. Something that constitutes what appears to be—even if it isn't—a totally harmonious view of the world system. Our naïveté, if nothing else, demands it."[112] To represent Jean's inevitable failure at form, DeLillo reprocesses the ancient metaphor of weaving as story-telling: "Earlier she had written a number of pages and now she was trying to busy herself in a different line of thinking. . . . She mumbled instructions to herself, not very successfully. The results, that is, were not successful, dangling buttons, loosely stitched seams; the mumbling itself was quite flawless."[113]

Given her failure to adequately match priceless thoughts to recalcitrant words, the obvious next step for Jean is to submerge herself in metafiction, an even further alienation from the reader than that proposed in the New Critic mindset: "There's a whole class of writers who don't want their books to be read. This to some extent explains their crazed prose. To express what is expressible isn't why you write if you're in this class of writers. To be understood is faintly embarrassing. What you want to express is the violence of your desire not to be read." In early interviews, DeLillo claimed that he alienated only those readers afraid of taking risks, in LeClair's terms "those wholly anesthetized readers who refuse the risk of loops."[114] He implied that there was an enlightened reader for whom he wrote: "The writer is driven by his conviction that some truths aren't arrived at so easily, that life is still full of mystery, that it might be better for you, Dear Reader, if you went back to the Living section of your newspaper because this is the dying section and you don't really want to be here."[115] Yet Jean's reflections suggest that this impulse is on a deeper level toward *no* reader: "If you're in this class, what you have to do is either not publish or make absolutely sure your work leaves readers strung along the margins."[116] Accordingly, DeLillo also stated: "this writer is writing against the age and he feels some satisfaction at not being widely read. He is diminished by an audience." The potential poet figure of *Great Jones Street* is nowhere in evidence, although fleetingly suggested in the illustrious figure of Chester Graylag Dent, a Nobel Prize winner in literature whose work very explicitly parallels the progress of DeLillo's career from "epic, piquant disquisitions on . . . the logic of games, the gamesmanship of fiction and prehistory" in *End Zone* to "famous 'afterthoughts' on the ethereally select realms of abstract mathematics" in *Ratner's Star.* This self-portrait seems in itself quite self-satisfied, but fails to explain what exactly the correlation is between a humanism "reflective of an incessant concern for man's standing in the biosphere" and a style "best characterized as undiscourageably diffuse."[117] This seeming contradiction proves damning when Dent eventually appears as a character in the narrative, consulted by Softly on Logicon. Dent carries on a peripatetic existence inside a submarine, "the quietest place on earth."[118] Much sought after despite having no apparent scientific qualifications, Dent seemingly functions to dispense DeLillo's message of solidarity, but he himself is impotent in self-exile, representative of the hypocrisy potential in any socially-conscious author, the misanthrope preaching unity.

Yet Billy himself seems to represent not only Dent's synthesis of the "outside world" and a heavily abstracted mode of science but also Bucky's potential to be a poet-figure to the masses. The latter prospect understandably frightens him: "Pretend you're the imperial mathematician. The emperor and his cousin the bishop want to know the meaning of a new star in the heavens. In the town square the witch-hunters are gathering twigs."[119] He is another ascetic, another elitist; his projected future home recalls the sparse apartment of Wolfe's pretentious young bus-rider with a "lamp with a crooked shade, manuscripts stacked in a corner of the room," the whole perfect for his "austere self-veneration." [120] Yet he nevertheless believes that his work "gradually reveals its attachment to the charged particles of other minds, men now historical, the re-discovered dead; to the main structure of mathematical thought; perhaps even to reality itself, the so-called sum of things."[121] But does it? His work to date has revolved around his theoretical construction of Zorgs, which, as he frequently points out, have no practical application. Which is the true ideal of *Ratner's Star?* Is it a dense and daunting work of art that nevertheless penetrates the human realm? To some degree it proves to be so, but only through its realistic depiction of Billy's past, not its mathematical material; Billy's life, not his work.

Billy is a traditional child hero; much younger then Bell, Harkness, or Wunderlick, he is a reincarnation of the plucky Skippy in *Great Jones Street* or the child who plays ball with Bell on an Indian reservation in *Americana's* lone moment of genuine transcendence; like them he possesses a mystical aura, a Wordsworthian innocence, to DeLillo's eyes: "I think we feel, perhaps superstitiously, that children have a direct route to, have direct contact with the kind of natural truth that eludes us as adults."[122] It is ironist Softly who reinforces Billy's function in the text, precisely at the point in the novel's concluding sections when Billy's centrality is compromised by the expansive discussion of Logicon. Softly reminisces about an Asian orphan adopted by his neighbors: "she possessed something unique. Moral authority. . . . Because she was tiny, virtually mute, because she was an Asian, an orphan, a victim of war, Phan was the ultimate moral force in that household."[123] Billy's background is not as tormented as Phan's, but the world of his youth, as opposed to the Wonderland-made-inaccessible of Field Experiment Number One, is one in which human values are tested, in which poverty, suffering, and genuine emotion factor. Such a background cannot be fully integrated into the text as a whole; its inclusion often seems as uneasy or unanticipated on DeLillo's part as the memory of Phan is on Softly's, as Edna points out to him: "It's unlike you to put things on a human level. . . . It's a pleasant change, truth be known."[124]

In his interviews, DeLillo insists that the "real world," our physical surroundings, our contemporary environment, must be elucidated in fiction: "So much modern fiction is located precisely nowhere. . . . Fiction without a sense of real place is automatically a fiction of estrangement, and of course this is the point . . . but I can't write that way myself. I'm too interested in what real places look like and what names they have. Place is color and texture."[125] Yet Bawer is correct in pointing out that "it's hard . . . to conjure up a clear picture of Logos College in *End Zone* or the huge futuristic scientific institute in *Ratner's Star.*"[126] DeLillo has failed to meet his own criteria in the novel at large, then, but he does fully flesh out the urban Hades of Billy's youth, the subway where his father Babe works, full of horrific but not unrealistic elements: rats, sparks, gloom, and twisted metal. DeLillo will look back to this scene, as well as a later visit to the Bronx zoo, in his landmark *Libra;* both scenes correspond to DeLillo's childhood memories, and as such are cornerstones of his movement toward a more realistic novel.

Babe is the anti-Softly, not because he represents any kind of moral advancement (he does not) but because he seems to exemplify realism as a value much as Softly, a born liar, exemplifies postmodern play. Whenever Billy's memories drift toward linguistic exegesis, Babe wrenches the narrative back with his colorful behavior, recollecting the father-figures of Tobias or Geoffrey Wolff:

> Later he'd sometimes grip the poolstick like a baseball bat and assume the batting stances of famous ballplayers of the past. Faye and Billy would be asked to identify the man whose stance he was imitating but neither ever knew and this annoyed Babe to the point where he'd pick up the phone and call his friend from the subways, Izzy Seltzer. He then resumed his stance, which Faye would have to describe to Izzy over the phone.[127]

Babe is not a harmless buffoon; there is rage in him, and paranoia, and the cause is in the dank subways, in the ever-present garbage ("much of local violence had garbage at its heart . . . a fester never ending, a mode and code of conduct"[128]).

When Babe, in a moment of paranoid lunacy, accosts a elderly, harmless passerby, we recall the bottled rage of Albert Schearl in Henry Roth's *Call It Sleep,* feral frustrations stemming from the failure of the American dream; frustrations of a naturalistic character, not a postmodern questing anti-hero.

Theirs is a realistically dismal world, peppered, in other words, with hope, humor, transcendence; completely realized. On the beach, fights are swelling to riot proportions, with answering violence from the police; motives are not given, but a boy does not need to understand: "he was soaked through with rain now but feeling lighter, more *sentient.*"[129] This is life in its awesome fullness, precisely what is missing from the much longer and denser focus of the novel, which is much opposed to this "death and sheepish laughter, *whomp,* dark sky and life."

The eclipse that Billy has predicted closes the novel, shrouding not only the static world of Field Experiment Number One but also a far less privileged realm of human poverty—starving Asian masses, diseased children, heaps of dung, presented to us in by-now-unaccustomed detail, "bodies of the starved abandoned on tiled verandahs, human experience."[130] But the reader finds himself thrust in the role of a "Ratnerian," and as such he occupies a state of "painless 'nonexistence,' the theoretical ideal of *n*-space."[131] This is a simile for literary detachment, representative of the overarching abstraction of the novel. Correspondingly, the ironic reader is rebuffed by these suffering masses much as the conventional reader might rebuff the postmodern author: "Why are you here? To unsnarl us from our delimiting senses? To offer protective cladding against our cruelty and fear? The pain, the life-cry speak our most candid wonders. To out-premise these, by whatever *tekite* whirl you've mastered, would be to make us hypothetical, a creature of our own pretending, as are you."[132] Here DeLillo's ideal reader, the reader he has created in the text, faces at least one instant, pivotally placed, of indignation. But this admission hardly seems enough to counteract all—and *how*—we have read, our grooming at the hands of "mastery." DeLillo has reached the melting point of literary self-absorption. In his next novels—*Players, Running Dog,* and *The Names*—he approaches the space of human suffering that such predilections minimize, abandoning a highly compromised elitism for a highly compromised populism, approximating Rorty's brand of irony by drawing attention to the human tendency to deny human tendencies in art.

Players and *Running Dog* represent a reactionary swing in the opposite direction of *Ratner's Star,* featuring pared-down plots, uncolorful but defined characters, and briskly comprehensible (and linear) narratives. Along with the more challenging *The Names,* they form a trilogy of genre works exploring the pulp thriller domain of the terrorist, the detective, the jaded world-traveler, the spy. As DeLillo explains, somewhat unnecessarily, the appeal of this vein of literature, of this or any other brand of pop culture art, is its simplicity, its offer of escapism: "Heart-throbbing romance and knock-about comedy and nerve-wracking suspense. History this weightless has an easy time of it, we learn, contending with the burdens of the present day."[133]

DeLillo disdains the reading public used to having its expectations sated in this way. Once again, pornography (which features prominently in the "espionage" of *Running Dog*) is DeLillo's metaphor for the reader's coarsest appetites; in *Players,* carnal lust and bloodlust seem to fit perfectly, casually, into the domestic scene, as Pammy's wandering gaze suggests: "the rows of paperback books set on the broad shelf between the portable TV and the wall. Mystery, mystery, spy, sex, mystery."[134] In *Running Dog,* he continues this personification of the average reader, equating him to a New York tourist in the seediest parts of town, perversely fascinated with the rubble and the rabble. When a pimpmobile makes it jaunty trip through Times Square crowds, a multitude of such voyeurs are on alert: "a conventioneer wearing an enormous name-tag crouched in the gutter, inserting a flash cube in his Instamatic."[135] This squalor is comfortably couched in the Novel's sense of order, as seen through the eyes of Del Bravo, the hero of the first chapter of *Running Dog,* who represents the detective ideal to be deflated by Auster in *The New York Trilogy:* "Trucks and earth-moving equipment. Derelicts around a fire. Experience told him what he'd see."[136] With such a sense of overall stability in place, it is safe to indulge in a pornographer's or voyeur's inclination: "he directed the light down under the bra, spotting dark bristles of recently shaved hair. Without touching the body he moved the flashlight slowly over her hands, face, hairline, neck and legs."[137]

Given this self-awareness, one might assume these novels to be disruptive in their genre analysis, very much akin to those works described by H.R. Jauss that can "evoke the readers' horizon of expectations formed by a connection of genre, style, or form, only in order to destroy it step by step."[138] Yet there is no doubt that these three novels constitute a movement *toward* that very same lascivious audience they decry. It is only to be expected that DeLillo's apprehension and abhorrence would steadily mount the closer he creeps toward the mainstream; as John Aldridge notes, this is a familiar anxiety for any modern writer injecting realism into the largely anti-realistic climate: "he may comfort himself with the knowledge that he will be read by millions of grateful readers, but he will surely be snubbed by critics and by his peers as meretricious and third rate."[139] All the conventions are there, as even LeClair himself acknowledges, and mourns; he labels *Running Dog* DeLillo's "least achieved"[140] novel on the grounds that it "too explicitly and consistently argues the destructive effects of the conditions it delineates."[141]

The novel's typically Pynchonesque conspiracies, for example, are surprisingly well-defined, supplying the reader with an unaccustomed sensation of authority. He or she does not have to wait very long, for instance, to learn the true nature of Radial Matrix, the hub of paranoia, bureaucracy and sprawling economics in *Running Dog:* "a centralized funding mechanism for covert operations directed against foreign governments, against elements within foreign governments, and against political parties trying to gain power contrary to the interests of U.S. corporations abroad." This type of explicit enumeration does not come easily to DeLillo; this dutiful description concludes with a perfunctory "so on, so on, so on."[142] But he enumerates all the same.

DeLillo wants his reader to recognize the salacious aspects of popular entertainment, not as much its lack of art but its affinity to violence, which has a political extension, as terrorist Kinnear in *Players* observes: "But they were our fantasies, weren't they, ultimately? The whole assortment. Our leaders simply lived them out. Our elected representatives. . . . All we had to do was know our own dreams."[143] Yet DeLillo wants to engage the reader in his own medium; he does not want to retreat into the avant garde. *Players* begins with passengers on a plane watching a film depicting a terrorist bloodbath on a golf course; the film is very much in Sam Peckinpah mode, bordering on camp: "we're steeped in gruesomely humorous ambiguity, a spectacle of ridiculous people doing awful things to total fools."[144] Instead of the film's soundtrack, there is a piano player contributing the carnivalesque tone of silent film, and thus the audience's interaction with this horrid violence is very much like that remote and self-satisfied demeanor that Bryson disparages in DeLillo's authorial stance, "appalled by the degree to which [his writing] had become unable to feel."[145] We ourselves are placed among this audience too, our presence suggested by those viewers whose faces are blotted out, "the top of not a single head visible over the high-backed mechanical chairs. We assume people are sitting there, content to sift among the images."[146] Even if we are not desensitized to violence, political strife, and moral atrocities, DeLillo questions whether we still capable of reacting to such issues when expressed through art, or whether we are merely "entertained" as Lyle is by television: "what he saw retained his attention completely even after it continued to dull his senses."[147]

Running Dog represents, to some degree, the art under exploration in the *Players* preface; it *is* the in-flight movie, in a sense, and it is not coincidental that the text has a cinematic quality that *Players* lacks: sweeping tableaus, a suggestion of vast space even within Manhattan's constricted streets, like that in a John Ford film, or in Kurosawa's *Seven Samurai;* indeed, the work of both these directors influences the novel's climactic scene, in which "hero" Glenn Selvy confronts Vietnamese "cowboys" on a desert plain, their pursuit having had "the foredained character of some classical epic, modernized to include a helicopter."[148] Kurosawa elected to compose violence in wide shots images to suggest its futility, diverging from the engagement of violence pursued by American cinema in its quick-editing and its worship of the heroic or villainous countenance in close-up. Yet DeLillo suggests, on the other hand, that the impression of separation afforded by wide shots allows the viewer to celebrate violence while maintaining a comforting sense of distance; close-ups, in contrast, wither the epic down to the human, as when cameras attuned to Hitler's last days—in the lost film hunted by everyone in the novel, from gangsters to government officials—reveal the pitiful humanity that has been at the root of all the slaughter and evil, reducing a tyrant to the level, as O'Donnell observes, of "everyone else, externalized and surveyed."[149] Many critics claim, though, that in this gesture DeLillo strips Nazism of its moral evil, his postmodernist interest in media leading him into all sorts of moral evasions.

Moral evasions are at the center of these novels, as Pammy's nature suggests: "Talk of violence made her sigh. Things in the street, just things she saw and heard day to day, forced her into subtle evasions."[150] Hers is the everyday manifestation of Lyle's more drastic evasion; Lyle, though drawn into a terrorist ring bent on targeting Wall Street, declines to pursue the connection between his own Wall Street employment and the poverty he sees all around him. Finance assumes a sublime aspect in Lyle's contemplation, both a horror and a glory, but beyond economics somehow, a locus not of greed but postmodern ambiguity: "He'd seen the encoding rooms, the micro-filming of checks, money moving, shrinking as it moved, beginning to elude visualization, to pass from paper existence to electronic sequences, its meaning increasingly complex, harder to name. It was condensation, the whole process, a paring away of money's accidental properties, of money's touch."[151] "Accidental properties" is a phrase from Elizabeth Bishop; her man-moth, seeing only the moon's "accidental properties," climbs from his underworld to try to peer through its hole, into its light, only to return, misled by his senses, bearing in his eye a precious, crystalline tear, romanticism's transforming imagination defeated by epistemological bafflement. Like the man-moth's moon, Lyle suggests, money is not what it seems to be; yet he may have everything inverted, his own idea of money the romantic one. DeLillo might have used this money, instead, as Frank Norris did grain in *The Octopus,* as the force shaping his characters, consuming them both figuratively and, in the case of a greedy businessman drowned in his grain, literally. Instead, as it shifts from the solidity of coin and paper to the formlessness and omnipresence of credit, "money" is, like the hole in the ground in O'Brien's *The Nuclear Age* (see chapter seven), both everything and nothing. By limiting this material to

Lyle's shallow consciousness, DeLillo admits his own evasions and yet still carries them out, as Updike observes: "the very intensity of Mr. DeLillo's wish . . . to say something new about the matter has evaporated the matter, leaving behind an exquisite ash-skeleton of elliptic dialogue and spindly motivation."[152]

But DeLillo does not maintain this reticence for long, for *Running Dog* is not nearly as equivocating or elusive about the harshest influence of capitalistic pursuits. Earl Mudger, a contemporary Milo Minderbender and the brain behind Radial Matrix, recognizes that there is no discernible difference between the techniques of wartime covert operations and the etiquette of the economic arena: "He uses the same message in business he used in espionage activities. That's why the firm's a whopping success."[153] Similarly, Richie Armbrister, a teenager in control of a powerful porn ring, recalls Gaddis's J.R., part of a new generation in which capitalist techniques are apparently inscribed from birth, stifling from the start the youthful impudence that is one of DeLillo's behavioral ideals: "They'll never find me. I have too much paper floating around. I'm very well hidden, believe me. Holding companies in four states. I don't exist as a person anymore."[154] Where DeLillo struggles here, though, is in suggesting the influence of that clandestine world on the surface world, the world of those *without* power, the reader's world. There is no domestic life to represent this world, as there was in *Ratner's Star* and there will be in *White Noise* and *Libra.*

Again, DeLillo's evasiveness is hard to separate from Lyle's. Lyle does not want to see "regular" people as cogs in a capitalist wheel, an admirable wish in itself, but instead he sees them only as a mob, a crowd better avoided but haunting his awareness: "Lyle hadn't been down here in years, the Lower East Side, that ethnic pantechnicon, *streets, people,* a history of flawless suffering."[155] In *Running Dog,* the pressure of the masses is growing stronger, overwhelming the spare plot with energy, potentially destructive, that recalls the carnivalesque Times Square of Coover's *The Public Burning.* In fact, Selvy's pursuit does lead him to Times Square; there is nowhere better, DeLillo suggests, to address the burgeoning life that is America in all its increasingly variable, and to many perverse, forms: "Everybody's in costume. Cowboys, bikers, drag queens, punk rockers, decoy cops, Moonies, gypsies, Salvation Army regulars, Process evangelists in dark capes, skinhead Krishna chanters in Saffron robes and tennis sneakers. Glitter and trash everywhere."[156]

These undefined masses protect their interests, however. They preserve the issue of the Vietnam War from that abstraction that many critics feel engulfs World War II in the novel. Moll, a presumably intrepid writer for *Running Dog* magazine, decorates her car with a snide "Vietnam—Love It Or Leave It" bumper-sticker, though she admits that she holds no real opinion, moral or political, on the war. She is elevating an anti-establishment facade over any sincerely held political conviction, and the denizens of the shadows correspondingly voice their disapproval: "And don't two guys come staggering out of a bar on Eighty-Sixth Street while I'm stopped for a light? And don't they see my sign and start pounding on my car until the whole thing gets out of hand and there's a mob of people and I end up with a broken ankle and my car gets wrecked?"[157]

But what of the individuals who make up the mob? DeLillo has said that his characters in these books are "ideas, vague shapes"[158] instead of "people I love or hate."[159] Yet at the same time they are "people I recognize."[160] This is confusing realism, to say the least. Updike observes that such shallow characterizing discourages "the considerable suspension of disbelief necessary to follow them into their adventures,"[161] yet, given that in "pure" genre fiction we generally accept such "vague shapes" without question, DeLillo, if nothing else, has exposed our own cruelties. For example, Moll suffers yet more abuses in the presence of Mudger, who makes sexual advances while she tills him for information. His appraisal of her is jolting: "Long legs like yours. You don't mind a little tough language, a touch of the unrefined. . . . Cunt. Bitch. Cunt."[162] Jarring and cruel as his assessment is, however, astute readers recognize that this indeed is the Moll that DeLillo has created for them, a standard pulp fiction woman defined by legs and snazzy dialogue—a type the reader might have accepted without reservation if unchallenged.

Moll is the ideal for Selvy because he wants nothing from a woman but a body; as birds hop "mechanically" in the grass outside, his thoughts drift to a "nondescript room, a bed with a naked woman straddling a pillow, no one he knew, and then sex, her body and his, relentless crude obliterating sex, bang, bang, bang."[163] Of course, this use of the imagination is to be expected given Selvy's line of work, which prevents his pursuit of "human links"[164] or emotional residue. However, Selvy meets his match in Nadine, a young woman whose company he acquires during the Times Square leg of his flight from Radial Matrix. Nadine represents the underprivileged and undeveloped citizen so often depicted by DeLillo only through the drunk, the homeless, and the wandering pervert. She herself is no innocent—Selvy rescues her from reading pornographic stories to the great and avaricious unwashed—but she certainly approximates innocence in comparison to the systemic violence perpetrated by Selvy, Mudger, and his cohorts at Radial Matrix. When the Vietnamese cowboys track Selvy down, Nadine expresses her befuddlement with a colloquialism so absurdly wholesome that it humanizes an otherwise coldly efficient depiction of combat: "I don't know more'n a monkey who they are."[165] Similarly, in their lovemaking Nadine denies Selvy his prerogative for reduction: "When they were in bed together, everything about her suggested an appealing healthiness. It bothered him. She seemed to think sex was wholesome and sweet."[166] Even more impressively, she continually forces Selvy's thoughts back from abstraction, asceticism, and irony—moral evasions—to fundamentals at hand, as in her description of her childhood home in Arkansas, far removed from the bacchanal of Times Square:

> "You ought to see the house. It's a shack, just about. Half the things in our house my mother made out of old feed sacks. Dish towels, face towels, napkins, even a lot of our clothes. Pillow cases. Feed sack pillow cases. Feed sack dresses and skirts."
>
> "Recycling."
>
> "Poverty," she said.[167]

DeLillo's inclusion of Nadine is perhaps his most important gesture in the novel; although ultimately she cannot dissuade Selvy from his bitter end, she provides a pivotal counter-balance to the omnipresent criminal element of the novel, pivotal because that criminal element often manipulates the rhetoric of solidarity to egregious ends. For example, in the midst of a standoff with Richie Armbrister over the Hitler film, small-scale criminal Talerico advises Richie's factotum Daryl to "spend more time with people. . . . You're alone too much. I don't like to see that. It's unhealthy."[168] Similarly, Mudger's avowed "business philosophy" is supposedly based on human understanding, the projection of alacrity toward all, none of which has anything to do with the cutthroat policies he actually employs. People, he observes, are what "systems planning is fundamentally lacking:" "I miss human interest. The war was full of human interest."[169] It falls to Nadine, as the type of person ignored or victimized by such monsters, to retrieve the moral message from this desiccation.

There is no equivalent to Nadine's subtle voice in *Players*. The only possibility for a healthy psyche lies in the stasis of marriage, no matter how pallid an option this might seem. Much commentary on the novel has focused on the functional and thus monotonous aspect of the Wynants's sex life, a common enough depiction of domestic sexuality in the contemporary novel: "It is time to 'perform,' he thought. She would have to be 'satisfied.' He would have to 'service' her. They would make efforts to 'interact.'"[170] LeClair, among others, insists that the Wynants's lack of play-energy is a fatal problem, the narrowing of "physical satisfactions" to "sexual satisfaction," that forbids or impedes "a more natural, playful mediation."[171] Yet DeLillo suggests that for all Lyle's claims of boredom, there is a festive element to their lovemaking, the salvation of sorts that Lyle, tragically, is too anti-social to perceive: "they ached and played, sunny as young tigers."[172] In like fashion, Lyle fails to note that without her, their apartment "hadn't nearly the same warmth."[173] Despite the marked absence of much discernible love, Pammy and Lyle need each other, their despair increasing when separated: "It would be nice, so nice, if he walked in right now."[174] Even if their interaction often seems obligatory, a chore, at least it shields each of them against the fear evidenced everywhere "outside." As Diane Johnson observes, "though freedom is what people ostensibly want, too naïve a definition of it buys a reaction as frightening as chaos."[175] Pammy and Lyle are made for each other, like Updike's Rabbit and Janice, who eventually manage a serviceable stability when together and nothing but upheaval and even death when apart. It is writer Moll who remains alone, still struggling to ward off mediocrity: "There was no danger here. No one watched or listened to her any longer. Security. Why did it feel so disappointing?"[176]

DeLillo's next novel, *The Names,* foregrounds the tension between the human and the "literary." Like its two predecessors, it is ostensibly a work of genre fiction, this time the expatriate novel, complete with exotic landscapes and jaded characters drinking too much and often wallowing in their own hard-as-nails world-weariness; it recalls a long line of novels, from *The Sun Also Rises* to *The Sheltering Sky* to *Under the Volcano.* Yet its characters are notably more complex than type, and than those in *Players* or *Running Dog.* Narrator James Axton assesses, for insurance purposes, the risk posed by various Middle Eastern countries to outside (American) business ventures; his wife, Kathryn, is a novice excavator laboring tirelessly to recover the Greece long-suppressed beneath the modern. Their shifting relationship, with its casual intimacies and frequent resentment, is complex and convincing, and they are surrounded by a transient but well-detailed circle of businessmen, researchers, and mercenaries. Yet for all the newfound surplus of character material, there is also a more postmodern/deconstructive aspect to the text than in the prior novels; LeClair believes that DeLillo's objective is to supply "consistently enriching relations between the transcultural observations of the New Realists and the semiotic skepticism of the metafictionists."[177]

At times, these contrasting elements merge beautifully, human and linguistic exploration for once, at last, coinciding: "Traceries of black Koranic letters covered the longer sides of the tomb with a smaller grouping on top. My hand moved slowly over the words, feeling for breaks between the inlay and marble, not to fault the craftsmen, of course, but only to find the human labor, the individual, in the wholeness and beauty of the tomb."[178] Yet at other points the landscape, such as the Middle East's "Empty Quarter," gives way entirely to language, as has many an "experimental" text: "I saw writing everywhere, the cursive beaded slant in tile, tapestry, brass and wood, in faience mosaics. . . . I looked up to see words turning corners, arranged geometrically on mud-brick walls, knotted and mazed, stuccoed, painted, inlaid, climbing gateways and minarets."[179]

DeLillo is facing his most pressing crisis of self-definition. The linguistic, metafictional aspect of postmodernism is epitomized by the character Owen Brandemas, who deserts his excavation and teaching to pursue a linguistically oriented death cult. His interests repel the audience, as Owen's trip to the National Museum emphasizes: "The Greeks made an art out of the alphabet. . . . No one is ever there. The caretaker follows me at a tactful distance." One might argue that the elitism of writers, not the rejection of readers, has caused the so-called death of the novel, but Owen delights in the end result in any case: "If I were a writer . . . how I would enjoy being told the novel is dead. How liberating, to work in the margins, outside a central perception. You are the ghoul of literature."[180] James is cognizant of Owen's own great failures as a storyteller: over-analysis, over-abstraction, defeatism: "But I don't want to surrender my text to analysis and reflection. . . . That's Owen too, Owen's voice coursing warmly through a half-dark room."[181] After one of his long and technical-linguistic digressions, Owen notes to Kathryn: "Your husband thinks all this is bookish drool." It is no surprise that Owen has no sympathy for the cult's victims: "The murders are so striking in design that we tend to overlook the physical act itself, the repeated pounding and gouging of a claw hammer, the blood mess washing out. We barely consider the victims except as elements in a pattern."[182]

James, despite his protestations, is dangerously attracted to Owen's ability to "de-individualize." In the novel's most ambiguous scene, James overwhelms Janet Ruffing, an associate's wife and novice belly dancer, with linguistic suavity, deconstructing her even as he pretends to restore the power of words by soldering her signifiers back to their signified: "There's a lack of connection between your words and the physical action they describe, the parts of the body they describe. . . . I want to put your voice back inside your body, where it belongs."[183] After a prolonged flirtation, she finally flees from him; he pursues, catches her, and they engage in frenzied, public intercourse. Kucich makes the expected connection between logocentrism (the structure of white male power) and rape, in this case, the rape of "a woman remarkable for her self-detachment."[184] DeLillo, in Kucich's view, dismisses the deeper issues involved, yet the text does contain a seemingly slight statement that draws the narrative back from the moral void. As they furiously couple against the wall, Janet makes a surreally innocent comment: "People just want to be held. It's enough to be held, isn't it?"[185] This moment is shockingly vulnerable, almost sweet, akin to Nadine's honeyed confession that she did not know "more'n a monkey" what was going on, a scene to which DeLillo explicitly harks back in order to counteract the appeal of Owen's descent into erudition and the blood-guilt of the cult. Owen, quizzing a former cult member in Sanskrit, learns: "The murderer has by this time become part of the dream pool of his self-analysis. The victim and the act are theory now."[186] Owen seems to agree, but for a moment, despite himself, he flashes back to a childhood memory in which his mother murmurs: "I don't know more'n a monkey what you're talking about," a suitably innocent rejoinder emphasizing just how far Owen has fallen from comprehensibility and conventional morality.

Owen is drawn to the Greek language but not to the Greeks, the Crowd all about him. In *The Names,* the attempt to suppress or ignore the crowd has even more of an unsavory political taint than in *Players* and *Running Dog,* as it is an impulse directed only toward those races that have not attained a suitably American level of affluence and imperialistic panache. Hantke reads this tendency as an anti-colonial undertone to the novel, a condemnation of America's narcissism: "these countries are invisible, inarticulate, insubstantial. Their invisibility is caused exactly by the fact that they are channels of power and not places where power resides."[187] Given this power structure, the American traveler-writer is free to judge the people, to *interpret* the people, by reading their cities as texts: "The streets that bend back on themselves or disappear, the miniature churches and narrow lanes, these seem a form of self-effacement, a way of saying there is nothing here worth bothering about. They are a huddling, a gathering together against the stark landforms and volcanic rock. Superstition, vendetta, incest."[188] DeLillo once again resurrects the image of savages around the fire.

Axton's risk-assessing duties lend him his own lofty vantage as he judges the destructive capacities of the people, the warmth of their bloodlust: "We have a complex grading system. Prison statistics weighed against the number of foreign workers. How many young males unemployed. Have the general's salaries been doubled recently. What happens to dissidents. . . . It's interesting because it involves people, waves of people, people running in the streets."[189] Axton does not seem to recognize the distance this vantage has put between him and those "running in the streets," but he is in fact systematizing, in rather inhumane terms, that very Joycean awareness of the people that he experiences firsthand while wandering through Athens, reflecting, Bloom-like, on the variety of life in this lush environment: "Up, into the world, crank the shutters open. . . . Today's a market day, a man is chasing peaches down the steep street below the terrace restaurants. A pickup has hit his, knocking a bushel off the end. . . . A boy stands under the mulberry trees, hosing down the floor of restaurants."[190]

Yet James, unlike Owen, is continually moving toward a deeper understanding of the Greeks, their richness of history: "there were Cypriots here, Lebanese, Armenians, Alexandrians, the island Greeks, the northern Greeks, the old men and women of the epic separation, their children, grandchildren, the Greeks of Smyrna and Constantinople. . . . Everywhere the pressure of remembrance. . . . Civil War. . . . children starving."[191] On the other hand, his young son Tap, a novice writer and the novel's most obvious writer surrogate, plucks out passersby for inclusion in his writing without the least interest in their specific context, their own stories: "A man standing near the edge of the quay lifts his cane to waggle a warning at some children playing nearby. Tap would use this detail in his novel."[192] But James himself cannot hold the mob, the very human mob, out of his consciousness; they refuse to be driven out of his focus by their venerable tongue: "The Greek in conversation crowds his listener and here we find the same unboundaried exercise of life. Families. People clustered, children everywhere."[193]

The Greeks epitomize family; Owen dismisses both family and marriage, including that of the Axtons: "How could you understand, he seemed to be asking. Your domestic drama, your tepid idiom of reproach and injury. These ranks of innocent couples with their marriage wounds. *He kept looking past us*" [italics mine].[194] James, conversely, finds his only solace therein: "Tap, coming along, reinforced the feeling that we were making it up day by day, little by little, but sanely, contentedly, with no huge self-seeking visions."[195] Family dynamics may be unfathomably complex, but they are grounding too: "We talked awhile about her nephews and nieces, other family matters, commonplaces, a cousin taking trumpet lessons, a death in Winnipeg. . . . The subject of family makes conversation almost tactile. I think of hands, food, hoisted children."[196]

DeLillo never reconciles these divergent aspects of the text, his Owen instincts and his James instincts. Instead, they lead, in the novel's most unconventional development, to alternate endings. The first is James's experience of resolution when he finally embarks on a long-delayed excursion to the over-touristed Acropolis; the second is a fictionalized account of an incident from Owen's youth, as written, quite remarkably, by Tap. Tap's story contains frequent misspellings that take on their own meanings; it is unclear whether this is meant to signify mistakes or intentional play on his part. The story itself depicts young Brandemas's flight from a strongly revivalist church; the church-goers fall into fits and seizures as they gain "voice," very much as in the climax of James Baldwin's *Go Tell It on the Mountain.* In Baldwin's vision, both call and voice are empowering yet paradoxical: the voice is the writer's voice, of course, the ability *to tell things as they are,* but is entwined also with conformity in the church, an inevitable subjugation to the social will, a concession to the Other, to society. Unlike John Grimes, Baldwin's boy protagonist, Owen elects to flee this writer's crisis; a child of the prairie, as he labels himself, engaging in the timeworn American motif of flight: "Why couldn't he understand and speak? There was no answer that the living could give. . . . This was worse than retched [*sic*] nightmare. It was the nightmare of real things, the fallen wonder of the world."[197]

The first ending, James's ending, concerns language also, but language successfully integrated into the psyche in a way that enables instead of inhibits human interaction and social progress. The tourist's communal Acropolis signifies not only the past, like Owen's scribbled-on museum fragments, but also the thriving life of the present: "I hadn't expected a human feeling to emerge from the stones but this is what I found, deeper than the art and mathematics embodied in the structure, the optical exactitudes. I found a cry for pity."[198] This realization takes the place of the scene we have been denied, the unkept promise of the Virgin's night, "pilgrims by the thousands,"[199] as Kathryn describes it, that provides an excuse for more intellectual banter on Owen's part but also brings to mind the starving Indian masses who appear unexpectedly at the end of *Ratner's Star* to challenge our way of reading. James's revelation is undoubtedly triumphant, but Tap's, more enticing to the academically minded, becomes the nexus of critical debate on the novel.

Of course, since the second ending is the *final* ending, one can easily argue that its celebration of language and play proves more satisfying to DeLillo than James's more humanistic understanding. Paula Bryant supports this common critical viewpoint: "a rebuttal to the typical modernist ending DeLillo has embedded within his narrative, [it] serves to shake both Axton and the reader by an exuberant, unsettling demonstration of the potential for human freedom inherent in the deliberate disordering and recreation of language."[200] Hantke, though, believes that play is only a last resort, an escape without any sense of whimsy or genuine liberty from a real world too horrible, literally, for words: "After the violent outcome of the two competing conspiracies—the cult murders and the assassination attempt in the park—anything situated outside of discourse, 'the nightmare of real things,' is tainted by this violence."[201] In opposition to both, John McClure sees the final chapter as a *criticism* of postmodern flights of fancy, a "parabolic retort to the postmodern narrative that discovers romance in conspiracy, a counter history in which wonder survives the crisis of desacrilization."[202] In truth, DeLillo abandons the narrative at an interpretive crossroads, segmented, divided, and arguably uncertain himself.

With this gesture DeLillo leaves us with the impression that literary interpretation is, in the end, impossible. Thus are James and his filmmaker friend Volterra frustrated by Vosdanik, a professional storyteller of sorts—"even incidents from his own life he recounted with a degree of awe"[203]—who professes to have information on the cult's history and practices: "Slow, we told him. Go slow, give us a chance to get it straight."[204] James and Owen prove an even more inopportune pair when they put their minds together; puzzling over clues to the enigmatic nature of the cult, they much recall Faulkner's Quentin Compson and dorm-mate Shreve piecing together the story of Thomas Sutpen's rise and fall in *Absalom, Absalom.* That novel, according to Brian McHale, marked a point of transition from modernist to postmodernist forms of writing (and reading), from problems of knowing to problems of modes of being. But if Quentin and Shreve's dilemma is largely the same as that faced by Axton and Brandemas, a significant difference lies in their standards of success. Faulkner's duo relies on circumstantial evidence and their own considerable imaginations, but apply the latter only with fiercely debated logic, not whimsy: "the two of them creating between them, out of the rag-tag and bob-ends of old tales and talking, people who perhaps had never existed at all anywhere."[205] In the end, Quentin and Shreve have pieced together a narrative of events in which they can feel secure, even while acknowledging those gaps their imagination has filled: "'Aint that right? Aint it? By God, aint it?' 'Yes,' Quentin said."[206] Such is not the case, however, with Axton and Owen: "Owen and I had spent several hours building theories, surrounding the bare act with desperate speculations, mainly to comfort ourselves. We knew in the end we'd be left with nothing. Nothing signified, nothing meant."[207] Notably, DeLillo will turn to a narrative akin to Quentin and Shreve's in *Libra:* a fictional history with the stability of truth.

In similar fashion James leaves us with a "provisional" history that represents a conditional victory. There has been an attempt on the life of his friend David Keller, an attempt that may have been meant for James, who has unknowingly been collecting information for the CIA. Typical postmodern confusion ensues; but James's final action in the novel, before his epiphanic trip to the Acropolis, is to sew together a clear story of espionage and the assassination attempt. Clearly, he does not have all the answers, muttering "let them muse on the plausibilities," but he does his part: "After I told the man from the Ministry what I'd seen in the pine woods, I told him everything else I knew, gave him all the names, Eliades, Rowser, Hardeman, all the tenuous connections. I gave him business cards, supplied approximate dates of conversations, names of restaurants, cities, airlines."[208] He gives him "all the names;" in one stroke the title of the novel shifts from a reference to absorption and linguistic abstraction in the cult, "scratching an enemy's name on a piece of pottery, then smashing it," to a contingent realism. Like Shreve and Quentin, James can live with the latter, which defines DeLillo's later direction.

Chapter Six

"Entropy and Efflorescence": To and From the Zero in the Early Novels of Paul Auster

Of the four authors discussed in this study, Paul Auster takes on the role of storyteller most self-consciously. He looks back to the origins of storytelling: "the greatest influence on my work has been fairy tales, the oral tradition of story-telling, the Brothers Grimm, the Thousand and One Nights—the kinds of stories you read out loud to children."[1] As a result of this interest, however, he is enmeshed in a peculiarly complex bind; in his view it is essential to understand stories, what they are, how they work, precisely because we need them so desperately, an atavistic, and decidedly non-elitist, need, in the blood: "stories are the fundamental food for the soul. We can't live without stories. . . . People do not necessarily need novels to satisfy their need for stories. They watch television or read comic books or go to the movies. It's through stories that we struggle to make sense of the world."[2] Yet while self-conscious writing, metafictional writing, is our by-now accustomed method of determining what stories are and how they work—as he claims early in "City of Glass," "the question is the story itself, and whether or not it means something is not for the story to tell"[3]—its detached dissection of storytelling's clichés, conventions, and universal appeal cannot in itself feed our souls, cannot supply us with what Auster feels we cannot live without. As he himself notes: "self-conscious experimentation is generally a result of a real longing to break down the barriers of literary convention. . . . most avant garde works do not survive."[4]

In Auster's first novel, *The New York Trilogy,* he shows no sign of being stymied by this tension, dissuaded from storytelling. Like an unpreserved Scheherazade, he peppers each installment of the trilogy—"City Of Glass," "Ghosts," and "The Locked Room"—with an eclectic variety of sub-stories, all of which are very clever but all of which digress from the plot. None of them resonate as particularly human; they thwart, not meet, the reader's expectations. Unlike the fairy tales that so influenced Auster, they do not have beginnings or endings, progressions or morals. When he tells of Arctic explorer Peter Freuchen, trapped in an igloo closing in as every breath hardens into a layer of ice, he neglects to reveal how Freuchen escaped his icy death: "Curiously, I do not remember how . . . needless to say, he did escape."[5] The reader's predominant impression is of a storytelling prodigy spinning his creative wheels.

Another example is his story of Bakhtin, holed away during the German invasion of Russia: "he smoked the only copy of one of his manuscripts, a book-length study of German fiction that had taken him years to write. One by one, he took the pages of his manuscript and used the paper to roll his cigarettes, each day smoking a little more of the book until it was gone."[6] This is a tragic story, a human story, but it is realized in a thin, crisp prose featuring a frugal sense of style, scarce descriptive detail, and no traces of human warmth or idiosyncrasy. For self-exiled writer Fanshawe, such stories "could help him to understand himself,"[7] but this is a writer's self-understanding only. The story is far more potent and more widely relevant when it reemerges, years later, in Auster's screenplay to the acclaimed Wayne Wang film *Smoke.* Here lonely widower and author Paul Benjamin (William Hurt) tells the Bakhtin story to young Rashid Cole (Harold Perrineau), who has saved him from being struck by a car and has subsequently moved into Paul's apartment for the immediate future. The story has now accumulated any number of added connotations and interpersonal subtexts, not the least of which is Paul's paying his debt to Rashid through the gift of storytelling; the numerous inflections and mannerisms of their interplay are what make the story work (along with Hurt's somewhat uncharacteristically expressive performance):

> Paul: It's 1942, right? And he's caught in Leningrad during the siege. I'm talking about one of the worst moments in human history. Five hundred thousand people died in that one place, and there's Bakhtin, holed up in an apartment, expecting to be killed any day. He has plenty of tobacco, but no paper to roll it in. So he takes the pages of the manuscript he's been working on for ten years and tears them up to roll his cigarettes.
>
> Rashid (*incredulous*): His only copy?
>
> Paul: His only copy. (*Pause*) I mean, if you're going to die, what's more important, a good book or a good smoke? And so he huffed and puffed, and little by little he smoked his book.

> Rashid: (*Thinks, then smiles*) Nice try. You had me going for a second, but no . . . no writer would ever do a thing like that. (*Slight pause. Looking at PAUL*) Would he?[8]

Here Auster not only emphasizes the flexibility of stories, their openness to retelling and re-experiencing, but he also plays up the human issues, the tragedy, the relevance beyond the sphere of the writer and his craft.

It is clear that there is a significant, even insurmountable, gap in Auster's understanding of the storytelling process between the world of *Smoke,* with its interpersonal sensitivity, and that of Auster's early, fleshless writing. Much of this difference lies, of course, in language, in an early prose style calculated to attain Roland Barthes's ideal of '*Ecriture,* which is a kind of writing (sometimes translated as "writing degree zero") characterized by absence and putatively lacking any ideological baggage. One of the pivotal analogies in "City Of Glass" is between language and a broken umbrella; Peter Stillman, whose childhood seclusion has rendered him peculiarly sensitive to the contingency of language when removed from social context, recognizes that a broken umbrella can no longer be called (or at least no longer *should* be called) an umbrella. Its functional definition, as a contraption designed to ward off the rain, no longer applies. Language, he observes, can never keep pace with shifting reality: "our words no longer correspond to the world. When things were whole, we felt confident that our words could express them. But little by little these things have broken apart, shattered, collapsed into chaos. And yet our words have remained the same."[9] Auster often stresses the difference between poetry and novel writing; particularly between the French poem and the English novel: "If English writing has staked out as its territory the world of tangibility, of concrete presence, of surface accident, French literary language has largely been a language of essences."[10] Many commentators have celebrated Auster's novels for their unique incorporation of the French poetic sensibility, but in truth they exclusively draw on the aspects of this poetry that parallel the more general deconstructive/postmodern agenda, exploiting the gap between word and function that Stillman emphasizes with the umbrella example. We can see this in Auster's description of Celan's poetry as "continually collapsing in on itself, negating its very premises, again and again arriving at zero."[11] The most constructive reading possible of the sparseness of Auster's prose is that he believes minimalism actually maximizes denotative stability. Given that the meaning of words is not perdurable, the less of them there are, the less likely miscommunication will occur. But the sparseness also suggests that rudiments of storytelling are all that are left us in the wake of decades of intensifying novelistic self-absorption.

Yet the overall critical consensus on Auster's work stresses his maintenance of overarching realism, or at least a "sufficient realism"[12] that Barone defines as "interested in old-fashioned morality, guilt and redemption, as well as new-fashioned philosophy."[13] It is true that such "old-fashioned" values have been Auster's interest in writing from the very beginning; a childhood essay written on Jackie Robinson paved the way: "It was 1961, and I was just fourteen years old, but composing that speech was one of the crucial events of my life. After that day, I knew that I wanted to become a writer."[14] In *Blue in the Face,* the very loosely cohering sequel to *Smoke,* he expounds on his feelings about Robinson when the ball player's ghost returns to our modern world to comment on our racial struggles: "After me, things started to change. I just don't mean for black people, I mean for white people, too. After me, white people and black people could never look at each other in the same way again."[15] Yet for the Auster of *The New York Trilogy* neither the social imperative nor "sufficient realism" carry much weight; instead, the novel is based on those values Auster finds in Knut Hamsun's novel *Hunger:* "a work devoid of plot, action, and—but for the narrator—character. By nineteenth century standards, it is a work in which nothing happens. The radical subjectivity of the narrator effectively eliminates the basic concerns of the traditional novel."[16] As its only value, Hamsun's novel advocates suffering: "although *Hunger* puts us in the jaws of misery, it offers no analysis of that misery, contains no call to political action."[17]

Though Sven Birkerts initially defended Auster's early approach, he later admits the hazards risked by *The New York Trilogy:* "the problem with self-reflexive fictions is that they obey the law of diminishing returns: unable to suspend his disbelief, the reader starts to find all revelations merely academic."[18] Indeed, each novella in the trilogy adheres to the same pattern, the postmodern pattern; Allison Russel summarizes, in wearying if accurate jargon, the deconstructionist program of "City Of Glass:" "Logocentricism, the term applied to the uses and theories of language grounded in the metaphysics of presence, is the 'crime' that Auster investigates in *The New York Trilogy.*"[19] This is why Auster admits that, "if a true reader of detective fiction ever tried to read one of these books, he would be bitterly disappointed."[20] The novella's hero, novice detective and professional writer Quinn, is "a paper-Auster," in Russel's view, "a mere linguistic construct of the author himself,"[21] who must cure himself of his desire for order, epitomized through the detective's role in case-solving, his supposed unraveling of confusion and restoration of the status quo via faith in his senses: "he had always imagined that the key to good detective work was a close observation of details. . . . The implication was that human behavior could be understood, that beneath the facade of gestures, tics and silences, there was finally a coherence, an order, a source of motivation."[22] Although defenders of the novel like McPherson assert that theory remains separate from story here—"the traditional notion of referentiality is preserved, for the thematic program that governs the novel achieves significance only outside the boundaries"[23]—a reader with any experience at all with postmodern texts can confidently predict how the program of the novella will unfold, specifically in those terms summarized by Tim Woods: "struggles against the restrictions of individual freedoms often result in epistemological or ontological anxieties, frequently precipitating crises of confidence in what separates reality from appearance."[24] In the end, the reader will be left with the usual irresolvable dichotomies; Quinn will fade from the narrative, dispersing like Slothrop in *Gravity's Rainbow.*

In "The Locked Room," the pattern will lead in the same direction. First, language is demystified: "there were times when no words came to my lips, when I struggled to say even the simplest things. There was a certain pleasure in this, I believe—to experience language as a collection of sounds, to be forced to the surface of words where the meanings vanish."[25] Then identity: "I was the sublime alchemist who could change the world at will. The man was Fanshawe because I said he was Fanshawe, and that was all there was to it."[26] "Ghosts" follows suit; the end result for the detective is a self-consciousness of his language that threatens to paralyze him: "words are transparent for him, great windows that stand between him and the world, and until now they have never impeded his view, have never even seemed to be there."[27]

This pattern suggests that the deconstructionist or postmodern novel today has been thoroughly mapped out to the point that there is little uncharted territory remaining for new waves of pioneers. It is no coincidence that passages in "Ghosts" are nearly identical to passages in *Ratner's Star,* published a decade earlier, particularly when the domestic world, the everyday physical environment, disintegrates into this ultrasensitive linguistic awareness, realism's final collapse. Initially, Blue is confident: "he sees the bed and says to himself, bed. He sees the notebook and says to himself, notebook. It will not do to call the lamp a bed, he thinks, or the bed a lamp. No, these words fit snugly around the things they stand for." But his self-satisfaction in the habitual assignments of language will eventually prove misguided: "and the moment Blue speaks them, he feels a deep satisfaction as though he has just proved the existence of the world."[28] Billy's mental processes in *Ratner's Star* run on the same track; he is at the next stage in the process: "the arms of the chair were called "arms" and that his arms were also called "arms" and it was just barely possible that this business of self-touching applied not only to parts of the body but to parts of the body and parts of other objects that happened to have the same names. Arms of chairs, legs of tables, hands of clocks, eyes of needles."[29]

As a result of this focus, authors of realistic contemporary fiction have begun to methodically and contrarily demonstrate to readers the feasibility of the reverse process, that "building up" from words to world we once took for granted. In a lengthy passage from Charles Frazier's best-selling, much-acclaimed, largely conventional *Cold Mountain,* hero Inman focuses on the somewhat inaccurate depictions of plant life in a weathered copy of *Bartram's Travels;* here we have a shrub, not a chair: "first he read it until each word rested in his head with a specific weight peculiar to itself. . . . That accomplished, he fixed in his mind the setting, supplying all the missing details of a high green forest: the kinds of trees that would grow there." The shrub is clearly envisioned, treated as real, even though Inman knows it is fiction: "it arose in his thinking as vivid as he could make it, though it in no way matched any known plant and was in several features quite fantastic."[30] Rorty is aware that such "pragmatic irony" is essential to the reading process, and insists that there is no reason to further destabilize the foundation it has been built on: "any argument to the effect that a familiar use of a familiar term is incoherent, or empty, or confused, or vague, or 'merely metaphorical,' is bound to be inconclusive and question begging. For such use is, after all, the paradigm of coherent, meaningful, literal speech."[31]

The real danger, of course, is that one person might view another in the same fragmented, conditional way as the chair or the shrub. Frazier's pragmatic reader can likely accept characters as human even while aware they are figments; certainly Frazier himself does not emphasize that Inman is a figment. Yet Rorty's philosophy insists that identity is a construct and Blue and Auster take advantage of the idea; we learn very little about "the future Mrs. Blue" except through Blue's imagination, centered condescendingly on her physical qualities. Blue can only approach her as Harkness approaches the female corpse in the car wreck, recreating a woman now as disassembled as one of Blue or Billy's chairs: "he reconstructs her body piece by piece, beginning with her feet and ankles, working his way up her legs and along her thighs, climbing from her belly toward her breasts, and then, roaming happily among the softness, dipping down into her buttocks, and then up again along her back, at last finding her neck and curling forward to her round and smiling face."[32] Yet this is actually one of the more human moments in "Ghosts," in which Auster otherwise reduces his characters to colors, to symbols in an allegory of reading that limits itself to the destructive, obsessive, and unsavory bond between writer (Black) and reader (Blue): "You were my whole world to me, Blue, and I turned you into my death. You were the one thing that turns everything inside out."[33]

The reading process underway, both entities are locked together until a culminating violence can be reached, whether separation or assimilation: "If he doesn't take care of Black now, there will never be any end to it. This is what the ancients call fate, and every hero must submit to it."[34]

Lavender insists that this interest does not detract from human concerns: "it can be argued that Auster's seemingly obsessive engagement of theory reduces the novel to an academic exercise [but] the value of the novel of critical engagement is that it clears a space where representation can once again close with politics and society."[35] Yet Auster himself recognizes that this is not the case and not his intent; if nothing else, he understands the reader's impatience with his self-consciousness, ascribing it to Blue, the reader's stand-in: "this book offers him nothing. There is no story, no plot, no action—nothing but a man sitting alone in a room and writing about books. That's all there is, Blue realizes, and he no longer wants any part of it."[36] Indeed, the only "human" issues and "human" moments of his text are digressions from his schematic plots, one example being a scene at the Heights Luncheonette, where the interplay between Quinn and the counterman, largely about baseball, has nothing to do with Quinn's case, and where the setting is, for once, rich with detail: "It was a bright yet dreary place . . . several tables for patrons, and a long Formica counter with swivel stools. . . . Ensconced behind the cash register, was the boss, a small balding man with curly hair and a concentration camp number tattooed on his forearm, lording it over his domain of cigarettes, pipes, and cigars."[37] The fleeting mention of the concentration camp number is the pivotal detail, of course, and suggests, given that both counterman and Quinn are long-suffering Mets fans, "the hopelessness of that passion . . . a bond between them."[38] A bond of suffering, and not the stuff of literary allegory; Quinn himself has lost his wife and son: "every once and awhile, he would suddenly feel what it had been like to hold the three-year-old boy in his arms . . . it was a physical sensation, an imprint of the past that had been left in his body, and he had no control over it."[39]

Auster does not develop such suffering in any detail, however, and instead incorporates it into a literary idea of absence. That said, Auster is clearly uncomfortable with such academic remove, and criticizes it severely, as DeLillo does, through an author-figure. As self-criticism, this is far more overt than in DeLillo, however, for this figure *is* "Paul Auster," sought out by Quinn, who hopes, unfruitfully, that he is the "Paul Auster" detective for whom Quinn has originally been mistaken on the phone. Instead, Quinn finds a "Paul Auster" writer, who uncoils for him a long exegesis on Cervantes's *Don Quixote* focusing on the identity of the author of the text within the text, an extremely facile reading that obviously suggests the maze of authorial relationships in "City of Glass" sketched out by Lavender as an impossibly entangled train of author figures from Auster to "Auster" to Quinn to William Wilson (Quinn's "detective writer" nom de plume) to Max Work (his detective hero), and forward and back again, in which "the illusion . . . is one of infinity."[40] This "Auster" represents the metafictionist Auster, the self-satisfied storyteller thick with irony who will tell the Bakhtin story without investing much in it; Auster is fully aware that many readers of *The New York Trilogy* may assess him just as Quinn assesses "Auster:" "Auster leaned back on the sofa, smiled with a certain ironic pleasure, and lit a cigarette. The man was obviously enjoying himself, but the precise nature of that pleasure eluded Quinn. It seemed to be a kind of soundless laughter, a joke that stopped short of its punch line, a generalized mirth that had no object."[41] In fact, he even suggests that the reader *should* assess him in such fashion; the unnamed narrator reproaches "Auster" for neglecting Quinn, much as Auster has neglected his character: "I began to feel angry that he had treated Quinn with such indifference. I scolded him for not having taken a greater part in events, for not having done something to help a man who was obviously in trouble."[42]

Still, this "Auster" figure has his family, which makes him the rare example in these books of an author who combines genius and mediocrity. Generally, the writer of genius and the writer of mediocrity are to Auster like argumentative twins born of the same egg, dueling elements of the same psyche. The mediocre writer, wracked by jealousy, is capable of startling violence; when the narrator of "The Locked Room" is writing an autobiography of Fanshawe, who vanished mysteriously before the publication of what was to become a classic body of work, he visits Fanshawe's mother and neglects his research to engage in violent intercourse with her, "fucking out of hatred,"[43] a startling near-incest given the nature of the childhood bond between the two. He seems to be displacing the Other—the author—by usurping his life, usurping even his Freudian anxieties; in similar fashion, he marries Sophie, Fanshawe's deserted wife, much as Peter Aaron, the narrator of *Leviathan,* will have an affair with the wife of his friend, the superior writer Ben Sachs.

The unnamed narrator of "The Locked Room" is the prototypical Auster protagonist, the merely adequate writer who covets, if subconsciously, the misanthropy and self-absorption that distinguish true genius, which stands out from the mundane on the basis of a certain opportunism, a faculty for plucking something momentous out of a flow of life that is no more than "a chronicle of chance intersection, of flukes, of random events that divulge nothing but their own lack of purpose."[44] When Fanshawe stretches out in an open grave at the precise moment of his father's death, it is coincidence, but a coincidence self-willed in an intangible way: "the open grave was there, and

Fanshawe had felt it calling out to him. Stories only happen to those who are able to tell them."[45] Our narrator, on the other hand, can make nothing artistic even of life's most fertile tensions; when Sophie confesses her affection, he can translate the event only into the most trite metaphors "of heat, of burning, melting down in the face of irresistible passions. I am aware of how overblown these terms might sound, but in the end I believe they are accurate."[46]

But his literary mediocrity remains equated with affection, with love, with family. The narrator cannot even grasp Fanshawe's capacity to reject his world: "no man would have left this woman of his own free will—especially not when she was about to have a child. . . . Even before I stepped into his apartment I knew that Fanshawe had to be dead."[47] Auster himself is clearly drawn to Fanshawe's seclusion and asceticism: "The stringency of his life disciplined him. Solitude became a passageway into the self, an instrument of discovery."[48] He has said of his characters that when "most confined, they seem to be most free,"[49] yet he is far more cognizant of the cost of greatness than the early DeLillo; take, for example, the pathos John Asberry inspires in him: "Asberry writes as an outsider, as one cut off from the possibility of a sustained interaction with the world, and no matter how sly or humorous he becomes, the essential feeling in his poems is one of homesickness."[50]

Auster complicates the distinction between the mediocre and the genius by suggesting that it is not the loving family man but the true artist who carries out the most pivotal acts of social mercy. As a child, Fanshawe is given a present by his mother to bring to a friend's birthday party, but instead he gives the present to a poor boy who is embarrassed because he has no gift to bring. Though this is a small gesture between children, Fanshawe makes it clear even then that he is acting according to principle, not sympathy: "not an act of charity so much as an act of justice."[51] In like fashion, Fanshawe will take a stand against racism during a stint in the merchant marines. Yet the writer-genius cannot be socially conscious *in writing.* Fanshawe's writings, his assorted stories, fables, and anecdotes, are, as mentioned earlier, antiseptic, designed to convey to us only the realization that "lives make no sense."[52] Our narrator, on the other hand, is at least aware that creative powers can be harnessed for the greater good; working as a census taker, he realizes that his lies could funnel much-needed financial resources to those more desperate areas of the city: "Everyone knows that stories are imaginary [but] I was offering my creations directly to the real world, and therefore it seemed possible to me that they could effect the real world in a real way, that they could eventually become real themselves."[53]

The New York Trilogy is clearly not such an exercise of the imagination. It does suggest, however, how to move beyond the confusion of life, though only in a most curious way. For Auster, everything comes back to Thoreau and *Walden:* "What [Blue] does not know is that were he to find the patience to read the book in the spirit in which it asks to be read, his entire life would begin to change, and little by little he would come to a full understanding of his situation—that is to say, of Black, of White, of the case, of everything that concerns him."[54] Yet Auster feels no need to characterize this understanding; such is not a part of his artistic program. He is not at all explicit about what Blue, or we, should hope to find; like Blue, we must read the book.

It is clear that *Walden,* like "Ghosts," presents a challenge. In fact, Blue's struggles with Thoreau seem a metaphor for the contemporary reader's struggle with Auster: "though he grudgingly admits that Thoreau is not as stupid as he thought, he begins to resent Black for putting him through the torture." In this respect Auster might seem to be looking to Thoreau only for a strong example of individualism, of solitude, of self-indulgence; this is the Thoreau that Auster often lionizes: "the idea of living a solitary life, of living with a kind of monastic intensity . . . the determination to reject everyday American life, to go against the grain, to discover a more solid foundation for oneself."[55] Scholars have often defended Thoreau against the charge of animosity toward society, a charge stemming from the isolationism that Auster celebrates. Certainly Thoreau decried much overt social involvement on the grounds that it interrupted his meditative pursuit: "probably I should not consciously and deliberately forsake my particular calling to do the good which society demands of me, to save the universe from annihilation."[56] Yet Thoreau quit jobs, lectured in public, and even spent time in jail to proclaim social causes such as abolition, the shielding of children from cruelty, and the defiance of tyrannical government. His personal reflections at Walden, while often seeming self-enclosed, were designed to instigate a profoundly moral response, with a specific economic message, as Sherman Paul observes: "he was to announce new symbols (new values) and galvanize public opinion, thereby saving society from the rot of materialism."[57] It is highly significant that, like the mythic hero who must restore the tribe, or like Bucky Wunderlick reemerging from his drugged limbo, Thoreau recognizes that a re-immersion in society, post reflection, is the all-important step. With *Walden* he is not a voice from afar in the forest, but a voice among us, a "sojourner in civilized life again."[58]

In this vein, Mary Elkins Moller insists that Thoreau would not have understood the appeal of his work to contemporary nihilists: "Loneliness, isolation, and alienation are key words, central problems of twentieth century literature, but Thoreau (who undoubtedly experienced them all) would have denied their validity."[59] Instead, she stresses his "feelings about love and friendship, his yearning for one to one relationships of an intimacy and intensity probably impossible to attain."[60] It is this aspect of Thoreau which proves most troublesome to Auster, the Thoreau who declared: "I think that I love society as much as most, and am ready enough to fasten myself like a bloodsucker for a time to any full-blooded man that comes my way."[61] In "The Locked Room," Auster explores this "democratic" relationship, the hyperintense link between individuals and between souls: "Fanshawe was always there. He is the place where everything begins for me, and without him I would hardly know who I am."[62] Like the bond between Ishmael and Queequeg, consummated by a night of shared bodily warmth the day before taking to sea, the relationship between Fanshawe and the unnamed speaker has symbolic connotations of matrimonial love: "when we were six, we asked . . . if it were possible for men to get married."[63] But "reality" inevitably severs and cauterizes this sanctified bond: "I had been struggling to imagine him, to see him as he might have been, but my mind had always conjured a blank. At heart, there was one impoverished image, the door of a locked room."[64] Alienation, then, remains unavoidable. Auster still casts his vote for relationship-oriented mediocrity, however, rescuing his protagonist from contingency and flux through personal redemption in the Other: "She had given up on me, and there were months of confusion before I finally won her back. . . . That is the only thing that matters. Beside it, the facts of my life are purely incidental."[65]

There are other aspects of Thoreau, though, that are even farther beyond the reach of many postmodern writers. Thoreau provides a Blake-like mantra that would belittle any writer claiming literary exhaustion, any writer for whom "the whole ground of human life seems . . . to have been gone over by their predecessors, both the heights and the valleys, and all things have been cared for." Instead, he insists that "Man's capacities have never been measured; nor are we to judge what he can do by any precedents, so little has been tried."[66] The ghosts of "Ghosts," however, are literary and historic figures; unlike the fleshed-out Bowery in *Great Jones Street,* the only city that retains definition for Auster is a literary-historical map: "Walt Whitman handset the first edition of *Leaves Of Grass* on this street in 1855, and it was here that Henry Ward Beecher railed against slavery from the pulpit of his red-brick church. So much for the local color."[67] Auster most obviously confesses his own lack of imaginative potency, of course, by sending us out to Thoreau for what he himself cannot provide.

In addition, he cannot bring himself to let the mediocrity found and celebrated by the speaker of "The Locked Room" stand as his final statement. Instead, he regresses to jaunty self-reflexivity, unifying (in a most degraded sense of the word) all three novellas by ascribing them to a single narrator. *The New York Trilogy* as a whole is much like Fanshawe's notebook: "each sentence canceled out the one before it, each paragraph made the next paragraph impossible."[68] Our final impression of it, therefore, is of a city in metaphorical cinders, its ideological and pragmatic underpinnings removed; the defining metaphor of Auster's next novel, *In The Country Of Last Things,* however, is the sifting of that garbage, the scavenging of what is still functional, the retrieving of umbrellas, broken or no, named or unnamed: "As an object hunter, you must rescue things before they reach this state of absolute decay. You can never expect to find something whole . . . but neither can you spend your time looking for what is totally used up. . . . What another has seen fit to throw away, you must examine, dissect, and bring back to life."[69]

The "country" of *In the Country of Last Things* is, to the extent of our very limited knowledge, one immense city, an embodiment of all our modern notions and fears of urban decay, in which poverty is universal and ferocious violence the norm. It is no stretch of interpretation, then, to read the novel as predominantly a work of economic and social criticism, in which the usual postmodern dilemmas of language, identity, and theory are secondary or else diagnosed and well-integrated; Katherine Washburn explains that object-hunting and its corresponding system of bartering "are emblematic of a society which has not only ceased to invent and produce but which, for nearly two decades, has inflated the value of real property, objects of art, and fetishistic junk alike."[70] The social concern of the novel is obvious; it was adapted to the stage and performed in Bosnia in 1994, and Auster has detailed a range of allusions including "the Warsaw ghetto and the siege of Leningrad, but also . . . events taking place in the Third World today—not to speak of New York, which is rapidly turning into a Third World city before our eyes."[71]

In order to write a novel of social observation, to create a dystopia readily translatable into contemporary reference (thus more like Orwell's Oceania in *1984* than one of Brian McHale's Zones), Auster needs to reconstruct the medium's communicative, conventional, and realistic functions. He must refute both the aesthete's imperative and the postmodernist's driving theoretical concerns. Correspondingly, Auster's language no longer features the somewhat absurdist or existential reductions that characterize *The New York Trilogy.* At the same time, it aspires to remain very efficient, straightforward; Auster does not take solace or find meaning in elaborate language as DeLillo does depicting the city at the end of *Great Jones Street:* "All the elegant passages, all the curious details, all the so-called beautiful writing—if they are not truly relevant to what I am trying to say, then they have to go. . . . You're telling a story, after all, and your job is to make people want to go on listening to your tale."[72]

Yet contradictory temptations have an obvious hold on Auster that is often impossible to ignore; he continually achieves and then represses moments of ingenuity that threaten to detract from the social horrors they describe. Note how his embellished description of the city's winter coating of ice—"weird configurations: bumps and ripples and whorls, entire waves caught in mid-undulation, a kind of geological frenzy in miniature"—quickly gives way to the brutal ramifications, to the victims, all hints of poeticism vanishing from his writing: "by morning, of course, walking would be next to impossible—people slipping all over themselves, skulls cracking on the ice, bodies flopping helplessly on the smooth, hard surfaces."[73] Such moments define Auster's brand of postmodernism, balancing imaginative indulgence with compassion: "Utter despair can exist side by side with the most dazzling invention; entropy and efflorescence merge."[74]

Yet Auster encodes the voids that bring on this despair in such a way as to suggest a literary theory of absence rather than a naturalistic one; again, issues of economic and political power (or powerlessness) threaten to fade, in favor of the grand realization conveyed in the poetry of William Bronk, whose work Auster trumpets and whose world-view coincides so exactly with the usual postmodernist view that one wonders why Auster felt the need to re-explain it: "Bronk's basic premise is that there is no inherent order or truth to the world, that whatever form or shape we feel it possesses is the one we ourselves have imposed upon it. We can speak not of *the* world, but rather of *a* world, *our* world, and it is constantly changing as we change. We cling to a belief in our world because we need to give coherence to our lives."[75] Yet ultimately in this novel those voids that recall French poetry stress tangible human loss: "I mourned the loss of one of my friends, felt pulverized by the weight of it . . . nothing more than a blank, a ravening null."[76] "Emotional residue" outstrips theory: "No matter what you might think, the problem here is never a lack of pity. Nothing breaks here more readily than the heart."[77] And isolation, so alluring to Auster in *The New York Trilogy,* represents the most unwise approach, even when traumatized by the death of a child: "It would be good, I suppose, to make yourself so hard that nothing could affect you anymore. But then you would be alone, so totally cut off from everyone else that life would become impossible."[78]

Therefore, the heroism of Anna Blume, bringing us her story—her search for her missing journalist brother against odds both material (poverty) and intellectual (the failure of perception and language brought on by the surrealism of the city)—is paralleled by the heroism of the author spinning a social narrative despite the burdens of postmodern awareness: "Your mind seems to balk at forming the words, you somehow cannot bring yourself to do it." The most affecting passages in the novel depict those who have lost their voice; Isabel, the dying woman tended by Anna in her last days of life, provides one grisly example: "the breakdown of muscle and bone finally reached her throat, and when that happened Isabel started losing the power of speech. A disintegrating body is one thing, but when the voice goes too, it feels as if the person is no longer there."[79] We have discussed how Auster values the poetry of what is *not* said, as in the work of Laura Riding—"Everything takes place in absence, in the distance between word and utterance, and each poem emerges at the moment there is nothing left to say"[80]—but in this novel any loss of word and utterance is grievous: "The story starts and stops, goes forward and loses itself, and between each word, what silences, what words escape and vanish, never to be seen again."[81] Thus it is that the conventional reader is likely to grant Auster the leeway that Anna asks for: "Bear with me. I know that sometimes I stray from the point, but unless I write down things as they occur to me, I feel I will lose them for good."[82]

In the process, Auster makes it clear that part of his own "heroism" is writing despite the despair inspired by the writer's marginality in the modern marketplace, the despair, discussed in our first chapter, which so often leads to resentful or resigned self-indulgence. This had been a factor in *The New York Trilogy* as well; Quinn's landlord ranks tenants based on a hierarchy of economic utility, in which the novelist did not fare well: "He doesn't like tenants who don't have jobs. . . . They use too much heat and run down the fixtures."[83] Matters are much worse in *In the Country of Last Things.* Charles Newman equates literature and economics by way of inflation; the worth of money and the worth of words are the same. Auster carries this relationship to the farthest extreme; in a world this impoverished, this collapsed, literature has *no* market value: "two shelves of Dickens, five sets of Shakespeare . . . a Jane Austen, a Schopenhaur, an illustrated *Don Quixote*—but the bottom had fallen out of the book market by then, and these things fetched no more than a trifle."[84]

Of course, as society grows more and more fragmented, broken down into monadic elements, the concept of a widely accessible work of fiction, let alone any idea of the Great American Novel, seems mere fancy: "In effect, each person is speaking his own private language, and as the instances of shared understanding diminish, it becomes increasingly difficult to communicate with anyone."[85] Auster does not devalue the idea of the monadic faction, seeing in it a kind of Faulknerian resilience; an example is the rabbinical group Anna encounters in an abandoned library, persistently carrying out its research and scholarship despite the crumbling of civilization. Lyotard sees in such splintered groups a source of important innovation; Woods sees the preservation of alternative, dissident voices, what he calls "unsanctioned histories."[86] But ultimately these individual stories are isolated to the point that they become shallow, puerile, unrewarding: "So many of us have become like children again . . . when hope disappears, when you find that you have given up hoping even for the possibility of hope, you tend to fill the empty spaces with dreams, little childlike thoughts and stories to keep yourself going."[87] Once again, the people are seen as boorish primitives; note Auster's description of Willie, a mentally retarded young man who embarks on a bloody rampage after his grandfather's death: "He was a prehistoric man, and the only way he could respond to death was to worship his departed ancestor, to think of him as a god."[88] The implicit need here is for the consolidating writer-priest.

Perhaps Blume's narrative can serve in this social capacity. Her storytelling diligence certainly stands as counterpoint to that of any number of artist-figures in the book who deny the storytelling call entirely. Ferdinand, Isabel's cruel and lascivious husband, is a skilled craftsman, a builder of intricate miniature ships, a fitting metaphor, like Jean's knitting in *Ratner's Star,* for a self-absorbed writer interested only in form: "his ships are remarkable little pieces of engineering, stunningly crafted, ingeniously designed and put together, and as long as he was furnished with enough materials . . . he was too absorbed in his work to stir up much trouble in the house."[89] Nor is there any consolation in play, as proved by Boris, who is a parallel to the "Paul Auster" figure in "City of Glass:" "fond of obscure pronouncements and elliptical allusions . . . he embellished simple remarks with such ornate imagery that you got lost trying to understand him."[90] Correspondingly, his notion of traveling the Country in a troupe of musicians represents a celebration of Bakhtin's sense of *carnival.* Although he is a benign figure, lending his assistance to Anna and her lover as they work in a temporary safe-house for the downtrodden, his little games and fables illuminate, or create, only his own little world: "they were part of an almost conscious plan to concoct a more pleasant world for himself—a world that could shift according to his whims."[91]

Instead, Anna's narrative seems designed to serve in place of those works of social realism aspired to by Samuel Farr, the one-time reporter who becomes Anna's husband: "I can't stop. The book is the only thing that keeps me going. . . . I'm going to take the manuscript back with me. The book will be published, and everyone will find out what's happening here."[92] Such accounts provide details of the past that can save the future, the *Schindler's List* ideal again. This social memory has both a personal and public function. In Robert Penn Warren's *All The King's Men,* Jackie Burden ultimately finds, in his past and our communal history, his future: "if you could not accept the past and its burden there was no future, for without one there cannot be the other. . . . If you could accept the past you might hope for the future, for only out of the past can you make the future."[93] Auster explores this possibility in the figure of Gold in "Ghosts," who perseveres for countless years in his investigation of a long-unsolved child homicide, laboring to rectify the past in order to equilibrate the present. That the country of last things is fictional, a surreal world, does not in Auster's eyes detract from this function; it helps engage it by catering to our ironism. Otherwise, we might be led to gloss over harsh memories altogether; in "Ghosts" we also have Gray, one of Blue's old cases, an amnesiac who forgets his wife, his name, and his past, yet starts an even happier life than he had before, the equivalent of Anatole Blumberg's dream in *End Zone*. It may be no coincidence that Nabokov, who mocked the social function of literature, concealed the harsher blows of his life in his autobiography *Speak, Memory*, the jagged spokes of memory involving the specifics of his father's death, his brother's homosexuality (fatal at the hands of the Nazis) and his wife's Jewishness (the impetus for their flight to America), in favor of delicate and entirely enclosed memories of house and land and flower and butterfly. Anna, on the other hand, has no memory to spare for anything beautiful, the lost world of her youth: "The whole family would go up north on the train for summer holidays. . . . Every year I would say to myself . . . try to memorize all the beautiful things you are seeing, and in that way they will always be with you, even when you can't see them anymore . . . but the trees and the sky and the water—all that is gone."[94]

Moon Palace, Auster's next novel, promises to continue the movement toward human issues that distinguished *In the Country of Last Things* from *The New York Trilogy*. Auster has stressed Anna's humanity, the fact that she is not one of DeLillo's figments; indeed, he can imagine nothing more noble than the fact that amid "the most brutal realities, the most terrible social conditions, she struggles to remain a human being, to keep her humanity intact."[95] Unlike the characters in "The Locked Room," Anna extends *beyond* her narrative: "You might have to stop, but it is only because you have run out of time. You stop, but that does not mean you have come to an end."[96] *Moon Palace* further solders *In the Country of Last Things* in reality, minimizing its more fantastic, fable-like qualities by concretizing Anna herself. Zimmerman, one of the novel's supporting characters, receives the letters of one Anna "Bloom or Blume, I was never sure of the spelling,"[97] who has "run off to join her older brother, William, who worked as a journalist in some foreign country."[98] He supplies the physical, objective description that had been missing from her own narrative: "a diminutive, dark-haired girl with a pretty face and a bristling, animated personality."

But *Moon Palace* resurrects not only Anna from *In the Country of Last Things* but the motif of the broken umbrella from *The New York Trilogy.* Orlando, a homeless mendicant, holds the spokes of his broken umbrella up to the rain, having evolved beyond reliance on his sensory input: "this was imagination in its purest form: the act of bringing non-existent things to life, of permitting others to accept a world that was not really there."[99] He is taking advantage of the fact that inevitably language and perception will fail, as protagonist Marco Fogg learns for himself while working as the eyes of Effing, his blind employer: "A fire hydrant, a taxi cab, a rush of steam pouring up from the pavement—they were deeply familiar to me, and I felt I knew them by heart. But that did not take into account the mutability of those things, the way they changed according to the force and angle of the light, the way their aspect could be changed by what was happening around them."[100] Here again is the postmodern rationale for play. Auster questions, however, whether Orlando's play might be a defense mechanism shielding him against all too real economic wear-and-tear, the harsh truths of New York life that the *Trilogy* displays but effectively downgrades. Orlando's illusions reflect those sought out by "the better part of New York's derelict population," who shield their pain watching escapist Hollywood films in a decaying, once grand theater, "a shrine, a temple built to the glory of illusion."[101] Imagination, the novel suggests, may often be negligence; when Marco spends his afternoons reading to Effing amongst his grandfather's riches, imaginative literature represents an indolent, luxurious detachment from the world: "it felt both odd and pleasant to be sitting indoors as the world went about its business, and this sense of detachment was probably enhanced by the books themselves. Everything in them was faraway, shadowy, fraught with marvels."[102]

But *Moon Palace* often seems to shield itself against poverty, or the social issues surrounding it, in similar ways. The kind of social exploration pursued in *In the Country of Last Things,* and in the American novel of social realism highlighted by Samuel's obsession, is highly problematized here, both in its formal aspect (mimesis) and its thematic one (social conscience). Certainly the nature of paradigmatic American art is very much on Auster's mind; he begins the novel with an epigram from Jules Verne: "Nothing can astound an American." This serves as a kind of rationale for egregious coincidences of plot; although *Moon Palace* would seem a very *traditional* novel, expressly recalling Dickens and the Victorian novel in its orphan motif, Auster's microscope is fixed on the entrenched formula of chance that is so often implemented by novelists under the guise of Fate, lurching the narrative to its appropriate resolution, its distribution of predictably just desserts, the orphan discovering his parents, resolving familial discord. His argument is that in our reading we habitually accept as realism protocols inadequate to life's model; yet at the same time he insists that coincidences are part and parcel of life, our national birthright, and thus his own use of chance declares him a realist "in the strictest sense of the word." He insists that "we are continually shaped by the forces of coincidence, the unexpected occurs with almost numbing regularity in all our lives."[103]

Yet moments such as the one in which Solomon Barber tumbles accidentally and fatally into an open grave immediately after admitting that he is the hero's long-missing father are, as Birkerts observes: "ominously close to campy self-parody. Too many coincidences overwhelm the ground of plausibilities that meaningful coincidences require."[104] Auster has not approximated realism but disrupted it in typical deconstructive fashion; we are left only with questions: "The synchronicity of these events seemed fraught with significance, but it was difficult for me to grasp precisely how. . . . Nothing but some crackpot solution could account for it: strange conspiracies of matter, precognitive signs, premonitions. [I] began exploring the question of coincidences, but I never got very far with it."[105]

Despite this apparently ambivalent process of destabilization, the novel does at times achieve the potency of the finest works of American realism; Marco, finished his schooling and out of work, finds himself beneath the sign of the Moon Palace Chinese restaurant:

> The pink and blue neon letters were so large that the whole sky was filled with their brightness. Then, suddenly, the letters disappeared, and only the two *o*s from the word *Moon* were left. I saw myself dangling from one of them, struggling to hold on like an acrobat who had botched a dangerous stunt. Then I was slithering around it like a tiny worm, and then I wasn't there anymore. The two *o*s had turned into eyes, gigantic human eyes that were looking down on me with scorn and impatience. They kept on staring at me, and after a while I became convinced that they were the eyes of God.[106]

The moment conflates Jonathan Edwards's famous sermon "Sinners in the Hands of an Angry God"—Marco as the sinning filth dangling from God's hand, writhing like a spider held over a fire—with Fitzgerald's eyes of T.J. Eckleburg, perhaps the most referenced image in contemporary American literature. As such, the scene incorporates Marco's sense of unachieved status in society, his lack of industrious contribution, his inability to live up to dictates of his culture that are in their own way as austere as any Puritan ideal of right and wrong, as judgmental as any estimation of sinner or saved. We see that there is still a land of gray ash consuming those who fall through the cracks, despite their best intentions. This latter category includes the Marco Foggs of the world, those whose artistic sensibilities are squashed by outside forces beyond their control, who find that their talents lack economic and social utility. Indeed, when there is any opportunity to earn his keep through storytelling, Marco eagerly seizes it; when plucked off the street by friends of future lover Kitty Wu, he unleashes his best stories: "that was the least I could do, I thought: sing for my grub, make them forget I had just licked their plates clean."[107]

But Marco is unwilling to work at anything *besides* storytelling. Starvation functions at times like a horrible social reality but more often as a choice, the artist's very individual choice. Perhaps there is good reason for Marco to feel shame after all, for his plight is largely of his own doing, starvation his ideal, just as for Auster prolonged deprivation is key to the development of voice: "Speech is a strangeness, an anomaly, a biologically secondary function of the mouth, and myths about language are often linked to the idea of food. . . . Mystics fast in order to prepare themselves to receive the word of God."[108] In the midst of his suffering we must remember that Fogg's college compatriots easily avoid his plight, while he has not even tried to find employment; Auster himself pursued a much different route than those of his college classmates: "That's what I'm still at a loss to explain. Why did my friends act so prudently and why was I so reckless?"[109] Thoreau may be Fogg's model here, but even in his withdrawal from society, Thoreau displayed constant industry, as evidenced by his elaborate accounting of daily tasks, consumption of supplies, etc. Fogg does nothing: "I decided that the thing I should do was nothing: my action would consist of a militant refusal to take any action at all. This was nihilism raised to the level of aesthetic proposition. I would turn my life into a work of art."[110] In addition, Thoreau would never have resorted to Marco's degree of pretentiousness: "For the rest of the night I just stood there in a trance of self-pity, waiting for the morning to come."[111] If we cannot, in the end, equate Marco's suffering with the epidemic and presumably involuntary suffering surrounding him in New York, Rorty's program of creating solidarity through "the imaginative ability to see strange people as fellow sufferers"[112] is short-circuited.

In keeping with Auster's "fasting mystic" parallel, Fogg's descent has not been without hints of artistic genius: "I was going mad, but I nevertheless felt a tremendous power surging through me, a Gnostic joy." Wordplay becomes his forte, as when he is reduced to scavenging garbage cans for food: "I gave funny names to the garbage cans. I called them cylindrical restaurants, potluck dinners"[113] Yet for all this he continues to blame his state on the economic realities of his time: "I was an instrument of sabotage, I told myself, a loose part in the national machine . . . living proof that the system had failed, that the smug overfed land of plenty was finally cracking apart."[114] It is not until reaching something akin to absolute zero that he realizes that his own inclinations are to blame; on the brink of embracing his newfound creative "power," tantamount to embracing death, he finally recognizes that one's mind cannot withdraw from his body, that corporeal needs cannot be dispensed with. In literary terms, he realizes that he cannot dispense with realism, for only it can adequately address the conditions toward which he had moved: "I had thought I was acting in courage; but it turned out that I was merely demonstrating the most abstract form of cowardice: rejoicing in my contempt for the world, refusing to look things squarely in the face."[115]

In the end, Auster manages to address poverty through Marco's abuse of the issue, but what of the more grand events of the time, events destined to be part of the cultural record, that would seem to demand Anna Blume's approach, not the ironist's? Marco abstracts himself out of time; the novel, though unwinding in the thick of sixties turmoil, deflects the questions raised by social unrest to focus on the starving artist dilemma. In *Hand to Mouth,* Auster describes the unrest at length; Columbia University became "a war" complete with "riots, slugfests and factual splits. Rhetorical excess abandoned, ideological lines were drawn, passions flowed from all sides."[116] Fogg is not oblivious to this—"by the spring of 1968, every day seemed to retch forth a new cataclysm"[117]—but his interest goes little deeper than this cursory observation. The reader's frustration at this omission is further compounded by Fogg's insistence that this negligence is actually metonymy, that his personal experiences of penury, naïveté and abstraction can be substituted for the larger canvas of the sixties: "My own story stands in the rubble of those days, and unless this fact is understood, none of it will make sense."[118] In *Armies Of The Night,* Norman Mailer showed that a writer's personality can serve as an example of his time; his second "reading" of the march on Washington, the more "outside," editorial reading, is only impactive on the basis of the unpredictable first half in which the bombastic, chaotic persona of Mailer himself seems to both embody and analyze the mood of the times and the issues under debate. But where Mailer openly engages his time, Marco never reacts to what is transpiring along the fringe of his awareness: "Woodstock. It had so little with what was happening to me just then, I didn't know what to think. Those people were my age, but for all the connection I felt with them, they might have been from another planet."[119] His attitude, and seemingly the attitude of the novel as a whole, is antithetical to the urge to uncover, to dig deep into histories, that so distinguishes Mailer or E.L. Doctorow in his *Book of Daniel.* Their type of pursuit has no value in Auster's eyes, apparently: "Everyone is familiar with the story of that time, and there would be no point in going over it again."

It is only when deriving *differences* between Fogg and the mood of his times that the novel achieves its rare moments of political and moral clarity. When the draft board rejects Fogg, it, like the landlord in "City Of Glass," groups the artist with "the simpletons, the grotesques, the young men who did not belong anywhere."[120] But invention (i.e. lying) has been embraced more, and more harmfully, by the "active" population. O'Brien will argue that lying to dodge the draft is a rational and moral choice, but Auster identifies such lies as the point at which misrepresentation was assimilated into the social dynamic, leaving an aftertaste in the general populace destined to sour any ennobling view of human nature; witness, as a case in point, the effectual irrelevance of charges of draft-dodging on Bill Clinton's first presidential campaign, despite blatant attempts by Republicans to milk the issue. As described by Auster, the artistically inclined might be too pure to even consider the prospect of avoiding the draft: "Unlike the vast majority of them, however, I had done nothing to prepare myself for the moment of truth. I did not have a note from a doctor, I had not gorged myself on drugs to distort my motor responses, I had not staged a series of mental disturbances to establish a history of psychological disturbances."[121] But it is significant to note his alienation is equally debilitating; as he attempts to explain himself to the psychologist at the draft board, he displays just how far he has removed himself from conventional forms of communication: "It was a horrible botch. My language became increasingly awkward and abstract, and eventually I could see that the doctor had stopped listening."

But Thomas Effing, Marco's employer (and through another implausible coincidence, his grandfather) provides an example of how the artistic soul moves beyond this state. Old, blind, and bitter, he has passed through many ideas of art. As a young painter known as Julian Barber, he aspired to absolute realism, traveling the nation in order to indulge his inclination toward "landscape, a passion for the real world."[122] Later, in the oblivion of an abandoned thieves' cave, an artist's withdrawn solitude, thief George Ugly Mouth supplies Effing with a new model for artistic expression that can only be seen as the postmodern norm: "rambling, half-formed narratives began to loop back among themselves with a certain frequency, intersecting at enough points to take on the structure of a larger, more unified story. Incidents were repeated, crucial passages were left out, events from the beginning were not told until the end."[123] Accordingly, Barber, in true postmodern style, gives up his former identity for a false one; Effing, his chosen name, is a pun on fucking.

But Auster denies us a glimpse of the art Effing produces in his solitude; Marco never finds his lost cave. What Effing leaves behind instead, however, is a gesture of benevolence toward both those who served him and the masses in general. After stipulating an inheritance for Marco and his other servants, he hands out the rest of his fortune on the streets of New York. In *Hand to Mouth,* Auster recounts his experiences with H.L. Humes, a fallen literary figure with delusions of inspiring "the greatest economic revolution in history" [124] by handing out a substantial inheritance to New York strangers. Auster admits that in those years he reacted to Humes's gesture in terms antithetical to Rorty: "my loner instincts were too ingrained, and I could never bring myself to climb aboard the great ship *Solidarity.*"[125] But in Effing Auster has stripped the political significance from Humes's gesture until only solidarity remains. The novel's second half, however, gives way entirely to Marco's obsessions and the ludicrous coincidences of his later life, squandering such possibilities.

The Music of Chance foregrounds this impulse toward solidarity but cannot reconcile it with Auster's more theoretic or philosophical interests. The novel is at once more realistic and more elliptical than *Moon Palace.* The realism lies in Auster's central characters, Nashe and Pozzi, two very different gamblers (Nashe is pragmatic, simple but not simple-minded, outwardly stoic; Pozzi is whiplash clever, energetic, and morally questionable) who lose their freedom in a card game but form a bond of sincere if perilous trust while futilely attempting to work off their debt by building a wall for Flower and Stone, two vastly wealthy friends, lottery winners, who have distinctive views on power and social status. It is in the scenes of wall-building that the novel takes on something other than a realistic tone, an existential feel beginning to permeate, as if it is Vladimir and Estragon standing and stacking brick: "Much better to think of things only in the most superficial terms—the debt, the contract, the hours they put in—and to bluster along with funny remarks and ironic shrugs of the shoulders."[126]

In most "biographical" respects, Nashe is a very typical Auster hero, a now-fatherless father bolstered by an unexpected inheritance and seized by the same wanderlust as DeLillo's David Bell: "Nashe did not have any definite plans. At most the idea was to let himself drift for a while, to travel from place to place and see what happened. . . . Speed was of the essence, the joy of sitting in the car and hurtling forward through space. . . . The car became a sanctum of invulnerability, a refuge in which nothing could hurt him anymore."[127] The characteristically American ideal of personal autonomy is an "abiding dream" identified by Tony Tanner as tainted with the "abiding American dread that someone else is patterning your life, that there are all sorts of plans afoot to rob you of your autonomy of thoughts and actions."[128] However, Nashe is in other ways clearly not the Auster norm; there is too much of him, to much *to* him. In the first few pages the reader accumulates a healthy amount of data about Nashe: his failed marriage; his more healthy ties to his daughter, sister, brother-in-law, and boss, a fire department captain; his elaborated finances; his love of classical music; his inheritance; his memory of a past trip to his negligent father's home; his lover Fiona and his conflicted emotions toward her and the prospect of another marriage. All of this comes in a rush in the opening scene, in addition to his encountering battered Pozzi on the side of the road, a flood of detail that would be nothing unusual for Updike, Anne Beattie, Thomas McGuane, or Larry McMurtry, but for Auster represents an unexpected freshet of enumeration, of "color," enough so that the expected postmodernisms, when they finally arrive, seem atypically real, more than the stipulations of an overarching conceptual blueprint: "Nashe understood that he was no longer behaving like himself. He could hear the words coming out of his mouth, but even as he spoke them, he felt they were expressing someone else's thoughts, as if he were no more than an actor performing on the stage of some imaginary theater."[129]

Yet the nature of Nashe's ultimate redemption, in which he finally earns his much coveted autonomy, is more problematic. He defines himself, at the novel's climax, by swerving his car into onrushing traffic. There are other people riding with him—unsuspecting Murks, the factotum of Flower and Stone, and his son—but their fate, their life or death, seems effectively irrelevant. Auster insists, though, that there is nothing equivocal about Nashe's choice: "The important thing is that he has triumphed. By the end of the book he has transcended everything he has been—he has become, I think, a great figure—a truly powerful human being who understands himself and what he's capable of (which was not the case at the beginning) and what this means is that he's willing to take the world as it comes to him."[130] The prospect of this kind of human triumph seems wonderfully strange to readers of the early DeLillo or of *The New York Trilogy,* yet such a reader must wonder, too, what the difference is, after all, between this self-willed car wreck and Nashe's death-wish in the early wanderlust sequences, in which: "he welcomed these close calls. . . . They added an element of risk to what he was doing, and more than anything else, that was what he was looking for: to feel that he had taken his life into his own hands."[131] The difference is a matter of inches; he may have gained fortitude since then, but what of the awakening of Nashe's communal instincts inspired by Pozzi? What is the value of becoming such a "great figure" after all?

He has made a choice, Auster argues, a Nietzschian gesture to cast off his passive acceptance of suffering. His choice to die is a choice to live; in an essay on Sir Walter Raleigh, Auster gives us the Wall, seamlessly tied into the wall over which Nashe labors:

> Each man approaches the wall. One man turns his back, and in the end he is struck from behind. Another goes blind at the very thought of it and spends his life groping ahead in fear. And another sees it from the very beginning, and though his fear is no less, he will teach himself to face it, and go through life with open eyes. Every act will count, even to the last act, because nothing will matter to him anymore. He will live because he is able to die.[132]

Nashe's story is a parable inscribing this sentiment in fiction. Yet in human terms his choice is a failure; it establishes Self but deprives all others: lover, child, friend. Indeed, Auster is not oblivious to this fact; despite his celebration of Nashe, there is an undercurrent of distinctively American pragmatism in the text that contradicts such existential notions of the Will (and the Wall). Fiona, for example, recognizes that the ideal of freedom so important to Nashe and to Auster is often only the trademark American male cowardice manifested by Rabbit: "This is America, Nashe. The home of the goddamn free, remember? We can all do what we want."[133] She embodies an embittered underside to the American dream of personal liberty, the deserving woman waiting forlornly for her immature lover to return. The subject of her criticisms is the early Nashe and not the later "hero," but her sense of loss pervades even Nashe's final suicidal gesture; chances are, Fiona will never see him again.

Similarly, although Nashe's earlier agreement to prolong his "labor camp" days may seem to represent a debilitating self-abnegation, his vow to preserve his daughter's college fund in the face of his financial and physical duress has heroic flavor: "The equation was too terrible: to pay off his gambling debt by stealing from his daughter's future. No matter what happened, it was out of the question. He had brought this problem down on himself, and now he would have to take his medicine. Like a man, he thought."[134] But his final decision may have stripped his daughter of him forever.

Pozzi's body, pummeled by a group of lawyers outraged over their defeat at cards, is a script of deprivation: "his naked torso was white, skinny, and pathetic, as if his body hadn't been out in the sun for years."[135] Nashe's final choice of self-definition counteracts his earlier decision toward definition through others, in which he saw this stranger "as a reprieve, as a last chance to do something for himself before it was too late."[136] It is also through Pozzi that Nashe recognizes the importance of a narrative embodying the pain of others, a narrative of solidarity: "Nashe would tell stories about the year he had spent on the road, or else he would talk about some of the big fires he had fought in Boston, dwelling on the most ghastly details for Pozzi's benefit, thinking it might get the kid's mind off his own troubles if he heard about what other people had gone through."[137]

This narrative is cast aside, however, for what may in the final analysis be another metaphor for the artistic drive that takes no quarter. Nashe and Auster both clearly share the same compulsion toward grand action, self-definition, as did Samuel Beckett and the patriarchal figure Hamm in *Endgame,* as seen by Bloom: "the will to live, in horribly decayed form, abides in [Hamm], and that always remains the daemon for Beckett. If you are an artist, you suffer your vocation's peculiar augmentation of the will to live, a craving for recognition initially and ultimately for immortality."[138] Literary immortality is so important because even the genius is as likely to live in misery as acclaim: "Haydn had lived to a ripe old age, honored with commissions and court appointments and every advantage the world of that time could offer. And Mozart had died young and poor, and his body had been thrown into a common grave."[139] For this reason, the artistic Will is uninterested in social definition, social compassion; Bloom continues: "Beckett seems to have been as good and decent a human being as any strong writer ever, and much more so than most: infinitely compassionate, endlessly kind though even more infinitely withdrawn. But as writer qua writer, he suffered as all writers suffer."

There is a much different and much less selfish *political* aspect to Nashe's gesture, although it is one Auster's statements on Nashe barely touch upon. It is an act of rebellion against the power of Flower and Stone, which is a power at once fated and random, the nature of American power: uninherited, unpredictable, unreasonable and yet nevertheless maniacal and self-important once established, as if royalty had always been in the blood (or, as here, in the cards). Stone reflects this sense of self-importance by constructing the vast, meticulously planned diorama "City Of The World," which represents an old-fashioned kind of art and authority based entirely on form and structure, on rigid class divisions and definitions; the city's heavy-handed punitive elements (there are disproportionately large numbers of prisoners and punishers inhabiting the diorama) create an atmosphere of Puritan doom and gloom, the entrenched belief, to quote Mailer's reading of Richard Lowell in *Armies Of The Night,* that Man is not good enough for God, an idea Flower and Stone further emphasize by looming over Nashe and Pozzi, "standing at a window watching them through a telescope or a pair of binoculars,"[140] overlooking the limbo of society's failures.

Woods observes how the nature of such authority seeps into the unconscious of everyone else, creating a nation of worker-drones responsive only to the ebb and flow of money: "the pervading aura of suppressed menace or threat is the critical link between American capitalism and the ethical imperatives of Puritanism."[141] Woods draws copiously from Foucault, who found in the modern penal system's conversion of convict to docile citizen a blueprint for the propagation of a sheeplike labor force: "it imposes on the convict the 'moral' form of wages as the condition of his existence."[142] Foucault's world is one in which sovereignty has given way to bureaucracy, in which the potent symbolism of the king's body and presence has become institutional, clinical, based on theories of normalcy; Stone's self-deluding model is more of a throwback, with elaborate ceremonies of public punishment at the scaffold and the firing line. Nashe comes to recognize this pretense, and understands that the only way he can strike a blow against the theatrical, monarchical tyranny of Flower and Stone is by striking them at the more genuine capitalist level, depriving his "employers" of their manpower, namely himself and Murks.

Murks is a fascinating figure in the book, Auster's equivalent to DeLillo's Globke, a "way in" the consciousness of the working man, in whose mindset labor can be an absolute good, not a penalization. He is our society's conception of normal, the family man, the pragmatist, the believer in the principle of work, to which end he reinterprets the wall: "There's no big mystery to it. You can see the wall going up, and after a while it starts to give you a good feeling. . . . When you work on a wall like this, you've always got something to show for it."[143] As a supervisor he is generally fair to his workers, sensing, we suspect, an innate kinship with Nashe, yet he seems to have no trouble executing the violent whims of his higher-ups, fully accepting his position in the hierarchy of power; he wears his gun as a sign of precautionary authority, and, in the novel's most infuriating ambiguity, he and his son might be the men who recapture and brutalize the escaped Pozzi. In either case, Murks does not question whether Pozzi deserves his fate, which may or may not be death; he is a part of the system. It is in Murks that Auster's most trenchant fears about the state of modern society strike home, yet it is his relationship with Nashe that supplies many of the novel's most redeeming human moments. It is very clear that Nashe's final gesture is not a railing against the Murkses of the world as it might have been for Nietzsche, but instead functions as an indictment of the nation's elite; as Pozzi bitterly ruminates (and this, we feel, is not just paranoia): "the whole world is run by assholes."[144] In this *The Music Of Chance,* once the self-conscious romanticism is assimilated and looked beyond, represents an example of that form of expression Effing was on the cusp of while lost in the desert, before retreating instead to his cave: the pent-up scream of frustration. The novel's diverted message of solidarity is an attempt to place a form of benevolent energy into play in creative and financial systems that have little use for it; like the music of long-dead composers, it tantalizes the reader with suggestions of another world not so arid that choosing to choose is in itself a heroic, even political, transcendence. Such utopian suggestions move to the center in Auster's later work.

Chapter Seven

"Nobody Would Believe a Word": Sincerity amid Terror in the Early Novels of Tim O'Brien

The literary interests of friends DeLillo and Auster frequently converge, a kinship distinguished, as Dennis Barone notes, by "frequent portrayals of an ascetic life," "obsessive characters," and "a loss of the ability to understand."[1] As we have seen, both authors, in their early work, recognize their artistic prerogative in the last of these interests, a prerogative that defines the experimental aspect of postmodernism. Tim O'Brien, in *his* early work, writes of the same matters, the same character types, the same loss, but in his unpolished sincerity he serves as a counterpoint to their prerogative, their sense of what the Novel should be. However, just as the relationship with the reader implied by his social imperative and his referential use of language proves increasingly magnetic to DeLillo and Auster, their early extremes of flamboyance and isolationism continually attract O'Brien, threatening to compromise his work. Taken together, these authors epitomize the schizophrenic prospects of the contemporary novelist.

O'Brien's first book, *If I Die in a Combat Zone, Box Me Up and Ship Me Home,* is a work of non-fiction. Despite the emergence in recent decades of such hybrids as the "nonfiction novel" or the "autobiographical fiction"—all the traditional distinctions growing increasingly blurry—this suggests a wholly different theory of writing than the works we have discussed thus far, the reader necessarily anticipating a credible attempt at verisimilitude, particularly from the war narrative. Correspondingly, there is no denying the rawness, even the awkwardness, of *If I Die in a Combat Zone,* a lack of intricate structure that would not sit well with the later novelist O'Brien, who is a precise, often delicate craftsman. O'Brien's strain of realism here is to pinpoint chance, randomness, as the integral force of modern life, as Steven Kaplan describes: "things just happen in this text, in the same way things just happen in Vietnam, and the process of sense-making is left to the reader."[2]

As we have seen, this same interest on Auster's part produced a sometimes unsatisfying tension between artifice and realism in *Moon Palace.* For O'Brien, writing nonfiction and plagued by higher stakes, the wavering is even more pronounced. Fully cognizant of all the "weaknesses" of the written medium exhibited by the postmodernists, O'Brien faces the prospect of proselytizing though aware that his "truth" is fated to slip into a limited, subjective murmur. Sharing too a novelist's elitist ideals, he is reluctant to concede his role to that of the "Vietnam writer," aspiring to be an artist, not a chronicler, to infuse his rigid subject matter, his lecture, his history lesson, with all the postmodernist's unfettered creativity. Yet all the while he believes he has a course of action too essential to abandon: his need to elucidate the Vietnam situation, both for his own unburdening benefit and for the social record: "I would wish this book could take the form of a plea for everlasting peace, a plea from one who knows, from one who's been there and come back."[3] This conflict characterizes all his earlier work, nonfiction or fiction; O'Brien continually questions the twin poles of American realism, commonplace mimesis and social didacticism, even as he intends to affirm them.

O'Brien is not drawn to postmodern writers, as DeLillo is, or to French poetry, as Auster is. Instead, he prefers writers who dwell in a more concrete realm, identifying with John Irving, Graham Greene, John Updike, Walker Percy, Norman Mailer, and Tom McGuane.[4] Even when his writing necessarily diverges from reality, he steadfastly tries to maintain a structure that illuminates rather than sterilizes the Real: "I tried to cast the scenes in fictional form. Dialogue, for example. Often I couldn't remember the exact words people said, and yet to give it a dramatic intensity and immediacy, I'd make up dialogue that seemed *true to the spirit* of what was said [italics mine]."[5] It is fascinating, therefore, that O'Brien's work often stands as a testament to the relevance of the *postmodern* novel, providing evidence that the "alternate worlds" it presents are indeed our own. While the moral crises of his book are certainly not new, World War I having provided any number of like ambiguities for Hemingway, Cummings, and Dos Passos to grapple with, the specific phenomenological and ontological crises new to this war are those that regularly thwart postmodern heroes.

Vietnam continually challenges realist urges. Even the most ostensibly "journalistic" Vietnam narratives, such as Michael Herr's *Dispatches,* read at times like prototypical postmodern texts; Herr dispenses, without compunction, with words, titles, and distinctions, the authority of strict realism abandoned to the wind: "names of places, of operations, of commanders, of weapons; memories, guesses, second guesses, experiences (new, old, real, imagined, stolen); histories, attitudes—you could let it go, let it all go."[6] Similarly, despite O'Brien's extensive research going in, war-torn Vietnam quickly becomes a Zone, an area of ontological ebb and flow: "We would seek out shapes in the dark. Impose solidity. We would squeeze our eyes shut. What we could not see, we imagined. . . . We would blink and rub our eyes and wonder about the magic of this place. Levitation, rumblings in the night, shadows, hidden graves."[7] In terms of postmodern parallel, the military establishment fills the role of logocentric authority, the antithesis of the unpredictable, unraveling forces of the jungle (which represent play, in a sense, or the contingency that stimulates play). Like the football program in *End Zone,* the military struggles to rely on its teleological spine, its absolute version of history, as demonstrated by Chaplain Edwards's insistence that mindless belief is an adequate all-purpose fail-safe: "But there's still faith, and you've got to have it. You've got to have faith in somebody."[8] His paradigm of such faith is President McKinley praying for guidance (and presumably receiving it) over the prospect of the Spanish-American war; Edwards and O'Brien have a contentious interchange over this idea of divinely supported conquest:

> "We read different books."
> "Different books hell! That's history."
> "That is McKinley's history."[9]

O'Brien's argument, like Rorty's, is that history is open to debate. The army counteracts, or attempts to counteract, this sensation of flux and interpretative breakdown, the day-to-day occurrences in Vietnam that, in Thomas Couser's terms, are "concrete, undramatic, and disorderly, so inert and devoid of meaning, that [they defy] both the nature and the purpose of narrative,"[10] with a monotonous routine best exemplified by the trudging of foot soldiers through the jungle, a repetitive, patterned, directionless movement recalling the entropic New York circles traced by Pynchon's "yo-yoing" Whole Sick Crew: "The left leg stretches with magnificent energy, long muscle. Lumbers ahead. It's the strongest leg, the pivot. The right leg comes along, too, but only a companion. The right leg unfolds, swings out, and the right foot touches the ground for a moment, just quickly enough to keep pace with the left, then it weakens and raises on the soil a pattern of desolation."[11] Herr describes the fundamentally entropic nature of the military order in similar terms: "there were times when the whole war itself seemed tamed of its vitality: epic enervation, the machine humming half-assed and depressed, fueled on the watery residue of last year's war-making energy."[12]

Of course, the prospect of order is a sham; in truth, the army represents a transient existence in which identity is denied, soldiers reduced to ciphers, sites: "You can go through a year in Vietnam and live with a platoon of sixty or seventy people, some going and some coming, and you can leave without knowing more than a dozen complete names, not that it matters."[13] As is typical of these novels, when identity goes, a freedom of imagination comes; O'Brien feels he is free to manipulate the people in his life, such as a girl from home whom he "creates" as Harkness created the car crash victim and Blue created his fiancé: "I lied about her, pretending that she wrote the poem for me. I compared her to characters out of books by Hemingway and Maugham. In her letters she claimed I created her out of the mind. The mind, she said, can make wonderful changes in the real stuff."[14] The result is less than satisfying, however; just as the chair for Billy Twillig can exist only in its semantic shambles, O'Brien's girl crumbles into dust and word before his eyes: "It was hopeless, of course, but I tried to visualize her face. Only words would come in my mind. One word was "smile" and I tacked on the word "intriguing" to make it more personal. . . . All there was to see was the word "face" or the word "eye" printed out before me. It was like asking a computer to see for me."[15]

The challenge for O'Brien and his realist notions is to be true to this postmodernized reality without taking on the accouterments of order that would compromise it. He purports, therefore, to let the events stand on their own without commentary or structure; without art: "I had witnessed things, smelled things, imagined things which struck me as startling and terrifying and intriguing in all sorts of ways. At this point I didn't care much for technique or language or structure or any of that craft stuff."[16] In this he aspires to the type of writing pioneered by Hemingway's *In Our Time,* as characterized by Edmund Wilson: "Mr. Hemingway is unperturbed when he tells us these things: he is not a propagandist even for humanity."[17] Note, for example, O'Brien's depiction of the nonsensical slaughter of cows by the soldiers in his troop: "The boys escaped, but one cow stood its ground. Bullets struck its flanks, exploding gobs of flesh, boring into its belly. The cow stood parallel to the soldiers, a wonderful profile. It looked away, in a single direction, and it did not move. I did not shoot, but I did endure, without protest, except to ask the man next to me why he was shooting and smiling."[18] O'Brien is seemingly apathetic here, suggesting only a hint of personal investment when insisting that he personally took no part in the action. O'Brien avers that there is nothing he could add to this: "Do dreams offer lessons? Do nightmares have themes, do we awake and analyze them and live our lives and advise others as a result? Can the foot soldier teach anything important about the war, merely for having been there? I think not. He can tell war stories."[19]

The cow scene will recur in most of his later war novels, however, and in each case its significance is different. Most troublesome is the way terrorists in *The Nuclear Age* twist the cow's agony to stand as a shining example of resilience under duress. Stories, O'Brien realizes, can never really be left to themselves. Thus it is that O'Brien cannot support an old battalion commander who shares his dream of epitomizing war without climbing up on a soapbox, without sentiment, without an over-analysis of the political causes involved: "Maybe I'll write a book. I remember when the Chinks swarmed across the river down into Korea. That would make a book. Trouble is, they want philosophy in with the real action. I'd like to write it straight, just how it happened, but I can see the rejection slips already."[20] O'Brien cannot support this ambition because the commander approves of the Vietnam War; the risk of shading, conscious or unconscious, is too great. O'Brien must take action despite himself. He must inject his narrative with conscience and support it with facts, with the names, to recall Axton's defining gesture: "Well, sir, there's little evidence that South Vietnam under the communists will be a worse place than a South Vietnam ruled by a Diem or a Khanh. I mean, there's no persuasive evidence, at least not persuasive to me, that all the lives being lost, the children napalmed and everything—there's no good evidence that all this horror is worth preventing a change from Thieu to Ho Chi Minh."[21] Such moments are fleeting, but the inclusion of those names and issues that Herr claims have lost their potency is striking given its rarity in our most celebrated depictions of the Vietnam War, whether in literature like *Paco's Story* or in films like *Apocalypse Now* or *Platoon.*

But O'Brien's approach here has severe limits, as emphasized by a comparison to George Orwell (notable given his central role in Rorty's scheme), particularly in his Spanish Civil War account *Homage to Catalonia,* which manifests its own reluctance toward political expostulation—"It is a horrible thing to enter into the details of inter-party polemics; it is like diving into a cesspool"[22]—but nevertheless pounds the drums when Orwell feels his readers are slumbering and no one else can rouse them. Whereas passages depicting Orwell's return to England condemn "the deep, deep sleep of England, from which I sometimes fear that we shall never wake till we are jerked out of it by the roar of bombs,"[23] O'Brien's final passages, as *he* looks out on the somnolent vista of his home, are all of personal involvement and reflection, not overt social censure: "And over Minnesota you fly into an empty, unknowing, uncaring, purified, permanent stillness. Down below, the snow is heavy, there are patterns of old corn fields, there are some roads. In return for all your terror, the prairies stretch out, arrogantly unchanged."[24] The disinterest of the natural landscape does suggest the arrogant disinterest of its inhabitants (in his first fictional work, *Northern Lights,* O'Brien depicts Minnesotans who are virtually oblivious to the war) but he will not goad his audience into waking, relying instead on that pathos inspired by the lone soldier, that pathos that many returnees discovered was not, in fact, forthcoming from the general populace.

O'Brien has tried to draw attention to himself as a figure representative of his era, as Auster did with Fogg: "I was bred with the haste and dispatch and careless muscle-flexing of a nation giving bridle to its own good fortune and success. I was fed by the spoils of 1945 victory."[25] But like Fogg, too, he is inclined to set himself apart from the rabble: "When nothing happened, I began to read. . . . The town's library was quiet and not a very lively place—nothing like a football field on an October evening."[26] Although he claims to accede to his draft summons out of a kind of civic loyalty (as Socrates accepted the unjust death sentence meted out by Athens), he persists in his superior attitude after arriving in Vietnam, displaying as much acrimony toward the common man as DeLillo's protagonists at their worst: "Laughing and talking of hometowns and drag races and twin-cammed racing engines—all this was for the others. I did not like them, and there was no reason to like them. . . . I was superior. Made no apologies for believing it."[27] The opening scene, in which the soldiers hunker around a fire like Neanderthals, indulging in their totemic practices, displaying their trophy body parts, trading their coarse stories of sex and aggression, meets our author/audience paradigm, repulsed storyteller O'Brien setting himself apart. Rorty has claimed that contrary narratives serve an essential democratic function, even in simplistic genre forms like those "platoon" movies that depict soldiers "of various ethnic backgrounds fighting and dying side by side."[28] Matters need not be so synthetic, as Orwell's example proves. Recognizing that such feelings of superiority only detract from the humanistic agenda at hand, he commences *his* battle memoirs with an adoring portrait of an Italian solider: "there were both candour and ferocity in [him]. I hardly know why, but I have seldom seen anyone—any man, I mean—to whom I have taken such an immediate liking." Orwell is fully aware of his fellow soldier's illiteracy, his lack of intellectual firepower, but this only endears him the more: "Obviously he could not make head or tail of the map; obviously he regarded map reading as a stupendous intellectual feat."[29] Such improbable and groundless affection redeems Orwell from faceless detachment, from the unctuous role of holier-than-thou pontificator.

O'Brien does himself realize, eventually, that he can separate himself only so far from his compatriots. In combat situations all defensiveness inevitably breaks down; through the grueling march, the individual, no matter how individuated, becomes absolutely dependent on the Other: "The man to the front is civilization. He is the United States of America and every friend you have ever known; he is Erik and blond girls and a mother and a father. He is your life."[30] This is a nightmare for the self-proclaimed artist, but for O'Brien it is his salvation as well, for there is a redeeming heroism to be gleaned from the universal perseverance of such "primitives," as exemplified by Captain Johansen, who represents, if nothing else, stoic endurance in the face of fear and death and chaos: "and those who are cowards not heroes, those men sweating beads of pearly fear, failing and whimpering and trying again—the mass of men in Alpha Company—even they may be redeemable. . . . You promise, almost moving your lips, to do better next time; that by itself is a kind of courage."[31] Herr depicts the same kind of heroism when he meets a battered soldier who has been in country for half a year: "He hadn't been anything but tired and scared for six months and he'd lost a lot, mostly people, and seen far too much, but he was breathing in and breathing out, some kind of choice all by itself."[32]

This aspect of O'Brien, the man *within* the group, becomes more central to later novels like *The Things They Carried.* His hesitancy to embrace this role is obvious and understandable, for to be "outside' is to resist being defined by the war, a threat of which he has more than an inkling even while in Nam: "The war and my person seemed like twins. . . . Twins grafted together and forever together, as if a separation would kill them both. The thought made me angry."[33] According to Daniel Zins, O'Brien has managed to reverse this process; Vietnam has not defined him, but has instead served as "the impetus and spark for becoming a writer."[34] But Herr recognizes the truth, that war is bigger than any man, no matter how self-actualized, no matter how potent an artist: "I went to cover the war and the war covered me; an old story, unless of course you've never heard it."[35]

Northern Lights, O'Brien's first admitted fiction, is an attempt to free himself from this destiny, to cut himself loose from the shackles of the war, and specifically from the war writer label, staking his claim as a realistic novelist without having to limit himself to the disruption of Vietnam, though that may well be the wellspring of his creativity. O'Brien does not ignore Vietnam entirely, however, for Harvey Perry, the brother of protagonist Paul, is a wounded veteran, blinded in one eye; yet Harvey's presence represents the *suppression* of the Vietnam experience, for he has no stories to tell, no nightmares to relate. Unlike Harvey, Paul is the sensitive type, the same type "O'Brien" was in *If I*

Die in a Combat Zone: "they were good guys and they worried and they were bad soldiers."[36] He is another youngish intellectual, allowing O'Brien to dwell on all those aspects of this psyche familiar to us from *If I Die in a Combat Zone,* the same artist dilemmas, only minus the scars, the war.

But without recourse to Vietnam, O'Brien struggles to supply Perry with convincing motives; in the novel's opening scene, Paul, oppressed by the forest nightlife, wakes from his tossing and turning with an unfathomable will to kill: "It was dark everywhere. The black can hissed in the dark, ejaculating sweet chemicals that filled the great forest and his father's house."[37] In the much more mature *In The Lake Of The Woods,* veteran and failed politician John Wade, amid the rustling and croaking outside, tosses and rises and lets loose his rage; but this rage is brought on by a wealth of motives, as we will see, of which Vietnam is central but not absolute or isolated. By contrast, O'Brien fails to convey Paul's anomie as anything more than the postmodern norm; he depicts Paul flatly, with all the defining characteristics of Pynchon's Benny Profane, "sweaty and anemic and flabby,"[38] practicing "melancholia and self-pity."[39] Perry is also sexually ineffectual, if not impotent; Grace, his wife (herself a trademark postmodern woman, fecund, the earth mother), caters to his every need, bringing him to orgasm only by hand when giving him his nightly "rub."

The fact that the only discernible motivation for his rage seems to be the sound of the forest is representative of one of the overt steps O'Brien takes to disentangle himself from Vietnam: he focuses not on the shift from warfront to homefront but from non-fiction to fiction. He infuses his narrative with realism—that is, with a newfound wealth of detail, character, and atmosphere—very self-consciously; our first impressions of *Northern Lights* are of *life,* a sense of the wide world with which every novelist must grapple and which author surrogate Perry finds is too plentiful for him: "mosquitoes and junebugs, dawn crickets, dawn birds, dragonflies and larvae and caterpillars, morning moths and sleeping flies, bear and moose, walleyes and carp and northerns and bullheads and tiny salamanders."[40] Moose and bear and multitudinous insect life are hardly the extent of O'Brien's ecosystem, however, as this fervid life includes humankind, human history as well; O'Brien is far from meager in his character backgrounds and definition, the very foundation that Auster disregards until his breakthrough in *The Music Of Chance;* he traces back through a rich Minnesotan history, laying out the chronicle of Sawmill Landing, telling of migrations and settlements of Germans, Swedes, and Native Americans, of racial striation and strife, of lives and deaths, none of which impact the narrative proper in tangible terms until Paul's grandfather, Pehr Peri, enters the storyline, bearing his motherless son into the wilderness. O'Brien populates his narrative with "colorful" caricatures, standard crusty Northern folk like mayor Jud Harmor, who is senile (or just mischievous?) to the point of perpetually confusing Paul for Harvey, and both for their father. He is good-hearted, somewhat prescient, and dying of cancer; Auster's "man behind the counter" in "City Of Glass" never emerges beyond the concentration camp number on his arm, but when Jud Harmor dies, the reader is meant, like Paul, to feel a pang of loss. The challenge all this life and all this history poses for Perry is that of *structure,* the very challenge of transition O'Brien has geared himself to face: "All collapsed around the few images. But even the images offered no natural sequences. They were random and defiant, clarifying nothing, and Perry spent the long night in myopic wonder, trying to sort them into an order that would progress from start to finish to start."[41] Accordingly, O'Brien braces his events with the most resolutely traditional narrative formula: the hero earning his rebirth through feats of fortitude both mental and physical.

Another very conscious step of disentanglement O'Brien takes is to write a novel that, while frequently touching on themes of past and future wars, is aggressively *non*-alarmist, an anti-didactic text in the sense of the political didacticism grudgingly conceded to in *If I Die.* Perry's father, an ambiguously Lutheran preacher, symbolizes warning incarnate, ranting in his sermons not only of perdition but of nuclear war, and at times his prophesies seem on the brink of fulfillment, as when the Cuban missile crisis looms: "ships moved to sea, alerts and realerts and anvil defense, and the craziest thing of all was that the old man's craziest prophesy was not really crazy."[42] At such moments, the reader senses another kind of fiction, an aggressively didactic text, latent beneath the surface, but the prospect of such a book evaporates as the Cuban missile crisis does, with a revitalizing gasp of air that proves Perry's father an ogre of negativity and presumption, the son realizing, finally, that the father *is* crazy after all, O'Brien celebrating the silence in which no bells are clamoring, even as he suppresses the urge to set them clamoring himself.

A more discordant step of disentanglement, though, is O'Brien's somewhat presumptuous use of Vietnam as metaphor; Perry's quest is not a metaphor for Vietnam, as some critical readers have asserted, but vice versa. When a ski trip with his brother goes horribly awry, leaving both stranded in uncharted territory, Paul must withstand the cold and the desolate whiteness; even though earlier in the narrative he proved too cowardly to even brain a rat transfixed by his headlights, he finds himself now in a world of violence and physical challenge, the realm of the mythic hero's conquest and also a surrogate Vietnam. O'Brien depicts the journey in long redundant sentences: "he was lethargic in a purely empty way, fatigued, spent, drained, hollow, weak, ballooned, oxygen-light, empty-headed, lightheaded. Sleepy, sleepy."[43] This repetition epitomizes the entropic nature of the military life described in *If I Die,* the grim soldiers' march, the regimented existence. Just as each marcher in *If I Die* feels that the man in front of him has become the sum of his existence, the U.S. entire, the world, Harvey assumes this role for Perry during the storm, becoming the Other that is All: "the harder [Paul] skied, the harder he pushed, the more his eyes burned, the faster Harvey's orange flaming rucksack receded. He chased and chased and the orange rucksack receded."[44]

But by "utilizing" the war in this way, as a metaphor for the trial-by-fire experience, O'Brien denies our understanding of *If I Die.* Perry often questions Harvey's motive in enlisting: "In the tangled density of it all, Perry sometimes wondered if the whole show were a masquerade for Harvey to dress in khaki and display bigballed outdoorsmanship."[45] Other authors have notably treated war as such "bigballed outdoorship;" Mailer in *The Naked And The Dead* seems energized by the idea of World War II as an arena in which Man defines himself against both his enemies and the elements, the same mentality, the same need, that *Why Are We In Vietnam?* aggressively criticizes. In light of the ordeal motif, we may wonder if O'Brien's comment about "bigballed outdoorship" is actually meant as self-criticism, for in reconstructing the Vietnam experience, so baffling and resistant to order in *If I Die,* as part of this straightforward story, he has supplied only a gross simplification, a right-wing ideal.

In his defense, O'Brien does insist that Perry must progress beyond the limits of the masculine narrative. He not only becomes leaner, stronger, and more intuitively agile through his journey, but also somehow evolves from lovelessness to love, from the automaton who must program himself to exhibit warmth or concern—"he told himself to be kind"[46]—to an unabashed husband expressing a deep dependency: "he would tell [Grace] that he loved her and mean it, mean it at precisely the moment he said it."[47] According to Milton J. Bates, Perry's maturation is a two step process, reflecting two kinds of courage, masculine and feminine, the latter which "shuns confrontation, seeking the safe, sheltered arena." [48] Masculine courage stems from the woods, the snow, the storm; feminine courage from the pond, the womb.

But O'Brien does not explain how this transformation comes about; indeed, his "feminization" is degraded by the fact that sexual temptation, sexual conquest, has had its usual place in the paradigmatic narrative of masculine challenge, Gawain tantalized by the Green Knight's wife. As in the Gawain myth, in which the hero does not quite take the bait but falters both by tolerating her advances and accepting her ribbon, Perry's submission is largely symbolic; although he does not lay a hand on Carol, the married woman with whom he lodges after emerging from the blizzard, they share a moment of sexual acknowledgment, implied guilt and desire, while Perry lies naked in bed: "When the curtain at last parted, he pretended to be asleep. He heard her straining for absolute silence."[49] In the morning she tells him, "I ain't gonna tell Arild nothin,"[50] Arild being her husband. Yet while Gawain's transgressions are a blemish, a source of deserved, if not fatal, guilt, Perry's constitute sexual triumph as a key element of his survival.

O'Brien may be perilously extracting our potential for feminization, for solidarity, from the Finnish *Kalevala*. Its symbols are much cherished by Perry's father, the myth-spinner for his Northern tribe, "a preacher of the elements, more pagan than Christian, appealing only to the only true emotion of his frontier congregations, which was fear." For him the central image is a bull, "the Bull of Karelia, a moose with antlers gone and head down in the dead of winter,"[51] a symbol of resistance, of fortitude, though O'Brien is well aware that the portent of the Bull is also of failure. The bull in question is slaughtered, after admittedly monumental resistance, for a wedding day feast, just as Harvey, afflicted with the nickname "The Bull," goes to Vietnam to prove himself worthy of it and inevitably becomes a victim. But O'Brien hints that there is another message to take from the myth, one easily overlooked; integral to the true spirit of *The Kalevala* is not only heroic resistance but brotherhood, a bond deeper than blood, sealed through duress:

> Beloved friend, my boon companion my fair boyhood comrade
> Start now to sing to me, begin to recite together,
> Now that we have come together, have come from two directions.
> Seldom do we come together, meet one another
> On these wretched marches, these poor northern parts.[52]

O'Brien does not elaborate on this aspect of the myth, instead sending us to find it, as Auster sent us to find Thoreau; it is the supplemental material that supplies what he could not but what we need to know. Though Paul saves Harvey, he never bonds with him as he finally does with Grace. Remembering childhood memories during the raging storm, he fails to recall the traumatic events of Harvey's childhood to which he was a witness, such as when their father forced him to fire his gun on Christmas morning. But the question that defines Harvey's role is insistent throughout, even if ignored by Perry: "I'm serious, you're really my goddamn *brother* aren't you. . . . I mean, what's a brother?"[53]

O'Brien stresses the love of man and woman more explicitly. After bathing in Pliny's Pond, flush with that multitudinous life that so dominates the novel's early pages, "sea of swamps, mother marsh, womb of man," he finally makes love to fertile Grace ("he thought son, son, son, son") whose body, like Myna's, is all earth-mother imagery and Joycean wordplay: "Chlorophyllrich and algathick and deep to the very bottom of things. Such breasts, he thought."[54] In such fashion the women in the novel fall into types. Perry is strung between sturdy, humanizing Grace and Addie, Harvey's lover, who is wild and exotic, "Asiatic, Indian, primitive,"[55] a man-swapper and a fitting embodiment of Fiedler's Dark Woman, the rose opposed to Grace's lily. Even Addie characterizes Perry's choice on these terms: "Grace offers you supper. I offer the badlands and Indian adventure and my lovely personality."[56] Grace is home life, mediocrity, and Perry chooses her, a definitive statement for O'Brien. For Perry, domesticity takes priority, though this domesticity must be without art. While Addie stresses the redemptive power of the imagination, "you have to have it,"[57] his climactic lovemaking with Grace is "unimaginative."[58] Excessive dreaming might infringe on the business at hand, rebuilding a marriage, conceiving a child.

Indeed, imagination is dangerous; Perry's defining realization in the midst of the Blizzard is that pragmatism must take priority over fantasy. While lost in the storm, he indulges in the same sort of flagrant exertions of the imagination that will later characterize Paul Berlin in *Going After Cacciato,* rewriting the past (a fictitious reconciliation with his father) and creating the present (pretending, prematurely, that the thaw has already begun), but such dreams eventually meet with scorn: "Everything was such a damned nice idea when it was an idea."[59] It is better, he insists, to apply one's mind to concrete planning: "The hunger had stopped him from thinking. No bloody thinking. That was the problem from the beginning, no thinking."[60]

Yet O'Brien emphasizes that Berlin, the protagonist of *Going after Cacciato,* is a dreamer who can use his imagination as a heuristic tool instead of "a way of escaping the world in his head."[61] Spec Four Berlin is on night watch at an observation post by the sea, musing on a series of nightmarish experiences, numerous deaths he has witnessed and one in which he has taken part, in allegiance if not in action: the murder of Lieutenant Sydney Martin, a by-the-books officer who insists on sending a man down each Vietnamese tunnel they come across. To avoid dwelling on such guilt, or perhaps to put it in perspective, Berlin engages in a flight of fantasy. A member of their platoon, Cacciato, has gone AWOL, claiming his intent to walk to Paris and evading all capture efforts, particularly as a result of Berlin's own incompetence. Berlin imagines a subsequent pursuit mission winding toward Paris, a thoroughly fantastic adventure that features chimerical catacombs beneath the earth, a narrow escape from beheading in Tehran, and Berlin's relationship with beautiful woman-child Sarkin Aun Wang. Reality for Berlin continually wavers: "Briefly Paul Berlin slipped back to his observation tower along the South China Sea. Partly here, partly there. Hard to tell which was real."[62] Consequently, readers may struggle to grasp the borders drawn between fantasy and reality, past and present, never was and might be.

O'Brien insists that such conjecturing is not necessarily impractical: "It was an idea. It was a working out of possibilities. It wasn't dreaming and it wasn't pretending. It wasn't crazy."[63] In his quaint dreams of thawing ice and his imaginary conversations with his father, Perry comes to realize the potential danger of fantasy masquerading as idea, but in Perry's world rational thought proves essential when lost in the storm, where in Vietnam the fiber of the jungle repels rationalism, and, indeed, often morality. In Berlin's effort to capture Cacciato, the real attempt that precedes the fantasy, his logical action may be an exertion of force, but Berlin's imagination depicts for him the fruits of this "practicality" in explicit detail: "Paul Berlin was suddenly struck between the eyes by a vision of murder. Butchery, no less: Cacciato's right temple caving inward, silence, then an enormous explosion of outward going brains. It scared him."[64] Immediately after this revelation, Paul's negligence allows Cacciato to escape, and while his folly is certainly involuntary (he defecates from fear), O'Brien suggests it is an instinctual response to brutal possibility, body and soul in tune with human issues even when reason is misdirected.

Yet at other times Berlin's imagination represents dalliance of the worst sort, a *turning away* from humanity. In acceding to the murder of Sydney Martin, Berlin may be doing what needs to be done; Martin's ethic of efficiency and decorum would likely have proved fatal in the long run. But at the moment of his decision Berlin evades the complexity of the situation, the necessity of being honest to himself, by choosing to be "elsewhere," conjuring images much in the same fashion as Perry taking solace in the illusion of thawing ice: "Paul Berlin was pretending it was the Wisconsin Woods. Indian guides. Deep green forests, true wilderness. He got up and moved to the tunnel and touched the grenade."[65] At such moments, Berlin's dreaming marks him as another descendent of Heller's Yossarian, fleeing from the memory of Snowden's gaping wounds by an absurdist's feat of rowing the ocean: "Sometimes, during the hot afternoons beneath the tower, he would look out to sea and imagine using it as a means of escape—stocking Oscar's raft with plenty of rations and foul-weather gear and drinking water . . . letting the winds and currents carry him away—to Samoa, maybe or to some hidden isle in the South Pacific."

Heller is O'Brien's most obvious influence in *Cacciato,* as he explores both the manner in which the soldier escapes his world through fantasy and how the world has *become* fantasy. His novel is both realism and surrealism, a depiction of war as dark comedy that reworks the world as dark comedy. O'Brien has stressed that since war is surreal, it is only "natural and proper" that the war novel be surreal.[66] Yet it is important, too, that the basis of this surrealism remain the bitter fact that "men were slaughtered like cattle for reasons that no soldier really understood." In *Catch-22,* the potential for fantasy, very human dreaming of independence and a better future, wins out, but it is necessary that the novel first descend into the more sparse and humorless episode in which Aarfy rapes and murders the "plain maid" Michaela, the concretization of everything the army has made of the soldier, the reality the dreamer must escape with his own reality. O'Brien's novel threatens to resort to mystery in a way that Heller never suggests, however; the mystery behind Yossarian's suppressed pain reveals itself gradually but in a far more methodical and less baffling manner than the distinctions between fact and fiction establish themselves in *Cacciato.*

O'Brien may have returned to Vietnam, but has his improving artistry rendered his work an indulgence rather than a moral and social instrument such as *If I Die?* To Dennis Vannatta, O'Brien's blend of fantasy and reality recalls the "more appropriate examples of magical realism,"[67] but this comparison does not sit well with O'Brien himself, who claims to have been unable to even finish *One Hundred Years of Solitude,* and insists, instead, that his text draws clear boundaries between fact and fiction. Yet Updike, probably our representative voice of the "quality" realistic writer, believes that O'Brien is led astray by an adherence to fantasy and to postmodern play. Updike admires O'Brien's depiction of the happenings of war, the nature of war, its most minute but salient details: "we do not doubt the reality of Mr. O'Brien's combat scenes."[68] At the same time, though, Berlin's elaborate fantasies "serve not as a relief from Vietnam but as a kind of excuse from it," in which the reader is dazzled by the romance and adventure of the Paris trek to the point that the brutal truth, the violence at issue, is "demeaned, lightened . . . there builds up a slightly insulating lacquer of self-conscious art."[69] In keeping with Updike's assertions, the novel features self-conscious imagery of artistic distance, such as the stone Buddha sitting smugly in the background of the opening scene: "Behind [the lieutenant] in shadows was the cross-legged Buddha, smiling from its elevated stone perch."[70] Johnson will celebrate the phenomenological fluidity of the Buddhist perspective, but for O'Brien the Buddha seems to represent less spiritual depth than amused safety, the smugness of the petty dabbler.

In this fashion, the novel would seem intended to tie into the ideal of art favored by those postmodern readers who find its true value in self-reflexivity and play. Tobey Herzog provides a good example: "the novel becomes a piece of metafiction, with the author's literary intentions overshadowing his portrayal of the politics and physical realities of war."[71] While theorists like Herzog or Michael Raymond do not devalue theme entirely, they are clearly more interested in technical details—what is dream and what is fantasy?—much like those Auster scholars who diagram the relationship of Auster to Quinn to "Auster" (and extensions ad nauseam) in "City Of Glass." They are interested less in O'Brien's answers than his questions: "what part was fact and what part was the extension of fact? What had really happened and what merely might have happened?"[72] Or "But what was the order? How did the pieces fit, and into what months?"[73] Raymond pushes the novel much further into abstraction by asserting that the observation post itself is a fiction, apparently delighted that as a result such "metaphysical considerations" as "courage and responsibility and such goals as understanding the war"[74] become fictions too. The basis of his reading is a sentence near the conclusion of the novel: "They talked of rumors. An observation post by the sea, easy duty, a place to swim and get solid tans and fish for red snapper. . . . It would become a war story. People would laugh and shake their heads, no one would believe a word."[75] Yet there is nothing else in the narrative to suggest that the post does not prove real, and O'Brien has never suggested any such possibility in his interviews; instead, the eventual *truth* of the observation post stands as testament to the potential veracity and efficacy of rumors and tall-tales, O'Brien having come full circle from the blasé soldier, story-inured, in the opening scene of *If I Die*. Raymond has bought into the cynicism, but O'Brien is attempting to redeem the concept of story from its war-ravaged funk, moving beyond Berlin's reluctance to talk, to write, sometimes even to think: "so trivial, so obvious and corny, that to speak of it was embarrassing. War stories. That was what remained: a few stupid war stories, hackneyed and unprofound."[76]

O'Brien does not truly intend to obfuscate; it is notable that Pynchon's Tyrone Slothrop disintegrates without much tangible trace, whereas O'Brien's postmodern "emblem" Cacciato leaves markers behind for the soldiers so that they might follow him. For O'Brien, experimentalism is "not for the joy of experimenting, but rather to explore meaning and themes and dramatic discovery."[77] When he omits those details essential to much traditional fiction, his intent is to heighten, not stultify, moral awareness; although he never reveals who actually murdered Sydney Martin, he is not trying to baffle his readers but instead indicating that the most important issue is Berlin's complicity in the act: "It doesn't matter to me who did it. It's like if you were doing a scene on the execution of Bundy and you suddenly were to concentrate on the executioner, who's really a stand-in. The key thing is that touching [of the grenade]."[78]

Fittingly, O'Brien imbeds his own latent desires in Berlin's psyche; he depicts a young man capable of ironist cruelty. Berlin plays the part, as "O'Brien" did in *If I Die,* of the fireside storyteller turned away from his fellows, ignoring their conversation, "playing solitaire in the style of Los Vegas."[79] He admits to viewing his compatriots as grotesques: "He would begin to smell like the others, even look like them, but, by God, he would not join them."[80] It seems almost a corollary that he possess elitist intellectual leanings; when he idealistically characterizes Germany as the fountain of logical prowess, of "decency, cleanliness, high literacy and low mortality, the pursuit of learning in heated schools, science, art, industry bearing fruit through smoke stacks,"[81] it is hard, in the midst of one inhumane war, not to recall the wars of the near past and the rhetoric that bolstered them, the notion of cleanliness bearing with it any number of atrocious connotations such as the fanatical pursuit of racial purity.

Like our other protagonists, he creates the Other to suit his needs. In fact, he does this in a more literal way than we have seen before; Sarkin Aung Wan is nothing but a figment, and a burdened one at that, representing not only fantasy and flight from the war but womanhood, home, youth, life: "'Unreal,' he thought. Just a creature of the of his own making—blink and she was gone—but even so he liked the way she closed her eyes to the music, the way her chrome cross bounced on her sweater, her braided hair swishing so full."[82] She is the only power still under Berlin's control, but also, paradoxically, everything that his "use" of her could potentially obscure, the human issues of the conflict so often neglected in war literature, a sensitivity to those of other races, to innocent victims of the conflict, let alone enemy soldiers.

Unsurprisingly, the Vietnamese are most intangible for him; there is a Manichean aspect to his character, as he desires to possess the Other (through a sensual-lascivious exertion of his imagination) yet is diffident, or even repulsed, in person. Both aspects are on display during a civilian search: "So, sure, he frisked them all: one by one in a row, patting along the thighs and rumps and breasts without daring to look, not feeling but not unfeeling, no touch in his fingertips."[83] His demeanor is professional and solicitous: "a smile of understanding, neighborly goodwill. *I'm with you,* he was saying."[84] But when those people protest, he cannot maintain his artificial composure toward the rabble unleashed: "*Savages,*" he whispered."[85] It is not a far cry from this attitude to the insensitivity to cruelty on display when the troop wrecks vengeance on a civilian village in retaliation for the death of Jim

Pederson: "The men did not cheer or show emotion. They watched the village become smoke. . . . 'Kill it,' Paul Berlin said, but without malice."[86] Much of this impassivity stems from life *before* his arrival in Vietnam, life by TV in the media age: "So when he saw the villages of Quang Ngai, he had seen it all before. He had seen, before seeing, hideous skin diseases, hunger, rotting animals. . . . He was not outraged or made to grieve. He felt no great horror. He felt some guilt, but that passed quickly."[87]

But O'Brien's point is not just that the American solider cannot comprehend his Vietnamese enemy; this misunderstood Other, the shadowy warrior in the jungle murk, is as likely to be a fellow American as a Vietnamese, such as Oscar, one of the blacks in Alpha company, who is an interpretive wash in Berlin's fantasies, his ghetto talk every bit a facsimile: "Not an act, but not quite natural. . . . With Oscar Johnson it was always hard to tell, and this gave him power."[88] The figures whose plight O'Brien is tempted to suppress, our marginalized figures, creep into the narrative by creeping into Berlin's psyche, his subconscious. Berlin's imaginary Delhi is an Americanized utopia until one reaches the fringes of the city that are also the fringes of his awareness, where lies a world of poverty and pain: "Beyond the houses was a wooden park. Beyond the park were tenements, and beyond the tenements were the shanties. He did not go to the shanties."[89] Similarly, in his Mandalay, the troop must pass through an impoverished urban sector, "past rows of mud shanties that soon gave way to concrete tenements." The inhabitants remain unseen, but their presence is not unfelt: "No people yet, but all the signs."[90]

This kind of peripheral interest encompasses U.S. as well as Vietnamese victimized. Auster set *Moon Palace* in sixties New York yet was unwilling to approach its violence and upheaval except through the most noncommittal means; O'Brien is so drawn to that domestic turbulence, American values in the crucible, that he manages to incorporate it into his Vietnam narrative. The precipitating frenzies of the era—the McCarthy hearings, the blacklist, the Rosenberg trial—are encapsulated in the beheading ceremony in Tehran, which has all the saturnalian splendor of the Times Square carousing in Coover's *Public Burning,* itself based on the Rosenberg trial: "Immediately the crowd surrounded the van. Men were jumping onto the fenders and running boards; others piled on the hood and rear bumper."[91] Even in Berlin's utopian Paris, the sixties rage and counter-rage that followed these incidents are very much pronounced: "The police wore plastic face shields and armored vests. The students were running from the gas."

Such moments ensure that, whatever the novel's "lacquer of art," *Going After Cacciato* remains a work of memory and not a gesture of evasion in itself; they also explain how Berlin could arrive at the same interpersonal awareness as Paul Perry: "Perhaps now you can see why I stress the importance of viewing obligations as a relationship between people, not between one person and some interpersonal idea or principle. An idea, when violated, cannot make reprisals. A principle cannot refuse to shake my hand. Only people can do that." [92] But unsurprisingly, Berlin's eventual acceptance of State, family, and mediocrity proves unacceptable to many critics; Saltzman contends that his position is plagued by the same rhetoric that supported the war: "At the same time he dreams of alternatives to reality, his mind abides by slogans perpetrated by the government."[93] But Berlin is in truth fully cognizant of the rhetoric employed by the State, the underlying guilt at issue. He elects to honor his responsibility to the society that has nurtured him *despite* this burdensome awareness; the Other he manipulates throughout the novel has become dominant: "Peace of mind is not a simple matter of pursuing one's own pleasure; rather, it is inextricably linked to the attitudes of other human beings."

Such explains O'Brien's diligence in memorializing the common soldier. Bernie Lynn dies immediately upon his appearance in the text, but O'Brien insists on a posthumous description, supplying a sense of the life that was lost: "A medium-sized, brown-haired kid with thin arms and tanned skin and wide-open eyes."[94] This does not seem a particularly consequential gesture until we recall O'Brien's admission in *If I Die* about how easy it is to forget the names of those dead in combat, or to never learn them at all; never to glimpse their visages. He insists here that even his most peripheral figures will meet a better fate.

In his elaborate defense Berlin serves to define liberal ironism, the pragmatic imagination: "Even in our imagination, we must be true to our obligations, for, even in the imagination, obligation cannot be outrun. Obligation, like reality, has its limits." While Berlin echoes Nashe's existential commitment to the choices one has made, Berlin's choice is made as much for others as himself, where Nashe's deathward act is entirely one of *self*-definition. Nevertheless, O'Brien does not celebrate Berlin's choice as Auster celebrates Nashe's; to him, his true hero is draft evader Will Cowling in *The Nuclear Age.* In that novel, the question of whether to flee or join the military is less important than the mending of the fragmenting American family. Whereas in *Going after Cacciato* making the choice for the Other is enough, in *The Nuclear Age,* removed from the violence of combat if not the paranoia, one must make this choice bear fruit.

In *Cacciato,* the only attempt at reaching home is a phone call to Berlin's parents that goes unanswered, an affecting moment of loss, distance, solitude: "He listened to the ring as he would listen to family voices, his father's voice and his mother's voice, older now and changed by what time does to voices."[95] For Cowling, too, the phone is a symbol of atrophied possibilities for intimacy, becoming the centerpiece in his own fantasies, in which he conjures up imaginary phone calls from girlfriends, friends, and family. Of course, in postmodern fiction the phone can represent the buffer of technology, as Pynchon's Benny Profane notes: "Along a 500-mile length of underground cable, there must be earthworms, blind trollfolk, listening in. Trolls know a lot of magic: could they change words, do vocal intonations?"[96] But often such observations ultimately serve to supply technological or media scapegoats for our own lack of personal responsibility. Here, the most affecting moments concern gestures that remain unmade, pledges that remain unspoken, a pivotal example being the funeral of Will's father, which the son, wanted by the authorities, can view only from afar, through binoculars, "down below, things looked much too small. . . . It was all in miniature, the coffin and the hearse and the flowers and my mother."[97] He muses over his opportunities missed: "You brave son of a bitch, I would've said. I love you."[98]

The novel's crisis is the struggle of domestic love in the emotional waste land of the nuclear landscape; for Cowling, who plots to "protect" his wife and daughter by sealing them in a gargantuan bomb shelter, it has become nearly impossible to carry out the most seemingly mundane act of affection, every hug a heroic endeavor: "Melinda squirms but I press close, and for a long time we lie there at the edge of the hole, father and daughter."[99] In *Something Happened,* Heller's Bill Slocum accidentally suffocates his son by embracing him to death, a final and brutal demonstration of his attenuated emotional prospects; Will is both more emotional and less sane than Slocum, and for him such an all-consuming embrace has become the decisive symbol of a victory over nihilism: "If I could, I would climb through the window and crush them to me with love. If I could, I would."[100] Cowling's obsession is truly a sickness, played to both comic and tragic effect, yet O'Brien is banking on the universality of Cowling's desire to function as the antithesis of any theories, policies, or misguided exercises of the imagination that could ever culminate in nuclear Armageddon. O'Brien is defining the modus operandi that will distinguish the later novels of all four of our writers: individual gestures of solidarity as the key to change.

Yet O'Brien also *explicitly* targets those theories, policies, and misguided exercises of the imagination; much of the narrative is devoted to Cowling's ranting, his exhorting of his readers to wake up, to survey their ideological surroundings, to recognize the dangers their nation is facing. O'Brien's didacticism, struggled with since *If I Die,* has finally moved to the forefront of his art. As if to avoid any confusion, O'Brien asserts that Cowling's didacticism, his use of "very tangible, realistic terms," is his own: "I want to butt people over the head with real bombs, real dangers, real perils, real possibilities."[101]

O'Brien and Cowling share none of DeLillo and Harkness's ironic delight in terminology, in euphemisms for destruction, inevitable death count tallies tripping off the tongue. Cowling uses such terminology, the Names, as blunt instruments: "I've presented the facts. I've named names: Poseidon, Trident, Cruise, Stealth, Minuteman, Lance, Pershing—the indisputable realities."[102]

Yet despite appearances, O'Brien has not conquered his earlier hesitancies. He is still unsure whether this type of novel is practical; he is hyper-aware, in fact, that his earlier "preaching" in regard to the Vietnam conflict—those specific names, places, leaders, and issues he broke precedent to recount—has been rendered obsolete by time: "Who remembers the convoluted arguments that kept us awake until five in the morning? Was it a civil war? Was Ho Chi Minh a tyrant, and if so, was his tyranny preferable to that of Diem and Ky and Du. . . . All those complexities and ambiguities, issues of history, issues of law and principle—they've vanished."[103] Thus O'Brien frets the value of his new book, with its strenuous goading and preaching, should the cold war end.

Correspondingly, careful readers will find Cowling, despite his apparent sincerity, an untrustworthy narrator to the point that it is quite possible to read the novel, despite itself and like *Northern Lights,* as a *rebuttal* of those who dedicate their lives to proclamations of doom. No matter his valuing of truth, O'Brien finds himself in that position well-explicated by Rorty: the liar lying to the audience for its own benefit. As a boy, Cowling invents apocalyptic "flashes" in order to alert his parents of the deeper issues: "I wanted them to feel better, give them something to focus on. They couldn't understand the real issue—nuclear war and sirens and red alerts—and so I had to concoct the flashes as a kind of handle on things, something they could lash onto. It was compassion."[104] Yet the demands of *artistic* lying, of mature fiction, prove at odds with any didactic program.

The demands of characterization provide a good example; cheerleader and terrorist Sarah Crouch proves inherently, exclusively symbolic, her beauty contingent on the political climate. Although she is beautiful when activism is alive if unfocused in the sixties, her looks give way to poetess Bobbi's beauty when political activism suddenly becomes antiquated, futile, and infiltrated by nihilism upon the day of Nixon's election: "She was not, I realized, beautiful. Hard and pretty but not beautiful."[105] Yet while Bobbi, Will's adulterous wife, possesses no voice in the narrative outside of her weak poetry, Sarah speaks for herself, clawing her way out of stereotype: "'What I despise,' she said quietly, 'is condescension. I'm a human being.'"[106] O'Brien would seem to concur in theory, a seeming point of contention with the early DeLillo: "A reader rightly demands and expects a dramatic, satisfying explanation for the behavior of people. These motives and sources needn't be spelled out directly, but the raw material should be there, built into the novel's drama and context."[107] Yet in Sarah he finds himself asking, as Will does, how much of this realism can he and his didactic narrative afford: "But how far can you dig into a personality? How much do you finally accept at face value? Do motives matter?"[108]

Even if O'Brien is able to deflect the characterization of Sarah and Bobbi, Will presents another challenge altogether. O'Brien cannot restrain himself; the conscientious craftsman, he delves deep into Cowling's psyche, even if by explicating Will's personality he risks suggesting that nuclear alarmism may be nothing more than a rationalization of personal problems; a motive single-minded, not many-minded. Will explains his noble rationale for building the shelter and for kidnapping his family ad nauseum before the reader finally discovers that Bobbi had threatened divorce long before his dig, his mania, his proclamations, his activism, began in earnest: "But why would she leave me? Why a separation?"[109] Indeed, the usual postmodern mantras become a habitual crutch reached for upon every frustration: "I can't find the fucking raisin bran. Entropy and dissolution, it's all around us."[110] Even Will's hole in the ground, which seems a source of enigma, flux and play in grand postmodern style, begins to collapse, drawing in on itself until all that is left is Bobbi's diaphragm, the tangible sign of her infidelity, "one of those objects whose absence reveals so much more than its presence."[111] It is no coincidence that Cowling's sexual problems predate his awareness of the nuclear threat; indeed, his penis is scarred from a childhood injury, a visible sign of his symbolic castration, "great big tread marks, as if I'd been sewn up by a blind man."[112]

Even more powerful than this impulse to characterization, though, is the impulse to liberty that in modern writers is so often an impulse to disruption. Indeed, what greater, more ambitious subject is there for an artist than the beginning or the end of the world (*The Nuclear Age,* like *Northern Lights,* begins with a prefatory quotation from Revelations); what greater challenge than to best Milton's romantic, tumultuous program, or to bring it to its fiery conclusion? Societal obligation is often merely a rationalization for creative self-indulgence, as Philip Roth illustrates in *Zuckerman Unbound,* in which young superstar writer Zuckerman attempts to console his bedridden, dying father by relating the story of the universe from big bang to inevitable big bang; the pretense is that he is soothing his father's anxiety of death with the idea of galactic rebirth, but his true motive, as his brother bitterly observes, is to flaunt his imaginative capacity at the expense of his vanquished father: "The origin of the universe! When all he was waiting to hear was 'I love you!'"[113] Accordingly, Will's fantasies, those pretend "flashes" he creates for his parents but later experiences for real, are not only self-willed but poetic rather than clinical, rife with as many images of birth as death, the fecund imagination in full bloom: "Oddly, I felt no fear. . . . There were dinosaurs. The grave yards opened. Marble churches burned like kindling. New species evolved and perished in split seconds. Every egg on the planet hatched. Clutching my pillow, I watched the moon float away."[114] If paranoia is creative rather than didactic, postmodern wordplay may be key after all; certainly the hole that Will digs so fervidly, that supposedly epitomizes modern despair, contingent lives lived in the warhead's bullseye, seems also to represent the elevation of wordplay over substance: "*I am all there is,* it says. *Keyhole, rathole, asshole, eyehole, hellhole, loophole, knothole, manhole, peephole, foxhole, armhole, sinkhole, cubbyhole, pothole, wormhole . . .* "[115] At such moments, though, imagination appears to be running down, babbling instead of aspiring to glory; in the sterile modern world, mechanized and intellectually regimented, that moon, romantic symbol of the imagination, has been lobotomized: "I detected a subtle crease at the horizon where the global halves had been stitched to perfect the whole."[116]

Accordingly, Cowling features the usual ironist elitism, in which his and O'Brien's exhorting of the audience takes on a more unsavory flavor. His high school and college plight play out in the most cliché terms: "I despised the whole corrupt high school system: the phys-ed teachers, the jocks, the endless pranks and gossip, the teasing, the tight little self-serving cliques."[117] Unlike DeLillo's Logos College, Peverson State College does at least have a legitimate bridge to the war material, as it is located "along the banks of Little Bighorn, ten miles from the famous battlefield, forty miles from SAC's northern missile fields . . . a danger zone, to put it mildly."[118] But Will's experiences remain universal ones, his observations more petty than perceptive: "football was still king and booze was queen and raw physicality was the final standard of human excellence."

Will's redeeming grace is that, unlike DeLillo and Auster protagonists, he is unconvincing in his elitist claims; he purports to admire Rafferty, Sarah's lover and a football star, for his obsessiveness, but he is really drawn to his bedrock pragmatism, his embodiment of an American ideal Cowling professes to disdain: "Grew up on a ranch. Like where the buffalo roam. All I ever wanted—that old home on the range. Deer and antelope."[119] After all, although Rafferty's approach to every situation, to "get the gist," draws Will's scorn, this in fact is Will's own aim, to get at the "gist" of the nuclear mindset: "the *heart* of it. . . . Real fundamental basics."[120] Correspondingly, the more effective of Will's apocalyptic fantasies stress a certain universality of experience, such as the image of an outfielding boy in the drop zone, "a boy in a baseball cap shielding his eyes, circling, waiting forever" for "a high pop fly that never quite came down."[121] As with DeLillo and Auster, baseball is the universal denominator; unlike Fogg or Bell or Bucky, however, when Will sees the masses as primitives, he often includes himself in the same category: "my motives may have been anchored in some ancestral craving for refuge, the lion's instinct for the den, the impulse that first drove our species into caves."[122] When his guard is down, in fact, his cravings are not solitary at all; he escapes his childhood intact only because of his father's company, huddling together in Will's first makeshift bomb shelter, built beneath the family's ping-pong table, "like the very first men on earth, or the very last, we gazed at my puny shelter as if it were a fire. . . . A cave, a few hairy apes with clubs, scribblings on a wall."[123]

O'Brien does satirize the middle-class value system, of course; what novelist can refrain? Will's family dilemma stems in part from his possessiveness, his conspicuous consumption of individuals as well as objects: "I'm well-established and there's no going back. My assets include a blond wife and a blond daughter, and expensive Persian rugs, and a lovely redwood ranch house in the Sweetheart Mountains."[124] Even his interest in geology, the most down-to-earth science, so to speak, "an example of how the world could be, and should be,"[125] leads him to scope out and excavate a mountain rich in uranium, the source of nuclear power, making him an active participator in nuclear proliferation. O'Brien seems to suggest, indeed, that all those who share such materialist values are at least silent partners in the stockpiling. Yet Adamson, whose name obviously suggests an everyman, demonstrates that the common man can overcome his selfish desires by converting his pragmatism into policy; he vaults for public office, running for governor, eager to serve a constructive social role. Thus it is that if the novel's final lines present a vision of post-war America that much resembles the inexcusably slumbering England to which Orwell returns, they also recall the affirmations of Paul and Grace Perry played out in more concrete terms than in *Northern Lights,* a resolute refusal to "say no in thunder" that for a moment supersedes O'Brien's irony:

> And when night comes I will sleep the dense narcotic sleep of my species. I will dream the dreams that suppose awakening. I will trust the seasons. I will keep Bobbi in my arms for as long as she will stay. I will obey my vows. I will stop smoking. I will have hobbies. I will firm up my golf game and invest wisely and adhere to the conventions of decency and good grace. Happily, I will take my place in the procession from church to grave, believing what cannot be believed, that all things are renewable, that the human spirit is undefeated and infinite, always. I will be a patient husband. I will endure. I will live my life in the conviction that when it finally happens—when we hear that midnight whine, when Kansas burns. . . . Yes, even then I will hold to a steadfast orthodoxy.[126]

Chapter Eight

"Father's Gift of Mythopoesis and Love": Conflicted Voices in the Early Charles Johnson

The Nuclear Age concludes with an embrace of conventionality that is seemingly at odds with many of O'Brien's writerly instincts. For Charles Johnson, whose similar instincts will ultimately lead to the fluidity of form and irreverence for historical fact that characterizes the later O'Brien as well as DeLillo and Auster, such an embrace is complicated still further by his status as an African American novelist. He writes from a position somewhat off-center and yet perhaps not far *enough* from center. To a large extent women writers, regardless of ethnicity, seem largely unaffected by the exhaustion that leads to self-referentiality, to play, perhaps because their tradition remains undernourished, not over-nourished; there is no shortage of tales still to tell, narratives to relate. The modern female novel, whether by Anne Tyler or Alice Walker, can still flourish in an atmosphere in which the precepts of Realism remain intact, as Joanne S. Frye's characterization suggests: "we use narrative to assess cause and effect in a pattern of significance, to relate ourselves to a sense of purpose, to claim a shared reality with other people, and to identify a specificity and continuity of self through memory."[1] But Johnson seems to have inherited the burdensome awareness of the male novelist, and despite the strong social purpose inherent in the voice of his first novel, he must eventually adapt the same innovative methods of our other three novelists to re-approximate this sense of purpose, community, and memory. The racial question makes it still more difficult to answer the writer's call, to accept the writer's voice.

When young Brandemas flees the church in the climactic scene of *The Names,* he flees both its secular community—the rural churchgoers and his family—and its promise of "mystical" or holy tongue; in the process, he rejects the paradigmatic American novelistic voice. This is a central image in this study, our new novelists reluctant to merge with "the people" and, further, to accept the idea that a language addressing "the people" can remain unambiguous, potent, and whole. The putatively divine voice seizing and emanating from Brandemas's fellow churchgoers is another manifestation of some lost Edenic tongue, implicitly linked this time with the Aramaic (not Arabic) dialect spoken by cult members near the Sea of Galilee, as Vosdanik avers: "No one can write it anymore. It is only sounds. It traveled in history with the Jews."[2] For young Jewish immigrant David Schearl in Henry Roth's *Call It Sleep,* Hebrew manifests the same powers, at least upon first exposure, instilling in him a sense of oneness with God that transcends language as David understands it: "Not Yiddish, Hebrew. God's tongue, the rabbi had said. If you knew it, then, you could talk to God."[3] While David does not stake out his artistic claims through Hebrew, he garners from his reading a sense of divine revelation as bestowed on prophets from on high, which he attempts to approximate by jamming his father's milk can into a train rail. He accepts what Brandemas flees; the resultant shock instigates a burst of Joycean understanding—a comprehensive awareness of, and involvement in, the experience and voice of all the people of his urban environs, whether Jewish or gentile. In addition, he gains the upper hand on his brutish father, significant because the idea of overthrowing the Father, the literary precursor, is another concept that our new novelists find difficult to accept.

The idea of the voice of God permeating the celebrant has its strongest footing in African American religious services, and thus it is that John Grimes, the hero of James Baldwin's *Go Tell It On The Mountain,* experiences *his* revelation, and gains, as David does, the upper hand on *his* overbearing father, within the walls and bounds of Church, on the threshing room floor: "to speak in tongues, as Elisha spoke, and with that authority, to confound his father."[4] The African American version of this transcendence, however, is by necessity more full of a sense of social issues, a sensitivity toward injustices, than its white counterpart. John's experience, unlike David's, is ripe with a "rage that had no language, which yet spoke now, to John's startled soul, of boundless melancholy, of bitterest patience, and the longest night,"[5] a melancholy laden with the vision of "the body in the water, the body in the fire, the body on the tree,"[6] visions bespeaking not only Christ but the lynched, abused, and suicidal black man, visions that resonate in the Grimes family history.

The fact that Johnson shares DeLillo's hesitancies is testified to by the church-going experience accepted and then rejected by Faith Cross, the protagonist of his first novel, *Faith and the Good Thing.*[17] She is cognizant of that same paradoxical synergy between the parochial concerns of the community and the "higher" linguistic powers that somehow insinuate themselves in their humble oblations: "Old men and wasted women she recognized as tireless sharecroppers and maids sang from chairs lining the interior of the tent; some spoke hurriedly, biting their tongues, in the lost language, while others spun like tops through the aisles."[8] In this case, the lost language is not Aramaic or Hebrew, of course, but an original, African tongue lost to Americanized memory. Faith is "possessed," or "taken," and falls to the floor; the limits of her perception widen, and she, like David Schearl, seems aware of everyone else in the community, her individual selfhood fading: "she saw it clearly—all the possible number of things in space, all forms that had ever existed in time reflected back into time like a man's image trapped in a room of mirrors. . . . Those [images] of Lavidia, the preacher, the undertaker, and Alpha were more real than she."[9] But Johnson insists that this moment of possibility is an illusion, particularly upon the death of Faith's mother, Lavidia, which leaves her an orphan: "But it didn't last. The silent kitchen said so." In this Johnson is also expressing his dissatisfaction with the social function that is especially a part of the African American literary tradition; the father Faith must contend with is Todd Cross, a raconteur of sorts who is also the representative victim, the "body on the tree" from Grimes's revelation, hung for refusing to cater to the idle whims of some white passersby youths.

Thus Johnson proves to have dual anxieties. The first is typical of the postmodern tradition, the postmodern legacy as a whole; he is attuned to the community's need for story that Auster emphasized, but is aware also of the artist's inherent need to transgress it. For Johnson, as for DeLillo, writing directly for the audience is the equivalent of pornography or prostitution; accordingly, Faith peddles not only her body but her father's tall-tales for cash: "in a world wracked by the incessant wars of billions of wills, it satisfied some ancient need to have completely, if only for an hour or an evening, a life in one's power—the other's, if not one's own."[10] But Johnson's other anxiety is regarding the "black novelist" label he bemoans as much as O'Brien does the "Vietnam novelist" designation. He resents "the circumscribed view of African American writing" in which, as Stanley Crouch describes, "any black writer who chooses human nature over platitudes, opportunism, or trends faces probable rejection."[11] In other words, the realistic form he is inclined to reject as a postmodernist he is *further* inclined to reject because it ties in with this sense of racial boundaries: "Our most sacred cliché . . . is that writers should 'write what they know' and for the Afro-American writer that inevitably means the black experience."[12] The African American writer is destined to be relegated to protest and naturalism, on which grounds white fiction is rarely celebrated: "claims are being made here for literature that have not been demonstrated at all. Is *The Great Gatsby* about despairing white people, is that what that's doing?"[13] It is on these terms that Johnson declares himself: "an American novelist, who also happens to be black."[14]

Yet *Faith and the Good Thing* clearly has a racially oriented social function, presenting, through both imitation and invention, a distinctive black voice, one set apart from, and sometimes against, the dominant European-hegemonic voice, the white voice. Folksy, musical, and peppered with euphemisms and digressive parables, this black voice posits the existence of another world, adrift with magical possibilities akin to those in Latin American fiction but held in abeyance by the more authoritative voice, the established power. At times, Johnson is the teller of tall-tales at ease before a willing audience: "Lynch wavered in the doorway, towering over her, so tall he could, at the same time, have gotten his hair cut in Heaven and his boots shined in Hell. He was *tall,* children."[15] At other moments he resorts to the dense and playful erudition of the witch-like Swamp Woman, as well as to a wealth of difficult and detailed philosophical exploration. Taken as a whole, his efforts recall Henry Louis Gates's explication of an ideal black voice that recapitulates the most contumacious qualities of the African trickster figure Esu, including "individuality, satire, paradox, irony, magic, indeterminacy, open-endedness, ambiguity, sexuality, chance, uncertainty, disruption and reconciliation, betrayal and loyalty, closure and disclosure, encasement and rupture."[16]

But does this voice stand out from the more general postmodern methodology? Note Auster's proclivity for chance, DeLillo's for disruption, Barth's for satire, Pynchon's for any of the above; Karl uses Jung's coyote, a trickster figure stripped of its most potent magic by the dawn of the white man but nevertheless still plying his tricks from the shadows, as a metaphor for the modern American novelist, white *or* black. Granted, critics like Jennifer Hayward have insisted that while Johnson's "technical innovations appear to be Postmodern," they are in fact "more closely tied to the organizational principles of the Afro-American literary tradition."[17] But these readers must surmount much contrary evidence, especially since Johnson often couches his stories very consciously in postmodern terminology, including tropes of deconstruction, as when he characterizes the mythical Good Thing that becomes the object of Faith's arduous search as "a wish, a possibility that can only be deferred. . . ."[18]

Why are such distinctions important? In *Mumbo Jumbo,* the paradigmatic example of racially themed writing in a distinctively postmodern mode, Ishmael Reed illuminates our perception of difference by using putatively authoritative modes of communication such as dictionary definitions, "factual" textual references, and entrenched literary quotations, to constrain facets of

Gates's signifyin' voice—colloquialisms, slang, poeticism—by bracketing them with quotation marks, defining them as medical abnormalities, or writing them off as "coon mumbo jumbo."[19] But Johnson seems less interested in such politics of difference than in modes of rebellion against the realistic *form*, the realistic novel, the novel of social protest, and thus the early Johnson ultimately finds himself in the same mire as the early O'Brien, writing literature putatively of heartfelt social protest that is actually inclined to deconstruct the idea of social protest in fiction.

Correspondingly, Johnson's short story "The Education of Mingo" is a racially themed story that questions both the feasibility and desirability of racially themed stories. The racial "sermon" appears explicit; Moses (a suitably ironic name for a slave-owner) purchases Mingo and attempts, regardless of his own lack of education, to school him on every decision and skill; another very overt example of the pandemic temptation to reconstruct the Other, "like standing, you might say, on the sixth day, feet planted wide, trousers hitched, and remaking the world so that it looked more familiar."[20] Where in DeLillo or Auster the interpreter is safely differentiated from the interpreted, however, Johnson depicts a racial system in which oppressor (interpreter) is interlocked with oppressed (interpreted) in a cruelly symbiotic relationship. Johnson recalls from Ellison's *Invisible Man* the image of the Sambo doll that for young communist-activist Brother Clifton comes to symbolize the manipulation of the stereotyped black man to political advantage; in Moses's nightmares, however, the puppet is two-bodied: "he and Mingo were wired together like say two ventriloquist's dummies, one black, one white, and there was somebody . . . yanking their arm and leg strings simultaneously."[21] Accordingly, everything in the story has a very deliberate allegorical and parabolic feel; despite the Faulkenerian sense of atmosphere and character type, the deeper metafictional nature of this world is introduced when Moses crosses over the boundaries between realism and symbolism, "into backcountry imprecise but startlingly vivid in spots as though he were hurtling headlong into a rigid New Testament parable."[22] All the while, though, Johnson distrusts what he is executing; he sympathizes with Moses's plight in the one-view world created by the writer-activist: "every time he moved his eyes he stared into a grim homily on the deadly upas of race and relatedness."[23]

In this vein, "Menagerie, A Child's Fable" is a self-conscious allegory that refuses to allow comprehensive interpretation. A "talking animal" story that recalls those of the Brothers Grimm and many of Aesop's fables, it references philosophical views ranging from Hobbes to Berkeley; in fact, its central character, a steadfast guard dog, is *named* Berkeley. Berkeley, setting himself against Locke's corpuscularian philosophy, held that God remained an active force in the world; his canine counterpart here strives and fails to maintain order in a pet shop when its owner, a God of sorts to the animals, vanishes. Yet Johnson does not allow the reader to address his story only as philosophical allegory; it is a social allegory too, and a literary one, and the different orders of interpretation are set against each other without hope of validation. The only certainty, in fact, is fear, fear of the untended rabble, the Hobbesian breakdown dreaded in the work of all four of our writers: "for all [Berkeley's] idealism, truth was decided in the end by those who could be bloodiest in fang and claw."[24] Yet Johnson's distrust of the masses is different than DeLillo's; where DeLillo fears the unmediated immersion of individuals into one heaving body, Johnson fears the community's spastic break-up into monadic and opposed fragments: "an entire federation of cultures, with each animal having its own indistinct, inviolable nature (so they said), the rows and rows of counters screaming with a plurality of so many backgrounds, needs, and viewpoints."[25]

The pluralism issue suggests a reading of "The Menagerie" as an allegory of our racial and sexual movements, our political rhetoric. There is a clear allusion to race-issue advocates when the fish under Berkeley's care whine that "they were handicapped in the competition for food, confined to their tanks, and besides, they were from the most ancient tree; all life came from the sea, they argued, the others owed *them.*"[26] The rabbits, on the other hand, represent women's rights advocates, especially after one in their number is raped: "Rabbit said that it was none of his [Berkeley's] business and he was as bad as all the rest."[27]

Does Johnson himself sympathize with the socially conservative outlook represented by beleaguered Berkeley? He complicates the matter by working the metafictional allegory, which has nothing to do with issues of racism or sexism. The monkey, instigator of much of the pet store confusion, seems to represent the idea of postmodern play, the trickster figure used by Karl to signify the counter-voice of much modern writing and by Gates to signify the similarly rebellious voice of exclusively African American writers: "He was downright wicked, a comedian always grabbing his groin to get a laugh, throwing feces . . . aping Mr. Tilford, which he did well, though Berkeley found this parody frightening, like playing with fire." [28] The monkey is opposed by the snakes, which represent a more exclusively aesthetic approach to literature, equally repulsive in its own way: "proud of being cold-blooded, [they] had an elaborate theory of beauty based on the aesthetics of scales."[29] Gary Storhoff manages to reconcile this metafictional/literary aspect with the philosophical one by linking both in a celebration of artistic consciousness cultivated from Berkeley's maxim that "there is no intelligibility in the world apart from the active imagination."[30] Storhoff's reading, though, nowhere takes into account the very pertinent social references, the social allegory that is clearly too pronounced to be left to the margins. Storhoff's attempts, like all attempts to find a cohesive key to the parable of "The Menagerie," are met with chaos—social, artistic, interpretive.

In *Faith,* the illusory Good Thing is equated with inviolable absolutes often deconstructed in literature that include not only "the fulfillment of a teleological principle inherent in all matter," but "doin' unto others as you'd have 'em do unto you," and also the idea of "abolishin' private property."[31] The defining principles social realism might be said to uphold are seen to feed the logocentric order. Johnson takes this stance because he is aware that novels written to expose society's problems all too often conform in the end to its most glaringly flawed precepts; the Horatio Alger rags-to-riches motif, for example, though certainly well-rebuked in classic American fiction like Dreiser's *American Tragedy,* has remained particularly viable for black writers, a prime demonstration being Wright's autobiographic *Black Boy,* which, while effectively depicting the lacerated psyche of a black youth floundering amid a racially splintered ideology, also depicts a rise, if not from rags to riches, then from south to north, from humble education to literacy, from obscurity to prominence in the intelligentsia. Note how closely the "story' of Faith's shallow husband, Isaac Maxwell, parallels Wright's, even in the urge to write that in both of them serves as a catharsis for feelings of rage, estrangement, blockaded creative outlets: "she remembered the salient elements of his life: attending one poorly equipped ghetto school after another, soaking up all the literature, books, and movies that presented an image of a more affluent life, and writing to purge himself of frustration. Unexpectedly, he won a scholarship to a junior college."[32] Unlike for Wright, though, Maxwell's pay-off is not genuine insight but only the most banal of philosophies: "Why, you can be as ugly as a witch, you can be evil and selfish and wicked, but cash money can make you beautiful."[33] Some readers of Joyce Carol Oates's *them* see an admirable resilience in the ascension from poverty carried out by Maureen Wendall through her loveless pursuit and capture of a married man, but Johnson makes it clear that we are by no means to celebrate Faith's similarly crass pursuit of Maxwell.

Yet instead the reader is tempted to read the novel, in its postmodern voice, as a celebration of fantasy, or escapism, akin to Faith's dreams of the "jinn, mermen, and fairy queens that filled her father's make-believe world." [34] This aspect of Johnson seems to be elevating the ideal of "telling lies" above Gerald Graff's plea for responsible art: "help us resist those influences, both material and intellectual, that would turn lying into a universal principle."[35]

As with O'Brien in *If I Die,* however, Johnson does in the end supply the nuts and bolts of realism, the Names, the cold hard data, the harshest statistics, the harshest *reality* about the African American experience: "But she remembered the statistics: 13,500 black men stricken dead as stone from hypertension, one out of every seven, the newspapers had said. They had twice the chance of collapsing from strokes as whites. Maxwell's life expectancy would, if he was lucky, be no more than 64.1 years."[36] Johnson deplores life lived under the onus of such statistics, identifying it as another facet of the same faulty middle-class drive that propelled Faith into her marriage in the first place, the idea that lives will confirm to a kind of social barometer, an "official" time table stipulating life and death. Yet at the same time he recognizes that such information is essential, validating the dangers, the pressures, and the despairs depicted in the narrative; it is here that Johnson evidences some of the influence of his mentor, John Gardner: "I do believe that art should be socially responsible. I do halfway believe most of the time in John Gardner's notion of moral fiction . . . whatever the work is . . . it's society that we interpret into the public space."[37]

It is to this end that Johnson, like DeLillo and Auster, uses the ironist, the author figure, to embody cruelty. Although at times Todd Cross's creative mendacity does provide a fleeting sense of equilibrium between the outer and the inner, the social world and the individual world, the body and the soul—the weight of reality, "in the world, on its streets, and behind the facade of buildings," balanced by "her soul's emanation, altering their world with compassion, her father's legacy of mythopoesis and love"[38]—the reincarnation of Todd in Alpha Omega Holmes displays the drawbacks of this freedom. With Holmes, her childhood lover now a painter and tale-spinner, Faith discovers sexual fulfillment and a seemingly kindred spirit but these are not enough to dupe her innate sense of right and wrong: "Liar! she thought."[39] Holmes confesses that he does not understand what his art is, but he knows what it is not, rattling off any number of standard theories, including the realism/escapism dichotomy ("One guy told me hit was supposed to show life as hit is, another said hit was wasn't no good unless hit made him forget all his problems") and the social/personal dichotomy ("A Muslim said my work was worthless unless hit was instrumental to his cause, and another guy—a damned fool!—said all that mattered was my puttin' all my feelings in hit"[40]). Each observing eye, he could claim, has its own independence. But relativity bothers Faith deeply as it likely bothers the reader: "If you don't compare what you know, or think you know, about the world to it, then how can you ever know if what you think is true?"[41]

Holmes's art is a regression from the world, a self-indulgence much in the vein of Marco Fogg's deliberate starvation; it is no coincidence that

Holmes's increasingly sparse apartment recalls Fogg's: "it revealed not property but a sort of voluntary retreat from the world, similar to the atmosphere of a treehouse or a cave where children hide from their parents and talk about girls."[42] DeLillo's ideal of childhood innocence is a factor here, but not in any fortifying way; on a very basic level, this is Peter Panism, an intractable rejection of the "growing up" process. For all his fluidity in the realm of art, Alpha proves to be as shallow in life as Maxwell, hiding behind his artistic pretensions to shirk, like Fanshawe, domestic responsibility. He tells Faith that he cannot care for their impending baby because he is "an artist."[43]

Johnson is obviously torn over the ascetic character. Rudolph, the protagonist of the story "China," also pursues a course of introspection rich in "a certain monastic beauty."[44] But he is entirely sympathetic; decrepit at age fifty-four, a typical modern middle-class buffoon-protagonist, he takes up the pursuit of martial arts, honing mind and body and spirit. The social barometer is maintained only by his wife, Evelyn, who is very much the unsympathetic shrew: "How could he see the world as "perfect"?—That was his claim. There was poverty, unemployment, twenty-one children dying every minute, every day, every year from hunger and malnutrition, over twenty murdered in Atlanta; there were sixty thousand nuclear weapons in the world . . . *good* reasons, Evelyn thought, to be 'negative and life-denying,' as Rudolph would put it.[45] Yet while Johnson insists that individual self-improvement, not cajoling, will promote the greater social good, his stressing of the wider world through Evelyn does remind the reader that the drive for personal self-improvement often threatens to be isolated, a form of masturbation.

In *Faith,* Johnson combines the impulse to social realism with Rudolph's sense of possibility in a scene in which he depicts the history of African American suffering, precisely the sort of writing he is so wary of in his criticism. After a naïve and painful encounter on the streets of Chicago that leads to her career in prostitution, Faith, innocence gone, becomes symbolic of this suffering from its point of genesis in the horror of the slave trade: "Around her, in the difficult Soosoo dialect, her own tribesman shout for mercy. But their gods are dead. They are separated, husband from wife, father from son, and tossed into the belly of *The Trinity* with tribesmen of a different tongue. Faith crosses the Atlantic in darkness. . . ."[46] Johnson fully acknowledges this history, but then, sensing its racial boundaries, he broadens Faith out even further, tracing her further back to the mystical source of life, long before racial distinctions became currency; he universalizes her: "It is she among them, a woman-thing with pointed ears and razor-sharp teeth; yet she is as strong as all the others, perhaps stronger, because within her loins is the mystery of being."[47]

Faith at such moments represents the idealized power in Johnson described by Hayward as "a glorification of the Eternal Feminine."[48] Thus it is that while as a lead character in these novels she stands aside only Auster's Anna Blume and (much later) DeLillo's Karen Hartke, her function, unlike Blume's, is limited to that of most of the supporting female characters we have encountered, namely a rebuttal to masculine intellectual preoccupation that involves little intellectual distinction on her part. Johnson does push Faith beyond this sense of fecundity, however; deserted by various lovers, she loses her newborn baby in a terrible fire, and is grievously scarred, transformed from a symbol of presence to a symbol of absence, from bounty to void: her nose is "two empty holes," her ears "gaps along the side of [her] head," and her mouth is nothing more than "a gaping, lidless maw."[49] Yet this horrible condition represents an equally ubiquitous flipside of the masculine perception of the female as bounty: femininity as death. She does ultimately achieve a kind of deliverance in her assumption of the Swamp Woman's role, and with it an alternative to time, age (linear narrative), and any lingering perceptions of absolute authority (or logos). She is Johnson's symbol of the human-in-progress, who has the potential to *transcend* race, to transcend gender. Given that the salvation of accepting phenomenological flexibility so stressed by defenders of the postmodern novel is rarely found in the novels themselves, *Faith* is something of a rarity.

Johnson's ideal is the process novel, in which a character is defined and shaped by experience but also by the various philosophies encountered, adopted, and discarded while being "squashed into a larger vision under the pressures of events."[50] This ideal is very much in keeping with cherished Buddhist precepts in which "all you have is this flow of impressions and sensations,"[51] but also with the theory of selfhood upon which Rorty embellishes his literary conjecturing: "the self is a centerless web of beliefs and desires which are constantly changing through a process of revealing. This revealing process takes place through perception, inference, and metaphor."[52] In his digression on "The Manumission of First-Person Viewpoint," Andrew Hawkins in *Oxherding Tale* stresses that a narrator (i.e. himself) is "in fact, nobody,"[53] "less a reporter than an opening through which the world is delivered: first-person (if you wish) universal." Thus Johnson often seems, despite the ideal of the process novel, to veer near the postmodern tenet of character as cipher or site, with its inevitable decline into shadow, non-existence, flux; when fugitive Andrew invents a white history in which he is the descendant of a Revolutionary War hero, he is perilously close to the state at which invention overwhelms self: "we all rearrange our past to sweeten it a little. Memory, as the metaphysicians say, is imagination."[54] But in the end, as in Auster's *In the*

Country of Last Things, most examples of character effacement in this novel serve to reinforce, not cast aside, the bitter reality of slavery and capitalism; lascivious plantation owner Flo Hatfield demands identity flux from Andrew, not for his own enjoyment, but for the sating of her own carnal pleasures: "the lover of Flo Hatfield's fantasy was polymorphous: husband, ravager, teacher, Galahad, eunuch, swashbuckler, student, priest."[55] She has assumed the liberating power of re-interpretation possessed by Ellison's narrator in the guise of Rheinhold and turned it *against* the downtrodden. At another point, Andrew studies the remains of a re-captured slave, and sees that character *is* indeed erasable—but only by the rope, the whip, the torturer's art: "he might have been anyone, given the decay, blisters, the green stains on his groin, gas ballooning his genitalia in a ghastly parody of eros."[56]

This novel, more than Johnson's other writing, epitomizes the conflict between the postmodern instinct and the social instinct. As a whole, the novel is self-consciously artificial, a work of imitation, history as conceptual (re)construct(ion). He does not pretend that his pre-bellum South is present, and accordingly the reader's view of the physical environment is often not through the eyes of narrator Andrew Hawkins but through those of a cataloguing historian plumbing source material for details: "A triple-chimneyed Andrew Jackson Downing house with cornices and arched windows, priceless furniture inside (John Henry Porter), paintings (Hudson River School), and curtained bookcases."[57] The form is self-consciously imitative too; a first-person account of an educated, mixed-race slave who escapes his bondage and past to eventually settle into white society, it is not only an examination of the traditional form of the slave narrative, but a reworking of much older, formative novels, many of them notably self-conscious themselves, including Fielding's picaresque *Tom Jones* and Sterne's prelude-to-metafiction *Tristram Shandy.* From Fielding and Sterne, Johnson has adopted the art of directly addressing the reader, commenting on the form at hand and in execution, even if apologetically: "In this second (unfortunate) intermission there is yet another convention of the Slave Narrative to consider. . . ."[58] Thus it is not surprising that, as with so many of these novels, most of its commentators have focused on the metafictional aspect of the text.

But the postmodern vision of imitation and exhaustion this suggests comes under attack through the character of Evelyn Pomeroy, the schoolteacher whose position Andrew takes on when he conceals his racial background, enters white society, and marries physician's daughter Peggy Undercliff. Pomeroy is a failed writer, who produced one critically acclaimed first novel at the age of twenty-six and thousands of pages but no finished work since—claiming much of Johnson's anxious sympathy, no doubt, as he himself threw away 2,400 laborious pages and spent many years writing *Oxherding Tale.* Pomeroy is nothing like Peggy, who embodies the postmodern ideal expressed in the novel through her "reshaping" of language in "a meld of puns, graveyard humor, her father's habit of posing the rhetorical question or ending her sentences with a stress, and dry wit."[59] Instead, Evelyn is respectful of decorum in life and art, dedicated to "the joy of literature and music" and to an ideal of fiction old-fashioned in both its adherence to character and plot and its intention of augmenting the social good. In fact, her comments on art recall O'Brien's on the state of contemporary fiction: "so sterile. . . . Certainly the things I've been reading are empty. No one seems intellectually equipped to write with truth as their motive. A novel *should* be an experiential *feast* . . . a whole world of people tied together by *plot.*"[60] Hers is the type of fiction explored by Jane Tompkins, who disputes the idea of the timelessly "strange" text celebrated by Bloom to focus instead on those marginalized works banished from view, study, and history on the grounds of their financial success or their explicit treatment of the social issues of their day; those works that "explore the way that literature has power in the world, to see how it connects with the beliefs and attitudes of large masses of people so as to impress on them deeply."[61]

Yet Evelyn's work is imitative—exhausted to the most postmodern degree—as Johnson expresses in Auster's usual terms: "the anxiety that these ghosts watch you at all times, tsk-tsking that you have let them down."[62] Evelyn's maternal figure, her precursor in Bloom's scheme, is Harriet Beecher Stowe, much celebrated by Tompkins. Pomeroy, feeling her own inadequacy, feeling perhaps that slavery, the greatest issue of her time, has already been definitively addressed by Stowe, writes a form of pastiche: "She found faults, first with her novel, then turned on the Novel itself. She dismissed it as dead. She wrote a parody of *Uncle Tom's Cabin,* a clever, sneering lampoon that was, after the first few laughs, *ugly*—ugly and spiteful because it burlesqued something it couldn't be, and all because Evelyn *did* love Harriet Beecher Stowe." In the story "The Sorcerer's Apprentice," novice sorcerer Allan lives in the shadow of his mentor, Reuben Bailey, and as a result is hyperaware of his own plebeian efforts. When he questions himself, when the act of writing (Rushdy's insistence that the story does not "make much of writing"[63] is inconceivable) is less important than queries about the cans and cannots of writing, a metafictional questioning, a stagnancy sets in: "it often happened that pupils came to mistrust their finest creations, those frighteningly effortless works that flew effortlessly from their lips . . . and left the apprentice feeling . . . as baffled as his audience and afraid for his future."[64] Allan can do nothing new, nothing except echo and ironize the work of Bailey and other greats of the tradition: "His talent was for pa(o)stiche. He could imitate but never truly heal; impress but never conjure beauty; ape the good but never again give rise to a genuine spell."[65] As a result, when he considers a most unwholesome self-destruction, summoning up a cadre of demons to bear him away, he is sorely rebuked for his art: "to labor on and will the work when you are obviously *beneath* this service is to parody them, twist them beyond recognition, to lay hold of what was once beautiful and make it a monstrosity. It becomes *black* magic."[66]

It is highly significant too that Bailey's legacy is one of magic wielded unselfconsciously for the social benefit: "the effects of his craft . . . comforted the sick, held back evil, and blighted the enemies of newly freed slaves with locusts and bad health."[67] Stowe, as Tompkins reiterates, represents the ability of the American novelist to exact measurable change on society. Accordingly, Bloom rails against Tolstoy's ranking of *Uncle Tom's Cabin* over *King Lear* on the grounds of its moral worth,[68] and Pomeroy, like O'Brien in *If I Die in a Combat Zone,* is both repelled and attracted to the idea of being a "journalist-muckraker."[69] Johnson himself criticizes Alice Walker's type of art, a modern equivalent in which "there *is* no history worth mentioning, only family scenarios of deprivation and bitter struggle;" unsurprisingly, Bloom rankles further when describing a student who prefers Walker's *Meridian* to Pynchon's *Gravity's Rainbow.* But Johnson's novel nevertheless admits its pursuit of the Stowe model. Andrew explains, in one of his asides, that there have traditionally been three kinds of slave narratives: after-the-fact interviews, "fraudulent" slave stories crafted for political/social ends by the Abolitionist movement, and authentic narratives that happen to parallel those of Puritan writers depicting the movement from sin to salvation.[70] Andrew, as one would expect, indicates that the third kind of narrative is his own, but the reader, located "outside" the text, recognizes, of course, that as a novel *Oxherding Tale* is necessarily closer in nature to the second type of narrative, a didactic novel, a socio-political message. Although Hawkins admits that "perhaps the narratives of Gustavus Vassa and Venture Smith are, as confessions, clearer about slavery and sexual politics,"[71] his narrative always returns to the wider issues, the relevant issues: "Sir, we were *already* in the midst of Civil War. Blacks and whites. Blacks and blacks. Women and men."[72]

Yet if this recidivism to the Real seems to be a gesture of accessibility, Johnson's philosophical modus operandi seems, in contrast, to be the harshest medicine. His preferred manner of novel-writing is to conjure up a wide range of established philosophic precepts and then fluidly debate their pros and cons, necessary in a world described by the Swamp Woman as "rife with conflictin' theories that bend and mutilate men like a computer card to explain them completely."[73] Johnson seems confident that if we look to the work of our greatest philosophers, we can find our way beyond familiar postmodern quandaries: "Does what you think direct what *is,* or is that what *is* controls what you *think?.* . . . If you choose the first way, you become a magician—like Nostradamus; if the second way—a metal ball on an inclined plane. An *automaton.*"[74] Washed-out philosopher Barrett, met by Faith on the streets of Chicago, returns from death to remind us of this possibility of deep thought that Faith ignores; he looms disapprovingly over her pursuit of Maxwell. But the philosophical approach, though the opposite of "telling lies" in many respects, is as equally daunting and dissuading as Johnson's impulse toward play. Note, for example, a passage from his short story "Alethia:" "But Scheler wrote—If I've got this right—that Mind, revealed by Kant to be only a relation in the worldweb, was a special kind of window, a gap in being, an opening that, if directed toward another, allowed him (or her) to appear—like Plato's form of "The Good"—as both moral and beautiful,"[75] and so on.

Often philosophy outweighs realism, characterization. "The Education Of Mingo" revolves around two very "simple" characters, a stiff challenge for Johnson, who is accustomed to speaking through and about more bookish, intellectual, or at least quick-witted types; as a result, Johnson strains to broaden the limited omniscience of his narrative voice to incorporate the necessary philosophic background: "*everything* about him and the African was as different from night and day, even what idealist philosophers of his time called structures of intentional consciousness (not that Moses Green called it that, being a man for whom nothing was more absolute than an ax handle)."[76] In *Oxherding Tale,* Johnson intensifies this type of exploration to the point that an extensive knowledge of philosophy is assumed; Ezekiel is "as thin as a line in Zeno,"[77] Flo Hatfield, "like Aristotle, couldn't stomach children,"[78] and Hatfield's paintings are positioned in order to draw attention to "the Y where corner and ceiling met, from the high ceiling to the chandelier, like logical implication in Spinoza's *Ethics.*"[79] Similarly, the novel relies on such representative tomes as "the anonymous *Cloud of Unknowing* that would someday be called 'brilliant' by people who still cared about the life of the spirit, and 'pretentious' by those who did not." [80] Johnson does realize that many of his readers will inevitably fall into the latter category, and will be bored by his most heartfelt and pressing exploration: "Faith tuned Barrett out, studying him from the great distance of objectivity, the way one reads a novel about philosophical ideas, with haste and indifference."[81] Unsurprisingly, Johnson seems to resent the recalcitrance of his readers, their refusal to take stock of things, their refusal to *think:* "It's only about once in a lifetime that you stumble on a first-rate philosophical metaphor, and when you do, people are bound to say 'Huh?' and take all of the starch out of it."

Yet if Johnson lets this frustration with his audience show even more than our other three novelists, his novel is even more suffused by a paradoxical envy for their families, their homes, their lifestyles defined by practicality: "It was this warm, dumb domesticity that destroyed Ezekiel . . . that we dismissed as *beneath* our sensibility: the quiet, dull, heroic life of the property owner too busy making biscuits, feeding the pigs out back, to ask the tedious question 'Why am I here?'"[82] Johnson segregates society as Rorty does: for the non-ironist, ignorance predictably proves to be bliss, materialism keeping one "honest. It brought out, begrudgingly, the best qualities in the bulk of humanity, whether humanity appreciated it or not."[83] The Soulcatcher, a preternaturally perceptive pursuer of escaped slaves, recognizes in Andrew the conflict between the artist's sense of righteousness and his coveting of what he disdains: "He wants what them poets hate: mediocrity."[84]

Johnson does recognize that the soul cannot be elevated without the secure footing provided by earning power: "these vain studies of things moral, things transcendental, things metaphysical were, all in all, rich food for the soul, but in Cripplegate's quarters all that was considered as making life worth living was utterly wanting."[85] Yet the capitalistic drives of the bourgeoisie, of mediocrity, have worked not only against the writer, but specifically against African Americans; at Andrew and Peggy's wedding, a drunken racist touches on the economic facts of life, so to speak, even as the nation wages war supposedly over racial equality: "if the Abolitionists get their way . . . the North and South will move to manufacture and no longer *need* the Negro."[86] The Negro, then, will be transformed from a unit of materialist acquisition to a unit without economic utility at all, and it is only through deceit, like Andrew's, that one can slip through the net.

It might seem highly problematic, therefore, that the novel ends triumphantly in marriage and the steady marriage life: "the business of rebuilding, with our daughter Anna . . . the world."[87] Andrew, maturation complete, seems immune now even to the conflicting ironies that plague Will Cowling in the concluding paragraph of *The Nuclear Age*. In addition, although Jonathan Little describes their union as the first non-disastrous mixed marriage in American literary history,[88] feminist readers have taken umbrage at this idealized presentation of marriage, since Peggy, formerly a strong character, has become subordinate. To his credit, though, Johnson very consciously admits the injustice of the neglected wives through the memory of Anna Polkinghorne, who, devastated by her husband's selfishly prurient whims, becomes a very literalized vision of the madwoman in the attic, "an irascible old woman who haunted the place like a dead man demanding justice."[89] She is given no voice—the scope of the novel hardly allows it—but Johnson at least evidences his regret over such necessary omissions by allowing her indignant presence to color the narrative, including the climactic marriage: "It is, at least, my father's vision of the story; I would tell you Anna Polkinghorne's, but I was never privileged to hear it."[90]

In relying on the institution of marriage to provide the novel's sense of closure, in which order is restored much as it is in the matrimonial climax of many a Victorian novel, Johnson relies upon the groundwork for prioritizing the domestic over the philosophical laid earlier in the scene with Karl Marx (discussed in our third chapter). Marx rebuffs Ezekiel's theoretical interests in favor of a much different form of humanism than that found in his seminal writings: "truth is some*one*."[91] Much in keeping with the Victorian conclusion of the novel, Marx represents the Victorian ideal of gentleman: "a *citizen* devoted first, and foremost, to his family: a droll Dickensian husband . . . going fat." Instead of attacking the money fetish, the materialism at the heart of the marriage/security ideal, he "diverted Ezekiel's conversation from social evil and deep-ploughing philosophy to the few pockets of well-being made possible by capital." Thus he does what American realism has always done—define the alternatives possible in a world in which the most drastic change is unlikely and even undesirable.

Nevertheless, Marx's divergence from his own famous view of the world as one of boss-and-worker strife parallels a similar divergence on Johnson's part, in that Andrew's recollection of the Marx encounter has interrupted a scene in which he and Reb are sentenced to work in Flo Hatfield's Yellow Dog mines, themselves very representative of Marx's more public, published fears of capitalism: "the land was blackened by the sites of old shafts and heaps of slate, the air was fouled by carbonic gas and smoke from blasting."[92] Here the exploitation of workers would be center-stage, the negligence toward human life that is born of over-intensifying greed: "they poured in—shovelers and wheelers, borers and slave teams—to replace those who perished from consumption. Silicosis. From dust particles in their lungs." But the novel sidesteps this world (Andrew relies on his white appearance to con his way to freedom) much as it often does the harshness of slavery, at least when compared to a traditional slave narrative like Frederick Douglas's or a modern work of social realism like Madison Smartt Bell's *All Souls' Rising*. Although the rhetoric of solidarity presented by Marx here is invaluable to Johnson, he recognizes at the same time that the novel must expose the injustices that can be concealed beneath such rhetoric.

Johnson understands that nothing inspires more intrinsic pathos than the breakdown of family. Though this is an essential component of the practice of slavery, characters white and black lose their families here; Ezekiel and

Peggy as well as Bannon and Reb lose their loved ones to abandonment, murder, suicide, plague. The American drive for movement and exertion, more so even than for money and power, works against the family dynamic: "We wanted to do something difficult—see?—like tame the West, spearhead a revolution, or pin the universe down like a butterfly on the pages of a book. . . . Something greater than merely *living* from day to day. . . ."[93] In Willa Cather's idyllic-on-the-surface *My Antonia,* frontier lives are routinely shattered by suicide, by domestic quarrels that lead to murder, the vastness of the American frontier grinding down the psyche even as it invites continued expansion. The simple contentment in the Other that Marx preaches is not an inherent part of the American make-up, which here is equated with the artist's gnawing, the novelist's inner drive.

It is highly significant that, no matter Johnson's own philosophical drive, nothing is more inexcusable here than giving up family for the pursuit of knowledge, for philosophy. Ezekiel tells Andrew the story of his Indian master/mentor Trishanku. Trishanku asks Brahma for the meaning of Samsara (the world of appearance). Brahma's initial evasions indicate that the answer will not lie in the usual crass pursuits: "How to gain a woman's heart, or gain wealth."[94] Asked to find a pillow for Brahma—apparently the explanation will be long indeed—Trishanku ventures off and is distracted by a domestic life in its entirety; he meets a woman, raises a family, becomes very commercially successful, only to see a flood wash away his kin and his belongings. Only then does Brahma ask for his pillow. Be careful what you wish for, Johnson tells us. Thus Andrew, the intellectual ironist, a "reader of dry, nerve-deadening books" who delights "in circuitous, literary conversations,"[95] threatens to be less like Trishanku than Kajichagulia from *Faith And The Good Thing,* who, in a tale told by the Swamp Woman, deliberately abandons his family to search for the ineffable Good Thing rather than be satisfied with the more domestic good thing he already has.

For Andrew to move beyond such selfishness (and for Johnson to consolidate Marx's personal admonitions with his public theory), he must settle the accounts of his past, including his obligations to his once-love Minty and to his father, George. He purchases Minty from a slave trader and he and Peggy nurse her through her final disease-wrought days; this "settlement of issues" is certainly presented in formulaic style (think of deathbed vigils from *Uncle Tom's Cabin* to *Gone With The Wind*), yet Andrews's reconciliation with his father can come only through the mediation of the Soulcatcher, who has pursued George, an escapee, to his death. In his awesome network of tattoos, Bannon incorporates all of black existence, a kind of Whitmanian panorama; here Andrew can reassess his small-minded father, put his bitterness into context, accept him for what he was and continues to be: "the profound mystery of the One and the Many gave me back my father again and again, his love, in every being. . . . I was my father's father, and he my child."[96] Here Johnson dismisses the idea of the Other—racial, sexual, generational—entirely; in so doing he has dismissed a norm of human interaction that has kept the nation afloat, but never more than floundering, since its conception, as drawn by Peggy's vituperative father from the ideal of Schopenhauer's "Parable of the Porcupines:" "the only tolerable condition for social intercourse is *keeping your distance*."[97] Through his de-individualizing experience with the Soulcatcher, Andrew has seemingly re-invigorated the institution of marriage; his union with Peggy is meant to celebrate his ability to make the economic/social order more supple, denying the rigidity of racial or sexual generalization, an utopian gesture, of course, with which Rorty would be quite pleased.

Yet this gesture still remains at odds with Johnson's explicit philosophizing; each saps the other. In his next novel, *Middle Passage,* Johnson will forefront depictions of the inherent cruelty of slavery at the expense of explicit philosophizing, to the point that the novel, in his words, "contains only a fraction of its predecessor's complexity."[98] *Middle Passage* crackles with his discomfort in this "dumbing down;" it is clear he is circumventing his most prized instincts for the painfully conceded good of the audience, refusing to flee the church, so to speak, streamlining his dense language, making it limpid, enough that he clearly sympathizes with Cringle, first mate of the slaver ship *Leviathan,* who is forced to conceal his most precious qualities from the dross that is his crew: "had he been a woman . . . he'd be the kind who could do Leibnizian logic or Ptolemaic astronomy but hid the fact in order not to frighten off suitors; or if a slave, one who could bend spoons with his mind but didn't so white people wouldn't get panicky."[99] Such are the sacrifices, in the end, of liberal ironist concession.

Chapter Nine

"The Days of Being a Shadow Are Over": The Ironic Narrative in Practice

This study has often referred to an ideal reader assumed, suggested, or demanded by these texts, but another ongoing dialogue within them concerns an ideal *author*—a debate that centers on the feasibility of a figure combining both art and action. In *Mr. Vertigo,* such a paragon can be found in the revered memory of Sir Walter Raleigh, the namesake of scrappy protagonist Walt Rawley; Aesop, the African American prodigy taken in by Walt's mysterious master, Yehudi, observes to Walt: "a man with my brains and your guts, and tall and handsome as well. That's Sir Walter Raleigh, the most perfect man who ever lived."[1] It is obvious why our authors would be drawn to such an imposing figure, for in him isolation and sociability merge; he can bring his influence to bear on society without compromising what passes for artistic integrity. For Peter Aaron, narrating *Leviathan,* friend Ben Sachs manages to approximate such a figure, as is evident from his hodgepodge physical aspect: "he resembled Ichabod Crane, perhaps, but he was also John Brown."[2] As such, Sachs seems almost a canceled character, set against himself, deconstructed, but Auster insists that this is not the case, that Sachs is strong—his eventual choice for activism, though ultimately disastrous, galvanizes Aaron, and Auster: "I want to stand up from my desk and do something. The days of being a shadow are over."[3] Sachs, though, may be too strong; Aaron, Auster's surrogate, feels inadequate in the face of his comprehensive nature, affronted even: "You're the funny little man who's been blowing up all these statues. A nice line of work if you can get it, but who on earth picked you as the conscience of the world? The last time I saw you, you were writing a novel."[4]

DeLillo shares Auster's fascinated ambivalence toward the Renaissance man. In *Libra,* he too presents an example of the isolated, literate thinker who is more than capable of dramatic political action; but Fidel Castro is certainly no Walter Raleigh: "Castro spent fourteen months in an isolation cell. He read Karl Marx. He read every Russian. He told us he read twelve hours a day. He read in the dark. Always studying, always analyzing. Years later I saw the executions of men who fought by his side in the mountains."[5] In *Mao II,* writer Bill Gray attempts to take action, taking a stand against the terrorism to which he is instinctively drawn, on some idealistic level, as an artist. Margaret Scanlan believes, however, that the climate is wrong for such aspirations: "this heroic, almost Byronic, mission fails in a manner calculated to illustrate the forces that oppose such romantic and humanistic narratives."[6] Yet Gray's failure—his death en route to Beirut, where he intends to trade himself for a hostage—is not the result of political conspiracy, or the whim of market forces, or the intrusion of technology into the human realm; he fails because he is struck by a car after wandering, absorbed in his own thoughts, into the street, and is not rational enough, mature enough, to seek immediate medical attention. Ultimately the forces that oppose "humanistic narratives" may come from within as much as without.

Nevertheless, these writers cannot bring themselves to look beyond the anti-romantic and anti-humanistic nature of today's market, in which, as Christian Moraru notes, "the audience, the media, and the publishing industry now make up a whole machinery of voracious consumption, an entire demonology of domestication, control and alienation."[7] We have discussed the correlation between writer and homeless man stressed in these novels; in *Mao II,* DeLillo delivers the final word on the subject. Gray's literary devotee Scott is wandering through a bookstore in Manhattan, one of those ubiquitous chain stores, no doubt, with their rows and stacks of "gleaming bestsellers,"[8] when a homeless man stumbles into the store, drawing all attention to himself, creating a scene. The world of *Mao II* is saturated by poverty; Karen, Scott's girlfriend (of sorts) later tours the province of the indigent, the deprived, the diseased. But this particular homeless man claims to be an author himself, arrived for his book signing. He might as well be, DeLillo claims, for art is suffering, art is to be neglected; there but for the grace of god, as Auster observes: "America swallows up its poets, hides them away, forgets them. Except for the few who become famous (often those of meager talent), the poet with no axe to grind or vogue to follow can expect little but neglect—or, at best, the admiration of his peers."[9] Indeed, financial pressures permeate everything in his *Leviathan:* "After David was born, the situation only grew worse. Money became my single, overriding obsession, and for the next year I lived in a state of continual panic. . . . Once when a publisher was slow in paying me for work I had handed in, I drove down to New York and stormed into his office."[10]

Yet there is in truth a significant space between the novelist and the tatterdemalion in the book store. Gray's books, "in their latest trade editions, a matched pair banded in austere umbers and rusts,"[11] represent, in fact, a steady cash cow, enough that he can afford to live locked away in his secluded bunker. Even the most idealistic writers in these novels have financial opportunities, as Sachs does: "the call from Hollywood had flattered his vanity, stunning him with a brief, intoxicating whiff of power."[12] Did Auster feel this way when the rights to *The Music of Chance* were purchased? DeLillo, when Paramount bid a million for *Underworld?* None of the authors in this study are in any way destitute, or living lives of literature-induced poverty; but the ideal of pain and asceticism remains.

In fact, Aaron's family life suffers more from this ideal than from real financial pressures. Compelled to carry on a schizophrenic existence in order to maintain both family and art, he removes himself to an adjacent shack when he wishes to write, just as Nicholas Branch in *Libra* pours over his ever-growing JFK archive in an incommodious extension built onto, but set apart from, his home. Aaron's workplace plays up all the ascetic requirements: "it is fallen into disrepair. The pipes have cracked, the electricity has been turned off, the linoleum is peeling up from the floor. I mention these things because that is where I am now—sitting at a green table in the middle of the larger room, holding a pen in my hand."[13] He seems to argue that writing is impossible without pain, self-indulgent pain, self-romantic pain. In *Mr. Vertigo,* flight, a fitting equivalent of writing, a fitting symbol of the imagination, is impossible to achieve without pain and sacrifice, in Walt's case an amputated finger: "what had once been a bloody mess of tissue and bone had smoothed over into a cold, soulless stump. I enjoyed looking at it now and running my thumb over the scar, touching that bit of me that was gone for ever."[14] Indeed, Gray's writing has a similarly gory aspect: "going over what he'd written during the day, the scant drip, the ooze of speckled matter, the blood sneeze, the daily pale secretion, the bits of human tissue sticking to the page."[15] Ultimately, this is a sham pain, a tool, as Gray admits: "I exaggerate the pain of writing, the pain of solitude, the failure, the rage, the confusion, the helplessness, the fear, the humiliation. The narrower the boundaries of life, the more I exaggerate myself."[16]

What kind of engagement with history does this attitude allow? What type of social involvement? For DeLillo, irony is the only constructive possibility. Faced with the surreal horrors of Beirut, Gray's photographer Brita wonders: "Isn't there supposed to be an irony, some grim humor, some sense of the peculiar human insistence on seeing past the larger madness into small or skewed practicalities, into off-shaded moments that help us consider a narrow hope?" Yet Murray Jay Siskind, Gladney's loquacious advisor in *White Noise,* identifies irony as part of a debilitating postmodern outlook in which he cannot help but share, an equation for either sterility or destructiveness: "self-depreciation, self-mockery, ambiguity, irony, subtlety, vulnerability, a civilized world-weariness and a tragic sense of history—the very things, he says, that are most natural to him."[17] The key must lie in Gladney's re-conceptualization of irony in his "night recitations" with wife Babette, in which they "create a space between things as we felt them at the time and as we speak them now. This is the space reserved for irony, sympathy, and fond amusement, the means by which we rescue ourselves from the past."[18]

This "rescue from the past" is not the same as forgetting, as O'Brien insists: "but the thing about remembering is that you don't forget. You take your material where you find it, which is in your life, at the intersection of past and present."[19] The key is to dissociate truth and fact, especially when faced with a reality as fluctuating as Beirut or Vietnam: "War is hell, but that's not the half of it, because war is also mystery and terror and adventure and courage and discovery and holiness and pity and despair and longing and love."[20] In his novels, it is never clear what is autobiography and what is invention, but soldier Mitchell Sanders, who often represents the reader's point of view, emphasizes the potency of this "unsubstantiated" truth: "I remember Mitchell Sanders smiling as he told me that story. Most of it he made up, I'm sure, but even so it gave me a quick truth-goose."[21] Such is the nature of Rorty's reconstruction, brought about by our authors in their later novels by identifying, and exploring, the point at which reconstruction became necessary.

For example, whereas Johnson in *Faith* fleetingly imagined the defining image of the slave ship, in *Middle Passage* he very specifically identifies the era of the slave trade as the point when literariness set in life, the point we can return to only through literary facsimiles diffused through exhaustion; accordingly, his epic or mock-epic tale is refracted though Melville's "Benito Cereno" and *Moby Dick.* Indeed, he makes it clear from his opening lines that, in fine postmodernist style, he has no reservations about re-telling, and potentially diminishing, his forefather's scope, his theme. Where Mellville's novel begins with Ishmael's famously grandiose and yet mordant vision of the sea and its call to men, Rutherford's motivation lacks all of Melville's sense of the mysteries of the soul, the conflation of bravery and despair: "of all the things that drive men to sea, the most common disaster, I've come to learn, is women."[22] In its opening pages *Middle Passage* reads like a parody of classic American fiction, recalling Barth's *Sot-Weed Factor,* for example, with its ribald spin on the Pocohontas/John Smith story.

In stripping Melville's individuals of their inflated personas, Johnson risks derailing Melville's sense of both the conflict in each man's breast and the potential attainable, perhaps, to men as a group. Cringle, first mate of the *Republic,* is Johnson's version of the *Pequod's* Starbuck, who in Melville's scheme represents the value of the domestic order, of hearth and home: "Let us home! Wife and child, too, are Starbuck's—wife and child of his brotherly, sisterly, play-fellow youth. . . . How cheerfully, how hilariously, O my Captain, would we bowl on our way to see old Nantucket again!"[23] Starbuck is Melville's voice from the shadows, as Nadine is for DeLillo in *Running Dog,* and he conveys the same message of necessary self-criticism that Sully preaches in *Americana:* "Ahab beware of Ahab; beware of thyself, old man."[24] Yet, while Cringle also represents domestic stability, he does so only in contrast to the rest of the disreputable crew: "his was the only [face] not pitted by smallpox, split by Saturday night knifescars, disfigured by Polynesian tattoos, or distorted by dropsy."[25]

The *Pequod* sailors as a whole, despite their ultimately disastrous end, are capable of startling moments of unity and collective purpose; the most evident example of this, to Ishmael's eye, comes as they squeeze the solidified whale sperm into liquid: "Come; let us squeeze hands all around; nay, let us all squeeze ourselves into each other; let us squeeze ourselves universally into the very milk and sperm of kindness."[26] According to Chase, Melville presents this moment only as an unrealizable dream, the paradigmatic gesture of a national literature that expresses solidarity only in "idealized momentary associations" always "precarious and doomed by the passing of time or by the mere anarchistic instinct of the individual."[27] It is important to note, however, that Ishmael is well aware that he is aiming too high in this image, and he correspondingly re-admits, still in the "Squeeze Of The Hand" chapter, Starbuck's fail-safe plebian virtues "in the wife, the heart, the bed, the table, the saddle, the fire-side, the country," as a more realizable consolation. Cringle's compatriots, though, represent a disorder that is antithetical to both Melville's "momentary associations" and any such consolatory domesticity: "The *Republic* was, above all else, a ship of *men.* . . . They gambled on who could piss the farthest over the rail, or on whose uncircumcised schlong was the longest, and far into the night lie awake in their hammocks swapping jokes about nuns sitting on candles."[28]

Not even Ahab maintains his potency in Johnson's retelling, shrunken (literally) from a grand symbol of tragic/heroic isolation to the diminutive Captain Ebeneezer Falcon, a paranoid, homosexual pedophile: "never mind that his sins were scarlet. He was living history. Of course, he stood only as high as my hips, and I had to fight the urge to pat him on his head. . . ."[29]

Falcon represents "the manifest destiny of the United States to Americanize the entire planet"; such a belief, a belief in the munificence of American colonial and ideological expansion, is linked with other, equally implausible dreams, "stories about El Dorado and the Fountain of Youth," which suggest the extremes of American logocentricism, the nation's habitual conviction in fantasies. All this faith is misguided, of course; Falcon never has the chance to establish even an illusion of Ahab's level of authority, as Rutherford informs the reader quite early in the narrative that Falcon is dead, and that he himself has inherited Falcon's logbook, the outsider in full command of the dominant voice, the black writer in full command of the white narrative. Of course, this is Johnson's relationship to Melville as well, seemingly the antithesis to Melville that the voice of *Faith* was to be to the white novelistic voice.

Indeed, Rutherford's coupe clearly invites a reading of the novel in terms of post-colonial theory, representing, as Brian Fagel describes, "the transcendence of coloniality via enunciation from the point of confinement."[30] In "Signs Taken for Wonders," Homi K. Bhabha discusses *Heart of Darkness* and coloniality in a way quite relevant to *Middle Passage,* examining the trope of a found English book that recurs in colonial literature like Conrad's. In Conrad a book on seamanship supplies "a measure of mimesis and a mode of civil authority and order," except for the reader well outside the English tradition, for whom reading the very book epitomizing his difference "displays the necessary deformation and displacement of all sites of discrimination and domination."[31] Yet Johnson cannot take comfort in Calhoun's similar coupe, because many of the Melville themes thereby displaced, themes of solidarity and domesticity, are those he wants to re-posit. In keeping with Buddhist notions of identity, he has no investment in strict dichotomies, in concepts of Self and Other still emphasized, if subverted, in Bhabha's gesture of appropriation, threatening disaster for a hybrid nation like America.

Hybrids in this text can represent ugliness; slave trader Owen Bogda, the offspring of a white slave trader and an African princess, is both an anglophile fop and a Kurtz-like tyrant. In him, all the boundaries in Conrad's precarious duality have been broken down; "refined" Kurtz and his "savage" African princess, drawn together and yet always apart, are blended inextricably here. Yet this is the fundamental nature of America, as the Allmuseri, who at first possess an understanding based neither in time nor individual identity, are to discover: "Ngonyama and maybe all the Africans, I realized, were not wholly Allmuseri anymore. We had changed them. I suspected even he did not recognize the quiet revisions in his voice after he learned English . . . how the vision hidden in their speech was deflecting or redirecting his own way of seeing."[32] This in-betweenness is the definition of a new young nation: "this weird, upside-down caricature of a country called America . . . land of refugees and former indentured servants, religious heretics and half-breeds, whore's sons and fugitives."[33] The slave trade represents the point in American history where the question of national identity is most complicated; it is the moment that precipitates the irony of contrasting voices Johnson implements in *Faith.*

It is through Rutherford's eyes that we watch the Allmuseri revolt. He sees the Allmuseri as the Other, just as Marlow does the Africans in *Heart of Darkness* or Captain Amaso Delano does the slaves in "Benito Cereno." In the latter, Delano encounters Cereno's wayward Spanish vessel and fails to realize, until nearly too late, that there has been a slave revolt, that former slaves have assumed control of the ship, using hapless Cereno as their puppet. Delano suffers only a nagging sense that all is not right in this Other, the black of their faces, the alienness of their motions, "the raw aspect of unsophisticated Africans."[34] Although many of the slaves on the *Republic* share names with those of "Benito Cereno," and their actions follow suit, one would expect Rutherford's perception of uprising slaves to be far different from Delano's. Instead, it proves to be very similar, a hazy perception of indescribable violence, an abstracted sense of the Other: "In disfiguring smoke that stung my eyes, someone from the world below, the hell of the hold, hunched over a sailor, who lay on his side like a body washed onto the shore, beating him about the head with a deskscraper, and when this blotched and spectral figure saw me, he faded back into the smoke."[35]

Steven Spielberg initially depicts the slave revolt in his *Amistad* in similar fashion, through dark, gory images in which identities are not discernible, only heaving black bodies, sweat, rain, blood. He realizes that this is likely the white way of perceiving such an incident, such black ferocity, and later works his way back, clumsily fleshing out the situation for his white lawyer protagonists through flashbacks and translations until viewers see the slaves for the individuals they are and see also how complicit they themselves have been in the process of dehumanization, of conceptual segregation. But Johnson is not white and neither is Calhoun. By portraying the strife of the novel in such a way, by interjecting Calhoun into these events as observer, not victim, Johnson confuses our ability to make habitual distinctions, exploring divisions between Self and the Other that go deeper than skin tone, even if in the process he deconstructs the very artistic persona he adopted to define himself in *Faith,* and, here, to confidently spoof Melville.

Unlike *Middle Passage, White Noise* contains few literary echoes; in fact, the world of the novel, very aggressively depicted as The World We Live In Now, is one in which alternative media has thoroughly supplanted the novel, wiping our memory clean, depriving us of our "inheritance," which is how

Johnson refers to "all knowledge, all disclosure, all revelation from the past, from our predecessors."[36] While "we still lead the world in stimuli,"[37] as Murray Jay Sisskind observes, television has claimed the center of all attention, and seems incapable of referring to other forms of art, being "sealed-off, timeless, self-contained, self-referring . . . a myth being born right there in our living room, like something we know in a dream-like and preconscious way."[38] The Neanderthals around the fire have finally found a replacement for that storyteller they have long distrusted. The younger generations have been rewired. But for DeLillo both narrative and memory remain essential, as exemplified by his participation in a program to help Alzheimer's patients retain memory by writing narratives.[39] *White Noise* and *Libra* function toward this end; taken together, they form a single extended narrative.

DeLillo views the assassination of Kennedy as the defining blow of the contemporary era, and accordingly it has had a magnetic effect on his writing: "my first eight novels seemed to be collecting around some dark center of the assassination."[40] The influence this event had on the nation is even more obvious, of course; it reduced a world of widespread faith in capitalism, technology, and the prospect of classless social harmony, a world described by Godfrey Hodgson as "confident to the verge of complacency about the perfectibility of American society,"[41] to a world in which both past and future history, and Man's place in relation to technological advances, is viewed with suspicion and dread, as in the world of Jack Gladney, in which "Man's guilt in history and in the tides of his own blood has been complicated by technology, the daily seeping falsehearted death."[42] In these two novels, the erosion and loss of fifties values and perception take on Edenic significance, Jameson's "lost object of desire."[43]

This Eden is a fictional construct, of course, replete with Emersonian and Arthurian elements, yet the continuing reverence for Kennedy, possessed even by those who never accepted his views or character in life, and persisting regardless of any number of posthumously disclosed scandals, is a perpetuation of this myth that testifies to its efficacy. JFK's death and the consequent sensation of overpowering loss invert, according to Hodgson, "the most universal and powerful of all human myths, in which the blameless king dies so that the people may live."[44] In Rorty's terms, in which history is nothing but a system of individual narratives replaced when their efficacy wanes, this is clearly a narrative of extreme potency, whereas the Warren Commission report has proved unsatisfactory to a majority of Americans. Distinctions between literal truth and fiction matter little; it is on these terms that Oliver Stone defended his controversial and factually loose *JFK* as "our alternative myth to the Warren Commission myth, an opportunity for people to rethink history."[45] DeLillo, like Stone, intends not to exploit or obfuscate but to allow focus, to allow hope, if only for that audience without an obsession for literal fact: "readers may find refuge here—a way of thinking about the assassination without being constrained by half-facts or overwhelmed by possibilities, by the tide of speculation that widens with the years."[46]

O'Brien characterizes this lost age of innocence through that quaintest of domestic images, the kitchen, the site of our most shiny new benevolent technology, our most glossy look; in *The Things They Carried,* he describes his last, loving, moments at home before departing for the war: "standing very still for a few minutes, looking carefully at the familiar objects all around me. The old chrome toaster, the telephone, the pink and white formica on the kitchen counters. The room was full of bright sunshine. Everything sparkled. My life, I thought."[47] Correspondingly, it is in this setting that DeLillo's Win Everett, the disgraced former operative who hatches the JFK conspiracy, likewise feels secure, at least at the beginning of the narrative: "a stir of the all-familiar, the heartbeat mosaic of every happy home, toast springing up, radio voices with their intimate and busy timbre, an optimistic buzz living in the ear. . . . Images wavered in the sunlit trim of appliances, something always moving, a brightness flying, so much to know in the world."[48] This "brightness flying" proves elusive, however, a conclusiveness that is always maddeningly out of grasp, and the optimistic buzz is what later evolves into the white noise of the Gladney family, an indecipherable barrage of technological murmurs continually wearing on our consciousness. Even as Everett spins his lies, constructing a false life for Oswald largely on paper, he senses those machines taking over, infiltrating his understanding of the world; he constantly frets over whether he remembered to turn off his oven, whether he is spied on at every moment by "spy planes, drone aircraft, satellites with cameras that can see from three hundred miles what you can see from a hundred feet."[49] For Everett, this process—devices making him pliant, a phrase that resurfaces here from *Running Dog*—culminates in the lie-detector, the invasive all-knowing apparatus that deprives him of his most compulsive urge: to lie.

For DeLillo, the chaos of the Bay of Pigs fiasco, like the chaos of Vietnam for O'Brien, reflects the first confluence of national policy and postmodern confusion, built on tactics Parmenter has already implemented when inventing a false war in Guatemala: "Rumors, false battle reports, meaningless codes, inflammatory speeches, orders to non-existent rebels. It was like a class project in the structure of reality."[50] T.J. Mackey, a Bay of Pigs veteran, recalls what it was like to be on the other side of the equation, the victim, the manipulated rather than the manipulator; in the midst of the action, the president, the grand father-figure of American dominance, fragments into a scurry of voices, communication channels, and alternate meanings: "the operation began to resemble something surreal . . . it seemed to him that something was running of control. There was strange and flawed material out there, a deep distance full of illusions, deceptions, eerie perspectives. The same ship used two names."[51] Everett, behind the scenes of many a covert action, emphasizes that there is always an inherent controlling force, even if out of view; even as his assassination plan, a mock-assassination designed to stir-up sentiment for another offensive against Cuba, veers far beyond his original design, he senses a comprehensibility in this, a surety in plot equivalent to the reader's accustomed sense of certainty in conventional narrative: "The tighter the plot of a story, the most likely it will come to death. A plot in fiction, he believed, is a way we localize the force of the death outside the book, play it off, contain it."[52] But his confidence is undermined when the plan truly spins out of control, he himself prematurely fading from the narrative, inconsequential; his murder barely merits a mention. With the assassination, DeLillo notes, Everett's world of confusions, secrets, codes, and murder, previously a self-enclosed world, the world of the operatives, spills into the world at large in its terrible variety, infesting the consciousness of the nation; the death of a president signaling the end of narrative surety.

DeLillo's type of irony, therefore, his openly fictional approach to historical fact, is only possible, or at least acceptable, after the event it addresses, just as Johnson's literariness, his rebel's voice, is possible only after his "defining moment." *Libra,* like *Middle Passage,* is an act of self-creation, a reassessment of national history in which the only method of retrieving confidence after the decisive and defining blow is through the imaginative recreation of the event itself.

DeLillo's vision of history is somewhat different, however, in his sprawling *Underworld.* He traces the triumphant baseball of the 1951 pennant game between the Dodgers and the Giants, "the shot heard round the world," through four decades of history and the errata-steeped lives of a variety of owners. On the same day as the monumental game, October 3, 1951, the Soviets tested the atom bomb, unleashing "the sun's own heat that swallows cities,"[53] and commencing the Cold War that would define life until the collapse of the U.S.S.R. Providing another serviceable construct of history, DeLillo revises his own timeline; the point at which It All Changed is no longer November 22, 1963 but October 3, 1951—Oswald's shot heard round the world supplanted by Bobby Thomson's. In a sense, he has reinvented the world of *Libra;* whereas Win Everett recognizes that all technology, right down to his every kitchen appliance, refers to the world of lies and covert espionage, here "all technology refers to the bomb."[54] DeLillo recognizes that with the Cold War over, this construct is now the superior method of addressing recent decades, and by reversing himself in this fashion he demonstrates Rorty's sense of interchangeable narratives, what DeLillo here calls "usable history."[55] His prime motive, indeed, is usability, not disruption; like protagonist Nick Shay, he hews "to the texture of collective knowledge," and provides "a single narrative sweep, not ten thousand wisps of disinformation."[56]

In retrospect, we realize that Auster had foreshadowed *Underworld* in *Leviathan,* which is dedicated, tellingly, to DeLillo (DeLillo later returns the favor in *Cosmopolis*). He describes Ben Sachs, drawn to "the vast follies and contradictions of history," in terms applicable to DeLillo: "he was able to read the world as though it were a work of the imagination, turning documented events into literary symbols, tropes that pointed to some dark, complex pattern embedded in the real." For him, "the bomb" marks a new generation: "Once we acquired the power to destroy ourselves, the very notion of human life had been altered; even the air we breathed was contaminated with the stench of death."[57]

DeLillo is somewhat more hesitant than Sachs to make the most tenuous connections, to indulge paranoia, and accordingly he has Shay ridicule *dietrologia,* the science of dark forces. On the whole, though, he and Sachs seem as one; yet while this passage suits *Underworld,* it does not in any way suit *Leviathan.* Though Auster attempts to parallel life under the bomb in general with Sachs's life in particular, he admits that they frequently diverge: "this was the early eighties, the days of the hostage crisis in Iran, the Khmer Rouge atrocities in Cambodia, the war in Afghanistan. Sachs's hair had grown lighter in the California sun, and his bronzed face was smattered with freckles. He looked good, I thought."[58] In addition, the incidents in which Sachs *has* tasted his age—he spent time in prison resisting the Vietnam draft, a very conscious gesture of civil disobedience—do not make their way into his fiction, or into *Leviathan:* "*The New Colossus* had nothing to do with the sixties, nothing to do with Vietnam, or the antiwar movement, nothing to do with the seventeen months he had served in prison."[59]

Auster does incorporate more of his own personal brushes with history into *Leviathan* than he did in *Moon Palace;* during his experiences at Columbia during the sixties, he became well-acquainted with a number of budding activists and terrorists, including one Ted Gold, who "blew himself to smithereens in a West Village brownstone when the bomb he was building accidentally went off."[60] Sachs suffers the same fate; a relatively obscure author, he eventually turns to activism, bombing replicas of The Statue of Liberty scattered across the country, until he accidentally becomes his own victim. Yet *Leviathan* nevertheless remains politically undirected, despite the critical bent suggested in its prefatory quote from Emerson, "every actual state is corrupt."

Thoreau remains central here, too: "America has lost its way. Thoreau was the one man who could read the compass for us, and now that he is gone, we have no hope of finding ourselves again."[61] Auster sets up a familiar expectation in the reader for that explanation, promised but undelivered in "Ghosts," of how Thoreau's writings can change or save our lives. In *Dreamer,* Johnson asserts Thoreau's contemporary significance through Martin Luther King's social program, "sending the city officials a collective Thoreauvian *no* to institutionalized inequality."[62] But Auster seems drawn less to this Thoreau than to the Thoreau that defies comprehension even when his writings are broken down, as they so often are, into pithy fragments; Arthur Saltzman writes: "It is fitting . . . that Thoreau is one of Sachs's champions. Certainly his celebrated civil disobedience sets a rousing example for events in *Leviathan,* but so does his stylistic incorrigibility."[63]

What is Sachs's statement exactly? What does he hope to prove? What does his failure signify? Auster does expose an eighties atmosphere in which political conviction is passé: "in the new American order of the 1980s, his position became increasingly marginalized. It wasn't that he had no audience, but it grew steadily smaller. . . . In the present climate of selfishness and intolerance, of moronic, chest-pounding Americanism, his opinions sounded curiously harsh and moralistic."[64] Yet Auster himself seems to refrain from politics not because the atmosphere is not right for it but because he shares Aaron's cherished belief that art is demeaned by didacticism: "his heavy-handedness often disturbed me—the way he kept hammering home his points, manipulating his characters to underscore his ideas rather than letting them create the action themselves."[65] It seems at this moment that Auster is more interested in writing of the uniquely precarious position of the modern committed artist than in *being* a committed artist himself, just as he is more interested in describing an ironic narrative than in providing one. Sachs's attempts at ironic narrative, ironic history, represent a gimmick to Aaron, who labels Sachs's sweepingly historical first novel a "fabulous contraption with blinking lights and ninety-eight different sound effects,"[66] even as he admits that its plot does "follow the historical record . . . there is no tampering with the laws of probability." In other words, an ironic realism pervades, just as in *Underworld* icons like J. Edgar Hoover, Frank Sinatra, Jackie Gleason, and Lenny Bruce interact with each other in ways that stretch our understanding of fact but not our sense of plausibility.

Auster does supply such a "contraption," however, in *Mr. Vertigo.* His tone is jauntier than DeLillo's or Sachs's; Walt begins his narrative with another example of history through celebrity: "that was 1927, the year of Babe Ruth and Charles Lindbergh, the precise year when night began to fall on the world forever." A dark note, certainly, but Walt, establishing a "tall tale" atmosphere, asserts that "what I did was greater than those two gents could have dreamed of."[67] Here Auster echoes Johnson's interest in *telling lies;* indeed, lying is well-supported in the text, and it is only a villainous hypocrite like Walt's uncle Slim who presumes to deny the value of the non-malicious lie: "Lying's a sin, Walt, you know that."[68] Everything about the novel bespeaks its status as facsimile—a close facsimile, to be sure, but a facsimile all the same—especially Walt's language, with its *faux* twenties talk exaggerated to the point of affectionate satire: "I was a boogie-toed prankster, a midget scatman with a quick tongue and a hundred angles."[69]

Auster's child protagonist sees the world as a source of stories, of tall tales, of "fibs," of monsters of a traditional variety, the vampire, the ghoul: "I'd let myself fall into the clutches of a monster, and if he turned out half as spooky as he looked, the odds were I would never see the dawn rise again."[70] Yehudi, the potential vampire in question, tells him: "you don't have to invent any tall tales for me,"[71] but no form could characterize a young America better, for it is a fairy tale country of sorts, an idealist's dream. The sense of a child's fear, innocent fear, heightens the moral tone of the novel; America in the young century, Auster is telling us, was like a young child in a brutal age, innocent yet beginning to scar. In *Leviathan,* Auster failed to convincingly link Sachs with the age of the bomb, the two timelines continually diverging; here he links a child and a nation much more effectively.

The novel's pervading sense of artificiality never overwhelms the reality of the age's horrors, such as the Saint Louis twister: "the twister shot through town like a cannonball from hell, and by the time it left five minutes later, a thousand buildings had been flattened, a hundred people were dead, and two thousand others lay writhing in the wreckage with broken bones and blood pouring from their wounds."[72] In *White Noise,* DeLillo suggests that media coverage has transformed atrocity into spectacle; the Gladney family sits glued to the television, "watching houses slide into the ocean, whole villages crackle and ignite in a mass of advancing lava. Every disaster made us wish for more, for something bigger, grander, more sweeping."[73] Auster, writing of the earlier half of the century, is writing of a time before the postmodern, when tragedy was still tragedy, a pathos that could be approximated through literary realism.

More than anything else, therefore, *Mr. Vertigo* is a narrative of our *entertainment* history, including both the rise and fall of Realism and the rise and fall of the Novel. Auster identifies the period of the first world war and the stock market crash as the point at which the writer could best supply the voice that the masses lacked, the point at which the author could come to grips with economic and social forces, with the plight of children, with the wreckage of a tornado, recognizing a call for action. It is the time of Dos Passos, Steinbeck, Cummings, Farrell. Walt certainly recognizes the state of the nation, the burgeoning poverty that helps make the crowd a mob: "the depression had already started in the hinterlands, and farmers and rural folks throughout the region were already feeling the pinch. . . . They needed Walt the Wonder Boy . . . and I must never forget the responsibility that entailed."[74]

The rise of modern science, however, has irrevocably diminished writing's place in the social sphere. Walt's ability to fly eventually yields to a more clinical universe, reverberating with echoes of Foucault's writings on the institutional and regulatory mindset: "every hour on the hour a different doctor would walk into the room and put me through my paces . . . they listened to my heart and looked into my ears; they X-rayed me from conk to toe. There was nothing to live for anymore except science. . . ."[75] This is a defining moment in lives and in art, Auster's "moment it all changed;" the priest-figures of this age are now doctors, scientists, and technocrats, not writers. This technological and institutionalized change takes place, significantly enough, at the dawn of Walt's puberty, a national loss of innocence compounded. In terms of our entertainment, this change parallels, too, the ascendancy of film, which in its sense of abridgment has changed our sense of time in such a way as to enable a rush through history at the end of the novel: "if this were a movie, here's where the calendar pages would start flying off the wall. . . . Ah, the old Hollywood razzmatazz. There's nothing like it for hustling things along. It may not be subtle, but it gets the job done."[76] This is precisely the approach to history Auster is using, an approach inconceivable before the ascendancy of film; Auster is free to peruse rather than delve, which can result in maddening simplicity. World War II provides a notable example when Walt, faced with jail time, enlists in the military: "The judge said the army would make a man of me, and if eating dirt and watching limbs fly off soldiers' bodies is proof of manhood, then I suppose the Honorable Charles P. McGuffin called it right. As far as I'm concerned, the less said about those four years the better."[77] Given O'Brien's work on Vietnam or the work of Mailer or James Jones or Joseph Heller on World War II, Walt's recalcitrance in withholding information here seems a severe omission, Auster's grand structure a force of trivialization.

Mr. Vertigo, in fact, much resembles director Robert Zemeckis's 1994 fantasy *Forrest Gump,* in which the title character wanders through a history, including a stint in Vietnam, in which events and social issues emerge only in a casual litany. When Jenny, Gump's brighter but less morally sound one-time lover, succumbs to AIDS after taking the 'low road' of 60's protest, free love and drugs, there is no sense of the horror of the disease, or the social issues surrounding it, only a fulfilled sense of obligation in that all the touchstones of modern life have been successfully incorporated into one fluid package. The film was monumentally successful in part because people enjoyed this simplistically dichotic view of history, in which there was, and is, a good route (do what your mother taught you) and a bad. Yet to Auster's credit, his approach is far more shrewd; in his rapid-fire foray through the period he often exposes the ***underside*** of conventional understanding, supplying, when describing the blooming of suburbia in the forties and fifties, the non-successes behind that glossy surface: "all those ranch houses and tidy lawns and spindly little trees wrapped in burlap—I was the guy that put them there. . . . In 1950, I moved across the river to a low-rent apartment in Newark, New Jersey, and started my ninth or tenth job since the war."[78]

Yehudi is clearly out of synch with the age of cinema, its rosy outlook, its glossing over of the complexities of life. When Walt urges him to pursue Miss Witherspoon more aggressively, his master chides him: "Just like the movies, eh, Walt."[79] His brand of entertainment has a tacky aspect to be sure, but fundamentally it is the display of one man's imagination, the storyteller, the autonomous artist, attempting to re-conquer the scientist's pedestal: "his mouth was one of the great huckster machines of all time, and once he got it going full tilt, the dreams poured out of him like smoke rushing through a chimney."[80] But there is no longer an audience for this type of art; the demand now, his pupil realizes, is for the easy visceral sensation, the complexities of the imagination no longer applicable: "that method was out of date, more suited to the corny prewar style he'd grown up with than to the jump and jangle of the new age."[81] This appetite grows coarser, fouler, eventually defining that world into which Walt falls after Yehudi's death: "gambling parlors, numbers operations, whorehouses, protection squads, slot machines."[82]

O'Brien's defining ironic narrative, like DeLillo's, extends through two novels; in *The Things They Carried* and *In the Lake Of The Woods,* he chronicles the creation of the postmodern condition during the war and the subsequent infiltration of that condition into stateside life. In examining this shift he beseeches his audience to make a defining choice that not only allows them to adapt to the postmodern condition but allows O'Brien himself to move beyond Vietnam determinacy.

The narrator of *In the Lake Of The Woods,* researching the mysterious disappearances of John and Kathy Wade after their disastrous run for a Senatorial seat, characterizes Vietnam as "a place where decency mixed intimately with savagery."[83] All moral distinctions, like epistemological ones, have blurred, or been obliterated altogether. Much has been written about the postmodern affinity for presenting waste and excrement as symbols of nullity, entropy, and the breakdown of our understanding; accordingly, O'Brien in *The Things They Carried* gives us the shit field, where good-hearted Kiowa is shot and lost, to represent the inauguration of a new, more complicated age: "I was afraid to speak directly, afraid to remember—and in the end the piece had been ruined by a failure to tell the full and exact truth about our night in the shit field."[84] O'Brien, though, is unwilling to grant his readers interpretive security in the Kiowa incident. That sort of certainty is no longer possible—*after* the Kiowa incident. Instead, he suggests at intervals that all of the experiences recounted in the book are fiction, including the characters, including Kiowa, even as he dedicates the novel to "the men of Alpha Company," also including Kiowa.[85] This is the most disruptive gesture of O'Brien's career, but his intent is to hammer home what continues to be his impression of realism: "in any war story, but especially a true one, it's difficult to separate what happened from what seemed to happen."[86]

This difficulty would seem to lead to despair, to the end of narrative: "you can't even tell a true war story. Sometimes it's just beyond telling."[87] *In the Lake Of The Woods* features as many challenges as *The Things They Carried*—first and foremost, it lacks a definitive answer to the question of whether John Wade murdered Kathy Wade on the night of September 20, 1986. Mitchell Sanders defends the concept of a satisfactory conclusion: "Jesus Christ, it's against the *rules*. . . . Against human *nature*. This elaborate story, you can't say, hey, by the way, I don't know the *ending*. I mean, you got certain obligations."[88] If the narrator of *In the Lake Of The Woods* is not up to such a responsibility, he at least is sensitive to the reader's perplexity: "Would it help to announce the problem early on? To plead for understanding? To argue that solutions only demean the grandeur of human ignorance? To point out that absolute knowledge is absolute closure?"[89]

Ultimately the reader's ability to consider various possibilities at once is essential to O'Brien because he wants us to recognize the social dangers of easy readings. He challenges his reader *not* to assume guilt, *not* to assume that the memory of Vietnam must inspire homicidal urges, or that the Vietnam vet will inevitably indulge them. He cleverly structures the novel to incrementally suggest that there have been other factors leading Wade to violence *besides* the war. There is male insecurity to consider; just as in *The Nuclear Age*, in which Bobbi's late-revealed infidelity seems more and more the cause of Will's unbalanced behavior, the reader here discovers, again relatively late in the narrative, that Kathy has had an affair with her dentist, Harmon. There are more factors still, most notably the influence of Wade's alcoholic, suicide father;

O'Brien insists that our usual reading proclivities and expectations in regard to Vietnam literature may be too narrow.

Could the veteran *not* be responsible? O'Brien asks; can the reader decide *against* the stereotype of the veteran that has so often appeared in fiction, in film, on television? O'Brien is particularly cautious neither to implicate nor exonerate Wade of the atrocities of My Lai. Present at the carnage, he flees, recognizing that: "this was not madness. . . . This was sin."[90] But still he leaves with blood on his hands. He kills a presumably harmless old man holding a hoe, because from the corner of his eye he perceives the hoe as a weapon. He also kills one of his fellow soldiers, PFC Weatherby, without any direct provocation; but Weatherby had been one of the most active participants in the slaughter. Is this second killing an act of justice? Is the first pardonable? From what O'Brien implies, Wade and Thinbill—another Native American, a parallel to benign Kiowa—are the only two soldiers on hand who attempt to refrain from "sin." The reader coming to terms with Wade must put his or herself in Wade's place, and come to understand the complications of war.

The violence of Kathy's murder, though, is horrendous; in the narrator's "re-enactment," Wade pours scalding hot water over Kathy's face. O'Brien spares none of the gruesome detail: "Puffs of steam rose from the sockets of her eyes. The veins at her throat stiffened. She jerked sideways. There were noises in the night—screechings—his own name, perhaps—but then the steam was in her throat. She coiled and uncoiled and coiled up again."[91] At the end of the narrator's investigations, though, the only proof attesting to this violence consists of scorched plants and a buried teakettle. The narrator himself is psychologically scarred by war; it has followed him back to America as it has followed Wade. He admittedly has his own rage—is he superimposing it on the facts? And if he cannot escape it, can O'Brien, no matter how unscathed he may claim to be? He covets a reader's validation, a reader's admission that this does not have to be.

In the end, his is a work of memory interested more in the future than in the past. He recognizes what Rorty often glosses over, and what reactionaries like Bawer and Aldridge bemoan: that the ironist reader is inherently more likely to adopt a moribund perspective toward events, toward the Other, their natural inclinations at odds with empathy and solidarity. O'Brien knows that novels of disruption such as his own can deepen this inclination, and therefore remains ever focused on Rorty's next step—considering the best possibilities along with the worst: "Are we so cynical, so sophisticated as to write off even the chance of happy endings . . . does happiness strain credibility?"[92]

Chapter Ten
"Others First": Approaching Solidarity

Narratives like O'Brien's maintain, as Rorty maintains, that our willingness to envision utopias is essential to the survival of a robust society, specifically a democratic society. But it is in highlighting the flaws of our own democracy as it is now constituted, the flaws we must overcome with utopian conjectures, that our authors face their most difficult choices. It is certainly clear that a dominant emotion in these novels is bilious rage; at one point in his Vietnam ordeal, O'Brien admits that "for all my education, all my fine liberal values, I now felt a deep coldness inside me, something dark and beyond reason."[1] Auster's Ben Sachs focuses this anger on our national fabric: "the dominant emotion was anger, a full-blown, lacerating anger that surged upon nearly every page: anger against America, anger against political hypocrisy, anger as a weapon to destroy national myths."[2] But an adherence to the postmodern fascination with media and symbol often seems to enervate any constructive aspect of this anger.

Although *White Noise* is acutely observant of modern times, for example, its observations can seem one-dimensional. Its most prime satirical moments have been well-explicated by now in the ever-expanding DeLillo critical industry: the Gladney family travels to the nation's most photographed barn, where the object of interest, the substance, is far less important than the capturing of the image, "taking pictures of taking pictures;"[3] a governmental department called SIMUVAC runs disaster drills during the unfolding of a real disaster, the airborne toxic event, a policy of which Gladney observes, "you saw a chance to use the real event in order to rehearse the simulation;"[4] consumers find their only transcendence, a distinctively atrophied transcendence, in the supermarket, since "even Tibet is not Tibet anymore;"[5] a deranged, possibly homeless man is dragged away from ATM machines, separated in ways inconceivable to any modern citizen from "the networks, the circuits, the streams, the harmonies."[6] Commodity and technology are supreme. Certainly in 1985 the time had come for a novel that could digestibly skewer our product-oriented society, the rarefied product with its "familiar life-enhancing labels."[7] But DeLillo has hardly broken new ground. His work on communication systems and marketing and the media-oriented psyche differs from that of Pynchon or Gaddis only in that he does not epitomize such confusions in *form* to the extent that they do. At the same time, he differs from many contemporary realists only in his honesty about his unidirectional focus. In Joan Didion's *Play It as It Lays,* derided by Wilde as the archetype of "catatonic realism," jaded protagonist Maria Wyeth meets her abortionist beneath a thriftmarket sign, an enormous T, "peculiarly illuminated against the harsh unclouded light of the afternoon sky,"[8] that overpowers the landscape with its bleakness, a modern equivalent of Fitzgerald's eyes of T.J. Eckleburg, but simplified, unelaborated, our waste land so much the desiccated realm of the marketed image that other significant determinants of human behavior seem negligible. DeLillo at least recognizes the limits of his approach; he satirizes the potential shallowness of his observations, implicating himself in Siskind's derision for the academic community's absorption in pop-cultural communication: "I understand the music, I understand the movies, I even see how comic books can tell us things. But there are full professors in this place who read nothing but cereal boxes."[9]

Leviathan embodies such limitations. Sachs channels his deep anger toward the United States into the image of the Statue Of Liberty, which once was a symbol of "all that is good within us," and indeed of all that Rorty feels the modern novelist must strive to emphasize: "one would be hard-pressed to find a single person willing to denounce the things it stands for: democracy, freedom, equality under the law."[10] As a symbol, though, it has been tarnished, the country straying from its ideals even as it has increasingly marketed its image of liberty to promote worldwide consumerism. In these terms, Aaron admits that Sachs's bombing of Lady Liberty replicas throughout the country has a sincere power, a true postmodern terrorism: "I had underestimated the power of the symbol . . . the Phantom [Sachs's terrorist nom de plume] had played a crucial part in resurrecting its meaning."[11] But Auster takes the corruption Sachs rebels against for granted, supplying few examples, if any, of the *lack* of "democracy, freedom, and equality under law" that runs counter to the Lady Liberty ideal. As such, ambiguities are sure to compound; fittingly, when Sachs as a boy first feels he understands the symbol—"I felt as if I'd struck a blow for democracy, as if I'd risen up in the name of oppressed people all over the world"[12]—it is only when carrying out a puerile rebellion against his mother's wish to have him dress up when visiting it. No more specific injustices are forthcoming in adult life; as a result, the symbol becomes more important not for what it represents but for its status *as a symbol,* suffering the degradation fated for symbols in the post-deconstruction era.

In the post-9/11 era, *Leviathan,* keenly aware of the implications of American political and economic iconography, seems at once prescient and naïve. In an article marking the first anniversary of the tumultuous event, Auster provides a much more clear explanation of the statue's significance than anywhere in *Leviathan:*

> Alone among American cities, New York is more than a place or an agglomeration of people. It is also an idea. I believe that idea took hold in us when Emma Lazarus's poem was affixed to the pedestal of the Statue of Liberty in 1903. Bartholdi's gigantic effigy was originally intended as a monument to the principles of international republicanism, but 'The New Colossus' reinvented the Statue's purpose, turning Liberty into a welcoming mother, a symbol of hope to the outcasts and downtrodden of the world.[13]

DeLillo has been equally, uncannily, unfortunately prescient. The twin towers loom mournfully on the cover of *Underworld,* which, in its roving discussion of American progress and warmongering, idealism and economic disparity, celebrity and criminality, explores the many significances of that image. "In the Ruins of the Future" crystallizes the latent connotations of our technological manifest destiny: "the World Trade Towers were not only an emblem of advanced technology, but a justification, in a sense, for technology's irresistible will to realize in solid form whatever becomes theoretically allowable. Once defined, every limit must be reached."[14]

Libra supplies far more specifics than either *Leviathan* or *White Noise.* It oscillates between the extremes of the postmodern and the naturalistic text. One of the Kennedy shooters, drifter Wayne Elko, appears as if straight from a Steinbeck novel, evoking, at least initially, some of the same pathos: "He was asleep ten minutes on the bench when a cop bounced his nightstick off Wayne's raised knee. It made a sound like he was built of hollow wood. Welcome to the Rockies."[15] Yet quickly a postmodern tone becomes clear, as DeLillo reveals how Wayne's vision of the world is only through film: "There were guys straight out of Wayne's favorite movie, *Seven Samurai,* warriors without masters, willing to band together to save a village from marauders."[16] Jameson insists that the political messages of Doctorow's *Ragtime,* despite seeming clear, are actually deliberately muddled, the novel "organized systematically and formally to short circuit an older type of social and historical interpretation which it perpetually holds out and withdraws."[17] Frank Lentricchia applies similar logic to the naturalistic story-line of *Libra:* "the social forces which obsess writers like Dreiser and Dos Passos—whom DeLillo most resembles in this book—are treated in *Libra* as forces whose capacity to shape as they differentiate the individual is decidedly on the ebb . . . displaced in DeLillo by the charismatic environment of the image, a new phase in American literature and culture."[18] DeLillo *is* clearly depicting the dawn of the media age, but Lentricchia oversells his premise by suggesting that DeLillo's interest in the postmodern aspects of life eventually supersedes his more traditional notions of economics, social injustice, urban decay, etc. Even though Oswald's path leads him to an unique end, a media apotheosis, the earlier sections of the novel, with their impressive reach in delineating various social spheres, retain their own unique force, and as a result of them Oswald stands as DeLillo's most convincing characterization to date, the naturalistic narrative still resounding.

Accordingly, DeLillo makes explicit his debt to canonical American writings without giving in to exhaustion. In his opening scene, he situates Oswald as an aimless passenger on the subway, and the scene echoes any number of traditional depictions of the railroad, perhaps the most durable yet conflicted image in American literature, emblematic of both freedom and oppression, both American ingenuity and American market forces out of control. Attuned to the mythological grandeur of the train and the progress it symbolizes, Thoreau sets down the prototype in *Walden:* "When I hear the iron horse make the hills echo with his snort like thunder, shaking the earth with his feet, and breathing fire and smoke from his nostrils . . . it seems as if the earth had got a race now worthy to inhabit it."[19] Thoreau is inherently distrustful of mechanization and the idea of collective identity, but here he projects the train as a symbol for what a nation of self-actualized Americans could achieve, given their mastery over nature and industry.

But while Thoreau believed governments should refrain from impeding business interests as well as individual aspirations, writers at the advent of naturalism were soon attuned to Machiavellian principles put into practice by big business with or without governmental controls. In *The Octopus,* Frank Norris depicted the unsubtle evil of the P. & S. W. Railroad Company of California, whose machines throttled the otherwise picturesque landscape: "the symbol of a vast power, huge, terrible, flinging the echo of its thunder over all the reaches of the valley, leaving blood and destruction in its path. . . ."[20] Correspondingly, in *Libra* there are few scraps left of transcendental self-reliance, only men living in quiet desperation; DeLillo presents a modern world of grim urban realities, of filth and vermin, of the grand image of the train regressed or degenerated into the subterranean subway car, which seems to power itself devoid of human influence—"they went so fast sometimes he thought they were on the verge of no-control"—and serves only as another transient shelter for the downhearted and frenetic people of a derelict nation: "He kept a watch for sewer rats. . . . Then the express stations, the creaky breaks, people bunched like refugees. They came wagging through the door, banked against the rubber edges, inched their way in, were quickly pinned, looking out past the nearest heads into that practiced oblivion."[21] For Oswald, the train goes nowhere, with no sense of manifest destiny available, no sense of destiny at all. Thoreau saw the train as a warning as well as a glory, knowing all too well that the individual had to emerge alongside but still outside the course of national progress rather than being wholly submerged, sublimated: "Every path but your own is the path of fate. Keep on your own track, then." But Oswald lacks the opportunity or the self-awareness to emerge; he is like one of Pynchon's Whole Sick Crew, who spend their time indolently riding New York buses in a closed circle of Manhattan, "yo-yoing," surrendering their identity to a course that does not advance: "It had nothing to do with him. He was riding just to ride."

For Oswald, the appeal of the subway is its seemingly directionless force, its "satisfying wave of rage and pain."[22] His pleasure in the sensation of "no-control" is merely a manifestation of the slave mentality, a satisfaction in enforced limitations. "No-control" is a lack of agency, the corollary of "no-choice." In the marines, Oswald will be brutally beaten after a grilling on marine rhetoric in which he repeats the correct responses verbatim; in explanation, the abusive officer tells him, "there are no right answers,"[23] a statement with the power of human reduction equivalent to that of the concentration camp guard in Primo Levi's *Survival In Auschwitz:* "There is no why here."[24]

There is little in Oswald's formative experience, the experience that eventually pushes him to action, which has changed much since the height of naturalism. His will to a power of rage and pain is a product of an imagination that is, like the type of stick figures he draws as a boy, "impoverished."[25] Tellingly, he lacks a father figure, his siblings are dispersed, and while his mother is immersed to the point of addiction in television, "Marguerite stayed up late watching the test pattern,"[26] their central problems are economic; mother and child live in incommodious basement rooms, often without heat. As Oswald explains, "I have a far mean streak of independence brought on by neglect,"[27] a horrifying deformation of transcendentalist concepts of self-reliance. Oswald thinks of his life in terms of "history out of George Orwell,"[28] an admission notable in terms of this study because for a large portion of this narrative DeLillo is writing as Orwell might write, earnestly, bluntly.

Margueritte, Oswald's mother, represents the voice of naturalism; even when the novel takes its turn toward the postmodern information age, she grasps for basic issues, and finds them: "I have struggled to raise my boys on mingy sums of money and today I am everywhere, newsreel and foreign press, but where are the sums for a decent burial?"[29] Magali Cornier Michael believes that her influence is lost in the novel's later stages, along with the naturalist flavor, "undermined by the novel's focus on the pervasiveness of the media and the overriding power of its languages of representation in the construction and fates of subjects."[30] Yet Margueritte perseveres until the final lines of the novel, and even if she herself ends up "everywhere" in the media, she is in this still following a naturalist pattern, DeLillo looking back to Dreiser's *American Tragedy,* in which Clyde Griffiths's own mother writes newspaper accounts on his murder trial.

Similarly, Auster's *Mr. Vertigo* is far more explicit about economic hardship and social violence than his earlier works. Auster does not hesitate to depict his own utopia in Yehudi's home, inhabited by a European immigrant, a paradigmatic American youth, a Native American woman, and an African-American prodigy: "All men are brothers, and in this family everyone gets treated with respect. [This] law is the law, and whoever goes against it is turned into a slug and wallows in the earth for the rest of his days."[31] Yet this utopia ends in ruin; outraged members of the KKK lay waste to the family while Yehudi and his airborne pupil are out, a moment that represents the random cruelty that is America in execution, the depiction missing from *Leviathan:* "I felt as if I had seen the sun explode. I felt as if I had just witnessed the end of the world."[32]

Auster depicts the slaughter swiftly, without embellishment: "they dragged Aesop and Mother Sioux out of the burning house, put ropes around their necks, and strung them up to the elm tree by the side of the road, each to a different branch. Aesop howled, Mother Sioux said nothing, and within minutes they were both dead."[33] O'Brien depicts human atrocity with a similarly detached but close observation. The slaughter at My Lai at the center of *In The Lake Of The Woods* is a prime example, saturated by the journalistic detail that was missing in the razing of civilian villages in *If I Die In A Combat Zone:* "the wind stirred up a powdery red dust that sparkled in the morning sunshine, and the little village had now gone mostly violet. He found someone stabbing people with a big silver knife. Hutto was shooting corpses. T'souras was shooting children. Doherty and Terry were finishing off the wounded."[34] Cruelty to children receives special attention: "He watched a little boy climb out of the ditch and start to run, and he watched Calley grab the kid and give him a good talking to and then toss him back and draw down and shoot the kid dead."[35]

Johnson's approach to violence is similar also: "A woman pitched her baby overboard into the waters below us. At least two men tried to follow, straining against their chains, and this sudden flurry of resistance brought out the worst in Falcon, if you can imagine that. He beat them until blood came."[36] His detachment has proven unpalatable to many critics. Vincent A. O'Keefe, for example, believes that Johnson creates a buffer zone between himself and the events of his narrative, an effective "rigor mortis," and, apparently, a moral failure. In like terms, one might argue that O'Brien's approach represents his continuing failure to fully empathize with the suffering of the Vietnamese: "What did these people want? What did they feel? Who was VC and who was friendly and who among them didn't care?"[37]

DeLillo recognizes that we may be drawn more to Auster's violent spectacle than his utopia: "Babette tried to switch to a comedy series about a group of racially mixed kids who build their own communications satellite. She was startled by the force of our objection. We were otherwise silent, watching houses slide into the ocean, whole villages crackle and ignite in a mass of advancing lava."[38] But the importance, both writers would argue, is in getting this historical violence down on paper. O'Keefe argues that for passages like Johnson's to hit home, the reader must experience not clarity but Calhoun's confusion, a confusion expressed through form, of course; Johnson fails by "telling the readers about his moments of disorientation, as opposed to showing the readers syntactically or typographically."[39] Such a postmodern disruption through form would, however, shift our focus from the significance of what is going on to merely the question of *what* is going on.

Auster shares on some level this view of the Novel as constructive social record, even when his own falls short; indeed, this is what brings Sachs to Aaron: "The story needed to be told, and better to you than to anyone else. If and when the time comes, you'll know how to tell it to others, you'll make them understand what this business is all about."[40] Despite his own hesitation, DeLillo eventually comes to recognize the necessity of remembering atrocity, and to this end he devotes a sizable portion of *Underworld* to like-minded preservationists; young urban activists paint an angel on a decrepit building every time a child's life is squandered: "the child's name and age were printed under each angel . . . as the van drew closer Edgar could see entries for TB, AIDS, beatings, drive-by shootings, measles, asthma, abandonment at birth—left in a dumpster, forgot in a car, left in a Glad Bag stormy night."[41] O'Brien takes the additional step of exploring the political significance of memory lapses; John Wade's evasion of My Lai parallels the claims of forgetfulness made by President Reagan in the Iran-Contra hearings, for example. It is no coincidence that a chapter recounting the testimony of true-life soldiers at My Lai, many of them pleading forgetfulness, precedes a chapter entitled "The Nature of Politics."

But these authors realize, as Rorty does, that the inclination toward solidarity must be stoked before all this specificity can lead to lasting political change, to realized utopia. In *Dreamer,* MLK's plan of action is conveyed by Johnson in liberal ironist terms: "first, changing the souls of men so that they not only protested for peace but in themselves *were* peace extended, loving in even life's smallest affairs. And second, he called for changing society so that the soul might have a field in which to flourish."[42] In other words, as he sums up: "Others first. Always."[43]

Johnson demonstrates this approach in *Middle Passage;* contemporary political commentary is very much on his mind, enough that he does not hesitate to compromise his sense of historical rectitude with anachronism, as in Falcon's dialogue: "crazy as it seems, I saw a ship with a whole crew of women. Yellow men were buying up half of America. Hegel was spewing from the mouths of Hottentots. Gawd!"[44] Of course, Johnson reminds us that in Falcon's time such advancements on the part of marginalized peoples were thoroughly impossible, given the ruthlessness with which white power maintained itself, a point not to be brushed aside in any contemporary debate; but we have stressed earlier how Johnson wants to move beyond racial distinctions, and this especially applies to politics. It is less important to pinpoint specific offenders than to identify the fundamental human drive that motivates them. After establishing Allmuseri uniqueness, an uniqueness in which there is no idea of uniqueness, Johnson reveals that even they had conformed to the usual social paradigm long before European intrusion: "they had been in chains before, I remembered. Taken in raids by other tribes."[45] Even within their own tribe, the same divisions of class and economics were in force, as Ngonyama observes: "you know, in our village I was a poor man, like you, but his father was well-to-do. Diamelo was used to getting his way."[46] Similarly, at the climax of the novel, Papa Zeringue, the black mob-type figure who rules the New Orleans underworld, "the cathouses, the Negro press, the gambling dens,"[47] admits to crimes against his own people that include funding *The Republic,* shipping slaves, and crating up the Allmuseri god. By this time, all distinctions have been blurred. Johnson is not demonstrating how well Zeringue has been indoctrinated into a white/European power system. His individual crimes demand individual guilt; his fault is his irony without empathy: "he held his dark kingdom, and all within it, in the greatest contempt."[48]

These novels continue the now-familiar motif of the shadowy observer, reading and re-casting his subject, his Other, from his hidden vantage.

Stalking is not merely a male/female issue; Wade stalks his wife, but late in the narrative we learn that as a boy he stalked his father as well. Gender issues serve primarily as a springboard to a discussion of human cruelty in general.

Not that the authors have fully matured in their treatment of women. Often females remain constrained, objects of physical desire. Isadora in *Middle Passage* is a key example; although Calhoun matures to the point that he can enter into a healthy relationship with her despite her homeliness and bland conformity, she slims down in his absence, making herself beautiful, desirable, a commodity, so that his climactic choice for her seems more a reward for his travails than the product of difficult, character-defining decisions.

Similarly, in "The Sweetheart of the Song Tra Bong," one of the stories in *The Things They Carried,* O'Brien presents a female ideal in the title character, a young cheerleader: "seventeen years old, fresh out of Cleveland Heights senior high. She had long white legs and blue eyes and a complexion like strawberry ice cream."[49] Kathy Wade, in her younger college years, has a similar quality of innocence, of purity through physicality: "back in college . . . she used to lie in bed and tell funny stories and giggle and roll around and be happy."[50] The bed is the true domain of the female, their sense of innocence not including virginity. Even the young cheerleader has a brusque attitude toward sex: "she gave off a kind of come-and-get-me energy, coy and flirtatious."[51] Auster's Fanny Sachs, Ben's wife with whom Aaron briefly carries on an affair, combines these same extremes. She is a man's (and especially an adulterer's) crassest sexual ideal in that she is unable to conceive children, but on the other hand is pure in that she is completely free of irony; there could never be a nihilistic gesture on part because "it presupposes a kind of cynicism that Fanny never really possessed."[52]

Even more significantly, the female cannot understand the male *writer.* After the narrator of *The Things They Carried* tells, yet again, the cow story, he is dismayed by the reaction of a woman in his audience: "it's always a woman. . . . She'll explain that as a rule she hates war stories; she can't understand why people want to wallow in all the blood and gore. But this one she liked. The poor baby buffalo, it made her sad. . . . I'll picture Rat Kiley's face, his grief, and I'll think, *You dumb cooze.*"[53] While Mark Heberle stresses that we need to remember that this outbreak "does not represent Tim O'Brien's trauma, but Rat Kiley's,"[54] critics like Lorrie Smith are quick to explicate the offensive nature of the narrator's attitude. But O'Brien recognizes that the fault ultimately lies not with a female reader but with a writer unable to communicate the truths of his experience: "you wake up and shake your wife and start telling the story to her, except when you get to the end you've forgotten the point again."[55]

Drawbacks admitted, our authors address their generalizing tendencies far more cogently than in their prior work. In "Sweetheart," Rat Kiley chides his fellow soldiers, as well as O'Brien and his audience, for harboring such puerile views: "You get these blinders on about women. How gentle and peaceful they are. . . . . Pure garbage. You got to get rid of that sexist attitude."[56] Through artist Klara Sax in *Underworld*, DeLillo tries to maintain a new ideal in his characterizations: "I like this girl because she is not amazonian or angelic or terrifically idealized."[57] Although often lost in abstraction herself, Klara wishes to rescue other women, even figments in works of art, from abstraction, from theory. Such is her appraisal of Whistler's mother in the famous painting: "looking into the depths of the picture, the mother, the woman, the mother herself . . . a strong and elegiac presence despite the painter's, the son's, doctrinal priorities."[58] In "Ruins," DeLillo shows, again, the novelist's affinity for the terrorist mindset, but it is clear, if it was not before, that he has recognized the dehumanization inherent in abstraction, in theory. He imagines a budding terrorist, shopping in a supermarket that could be a setting in *White Noise:* "Does the sight of a woman pushing a stroller soften the man to her humanity and vulnerabilities, and her child's as well, and all the people he is here to kill?" His conclusion is sobering: "He knows who we are and what we mean in the world—an idea, a righteous fervor in the brain. But there is no defenseless human at the end of his gaze."[59]

O'Brien's portrait of Kathy Wade displays sensitivity to the female beyond that of his earlier novels. He is far more conscious of the role to which he has confined her—that of the veteran's wife. Indeed, although the narrator supplies excerpts from *Recovering From The War: A Woman's Guide To Helping Your Vietnam Vet, Your Family, And Yourself*, therefore seeming to limit her role to the veteran's wife and nothing but the veteran's wife, there are murmurs of a new feminized understanding, an awareness of a woman's course of life, on the fringes of the text: "the old lady—Mrs. Brandt—she had banalities to burn. A jingle for every occasion: birthdays, menstruation, first love."[60] Such admissions may admittedly be basic, reductionary, and clichéd, but they nevertheless represent a new depth by O'Brien's standards. Correspondingly, even Kathy's affair with Harmon does not place her in the same morally questionable category as Bobbi Cowling; unlike Bobbi, her decisions, her guilt, are as fleshed out, as understandable, as possible: "it was a very terrible unsticking thing she had done, and . . . after it was over, all she'd wanted was to keep it secret, but the secret had soon become worse than the terrible thing itself."[61] In fact, her eventual confession suggests integrity in light of Wade's tendency to conceal the festering rot of his past. As a result of this fleshed-out portrait of Kathy Wade, the appearance of a female corpse in that past, in the long-suppressed memory of the massacre at My Lai, has added impact because O'Brien has resurrected the feminine from an objectified plane: "they came across a young female with both breasts gone. Someone had carved a C in her stomach."[62]

This example appropriately links the female Other with the racial Other; the same correspondence eventually applies to the Sweetheart: "she wore a bush hat and filthy green fatigues; she carried the standard M-16 automatic assault rifle; her face was black with charcoal."[63] In *Underworld,* DeLillo, in typical liberal ironist style, carries out an act of effacement on the issue of race but then confesses this proclivity. The novel's prologue, centered on the pivotal ball game, was initially published as the highly acclaimed novella "Pafko At The Wall;" in incorporating "Pafko" into *Underworld,* DeLillo made several at-first-glance minor changes that under closer examination reveal that he has removed his most trenchant social observations. The protagonist of the *Underworld* prologue, and thus the protagonist of "Pafko" as a whole, is Cotter, a fourteen-year-old African American schoolboy ducking classes to attend the big game. In "Pafko," DeLillo hints at the nature of African American existence in the fifties, an existence that sets Cotter apart from the truant white boys who have also infiltrated the stands. His glasses are inherited from a cousin, "Trumaine Martin, dead at twenty-six of being in a room that contained a discharging pistol."[64] This is a life of hard knocks and Johnson's harsh statistics, a domestic world inextricably linked with violence, sudden death. Such asides assume the foreground when Cotter, having left the stadium with the historic baseball in hand, is followed most of the way home by white businessman Bill Waterson, who has until that point acted as his friend, another example of American solidarity through the game of baseball. Now, though, Bill is intent on retrieving the ball for his own, offering money and new sporting equipment in exchange for memorabilia. Cotter does not bite, and eventually Waterson loses his cool: "Don't be so god-damn almighty nigger-ish. Not with me, okay?"[65] After losing his self-control in this way, Bill cannot leave the moment unexamined: "Goddamn, you made me say it and there's no forgiving the fact, is there? Aw shit, good Christ, but I'd a never said it if you hadn't made me. Jesus in heaven, I'm completely mortified." DeLillo probes the racial attitudes that are as ingrained in the American psyche as they are in sport; that persist in combustible combination with the idea of progress exemplified in the gestures of goodwill carried out by Bill for eight and two-thirds innings.

All of these passages from "Pafko" are gone from *Underworld,* however; Cotter has no cousin, and though Waterson follows Cotter, he doesn't make his slip of the tongue. DeLillo would seem to be broadening his focus; in the new opening line, Cotter has been universalized: "He speaks in your voice,

American, and there's a shine in his eye that's halfway hopeful."[66] Indeed, the threat of the bomb overwhelms any other social crises, its unleashing promising, like its weaker cousin the X-ray, "a flash too bright to make racial niceties."[67] But DeLillo has demoted Cotter as protagonist in favor of Nick Shay, who often seems to speak for DeLillo, both autobiographically and metafictionally; now the teen in a room with a discharging pistol is not Cotter's cousin but Nick, whose adulthood begins after he accidentally shoots a heroin addict. DeLillo has chosen to focus again on the criminal aspect of the author, the terrorist quality, his transgressive force.

Yet DeLillo does not leave this shift in focus unquestioned. He parallels his own act of effacement to that epitomized by "Long Tall Sally," a woman drawn on the side of a bomber rendered obsolete by the end of the Cold War. Klara, converting these bombers into a grand work of art, has many favorable things to say about Sally, who is drawn as a spirited white woman, but Louis, who was a crewman on that same plane back when it was still in service, notes the truth behind the song that inspired her, the truth obscured by the white soldiers who drew her: "this song is written by a black woman from Appaloosa, Mississippi. [Little] Richard add the little touches. I guarantee, brother, this Sally we're talking about ain't no skinny blond playing kissy-face in no back seat. She's an advance class of entertainment."[68] She is also black.

Auster also self-ironically depicts how the author-figure, the novelist, can subsume this issue of the Other—any Other. Aaron claims that he needs the answers to Sachs's death to honor the depth of their friendship, but Auster indicates that what is really at stake, before Aaron has allowed himself time for self-reflection, is only the writer's instinct, on the trail of future narratives like a news-hound on the hunt. In the momentum of his investigation, Aaron becomes entirely unconcerned with issues of human life, entirely unmoved, for instance, by the devastation wrought by a tumultuous earthquake: "collapsed highways, burned buildings, crushed and mangled bodies—these disasters meant nothing to me except insofar as they could prevent me from talking to Lilian Stern."[69]

Thus it is that the author-figure in these books must move beyond a compulsion to empathize that is based only in fitting the Other into a mold: human compassion stirred up only for the victim with literary aspirations. DeLillo's Bill Gray is initially drawn into activism only because there is a writer in need, a Swiss writer taken hostage in Beirut, an incident with unsubtle allusions to the Salman Rushdie death threats, against which DeLillo has publicly spoken. In *The Things They Carried,* O'Brien's narrator (putatively O'Brien) studies the corpse of a man he has killed, both fascinated and horrified; he survives this moral crisis point, according to Lorrie Smith, only in the most superficial and perhaps offensive manner: "the narrator recognizes himself in the dead man but also makes him absolutely other, that is, womanly. Recovery from his trauma . . . rests on asserting the living, masculine self in opposition to the dead, silent, feminine Other."[70] Smith is correct in observing that O'Brien has undeniably feminized his victim; he relates an imagined history of the dead youth, which includes the fact that "his eyebrows were thin and arched like a woman's, and at school the boys sometimes teased him about how pretty he was."[71] But O'Brien is not distancing himself from the Other. Rather, he is breaking down the concept of Otherness by bonding with the man he has killed by identifying both as "sensitive soldiers," to recall the term used in *Northern Lights*. The victim may be feminine, but this is because he represents O'Brien's much-cherished image of the abstracted and ostracized author-figure open to the "feminine" ideal of courage: "his chest was sunken and poorly muscled—a scholar, maybe."[72] But what is really needed is not this pigeon-holing but something akin to Johnson's rare moment of "gratuitous" empathy; forced to toss a corpse overboard, Calhoun imposes on it only the most general terms of brotherhood: "judging by what little was left of his face, hard as wood on one side and melting into worm-eaten pulp on the other as rigor mortis began to reverse, he was close to my own age, perhaps had been torn from a lass as lonely as, lately, I now saw Isadora to be, and from a brother as troublesome as my own."[73]

Eventually, for Gray the Novel can no longer be seen as a revelation open only to the privileged, the elite: "Do you want to know why I believe in the novel? It's a democratic shout. Anybody can write a great novel, one great novel, almost any amateur off the street."[74] It is no coincidence, then, that even if he does not survive to carry out his grand political gesture, he dies in the midst of a Whitmanlike sense and celebration of the Crowd, the democratic impulse flourishing even en route to Beirut, where one might have expected the Crowd to take on the aspect of a ravenous, murderous body: "He stood on deck and was surprised to see them come aboard, easily a hundred people. . . . He thought it was touching and brave and these people were dear to him, families, cartons, shopping bags, babies, the melodious traffic of a culture."[75] DeLillo concedes his tendency to disparage the Crowd for its literary fodder, resembling J. Edgar Hoover in *Underworld*, who is unduly sensitive to "newspapers, guidebooks, Gideon bibles, erotic literature, subversive literature, underground literature, literature—whatever people read in hotels, alone, thumbing and breathing."[76] Yet here he is more open to the Crowd, provided he can pinpoint the individuals in it, just as a concerned father pinpoints his daughter amid a mass wedding presided over by Sun Young Moon in *Mao II*, defining her in the face of a religious de-individualization: "healthy, intelligent, twenty-one, serious-sided, possessed of a selfness, a teeming soul, nuance and shadow, grids of pinpoint singularity they will never drill out of her."[77] Similarly, when the Wades are considering campaign strategies, shrewd manager Carbo advises them to reach for the masses by targeting the individual within them. As an additional challenge, this hypothetical voter, this "way in," is to be viewed as female: "because this girl's human just like you and me. She's got an ego. She got her dignity. I mean, she's a living, breathing, piece of ass and you got to respect that."[78]

This "pinpointing" tendency allows the author to re-engage with the social implications of his world, its forces of dehumanization; Nick muses over the contrary process that has created his Lexus: 'there's nobody on the line with caffeine nerves or a history of clinical depression. . . . Robots tightening bolts, programmed drudges that do not dream of family dead."[79] Thus Matthew Shay, in a state of moral turmoil while working on the bomb project, has a need answered more by DeLillo than by Nick: "maybe he would give the kid advice about the moral and ethical aspects of this kind of work. Mainly what Matt wanted was a show of interest."[80] A "show of interest" defines DeLillo's storytelling technique in this novel, in which characters mentioned seemingly in passing in one chapter are soon after given a chapter of their own, the smallest leads explored, the most minor lives expanded, given substance. Albert, Matt's old teacher and chess mentor, sees Sister Edgar from a distance and remembers her reputation as a tough disciplinarian; she catches his interest only for a moment, in passing, yet the next chapter begins: "The old nun rose at dawn, feeling pain in every joint. She'd been rising at dawn since her days as a postulant, kneeling on hardwood floors to pray. . . ."[81] DeLillo has come full circle from his earliest statements on characterization in regard to *End Zone;* here, each individual warrants a fullness of character.

In "In the Ruins of the Future," DeLillo makes the identical gesture; walking "among crowds of people, the panethnic swarm of shoppers, merchants, residents and passersby," he spots "the woman on the prayer rug" who is "partially concealed by a couple of vendor's carts and no one seemed much to notice her." The keen eye of the increasingly sensitive artist has pinpointed the Other, and sees her not as different but as part of "the daily sweeping taken-for-granted greatness of New York," in which difference is "surrendered to the impact and the flash,"[82] unmistakably recalling the flash that annihilates racial "niceties" in *Underworld.*

In humanizing the individual in the Crowd, DeLillo is not denying the desirability of cooperation, interaction, communication. Instead, he presents a model of functional social unity in the family, despite the fact that in *White Noise* Sisskind characterizes family as an institution "strongest where objective reality is most likely to be misinterpreted."[83] The Gladneys do seem to substantiate his claim, for they represent an aggregation of misinformation, of facts improperly remembered from school. Sheltered in their shared but questionable knowledge, they demonstrate the pandemic ignorance spread down from the top during the JFK years, in which "the White House was . . . the summit of unknowing,"[84] a process begun with the Everett family in *Libra,* in which Suzanne represents the first generation infected by post-assassination consciousness. Saturated by her father's lies and tormented by vague premonitions that all is not right in the world, she recognizes on some primal level that the comforting illusion of the fifties family is no more than a comforting illusion, and clings to her toy family, "with little black dots for their eyes and mouth," relying on surrealism because she can no longer have faith in the integrity of real domesticity, in the stability of identity: "she had to keep them near and safe in case the people who called themselves her mother and father were really somebody else."[85] By the time of the Gladneys, the illusion of stability has crumbled to the point that the family is in perpetual flux, spread out over the world, children from various marriages coming and going, ex-wives and ex-husbands visiting unannounced. Understandably, it at first glance hardly seems a healthy unit: Babette and Jack obsess over which of them will die first; Wilder cries for hours at a time without any tangible provocation. According to Ferraro, the transient nature of the family, "forced to configure to alternative households," eradicates "genuine warmth and mutual need."[86]

Yet despite Wilder's crying and Heinreich's moribund nature, the children in *White Noise* are not paranoiacs, and are not, like Suzanne, afraid of their parents. In fact, despite Ferraro's assertions, the Gladney family, as a type of the amorphous modern family, is not unhealthy at the core. Jack loves Babette; Babette loves Jack; they love the children. Their moments of solidarity through petty misinformation are actually depicted warmly if bemusedly by DeLillo. The children are at the center; DeLillo maintains their quality of salvation. In fact, children such as Wilder have approximated the heroic storyteller's journey more purely than the novelist: "it was as though he'd just returned from a period of wandering in some remote and holy place . . . which we in our ordinary toil can only regard with the mingled reverence and wonder we hold in reserve for fears of the most sublime and difficult dimensions."[87]

This transcendence, this salvation, is well within the grasp of even the most ill-fated characters. Parmenter jokingly tempts Everett to follow his family instincts, but in truth if he had there might have been no assassination, and he might never have been murdered: "Win. What the hell. Why not settle in, raise your little girl, sign up for the concert and drama series. The school's bound to have one. No, I mean it."[88] Instead, Everett rejects the mediocrity offered by wife Mary Francis, "who knew how to use the sound of her own voice to bring him back to what was safe and plain."[89] Similarly, although Oswald claims that happiness "does not consist of a small home, of taking and getting,"[90] his last-minute reconciliation attempt with his Russian wife Marina the day before the assassination could have changed everything; it is a biblical motif, Peter rejecting Christ three times before the cock crows: "three times he'd asked her to live with him in Dallas. Three times she'd said no."[91] It is too late for Oswald, who has physically abused Marina in the past, but these alternative possibilities haunt. Once again, the rhetoric surrounding Johnson's Martin Luther King and his followers suggests the reconciliation through mediocrity suggested throughout these novels: "the family . . . was far more than a group bonded by blood . . . it was the finest opportunity anyone would have for practicing selflessness."[92]

Through television, the individual family has become the global family. Beryl, Parmenter's wife and another shrewd analyzer of American culture, wrestles with moral issues while watching coverage of the Oswald shooting, recognizing the transcendent force of the captured scene and Oswald's knowing face in it: "a glance at the camera before he was shot, that put him here in the audience, among the rest of us, sleepless in our homes—a glance, a way of telling us he knows who we are and how we feel, that he has brought our perceptions into his sense of the crime."[93] Hantke correctly assesses the significance of her response: "unlike Branch, who is concerned with establishing factual truth, Beryl's hard-earned response is that of collective moral responsibility."[94] The emphasis is on the collective; to achieve this moral understanding, Beryl must overcome a reluctance to incorporate herself into the crowd that very much resembles the writer's elitist sensibilities: "she didn't want these people in her house."[95] This reluctance is very characteristic of DeLillo's; at the time he did not "join in" the media coverage: "I didn't watch much television that weekend. I didn't watch much of the funeral. I think I have a kind of natural antipathy to formal events of that kind."[96] His novel is a modern approximation of what he at that time avoided; as a gesture, it replaces antipathy with compassion.

Similarly, in the face of Rorty's potentially disheartening spectrum of contingent narratives—"they had presented me with two versions of the truth, two separate and distinct realties, and no amount of pushing and shoving could bring them together"—Aaron, and through him Auster, insists that "the only justifiable response was compassion."[97] Thus in *Mr. Vertigo* the power of Walt's turbulent genius, "in order to lift you off the ground, we have to crack the heavens in two. . . . We have to turn the whole bloody universe inside out,"[98] is always offset by a deeper notion of community: "if you look in someone's face long enough, eventually you're going to feel that you're looking at yourself."[99] Although Yehudi's utopia is dashed, Walt will eventually redeem himself for an erratic life through his devotion to Molly Fitzsimmons: "the master had forgiven me. He'd canceled out my debt to him because of Molly, because of how I'd loved her and married her."[100] Similarly, although Johnson's Allmuseri god has a postmodern trenchant for destabilizing language in which "to say anything was to fall short of ever saying enough," [101] he compels Rutherford to break down all those barriers between Self and Other that his irony, Johnson's irony, has raised: "the Allmuseri god is everything, so the very knowing situation we mortals rely on—a separation between knower and known—never rises in its experience."[102] It is only after this experience that Calhoun, for the first time, can immerse himself in the suffering of others: "the first thing I was forced to do was forget my personal cares, my pains, and my hopes before repairing to the deckhouse where the sufferers were sprawled. I placed a hand on each of their foreheads and listened—though tired and sleepless."[103] He dedicates himself to saving Baleka, a young slave girl aboard ship, recalling Bucky Wunderlick and his mentorship of Skippy; like Cringle, who donates his expiring body for the consumption of the wayward, starving crew, Calhoun recognizes that his crewmates have become his all: "I knew I was dying, no doubt about that, and I did not care for myself anymore, only that my mates should survive."[104] Accordingly, Peter Aaron will berate himself for his failure to pursue such selfless gestures; indeed, his recalcitrance may have cost Sachs his life: "I should have told him he was crazy and made him stop. If there was ever a moment when I failed Sachs as a friend, it was that afternoon four years ago."[105]

There are numerous impediments to this compassion in the world of *White Noise,* in our world, as epitomized by the obsession with Hitler upon which Gladney has built an auspicious career. At its rotten core, "Hitler Studies" represents an obsession with power: "Some people carry a gun. Some people put on a uniform and feel bigger, stronger, safer."[106] This is not merely an affinity for the icons of the past, the postmodern approach to history without context; it is an affinity for power devoid of restraint and it continues into the here and now, as ex-wife Tweedy Browner indicates: "Malcolm and I once took tea with Colonial Qaddafi. A charming and ruthless man, one of the few terrorists we've met who lives up to his public billing."[107] Paul Cantor insists that "DeLillo is not a participant in the Hitler phenomenon, but as its pathologist [he] understands the psychological appeal of totalitarianism."[108] In Rortyian fashion, though, DeLillo understands it precisely because it is close to him. As Gladney himself observes of one of his fellow academicians: "brilliant people never think of the lives they smash, being brilliant."[109]

Gladney compares his comfort in Hitler to the security of owning a gun; when his father-in-law gives him a pistol, it provokes the same sensation: "It occurred to me that this was the ultimate device for determining one's competence in the world."[110] He considers murdering Mink, who has taken advantage of Babette's weakness; implicit in Jack's act is the American heritage of regeneration through violence, the desire, as explained by Richard Slotkin, to slay the threatening Other, incorporating his coveted power, his strangeness, as one's own, as Sisskind asserts in one of his rambling, improvisational monologues: "Think how exciting it is, in theory, to kill a person in direct confrontation. If he dies, you cannot. To kill him is to gain life-credit. The more people you kill, the more credit you store up. It explains any number of massacres, wars, executions."[111] In "Ruins," this is the modus operandi of the fanatic: "Kill the enemy and pluck out his heart."[112] As if to protect himself, Murray reiterates the artist's usual excuse for irresponsibility: "I'm talking theory."

But Gladney fails in his murder attempt, a failure not of competence as much as will. As N. Katherine Hayles observes: "the fantasy is shattered when Mink, perhaps accidentally, shoots Jack in the wrist. The act that Jack intended to mark his distance from those who die ends by establishing his connection to mortality."[113] In these terms, Gladney's epiphany seems entirely self-absorbed, as self-absorbed as the killing would have been, but DeLillo stresses that this revelatory moment, like Calhoun's interaction with the Allmuseri god, has a quintessential social aspect: "I looked at him. Alive. His lap a puddle of blood. With the restoration of the normal order of matter and sensation, I felt I was seeing him for the first time as a person. The old human muddles and quirks were set flowing again. Compassion, remorse, mercy."[114] These "old human muddles" are the converse of the "subjects remote" that we remember as Owen Brandemas's contribution to *The Names,* which symbolized DeLillo's postmodern interests.

Similar acts of compassion saturate *Mao II* through the character of Karen, who discovers in New York a more concrete equivalent of Auster's Country of Last Things. This is no parable, no science fiction, but "a world apart but powerfully here, a set of milling images with breath and flesh and a language everywhere that sounded like multilingual English."[115] As in Auster, unfortunate wastrels prowl the terrain with their shopping carts: "pushed, dragged, lived in, fought over, unwheeled, bent, rolling haywire, filled with living trivia."[116] When Karen pries "a real spoon with impacted food that was also real"[117] from an abstract work at an art gallery, she reminds us that despite Auster's conflation of art and hunger, hunger remains a true-life need, not an artistic statement. Similarly, the grotesquerie of the common man so harped upon in DeLillo's earlier fiction, a grotesquerie epitomized in *Underworld* by the mutated freaks in the newly discovered Eisenstein film *Unterwelt,* become literalized in the Chernobyl victims encountered by Nick when he travels to Kazakhstan at the end of the novel. No abstractions are possible.

Acts of compassion are increasingly pivotal to O'Brien as well. The Rasmussens, the wizened couple who befriend Wade after his wife's disappearance, prove that gestures of solidarity, and true bonds of love, remain feasible. Earle stresses that self-reliance must paradoxically be built on charity. A "meat and potatoes" man who believes that one should "say what you mean, mean what you say"[118] (simultaneously discrediting both the political machine and deconstruction), he eventually provides John with the boat in which he makes his final escape into the fog, into the reaches of The Angle, the borders of the nation. In a moment of revelation, John recognizes that "he had a genuine friend in the world."[119] The Rasmussens' gesture stands outside any epistemological crises in the novel; O'Brien is echoing a moment in *The Things They Carried* in which grizzled Elroy Berdahl, who also resides on the borders of the lake, lends a boat to young and conflicted draftee O'Brien, giving him his option to flee. For O'Brien, torn by indecision, self-doubt, horror, disgust, this gesture is everything, even if he does not elect to escape, even if he makes the wrong decision: "the hero of my life. How do I say this without sounding sappy? The man saved me."[120] This statement has a meaning ultimately outside of language, allowing no confusion, no abstraction, no concessions to contingency, even though such precepts are integral to O'Brien's novelistic style by this point: "the old man understood that words were insufficient. The problem had gone beyond discussion. . . . Intellect had come up against emotion."[121] This event never happened to the real O'Brien; he is inventing a useful personal history as well as a national one, a moment of unequivocal certainty of the sort that eluded his grasp since his more tormented attempts at sincerity in *If I Die in a Combat Zone.*

For some readers, such gestures of comprehensibility, utility, and solidarity are not enough to counteract the anti-traditional elements of these novels. Though *Entertainment Weekly,* a publication consciously crafted to appeal to the Crowd, celebrated the mainstream commodity of *Underworld,* "never mind that PEN/Faulkner Award—he's still in the best-selling company of schlocky Sidney Sheldon,"[122] its book critic Tom De Haven struck a discordant note, acknowledging the novel's brilliance but insisting that "in DeLillo's fiction, locating the ideas and organizing principles is always easier than finding and engaging with the story. That seems especially true here."[123] Tony Tanner bemoans the non-linear narrative structure, stressing that in many experimental narratives, but not in here, "you usually feel that the scramblings and wretched juxtapositions have some point."[124] For LeClair, the novel, though offering "ease of access," marks a return to that "experimental, breakout vigor" that distinguished DeLillo's earlier, more challenging works.[125] In other words, LeClair can again pursue readings based on extensive research, on re-readings and more re-readings; an archivist's delight, an "archeologist's patience," as he calls it, a brand of enthusiasm that seems akin to that of a Nicholas Branch but beyond that possible or desirable for the average reader: "not all the pieces are equally interesting, but detritus can be put aside for later examination."[126]

The clash of values between De Haven's and LeClair's schools of reading comes to the fore in the novel's final long paragraph, a dazzlingly constructed encomium to the word "peace," which is expectedly lush with significance in the post cold-war world: "a word ever expanding outward, the tone of agreement or treaty, the tone of repose, the sense of mollifying silence, the tone of hail or farewell."[127] Of course, these are just dictionary definitions, and some of them are contradictory; given the damnable surplus of meaning in each and every word, this could be seen as one final resignation to the fact that all attempts to decipher meaning are doomed, especially where 827 page metatexts are concerned. LeClair, though, sees a far grander meaning in the final resounding *Peace:* "the final words of *The Waste Land* are 'Shantih shantih shantih,' the 'Peace that passeth understanding.' The final word of *Underworld* is 'Peace.'"[128] But Eliot is not the best model for moral or social understanding, and with the *Waste Land* reference LeClair is in effect positioning *Underworld* as another worthy addition to our rich literary legacy of obfuscation, esoterica, and mastery. Fittingly, just as readers have struggled for decades to ascribe meaning to Eliot's final lines, here a disgruntled De Haven finds it hard to ascribe any at all to DeLillo's: "the last word in this massive, brilliant but meandering and too-often undramatic 800-plus page novel is *Peace.* I'm pretty sure we're supposed to laugh, that it's meant as a bitter joke."[129]

It is true that DeLillo, far more than Auster, O'Brien, or Johnson, harbors still an aspiration toward the grandness, the grand bafflement offered by Pynchon and Gaddis. For this very reason, though, the fact that his own grandest text stresses something more is highly significant of the movement toward postmodern reconciliation. Klara Sax, in her first appearance in the novel, characterizes her vast desert art project as just that, "an art project, not a peace project."[130] Though he generally gives DeLillo's social warnings their due, LeClair also clearly favors "art projects" to peace projects. Yet with its final lines, with its final, magisterial "peace," *Underworld* rebukes all of Klara's presuppositions.

It is highly significant too that the final paragraph, whatever its stylistic grandeur and Pynchon-like sweep (equal parts abandon and rigorous control), is unremoved from the real. It depicts a scene very familiar from Auster's work:

the writer at his desk, while outside in the world children play, life bustles. In Auster's work, such scenes emphasize the fissure between author and world, characterized with both wistful sadness and self-important gratification. But here the author is us ("and *you* can glance out the window for a moment") and seems an equal part of that world outside: "its your voice you hear, essentially, under the glimmerglass sky." His study—*our* study—does not seem to be an ascetic's sparse retreat—Aaron's crumbling shack, Marco Fogg's apartment, Lyle Wynant's blank hotel room. Instead of being erased from reality through abstract thought, it is flush with detail, with copious realism: "you look at the things in the room, offscreen, unwebbed, the tissued grain of the deskwood alive in light, the thick lived tenor of things, the argument of things to be seen and eaten, the apple going sepia in the lunch tray, and the dense measures of experience in a random glance."[131] In *The Names,* James's voice, the relatively concrete voice, the family voice, the fully developed voice, peters out somewhat as the novel progresses, giving way to Owen's dense, anchorite perception. The movement in *Underworld* is in the opposite direction, regressing into the past, into the world of Nick Shay's youth in its great, shabby detail: living and breathing characters coming and going, stolen cars and pool halls, drugs and childhood pranks, fledgling lusts, families under duress, hard labor, passionate sex, boyhood and manhood. It is Oswald's childhood world revisited, but explicated at greater length, more resistant to the fragmenting focus provided (enforced?) by global media, represented here by that monitor flickering in front of us, offering its putative, expendable miracles. "Peace" in all its variable meanings has resonance not as something ever fully realizable but in the sense of new possibilities, "a word that spreads a longing through the raw sprawl of the city and out across the dreaming bourns and orchards to the solitary hills." A hope for peace is indeed a gesture of solidarity, perhaps the one solidarity that can truly unite our full variety of sufferers, whether dwelling in the "sprawl" of Wolfe's socially diverse cities or in the "solitary" reaches haunted by our most putatively anti-social writers.

Afterword

"Create the Counternarrative": Writings in a New Century

The novels discussed earlier in this study are products of a period in which writers felt the urge to stand outside common perception, uprooting the anxieties, threats, and disheartening political and economic agendas that were arguably ignored by the public and the media (this has always been a fundamental urge for novelists, of course, but rarely so matter-of-factly acknowledged). The opening salvo of the new century has presented much different challenges, however, as millennial apprehensions quickly gave way to questions about the storyteller's role in an age of war, heightened terrorist threat, and a revised assessment of America's role on the global stage. If these novelists have not produced a masterwork in the last few years, a critical and commercial breakthrough on the order of *White Noise, Middle Passage* or *The Things They Carried,* their work has nevertheless continued to evolve in ways that reflect both their ambitions as artists and the troubled realities of our sociopolitical climate.

Those earlier breakthroughs have made it difficult to cling to notions in which poverty and obscurity have an innate value, or even glory. The motif of the starving, neglected artist continues to recur, as incarnated, for example, in self-proclaimed vagabond Willy G. Christmas in Auster's *Timbuktu,* who perishes on the steps of Edgar Allen Poe's Baltimore home, his reams of writing, "poems, stories, essays, diary entries, epigrams, autobiographical musings, and the first eighteen hundred lines of an epic-in-progress"[1] to remain forever unpublished and unread. But writer-figures straining to cope with notoriety and financial security receive increased attention. In *The Book of Illusions,* David Zimmer, an Auster/author surrogate who previously appeared in *Moon Palace,* finds himself bereft of loved ones but flush with money, "a grotesque situation, a sickening excess of wealth."[2] A hilarious segment of O'Brien's otherwise somber *July, July* depicts one Marv Bertel, overweight manufacturer of industrial mops, who sheds his excess pounds and then celebrates by pretending, to any moderately intoxicated woman who will listen, to be an athlete, a surgeon, a convict. The glamorous identity that finally trips him up, however, is that of a writer, the "highly regarded, largely unread, obsessively reclusive"[3] Thomas Pierce, an obvious stand-in for Thomas Pynchon given his "grotesque fictions, freakish and scary, ruled by entropy."[4] When Marv's wife-to-be eventually ferrets out his deception, she insists that he prolong the charade indefinitely. She had never read Pierce before meeting Marv, and neither had her friends or family, but the status of the unreadable novelist is, apparently, too lofty to relinquish lightly.

O'Brien, despite his iconoclastic instincts, is unable to condemn characters like Marla, the affluent housewife who insists that "there was nothing evil about a decent home, a decent income, summer excursions to London or Venice or Nassau."[5] Mr. Bones, the canine companion of Willy Christmas in *Timbuktu,* also comes to the realization that "he had landed in the America of two-car garages, home-improvement loans, and neo-Renaissance shopping malls, and the fact was that he had no objections."[6] But dogs do not need to speak out against their age; how can the comfortable novelist conjure up sufficient fervor? Nothing stifles creativity like contentment, as learned by Hector Mann, filmmaker counterpart to writer Zimmer in *Book of Illusions,* who admits that with happiness comes "a fatal lack of ambition."[7]

But any sense of status and security is haunted at best. Haunted indeed; ghosts have prowled many of the novels in this study, even claiming the title of one chapter of *The New York Trilogy,* but recent works are flush with apparitions from the past and the grave. Ghosts of faded centuries plague the dawn of the new one; recent victims of conspiracy and conflict torment contemporary awareness. In *July, July,* the Class of 1969 seems too tormented by memory to cross the threshold of the 21st century; ghastly plane crashes figure prominently in both that novel and *The Book of Illusions.*

For Charles Johnson, to write *Soulcatcher and Other Stories* was to encounter ghosts not only long dead but long forgotten. The stories, written in conjunction with the six-part PBS documentary *Africans in America,* recreate neglected fragments of the historical record of American slavery, from the seventeenth century through the Civil War. According to Johnson, the daunting accumulation of research uncovered for the creation of the series gave him pause. His first inclination, typical of our authors, was to withdraw into formalism, technique; while unsure what to write about, he was certain of his writerly prerogative: "I dreamed of dramatizing the history covered by the series, of course, but I also wanted to bring a specific technical challenge to every one of the tales, regardless of their content."[8] Indeed, the list of technical challenges he envisioned, and ultimately employs, much resembles the grab bag of genres composing Willy Christmas's unread body of work.

The prospect of writing "message" fiction is even more troublesome than the trial of sifting though a seemingly endless supply of true-life accounts. Johnson is no more comfortable with the "black writer" or "slavery writer" moniker than he was during the writing of previous slave narratives *Oxherding Tale* and *Middle Passage.* In the story "Poetry and Politics," Johnson explores the dilemma that Phyllis Wheatley presents for contemporary readers. Though the first widely recognized African American poet, Wheatley wrote more about religious piety than the injustice of slavery, complicating, for many, the legitimacy of her status in the canon. As imagined by Johnson, she clearly anticipates the conflicted response that her work will later inspire: "Will it not be odd, a hundred years hence, when readers open *Poems on Various Subjects, Religious and Moral* by Phillis Wheatley, and discover that in not a single poem do I address the anguish of bondage, the daily horror that is happening around us"?[9] But she cannot turn her back on her true artistic imperative, her creative mettle: "as soon as I turn my pen to painting a portrait of a slave suffering beneath my lash, I cut myself off from what flows most easily from me—the things I love."[10]

Despite Johnson's many reservations, the *Soulcatcher* stories reflect his continued movement toward realism and straightforwardness, as evident by his presentation of philosophical themes. As is usual in his fiction, characters habitually make reference to philosophical writings, even when such knowledge on their part might seem unlikely, or indeed historically impossible. A reader of "Confession" notes the overt echoes of Plato's *Republic* in the meandering account of slave Tiberius, captured after having been swept up in bloody revolt: "like I'd lived alla my life in a cave, believin' the shadows I seen were real until Jemmy held up a light and they melted away."[11] Yet we can believe that Tiberius would stumble on this trope on his own; Johnson maintains strict realism in his character portraits in a way he did not in the *Sorcerer's Apprentice* stories. The clumsy injection of high philosophy into the mind of Mingo in "The Education of Mingo," discussed in chapter eight, provides a point of comparison.

Although an anthology, *Soulcatcher* has a coherent overarching narrative. Collectively, the stories recreate, or rewrite, the entire tumultuous slavery era from the African American perspective (Johnson obviously draws heavily from the accounts of Frederick Douglas, whose perspective he inhabits in "The Lion at Pendleton"). A central precept of this narrative is its presentation of the Other, that grappling with difference so pronounced in many novels in this study; but while *Middle Passage* rescues the black Other from the white gaze, the *Soulcatcher* stories turn the tables entirely. "The Transmission" submerges us in the consciousness of yet another Allmuseri tribesman, Malawi, terrified and confused in the midst of his own middle passage, certain only that they are "in the hands of white demons taking them to hell where they would be eaten."[12] In "The Plague," Richard Allen, during a 1784 outbreak of yellow fever in Philadelphia, tries to discern the humanity in one of the white victims, a church trustee who had expelled black parishioners: "I believe it was him, but the decomposition of his face made a definite identification difficult."[13] (In both stories, Johnson's play is confined to his titles, in which there is always double meaning; "The Transmission" refers to both middle passage and the transmission of stories, whereas "The Plague" is both yellow fever and the peculiar invention of slavery.) Such vantages, which might seem devoid of compassion, suggest to William R. Nash that African American solidarity has supplanted *human* solidarity as Johnson's overriding agenda.[14] Yet Johnson always asserts the necessity of connection and communication despite boundaries. Malawi's characterization of sailors as white demons clearly recalls terminology used by Malcolm X and the Nation of Islam, but the story's conclusion reaffirms the impossibility and undesirability of separatism. Malwai, who carries with him his tribe's histories, ultimately passes on this legacy not to another prisoner, but to a receptive demon: "Malawi sang and the phantom listened."[15]

Potential fodder for the separatism argument can also be found in "The People Speak," which recounts a momentous meeting of the African Colonization Society in 1817 Philadelphia, a vote by free blacks on whether they should remain in America or return en masse to Africa. One by one, distinguished historical personages take the floor and speak their piece, emphasizing the horrors of the past and the perilous nature of the future, all of them urging re-colonization. Their arguments are convincing, to say the least. As in *Dreamer,* when Chaym Smith, MLK's look-alike and antithesis, rebukes the peaceful fight for equality, Johnson is committed to alternative voices (indeed, *Soulcatcher* is, if nothing else, a collection of contrary arguments and perspectives) even when they dissent from the grand American narrative he envisions. The vote goes down to unanimous defeat, however, and the eloquent speakers, rebuffed, show signs of bafflement: "Whatever our future is to be, you have decided that it will be *here,* on these shores. God help us all . . ."[16] Once again, the prevailing voice is not that of reason but of the Crowd, the unpredictable, uncontrollable masses that our writers cannot help but fear and disdain. Still, Johnson recognizes that theirs is the American voice; writers can proffer any number of narratives of past, present and future, but in the end the assessments rest with others.

The narrative Johnson offers them here is, like so many of the historical constructs we have discussed, highly fictionalized, and Johnson is in no way demure about that fact. Crowd or no Crowd, he is confident that his readers, modern as they are, will offer no objections. A footnote to "The People Speak" states that "fiction often changes the facts for dramatic effect,"[17] and goes on to detail those changes, some of which simply streamline the storytelling (the actual vote was by voice, not paper ballot) while more substantial ones emphasize solidarity and democracy. At the actual meeting, for example, there were no women. Poetic appropriateness supplants historical rectitude; indeed, the process of American mythologizing, whether calculated or unconscious, is a major subtext of *Soulcatcher.* In "Martha's Dilemma," widowed Martha Washington comments sardonically on the deification of her husband, on the new, bolder histories congealing as accurate memory fades, "the well-meaning mythmakers who began enlarging his legend before we could properly bury him in Mount Vernon's family tomb."[18] The most ironic of these lies, of course, is that their subject was himself incapable of lying: "He could lie, oh yes. He was, after all, a *politician.*"[19] (45). Yet Johnson is not interested in uprooting the Washington mythology, though Martha comes across in comically unflattering terms; he concludes his Wheatley tale with a congratulatory letter from the President, signed, significantly, "your servant." To commemorate a new century, Johnson is supplying a revised but positivistic narrative, thoroughly aware of the legacy of past injustice but imbued just the same with American possibility.

Fittingly, it is Thoreau, so often the crucial figure for our novelists, who provides the final word. In keeping with Auster's novels, his true nature remains unknowable; in the concluding story, "Murderous Thoughts," his is the last in a chorus of unidentified voices, though the reader easily recognizes him as "a mystic, a transcendentalist, and a natural philosopher."[20] Thoreau, disgusted that the government would ship an escaped slave back South to his owner, offers a lacerating assessment of a potentially unredeemable nation: "when this stain on our souls has been scrubbed away by Revolution, perhaps men and women of God, blacks and whites, can rebuild America with wood less crooked than that used by the Founders."[21] From our much-removed vantage, we watch him construct his counternarrative, prophesizing the Civil War and speculating as to the latent potential beyond it. In formal terms, Thoreau's statement directly parallels the one with which Johnson concludes his preface, in which he implicitly explains how through *Oxherding Tale, Middle Passage* and now *Soulcatcher* he has been providing a counter-history in which the African American experience has played a significant part in "the on-going adventure of democracy and the creation of the republic in which we presently live."[22]

At first glance, Auster's intent in *Timbuktu* could not seem any more different, any more lacking in Johnson's grand ambition. Critics were taken aback by this largely straightforward dog's tale, and many assumed that Auster's creative impetus, like Johnson's initial engagement with *Soulcatcher,* must have been one of formal experimentation, namely, the stylistic panache necessary to describe the world through the limited capacities of Mr. Bones. Most of these critics ultimately dismissed the novel as child's play, as if the concept of such a story should have been anathema to a writer of Auster's stature, despite his frequent claims that fairy tales and children's narratives have had a profound influence on his fiction. Johnson certainly notes the "adult" potency of children's lit forms, which simultaneously inspire ironic engagement and primal receptivity. He couches "The Mayor's Tale" in the form and voice of a fable, even though his subject is the vital social and economic role that escaped slaves played in the civic operations of northeastern cities even prior to the Civil War.

In much the same terms, Auster is clearly writing for adults. The oft-explored theme of identity flux comes into play within the opening pages of *Timbuktu,* much as it does in *Soulcatcher,* in which Johnson uses our fluidity of self as not only a metaphor for slavery, as in *Oxherding Tale,* but as a way of incorporating women into his narrative (often a stumbling block for him). In "A Solider for the Crown," slaves reinvent themselves when they hear that they can obtain freedom by fighting on the British side in the Revolutionary War: "how sweet this business of renaming oneself felt, and that you wanted to toy with a thousand personalities—each name promising a new nature."[23] At the conclusion of the story, however, Johnson reveals that his speaker is a woman, reinventing her gender along with her name. Yet Mr. Bones is neither man nor woman, and such familiar postmodern identity dilemmas seem more incongruous applied to him than in Johnson's scenario: "it was more than just love or devotion that caused Mr. Bones to dread what was coming. It was pure ontological terror. Subtract Willy from the world, and the odds were that the world itself would cease to exist."[24]

Yet it is this simple love and devotion that is the focus of the novel, not philosophical delving; Johnson's slavery books necessarily explore notions of the Other, but Auster's dog protagonist can break down all barriers: "they might not understand the nuances of their master's thoughts, but they feel what they feel."[25] How better for a postmodern writer to urge solidarity than with a character for whom postmodern doubts necessarily and instinctively factor less than devotion and unbridled affection? For all of Mr. Bones's moments of doubt, and there are many, he remains unfragmented, an ideal: "he was first and foremost the thing he appeared to be."[26] Such is the holy grail of postmodern fiction, the essentially sound word, concept, or being. The *New York Trilogy* exposes the allegorical or otherwise artificial nature of its characters, and by extension our notions of self, but as Christmas tells Mr. Bones, "you're no trope, my boy, you're as real as they come."[27]

Auster has no interest in presenting the world as benign or suggesting that solidarity is easily achieved. Mr. Bones ultimately imitates Nashe's existential statement at the end of *The Music of Chance,* wandering into onrushing traffic to end his life. His statement is not as hopeless as it appears; whereas Nashe's suicidal driving cuts off all possibility of reuniting with his daughter and his lover, Mr. Bones, desperately ill, wants only to reunite with his deceased master, who is waiting, so Mr. Bones believes, in Timbuktu. The world remains a brutal place; Mr. Bones has learned "to assume the worst in people until they had demonstrated their best intentions," which is, as he understands, "a sad lesson to be learning so late in life."[28] But Auster nevertheless presents a straightforward moral, one so forthright in address and seemingly free from irony that critics had no use for the novel, despite (or because of?) strong sales: "Good begets good; evil begets evil; and even if the good you give is met by evil, you have no choice but to go on, giving better than you get."[29]

Mr. Bones appears in *The Book of Illusions.* Drunken David Zimmer, also wallowing in despair, swerves to avoid a dog walking boldly toward his headlights. Still, connections between the two novels are minimal, as *Book of Illusions* has a more complex plotline and is flush with Auster's usual preoccupations, so much so that some readers have wondered whether he is stuck in a holding pattern, "writing the same book again, a book about a lonely man searching for meaning in random events while thinking ambitious thoughts about French literature and Nathaniel Hawthorne."[30] Yet the novel resumes and expands, not reiterates, Auster's ongoing narrative about America's appetite for entertainment. Filmmaking, one of the first media to push the novel toward the margins, now dominates the discussion.

We earlier discussed *Smoke,* Auster's successful entrance into the screen trade (*The Music of Chance* had been previously adapted for film, but Auster was not involved in the Philip Haas project). The popular and well-reviewed independent film immediately established his credibility in the cinematic world, and indeed Auster would later serve on the jury at the Cannes Film Festival. His informed understanding of the challenges of script writing factors into the structure of *Book of Illusions.* If *Timbuktu* poses the challenge of translating the "speech" of a canine lead character, *Illusions* demands the translation of film into literature, instead of the customary reverse: "All the visual information had to be there, the physical details of the action—so that the reader could 'see' what was happening—but at the same time, the prose had to move along at a quick pace, in order to mimic the experience of watching a film, which is rushing by you at 24 frames a second."[31] Auster's inclination is not only to epitomize the experience of film creation and film viewing but to carve out a space, if a theoretical one, in which the novelist can consume and control this process. *Smoke,* along with its improvisational companion piece *Blue in the Face,* mark Auster's only unambiguously successful cinematic forays thus far; later efforts have been significantly more problematic in execution and reception, and it hardly seems an interpretive leap to detect resultant frustrations lurking in *Book of Illusions. Lulu on the Bridge,* Auster's debut as a director in a conventional sense of the title (*Blue in the Face* was more of an experimental, unstructured piece), never received theatrical distribution in the United States, though it appeared later on DVD. Despite less than promising reception to the film at Cannes and other festivals, Auster attributes the plight of *Lulu* not to art but to the business of show business: "It was a complicated business screwup. But there was nothing I could do about it."[32] Accordingly, *Book of Illusions* exposes "the business of Hollywood in all its worm-eaten glory."[33] Auster's experiences as a screenwriter of *The Center of the World* likely compounded such feelings of powerlessness. Auster, along with his wife Siri Hustvedt, wrote the initial script for this examination of sex and commerce for his *Smoke* collaborator Wayne Wang. Wang's interpretation and reshaping of their efforts deeply displeased Auster, however, and he attempted to have his name removed from the credits: "It's really not our work. These things happen in movies all the time."[34] If Auster seems more resigned than resentful here, his declaration that he will never work again with Wang suggests a deeper dissatisfaction with both the process and economic imperatives of filmmaking.

Book of Illusions re-ignites Auster's narrative history of entertainment in the midst of the period central to *Mr. Vertigo,* in which stage shows and vaudeville acts yielded to cinema. Zimmer, who has lost his wife and children in a plane crash, finds solace in the silent films of (fictional) comedian Hector Mann. For many film aficionados, the end of the silent era is a break to be looked upon with mournful nostalgia, when, as Zimmer explains, the presentation of films became an isolated, self-enclosed spectacle, devoid of live accompaniment and accessory performing arts: "The movies talked now, and the flickering dumb shows of the past were forgotten. No more clowns, no more pantomimists, no more pretty flapper girls dancing to the beat of unheard orchestras."[35] Concomitant with the loss of the stage show atmosphere come decisive changes in the medium itself. For Zimmer, there had once been a magic to the movies independent of its ability to capture reality, despite that myth of total cinema so fundamental to film theorists such as Andre Bazin. Each new innovation—and certainly film's ever-shifting form, its technological basis and determinacy, serves as a counterpoint to the novelist's chosen medium—adds to the sensation of loss even as the notion of movies *as* "sensation" grows more pronounced: "the paradox was that the closer movies came to simulating reality, the worse they failed at representing the world—which is in us as much as around us."[36] This cinematic shortcoming provides refuge and opportunity for the writer (Zimmer is certainly linked here with Auster; one always hesitates to read too much into the parallels between author and narrator, but Zimmer's work, like Auster's, includes translations from French, numerous reviews and "a book about writers who had given up on writing, a meditation on silence"). The skilled writer can make a near-divine link which escapes most cinema; Auster has claimed that "the reason why writing is never going to die out, in spite of all the dire predictions that are made about fiction" is the nature of the form itself, in which "two absolute strangers can meet on the deepest level." Unprompted, he adds: "You don't feel that in a movie."[37]

The purity of this meeting between individuals is, of course, threatened when it takes on the tone of a financial transaction. Auster depicts the harsh economic realities of which he has first-hand experience. Hector's final films, his last creative gasps before the intrusion of sound, are complicated by the extravagancies and incompetence of his producer, who "borrowed from his distributors against future box-office revenues, and when he reneged on several of these deals theatres began to refuse to show his films."[38] Like Auster with *Lulu on the Bridge,* Hector believes that he "was doing his best work at this point, but the sad fact was that fewer and fewer people were able to see it." Hector's fade from public awareness receives little media attention except stories about "business practices and the rise of the criminal element in the motion picture industry."[39]

The move-going audience has also been complicit in the degradation of their preferred medium. The logical extension of Hollywood's callous commercialism and stupefying simulation is pornography, as Hector comes to understand when, on the run from a murder in which he bears some responsibility, he takes on a "career" performing in live sex shows. Though the show is of course real, it is very much in line with the new market for "stag films, blue movies,"[40] and the unsavory lust of the populace is the motivating force behind both: "there was good money to be made from daring to show people what they wanted."[41] Understandable, then, that the overriding temptation for the committed artist is to create art sans audience. Like so many other artist figures we have discussed, Hector hides himself away; in the confines of his secluded New Mexico ranch, he is a true auteur, fashioning "movies for the pure pleasure of making movies," a gesture that is "an act of breathtaking nihilism."[42] The appeal of this approach is obvious, but it denies that essential link between individuals, between author and audience, that Auster has celebrated. Unlike Willy Christmas, who fights for the publication of his writings until his dying breath, Hector makes an inexcusable choice when he mandates the destruction of his films in his will.

DeLillo has supplied his share of comparably nihilistic artists, and in "The Body Artist" he gives us Rey Robles, a filmmaker who, while not embracing such a pronounced retreat as Mann's, certainly imposes an avant-garde mentality on his commercial productions. Certainly we recognize a kindred spirit to Mann in the creator of "*Polaris,* a tense American drama with an undercurrent of Spanish surrealism," whose calling card is the depiction of "people in landscapes of estrangement."[43] Perhaps the inevitable compromises of making such films within the studio system, without flight to New Mexico, without unfettered auteurism, ultimately contribute to his suicide. Once again, ghosts stand as representatives of (from?) this landscape of estrangement. In *Book of Illusions,* Auster parallels the cinematic echoes of Mann and his fellow film actors, speaking "more deeply to us now than they had to audiences of their time" simply "because they were dead,"[44] with Zimmer's more personal memories of his lost family, which are always with him in his movie-going research. In *The Body Artist,* Lauren Hartke, the performer of the title, is not only haunted by the suicide of her husband Robles, but also by one Mr. Tuttle, an unidentified intruder in her home who possesses an uncanny, unexplained remembrance of her husband's words and actions. As Lauren gradually comes to understand, he even "remembers the future,"[45] muttering nonsense that she later recognizes when it emerges in their conversations. Although Tuttle's fragmentary nature has a decidedly postmodern edge—"she thought maybe he lived in a kind of time that had no narrative quality"[46]—his omniscience over time recalls that of any variety of novelist, as Cowart explains: "the literary artist can do these things as well—and in narrative that need not proceed in a linear fashion."[47] When Tuttle vanishes as mysteriously as he appeared, Hartke can return to her work, the most debilitating aspect of her grief now filtered into her art. This scenario duplicates exactly the plotline of *The Inner Life of Martin Frost,* the only of Hector Mann's lost final films that Zimmer is able to view before its destruction. The film depicts a mysterious woman who appears to a novelist suffering from writer's block.

Having sparked his creativity, she vanishes, literally, as he completes his last page; she is, like Tuttle, "a spirit, a figure born of the man's imagination, an ephemeral being sent to become his muse."[48] Mann's film parallels Zimmer's reality; he finds a cure to his guilt and loss in the unsubtly named Alma, who appears out of nowhere to force him, at gunpoint, to travel to Mann's ranch in the unsubtly named town of Tierra del Sueno. After Alma's love leads Zimmer to renew his writing and his life, including his first undrugged plane trip since his family's death, she commits suicide, leaving him again in grief but with a newfound ability to adapt and change, one rooted in a more flexible understanding of time: "the gods had decided that I wouldn't be allowed to have a future until I returned to the past."[49]

The process of grappling with memory and conceptualizing the future is fraught with an uncertainty that permeates even the most domestic moments between Lauren and Ray in *The Body Artist,* in which "everything is slow and hazy and drained and it all happens around the word *seem*"[50] and the most loving ones between Zimmer and Alma in *Book of Illusions,* learning from Mann's films "not to trust in the surface of things, to doubt the evidence of our own eyes."[51] We are accustomed by now to the semiotic tone of these dilemmas, but in both cases we never sense that theoretical structures outstrip emotional content. Indeed, Auster has taken pains to emphasize that we should recognize Zimmer's anxiety and trauma as his primary interest, that what sets his new novel apart from his past efforts is "the mournful, grief-stricken tone of the narration."[52] The same claim could be made of *The Body Artist,* somewhat uniquely among DeLillo's canon.

O'Brien's *July, July* is also about coming to terms with ghosts and memory. Heberle has convincingly described O'Brien as a novelist of trauma, not specifically Vietnam,[53] and *July, July* supports the claim; this is the most haunted of our books. Darton Hall College, the reunion site of a profoundly traumatized class of '69, has "a forlorn, haunted feel to it, many memories, many ghosts, which seemed appropriate."[54] Appropriate not only because a murder has recently stripped them of one of their classmates, but because loss and death have been the defining characteristics of their age. As in *The Body Artist* and *Book of Illusions,* their timeline is skewed. Johnny Ever, a sardonic voice first overhead on the radio during a grisly debacle at the Song Tra Ky, becomes a Tuttle-like omniscient apparition for severely-wounded, morphine-groggy David Todd: "Ten, twenty years down the pike, here comes the survivor guilt. Ghosts galore."[55] The voice persists until the present day, prophesizing the future and refusing to release the past, always in the process a fitting representative of contemporary consciousness: "Irony? Invented it."[56]

It is not only the veteran whose perception of time and fate becomes confused; his classmates, the women especially, have similar experiences. O'Brien's previous novel, *Tomcat in Love,* suffered the usual assault from critics affronted by his depiction of female characters. Heberle attempts to rationalize the novel as a representation of Clinton America, and a revisionist one at that, in which "misadventures with variously foul-mouthed, previously abused, sexually provocative, and/or shrewdly manipulative predatory females reverse the normal myths of male control and conquest."[57] In *July, July,* O'Brien for once equates his men and women; if amputee David carries with him the anguished legacy of war, Dorothy Stier carries with her the ongoing anguish of breast cancer. She even has her own Johnny Ever, her own Tuttle, in neighbor Freddie Engelmann, a CIA operative who knows everything about her past and her future: "Eight nodes, that's a killer. Some gals make it. Not you, I'm afraid. I'll give it five years. Five years, two months, handful of days."[58]

O'Brien has not entirely put his discomfort with female characters behind him; we witness the story of the novel's most sympathetic female lead, the ex-minister Paulette, only through the awareness of the decidedly unsympathetic Janice, who suspects Paulette of seducing her husband and condemns her outright for removing God from her sermons. But even Janice is haunted: "Rudy had become more of a ghost than a husband, rarely uttering a complete sentence for days at a time."[59] The Evers in the book, and each significant character has one, remind us always of wider historical traumas in addition to personal ones. Through Ever, David experiences decades of horror, only the final of which recalls his own wartime nightmare: "he scrubbed the ovens at Dachau, rode point at Washita, sat in on LBJ's war briefing, attended a mediocre comedy at Ford's Theatre, and listened to the insane blather of Hector Ortiz's transistor radio."[60]

Some commentators on the novel have derided O'Brien's postmodern litany of dates and names, but in comparison to the fond millennial recollections and "best of" lists that marked the end of the nineties, there is a more barbed edge to his agenda than a superficial awareness of historical touchstones. So it is also with Auster, who positions Zimmer's pain as a counterpoint to a period of alternating media celebration and sensationalism (thanks to apocalyptic Y2K conjecture): "I note with a certain grim satisfaction that we are also closing in on the last weeks of the century—Hector's century, the century that began eighteen days before he was born and which no one in his right mind will be sorry to see end."[61]

Both books not only look back to the changing of the millennium but reflect the doleful post 9–11 reality that supplanted it. Inveterate New Yorker Auster was one of the first wave of fiction writers to play a public role in addressing the emotional and sociopolitical repercussions of the incident. In addition to his participation in National Public Radio programs, he contributed a short story to the anthology *110 Stories: New York Writes after September 11,* entitled "Random Notes—September 11, 2001, 4:00 PM; Underground." The story provides a final answer, in a way, to the scenario of the self-willed isolationist that has run through so many of these books. In chapter three, we pinpointed Wolfe's subway rider, disdaining her fellow travelers and their unchallenging choice of reading material, as a fitting stand-in for modern authors dedicated to high art. But in the "Underground" section of his story, Auster shows that such distinctions no longer exist for him in the new New York. Riding on a subway, he does indeed assess the state of the literary audience: "Counting the newspapers not written in English, scanning the titles of books and watching people read (the mystery of it, the impossibility of entering another person's mind)."[62] The assortment of reading material, surely a mixed bag for the ambitious novelist, includes "trashy novels, comic books, Melville and Tolstoy, *How to Attain Inner Peace.*"[63] But his tone toward his "fellow New Yorkers" is unequivocally benign, and the uncertainty of "entering another person's mind" is a source of wonder, not fear; the Joycean mindset has won out: "floored by the singularity of each person's nose, each person's chin, exulting in the infinite shufflings of the human deck."

But "Random Notes" is an appropriate title to this very brief story, which is hardly intended to serve as a comprehensive statement on September 11th. In fact, Auster has stated that the great literature on this period of history might be a long time in coming. In a NPR interview, he and friend Salman Rushdie observe that *The Red Badge of Courage* came some years after the conflict it depicts; *War and Peace* decades. [64] Yet, Auster also speaks of approaching the residue of the incident "obliquely" in fiction, and in those terms it is difficult not to sense echoes in *Book of Illusions,* in Zimmer's loss, in the ghostly apparitions, in the theme of love's capacity to overcome grief: "A plane falls from the sky, and all the passengers are killed. A woman falls in love, and a man falls with her, and not for an instant as the plane goes down does either of them think about death."[65] Auster has claimed that the book was finished three weeks before 9/11,[66] but his apparent prescience puts a reader in a difficult interpretive position, though not an unusual one for readers of Auster or DeLillo. Ryan Simmons, for example, struggles to explain his arguments linking DeLillo's *Mao II* and the Unabomber, given that our awareness of the latter came only after publication of the former: "I do not mean to suggest that DeLillo literally predicted the future when writing *Mao II* . . . DeLillo was deeply engaged with currents of thought and actions that (in many cases) only became fully exposed when the Unabomber became associated with a face and a name."[67] Perhaps Auster didn't forecast 9/11, but in *Book of Illusions* he certainly sets down his pattern of dealing with grief. In the NPR interview, Auster describes the importance of laughter in the world after 9/11 and his turning to vintage Hollywood comedies for solace; to *Sullivan's Travels,* not to Hector Mann, but the parallel with Zimmer is uncannily clear. There is no such ambiguity when dealing with *July, July,* for O'Brien speaks openly of the impact of terrorist attack on his novel's promulgation of ghosts: "September 11 made me want more Johnny. . . . The voice became more cynical and hard, because that's how I felt after 9/11."[68]

Thus O'Brien's usual discussions about the importance of narrative-writing, to life as much as art, take on a new tone. His phrasing is often identical to his earlier novels; for David Todd, as for John Wade of *In the Lake of the Woods,* the greatest potential failure is a "failure of nerve, which was also a failure of imagination, the inability to divine a happy ending."[69] The novel's characters represent a spectrum of narrative potential. David and Dorothy, too jaded to trust to happy endings, can only hope to eke out a hardened existence, a tough-fought survival. Conversely, only those who trust that they can create a new narrative, re-writing their lives, have a chance for future happiness. Paulette the progressive minister and Billy McMann the draft-dodger, whose defining decisions represent a synthesis of political and personal activism, find a future together. But what of those who forestall the possibility of happy endings, who see no potential reality in "the essential renewing fantasy of splendid things to come"[70]? Although Marv and aging man-magnet Spook Spinelli carry out a whimsical facade of romance while sitting together on the flight home, they openly note that their dalliance is fantasy, not possibility; they perish together, we assume, in the fiery conflagration that ends the novel, "the bleak flaming grasslands"[71] that mark their crash.

DeLillo's "In the Ruins of the Future" discusses the role and responsibilities of storytellers in the post-9/11 era. Rorty's responses to the tragedy have seemed to shy away from his core theories, as if he felt that his own embrace of contingency would seem irrelevant or perhaps irreverent in public debate. The nature of the terrorist threat, the nature of the terrorist himself, which we cannot quite grasp—"we do not really have any pigeonholes in which he fits, nor any sense of what institutions and practices will be required to cope with him"—seem to necessitate a straightforward, pragmatic, unironic address to his readership. While the title of his 2002 opinion piece "Fighting Terrorism with Democracy" suggests an efficacious use for narrative creation in a fragile environment, the article itself, largely a condemnation of Bush administration policies on homeland security and military aggression overseas, mourns the lack of viable political narratives without suggesting alternatives: "Democratic politicians can hardly tell the public the truth: that they are as baffled as Republicans to insure that no other American cities will be attacked."[72] DeLillo, on the other hand, addresses the newfound narrative void in prototypically Rortyian ways. As Bill Gray in *Mao II* always feared, the terrorists have written a paradigm-changing narrative: "Terror's response is a narrative that has been developing over years, only now becoming inescapable. It is our lives and minds that are occupied now."[73] DeLillo, like Rorty, frets over possible compromises to the noble nature of our democracy, "OUR tradition of free expression and our justice system's provisions for the rights of the accused," yet he recognizes the possibility of constructing narratives rooted in such nobilities, even if the Bush administration, previously left high and dry at the end of the period encapsulated in *Underworld,* "feeling a nostalgia for the Cold War," may not be the agency best suited for their creation. He puts the matter bluntly: "The narrative ends in the rubble and it is up to us to create the counternarrative."

"In the Ruins of the Future" begins to do just that. DeLillo notes that personal narratives about September 11th, "stories about heroism and encounters with dread," have proliferated quickly, finding easy access to the media. The need they fill is obvious, for they "take us beyond the hard numbers of dead and missing and give us a glimpse of elevated being." Auster supplies some himself; in "Random Notes," he tells of his daughter's first solitary subway ride on that fateful day, and of his view of the collapse from the top floor of his house. He relates first-hand accounts from his barber, his sister-in-law. "Ruins" also provides a series of narratives, some relayed in first-person, but unlike in Auster's piece the reader is uncertain of the truth of any of them. Are they facts or figments? As with Johnson in "The People Speak," DeLillo is confident that his readership is open to creative license even in the address of momentous historical happenings. Marco Abel sees in these accounts a highly cinematic attempt to counter our "seeing" of the attack footage as televised repeatedly in all media outlets.[74] Such a stance can be seen to rescue the attack from the manipulation of politicians and spin doctors; DeLillo sees something more transformative in these accounts, though, in both the heroism and the dread, even if both are fictional parts of "a shadow history of false memories and imagined loss." Most essential to this program are those accounts that suggest a potential rebirth of solidarity, "hands and spirits joining, human beauty in the crush of meshed steel."

In light of "Ruins," *Cosmopolis,* DeLillo's latest novel, presents an interpretive quandary. This day-in-the-life of Eric Packer, billionaire business guru, seems a throwback to early DeLillo novels in its playfulness, disengagement from realism, and nihilistic flavor. It recalls early Auster novels as well, and its dedication to Auster is fitting in that Packer embodies his well-established artistic interests: "he liked spare poems sited minutely in white space, ranks of alphabetic strokes burnt into paper."[75] Once again, we question the barriers to readership that such poetry represents, and we wonder if *Cosmopolis* is meant to baffle us much like those revered paintings in Packer's collection that "his guests did not know how to look at."[76] Correspondingly, much of the initial critical response to the novel recalls the naysaying of DeLillo's early texts. Indeed, Updike, our representative modern realist, objects to the "lobotomized quality of the novel's dialogue," [77] and frets over the glibly artificial scenes in which Packer discusses social conditions with his "theory advisor, " conducts business dealings while having his colon examined, or kills, for no readily apparent reason, his bodyguard Torval. Updike notes that DeLillo, in his best writing, is not at all like Auster, who keeps on a "fantastic plane undeviatingly" and he regrets that *Cosmopolis* largely resists DeLillo's natural instinct to "drop us down into the quotidian mundane, where we can be wounded." The novel offers more theory than cogent info, even regarding the economic and social confusion in which Packer thrives; Updike advises us that "for what it's like to be a young Master of the Universe, read Tom Wolfe instead." (This is a somewhat striking suggestion, given Updike's many well-publicized, derisory comments about Wolfe's literary agenda and execution).

But if *Cosmopolis* seems an archaic DeLillo narrative, that is by design. The novel embodies, for a post-9/11 world, the narrative that suggested the terrorist counternarrative. In "Ruins," DeLillo characterizes our altered mindset: "the new Palm Pilot at a fingertip's reach, the stretch limousine parked outside the hotel, the midtown skyscraper under construction, carrying the name of a major investment bank—all haunted in a way by what has happened, less assured in their authority, in the prerogatives they offer."[78] *Cosmopolis* is a novel rooted in electronic connectivity, skyscrapers, investment banks, and especially stretch limos such as the one in which Packer spends his last day. Indeed, Packer surmises that this "global era" will "officially end" when "stretch limousines begin to disappear from the streets of Manhattan."[79] The stretch limos have not disappeared, but their significance has changed; writing in a new global era, DeLillo tells us that we are haunted, and the ghosts are indeed everywhere in *Cosmopolis,* even if Packer is not cognizant of them. They are in his building, "the tallest residential tower in the world, a commonplace oblong whose only statement was its size,"[80] and in the bank buildings, "made to be the last tall things made empty, designed to hasten the future."[81] They are present, too, in the specter of capitalism, the specter "haunting the world,"[82] at least in the eyes of the protestors who envelop Packer's limo in the novel's most potent depiction of contemporary chaos.

Our vantage on such action, and on the novel in total, is strangely bifurcated, rooted as we are in both the present of the novel and our post-9/11 present. This time-spanning status is incorporated into the plot. Packer's job, at least as much as we can understand it, is to indulge in prophesy, "to believe that there are foreseeable trends and forces, when in fact it's all random phenomena."[83] But ultimately it is in his security cameras that he sees the future, namely his death, the end of his narrative on both a personal and historical level: "Why am I seeing things that haven't happened yet"[84]? Just as Auster's Zimmer seems preternaturally aware of impending disaster—"when I saw that look in her eyes, I knew that she was carrying a gun in her purse, and I knew that within three or four seconds she was going to stick her right hand into her purse and pull out her gun"[85]—Packer transcends time, often in explicitly cinematic terms. The moment of his murder, and even what happens beyond, unwinds onscreen, on his newfangled watch: "He knew, he sensed the zoom shot that would follow. He thought of covering his watch but did not. He saw the tag in tight close-up now and read the legend printed there. Male Z."[86] Even as trauma unwinds in the present, and off-screen, filmic awareness remains; standing outside the hovel of his murderer-to-be, his bodyguard's gun in hand, Packer reflects on childhood movie-going: "I saw two hundred situations where a man stands outside a locked room with a gun in his hand."[87] In *The Body Artist,* Lauren is also aware of Hollywood's poor presentation of reality: "real people don't look at ringing phones."[88] But here, as in *Book of Illusions,* as in the slavery-era testimonials in *Soulcatcher* "delivered to an off-camera reporter,"[89] as in the cinematic "editing" in the closing chapter of *July, July,* cinematic time and cinematic reality may have won out. Even the crowd scenes so fundamental to DeLillo are camera-bound, staged rather than recorded. Packer serves as an extra in an unidentified film in which a crowd lies naked in the street, presumably representing victims of some grisly tragedy. He later attempts to compensate for the overpowering nature of the experience, "so total and open he could barely think outside it,"[90] by having ferocious sex with Elise Shifron, his wife, another extra, "the two lovers, in isolation, free of memory and time."[91] We can hardly tell whether this instinct and act have any impact on Packer, but they are clearly crucial to the post-9/11 narrative that will succeed him, in which the omnipotent camera finally falls short. Critics such as Jeremy Green have discussed the role of publicized tragedy in DeLillo's work: "exposure to these brutal images on the airwaves forges a palpable link between the faceless loner's violent action and the faceless crowd's spectacular consumption of such actions, such violence."[92] No matter how many times the Towers fall on camera, however, DeLillo insists that, for once, "the event dominated the medium."[93]

"Ruins" suggests that, for now, the narrative of the terrorist has won out. *Cosmopolis* presents the self-named Benno Levin, Packer's eventual killer, and DeLillo takes pains to isolate him from any accustomed analysis of writer/reader relations: "I did not read for pleasure, even as a child."[94] Throughout the novel, DeLillo suggests that terrorist actions shuck off theoretical recapitulation. In the midst of the protestor's march, Packer witnesses a self-immolation, an act that successfully defies both interpretation and capitalism. The market "could not claim this man or assimilate his act. Not such starkness and horror."[95] Of course, this is not technically an incident of terrorism; in "Ruins," DeLillo claims that public protests against capitalism, despite occasional violence, are well-intentioned efforts to "slow things down, even things out, hold off the white-hot future." Terrorists, on the other hand, "want to bring back the past."[96] He has given us both varieties of protest in *Cosmopolis,* in the Manhattan throng and in resentful Levin, a former Packer employee who blocks all efforts at categorization. Packer tries to understand how Levin fits into the world he knows: "Violence is meant to be real, based on real motives, on forces in the world that what. That make us want to defend ourselves or take action. The crime you want to commit is cheap imitation."[97] Packer is notably interpreting Levin in postmodern terms, but is coming up empty. As "Ruins" tells us, "There is no logic in apocalypse. They have gone beyond the bounds of passionate payback."[98]

Who does Levin (apparently) murder? He murders a man representative of cold war paranoia and warmongering, who "wanted to be buried with his nuclear bomber, his blackjack A."[99] He murders a man incapable of seeing beyond difference; Packer doesn't know his wife's eye color, repeatedly cheats on her, and dismisses her poetry as "shit." Levin, "without irony,"[100] kills a man defined by it: "the self-totality. The lack of remorse. These are your gifts."[101] *Cosmopolis* is itself an act of self-immolation, a defining expression of Rortyian self-criticism. It clears a space for narratives that re-assert the democratic agenda; again from "Ruins": "With the end of communism, the ideas and principles of modern democracy were seen clearly to prevail; whatever the inequalities of the system itself. That is still the case."[102] In this DeLillo sounds much like Johnson's Thoreau, whose mourning for the present suggests architecture for the future: "Now please excuse me. I must return to my room for a time to write down all the details I can remember of this monstrous day. One of the most important things we can do, young man, is never forget . . ."[103]

Notes

NOTES TO CHAPTER ONE

1. Richard Rorty, *Contingency, Irony, and Solidarity* (1989; New York: Cambridge UP, 1993), 37.
2. Ibid., 22.
3. Ibid., xv.
4. Richard Rorty, *Philosophy and Social Hope.* (New York: Penguin, 1999) 262.
5. Alan Wilde, *Middle Grounds: Studies in Contemporary American Fiction* (Philadelphia: U of Pennsylvania P, 1987) 4.
6. Ibid., 162.
7. Thomas Berger, *Who Is Teddy Villanova?* (1977; New York: Dell, 1978) 165.
8. Wilde, *Middle Grounds,* 165.
9. Tim O'Brien, *If I Die In A Combat Zone, Box Me Up And Ship Me Home* (New York: Delacorte, 1973; New York: Dell, 1987) 96. Citations are to the Dell edition.
10. Hans Robert Jauss, *Toward an Aesthetic of Reception,* trans. Timothy Bahti (Minneapolis, U of Minnesota P, 1989) 25.
11. Paul Auster, *Leviathan* (New York: Viking Penguin, 1992; New York: Penguin, 1993) 75. Citations are to the Penguin edition.
12. Don DeLillo, *Mao II* (New York: Viking Penguin, 1991; New York: Penguin, 1992) 141. Citations are to the Penguin edition.
13. Sigmund Freud, *Group Psychology and the Analysis of the Ego,* Trans. James Strachey (1922; New York: Norton, 1989) 88.
14. John Gardner, *On Moral Fiction* (New York: Basic, 1978) 36.
15. E.M. Forster, *Aspects of the Novel* (1927; London: Arnold, 1963) 27.
16. Joseph Campbell, "Mythological Themes in Creative Literature and Art," Myth, Dreams, and Religion (New York: Dutton, 1970) 162.
17. John Barth, "The Literature of Replenishment: Postmodernism and the Rebirth of the Novel," The Atlantic June 1980: 70.
18. Ian Watt, *The Rise of the Novel: Studies in DeFoe, Richardson, and Fielding* (1957; Berkeley: U of California P, 1974) 32.

19. Tzvetan Todorov, "Reading as Construction," The Reader in the Text: Essays on Audience and Interpretation, ed. Susan Suleiman and Inge Crosman (New Jersey, Princeton UP, 1980) 68.
20. Rorty, *Contingency,* 5.
21. Brian McHale, *Postmodernist Fiction* (New York: Methuen, 1987) 27.
22. Ihab Hassan, "The New Gnosticism: Speculations on an Aspect of the Postmodern Mind," Paracriticisms: Seven Speculations of the Times (Urbana: U of Illinois P, 1975) 141.
23. William S. Burroughs, *Naked Lunch* (1959; New York: Grove Weidenfeld, 1990) 74.
24. Frank Kermode, *The Sense of an Ending: Studies in the Theory of Fiction* (London: Oxford UP, 1967) 4.
25. Ibid., 117.
26. Susan Sontag, "Against Interpretation," Against Interpretation and Other Essays (1961; New York: Dell, 1966) 43.
27. Philip Stevick, *Alternative Pleasures: Postrealist Fiction and the Tradition* (Urbana: Uof Illinois P, 1980) 40.
28. Sontag, "Against Interpretation, 10.
29. Richard Rorty, "Philosophy & the Future," *Rorty and Pragmatism: a Philosopher Responds to his Critics,* ed. Herman J. Saatkamp Jr. (Nashville: Vanderbilt UP, 1995) 198-199.
30. Fredric Jameson, *Postmodernism: or, The Cultural Logic Of Late Capitalism* (Durham: Duke UP, 1993) 369.
31. Rorty, *Contingency,* 87.
32. David L. Hall, *Richard Rorty: Prophet and Poet of the New Pragmatism* (Albany: State U of New York P, 1994) 155.
33. Charles Hartshorne, "Rorty's Pragmatism and Farewell to the Age of Faith & Enlightenment," Rorty and Pragmatism 20.
34. Saul Bellow, *Seize the Day* (1956; New York: Crest, 1965) 21.
35. Josephine Hendin, *Vulnerable People: A View of American Fiction Since 1945* (New York: Oxford UP, 1978) 13.
36. Philip Roth, *Operation Shylock: A Confession* (1993; New York: Vintage, 1994) 215.
37. Peter J. Rabinowitz, "What's Hecuba to Us? The Audience's Experience of Literary Borrowing," *The Reader in the Text,* 245.

NOTES TO CHAPTER TWO

1. Brook Thomas, *American Literary Realism and the Failed Promise of Contract* (Berkeley: U of California P, 1997) 138.
2. Lee Lemon, "John Barth and the Common Reader," *Review of Contemporary Fiction* 10-2 (1990): 42.
3. Ibid., 47.

27. Charles Johnson, *Oxherding Tale* (Bloomington: Indiana UP, 1982; New York: Plume, 1995) 87. Citations are to the Plume edition.
28. DeLillo, *Players,* 205.
29. Henry Miller, *Tropic of Cancer* (New York: Grove, 1961) 60.
30. Charles Johnson, *The Sorcerer's Apprentice: Tales and Conjurations* (New York: Atheneum, 1986; New York: Plume, 1986) 118. Citations are to the Plume edition.
31. Rorty, *Rorty and Pragmatism,* 15.

NOTES TO CHAPTER FOUR

1. Ihab Hasan, "Culture, Indeterminacy, and Immanence," *The Postmodern Turn: Essays In Postmodern Theory And Culture* (Ohio: Ohio State UP, 1987) 83.
2. Harold Bloom, *The Western Canon: The Books and Schools of the Ages* (New York: Harcourt, 1994) 30.
3. Arthur M. Saltzman, *Designs of Darkness in Contemporary American Fiction* (Philadelphia: U of Pennsylvania P, 1990) 115.
4. William Gass, *Fiction and the Figures of Life* (New York: Knopf, 1970) 183,
5. Rorty, Contingency, 91.
6. Jean Bethke Elshtain, "Don't Be Cruel: Reflections on Rortyian Liberalism," *The Politics of Irony: Essays of Self-Betrayal,* ed. Daniel W. Conway and John E. Seery (New York: St. Martin's, 1992) 211.
7. Richard Rorty, "Robustness: A Reply to Jean Bethke Elshtain," *The Politics of Irony* (see note 6) 219-223.
8. Elshtain, "Don't Be Cruel," 202.
9. Stanley Fish, Is *There a Text in This Class? The Authority of Interpretive Communities* (Cambridge, Harvard UP, 1980) 319.
10. Kay Haugaard, "Suspending Moral Judgment: Students Who Refuse To Condemn The Unthinkable-A Result Of Too Much Tolerance?" *The Chronicle Of Higher Education 27 June* (1997): B5.
11. Don DeLillo, *White Noise* (New York: Viking Penguin, 1985; New York:Vintage, 1985) 200. Citations are to the Vintage edition.
12. Joseph Oran Aimone, L. Ross Chambers, et al., "Teaching Literature In The Academy Today: A Roundtable," *PMLA* 112 (1997):104.
13. Don DeLillo, *Americana* (Boston: Houghton Mifflin, 1971; New York: Penguin, 1989) 364-365. Citations are to the Penguin edition.
14. Farrel, *Subjectivity, Realism and Postmodernism,* 2.
15. Irving Howe, *Politics and the Novel* (1957; New York: Columbia UP, 1992) 36.
16. Rorty, *Contingency,* 172.
17. Milan Kundera, *The Art of the Novel* (New York: Grove, 1986): 12.
18. Rorty, *Contingency,* 173.
19. Ibid.,165.

20. Ibid., 192.
21. Terrence Rafferty, "Book Review: Vineland," *The New Yorker 19 February* (1991): 108.
22. Richard Rorty, *Achieving Our Country: Leftist Thought in Twentieth-Century America* (Cambridge: Harvard University Press, 1997) 6.
23. Thomas Pynchon, *Mason & Dixon.* (New York: Holt, 1997) 698.
24. Ibid., 699.
25. T. Coraghessan Boyle, "Review: Mason & Dixon." *New York Times Book Review* 18 March 1997.
26. Pynchon, *Mason & Dixon.* 752.
27. Tim O'Brien, *The Things They Carried* (Houghton Mifflin/Seymour Lawrence, 1990; New York: Penguin, 1991) 260. Citations are to the Penguin edition.

NOTES TO CHAPTER FIVE

1. John LeClair, *In the Loop: Don DeLillo and the Systems Novel* (Urbana: U of Illinois P, 1987) 33.
2. Ibid., 18.
3. Keesey, *Don DeLillo,* 14.
4. DeLillo, *Americana,* 199.
5. Ibid.,137.
6. Ibid.,16.
7. Ibid.,22.
8. Ibid., 60.
9. Ibid.,91.
10. LeClair, *In the Loop,* 10.
11. DeLillo, *Americana,* 28.
12. Burroughs, *Naked Lunch,* v.
13. Thomas Pynchon, *The Crying of Lot 49* (New York: Harper, 1966) 24.
14. DeLillo, *Americana,* 36.
15. Ibid.,176.
16. Interview. "An Outsider in this Society: An Interview with Don DeLillo." Ed. Anthony DeCurtis, Introducing Don DeLillo, ed. Frank Lentrecchia (Durham: Duke UP, 1991) 59.
17. DeLillo, *Americana,* 33.
18. Saul Bellow, *The Adventures of Augie March* (Greenwich: Fawcett. 1953).
19. DeLillo, *Americana,* 51.
20. Ibid., 311.
21. Rorty, *Contingency,* 157.
22. DeLillo, *Americana,* 315.
23. Ibid., 33.
24. Ibid., 30.
25. Ibid., 341.
26. Ibid., 348.

27. Ibid., 129.
28. Ibid., 289.
29. Ibid., 118.
30. Ibid., 120.
31. Ibid., 322-331.
32. Don DeLillo, *End Zone* (Boston: Houghton Mifflin, 1972; New York: Penguin, 1986) 112. Citations are to the Penguin edition.
33. DeLillo, *End Zone,* 111-112.
34. LeClair, *In the Loop,* 59.
35. Bruce Bawer, *Diminishing Fictions: Essays on the American Novel and its Critics* (St. Paul, Graywolf, 1988) 253.
36. Ibid., 253.
37. DeCurtis, "An Outsider in This Society," 61.
38. DeLillo, *End Zone,* 206.
39. Ibid., 57.
40. Gass, *Fiction and the Figures of Life,* 35.
41. Ibid., 36.
42. "An Interview with Don DeLillo," *Anything Can Happen,* 81.
43. Delillo, *End Zone,* 3.
44. Ibid., 6.
45. Ibid., 40-41.
46. Ibid., 3.
47. Ibid., 45.
48. Ibid., 89.
49. Ibid., 71.
50. Ibid., 71.
51. Ibid., 73.
52. Rorty, *Contingency,* 89.
53. DeLillo, End Zone, 65.
54. Joseph Campbell, *The Hero with a Thousand Faces* (1949; New York: Pantheon Books. 1961) 116.
55. John Updike, *Rabbit, Run* (1960; New York: Fawcet, 1991) 79.
56. DeLillo, *End Zone,* 228-229.
57. Ibid., 43.
58. Ibid., 21.
50. Michael Oriard, "Don DeLillo's Search for Walden Pond," *Critique* 20 (1978): 16.
60. DeLillo, *End Zone,* 197.
61. *EZ* 224.
62. Ibid., 85.
63. Ibid., 207.
64. Ibid., 80.
65. Campbell, *The Hero with a Thousand Faces,* 308.

143. DeLillo, *Players,* 105.
144. Ibid., 9.
145. Norman Bryson, "City of Dis: The Fiction of Don DeLillo," *Granta* 1.2 (1980): 156.
146. DeLillo, *Players,* 5.
147. Ibid., 17.
148. DeLillo, *Running Dog,* 209.
149. Patrick O'Donnel, "Obvious Paranoia: The Politics of Don DeLillo's Running Dog," *The Centennial Review* (1990): 59.
150. DeLillo, *Players,* 51.
151. Ibid., 110.
152. John Updike, "Layers of Ambiguity," *New Yorker* 27 March 1978:128.
153. DeLillo, *Running Dog,* 76.
154. Ibid., 49-50.
155. DeLillo, *Players,* 143.
156. DeLillo, *Running Dog,* 114.
157. Ibid., 112.
158. "An Interview with Don DeLillo," *Anything Can Happen,* 83.
159. Ibid., 81.
160. Ibid., 82.
161. Updike, "Layers Of Ambiguity," 127.
162. DeLillo, *Running Dog,* 172.
163. Ibid., 26.
164. Ibid., 83.
165. Ibid., 185.
166. Ibid., 182.
167. Ibid., 155.
168. Ibid., 205.
169. Ibid., 139.
170. DeLillo, *Players,* 35.
171. LeClair, *In the Loop,* 152.
172. DeLillo, *Players,* 35.
173. Ibid., 88.
174. Ibid., 71.
175. Diane Johnson, *Terrorists and Novelists* (New York: Knopf, 1982) 110.
176. DeLillo, *Running Dog,* 213.
177. LeClair, *In the Loop,* 177.
178. Don DeLillo, *The Names* (New York: Alfred Knopf, 1982; New York: Vintage, 1989) 272. Citations are to the Vintage edition.
179. Ibid., 137.
180. Ibid., 77.
181. Ibid., 20.
182. Ibid., 171.

183. Ibid., 228.
184. John Kucich, "Postmodern Politics: Don DeLillo and the Plight of the White Male Writer," *Michigan Quarterly Review* 27 (1988): 335
185. DeLillo, *The Names,* 230.
186. Ibid., 291.
187. Hantke, *Conspiracy and Paranoia,* 122.
188. DeLillo, *The Names,* 72.
189. Ibid., 33-34.
190. Ibid., 38.
191. Ibid., 104.
192. Ibid., 18.
193. Ibid., 119.
194. Ibid., 79.
195. Ibid., 39.
196. Ibid., 31.
197. Ibid., 339.
198. Ibid., 330.
199. Ibid., 24.
200. Paula Bryant, "Discussing the Untellable: Don DeLillo's The Names," *Critique* 29 (1987): 16-17.
201. Hantke, *Conspiracy and Paranoia,* 127.
202. John McClure, "Postmodern Romance: Don DeLillo in the Age of Conspiracy," *Introducing Don DeLillo* (see note 16) 113.
203. DeLillo, *The Names,* 149.
204. Ibid., 151.
205. William Faulkner, *Absalom, Absalom!* (1936; New York: Vintage, 1990) 243.
206. Ibid., 287.
207. DeLillo, *The Names,* 216.
208. Ibid., 328.

NOTES TO CHAPTER SIX

1. "Interview with Larry McCaffery And Sinda Gregory," *The Art of Hunger: Essays, Prefaces, Interviews, and the Red Notebook* (New York: Penguin, 1993) 304.
2. "Memory's Escape: Inventing the Music of Chance, A Conversation with Paul Auster," ed. Mark Irwin, *Denver Quarterly* 28-3 (1994): 119.
3. Auster, *New York Trilogy,* 3.
4. "Itinerary," *The Art of Hunger,* 26.
5. Auster, *New York Trilogy* 301.
6. Ibid., 299.
7. Ibid., 299-300.
8. Paul Auster, *Smoke & Blue in The Face: Two Films By Paul Auster* (New York: Hyperion, 1995) 101-102.

9. Auster, *New York Trilogy*, 92.
10. "Twentieth-Century French Poetry," *The Art of Hunger*, 204.
11. "The Poetry of Exile," *The Art of Hunger* 97.
12. Dennis Barone, ed., *Beyond the Red Notebook: Essays on Paul Auster* (Philadelphia: U of Pennsylvania P, 1996) 6.
13. Dennis Barone, "Review of Leviathan," *The Review of Contemporary Fiction* 12-2 (Fall 1992): 193-194.
14. Auster, *Smoke & Blue in the Face*, 194.
15. Ibid., 193.
16. "The Art of Hunger," *The Art of Hunger* 10.
17. Ibid., 11.
18. Sven Birkerts, "Reality, Fiction, and In the Country of Last Things," *The Review of Contemporary Fiction* 14-1 (1994): 66.
19. Alison Russel, "Deconstructing The New York Trilogy: Paul Auster's Anti-Detective Fiction," *Critique* 31 (winter 1990): 72.
20. "Interview with Larry McCaffery and Sinda Gregory," The Art of Hunger, 303.
21. Russel, *Deconstructing the New York Trilogy*, 73.
22. Auster, *New York Trilogy*, 80.
23. William McPherson, "Remaking Narrative," *Poetics Journal* 7 (1987): 142.
24. Tim Woods, "The Music Of Chance: Aleatorical (Dis)harmonies Within 'The City Of The World,'" *Beyond The Red Notebook* (see note 12),143.
25. Auster, *New York Trilogy*, 338.
26. Ibid., 348.
27. Ibid., 174.
28. Ibid., 176.
29. DeLillo, *Ratner's Star*, 59.
30. Charles Frazier, *Cold Mountain* (New York: Atlantic, 1997) 100-101.
31. Rorty, Contingency, *Irony and Solidarity*, 8-9.
32. Auster, *New York Trilogy*, 174.
33. Ibid., 230.
34. Ibid., 222.
35. William Lavender, "The Novel of Critical Engagement: Paul Auster's City Of Glass," *Contemporary Literature* 34 (1993): 238-239.
36. Auster, *New York Trilogy*, 202.
37. Ibid., 43-44.
38. Ibid., 44.
39. Ibid., 6.
40. Lavender, "Novel of Critical Engagement," 223.
41. Auster, *New York Trilogy*, 120.
42. Ibid., 157.
43. Ibid., 314.
44. Ibid., 256.

45. Ibid., 260.
46. Ibid., 274.
47. Ibid., 237.
48. Ibid., 327.
49. "Memory's Escape," 111.
50. "Ideas and Things," *The Art of Hunger,* 106.
51. Auster, *New York Trilogy,* 250.
52. Ibid., 298.
53. Ibid., 295.
54. Ibid., 194.
55. "Interview With Joseph Mallia," 271.
56. Henry David Thoreau, *Walden, or Life in the Woods* (1854; New York: Quality Paperback Book Club, 1997) 94.
57. Sherman Paul, *The Shores of America: Thoreau's Inward Exploration* (Urbana: U of Illinois P, 1958) 11.
58. Thoreau, Walden, 1.
59. Mary Elkins Moller, *Thoreau in the Human Community* (Amherst: Uof Massachusetts P, 1980) 12.
60. Ibid., 20.
61. Thoreau, Walden, 184.
62. Auster, *New York Trilogy,* 235.
63. Ibid., 252.
64. Ibid., 345.
65. Ibid., 354.
66. Thoreau, *Walden,* 10.
67. Auster, *New York Trilogy,* 163.
68. Ibid., 370.
69. Paul Auster, *In the Country of Last Things* (New York: Viking Penguin, 1987; New York: Penguin, 1988) 36. Citations are to the Penguin edition.
70. Katherine Washburn, "A Book at the End of the World: Paul Auster's In The Country of Last Things," T*he Review Of Contemporary Fiction* 14-1 (spring 1994): 63.
71. "Interview with Larry McCaffery and Sinda Gregory," 314.
72. "Interview with Joseph Mallia," 273.
73. Auster, *Country of Last Things,* 91.
74. Ibid., 29.
75. "Native Son," *The Art of Hunger,* 141-142.
76. Auster, *Country of Last Things,* 114.
77. Ibid., 16.
78. Ibid., 19.
79. Ibid., 78.
80. "Itinerary," *The Art of Hunger,* 21.
81. Auster, *Country of Last Things,* 38.

82. Ibid., 38.
83. Auster, *New York Trilogy,* 149.
84. Auster, *Country of Last Things,* 178.
85. Ibid., 89.
86. Woods, "The Music of Chance," 127
87. Auster, *Country of Last Things,* 9.
88. Ibid., 179.
89. Ibid., 53.
90. Ibid., 146.
91. Ibid., 147.
92. Ibid., 104.
93. Robert Penn Warren, *All the King's Men* (1946; San Diego: Harcourt, 1982) 435.
94. Auster, *Country of Last Things,* 87-88.
95. "Interview with Larry McCaffery and Sinda Gregory," 315.
96. Auster, *Country of Last Things,* 183.
97. Paul Auster, *Moon Palace* (New York: Viking Penguin, 1989; New York: Penguin, 1990) 88. Citations are to the Penguin edition.
98. Ibid., 89.
99. Ibid., 209.
100. Ibid., 122.
101. Ibid., 52.
102. Ibid., 112.
103. "Interview With Larry McCaffery and Sinda Gregory," 278.
104. Sven Birkerts, *American Energies: Essays on Fiction* (New York: Morrow, 1992) 346.
105. Auster, *Moon Palace,* 233-234.
106. Ibid., 69-70.
107. Ibid., 37.
108. "New York Babel," *The Art of Hunger* 33.
109. Auster, *Hand to Mouth,* 6.
110. Auster, *Moon Palace,* 21.
111. Ibid., 67.
112. Rorty, *Contingency and Irony,* xvi.
113. Auster, *Moon Palace,* 60.
114. Ibid., 61.
115. Ibid., 73.
116. Auster, *Hand to Mouth,* 34.
117. Auster, *Moon Palace,* 25.
118. Ibid., 25.
119. Ibid., 46.
120. Ibid., 81.
121. Ibid., 75.

122. Ibid., 150.
123. Ibid., 175.
124. Auster, *Hand to Mouth,* 41.
125. Ibid., 35.
126. Paul Auster, *The Music of Chance* (New York: Viking Penguin,1990; New York: Penguin, 1991) 127.
127. Ibid., 11-12.
128. Tony Tanner, *City Of Words: American Fiction 1950-1970* (New York: Harper, 1971) 15.
129. Ibid., 36.
130. "Memory's Escape," 116.
131. Auster, *Music of Chance,* 13.
132. "The Death Of Sir Walter Raleigh," *The Art of Hunger* 81.
133. Auster, *Music of Chance,* 16.
134. Ibid., 106.
135. Ibid., 24.
136. Ibid., 1.
137. Ibid., 136.
138. Bloom, *The Western Canon,* 498.
139. Auster, *Music of Chance,* 216.
140. Ibid., 116.
141. Woods, "The Music of Chance," 150.
142. Michel Foucault, *Discipline and Punish: The Birth of the Prison* (1975; New York: Vintage, 1979) 243.
143. Auster, *Music of Chance,* 148.
144. Ibid., 135.

NOTES TO CHAPTER SEVEN

1. Barone, *Beyond the Red Notebook,* 11.
2. Steven Kaplan, *Understanding Tim O'Brien* (Columbia: U of South Carolina P, 1995) 34.
3. O'Brien, *If I Die,* 31.
4. *Anything Can Happen,* 278.
5. "Two Interviews: Talks with Tim O'Brien and Robert Stone," ed. Eric James Schroeder, *Modern Fiction Studies* 30 (1984): 136.
6. Michael Herr, *Dispatches* (1968; New York: Vintage, 1977) 18.
7. O'Brien, *If I Die* , 36-37.
8. Ibid., 65.
9. Ibid., 65.
10. Thomas G. Couser, "Going After Cacciato: The Romance and the Real World," *The Journal of Narrative Technique* 13 (1983): 2.
11. O'Brien, *If I Die,* 35.
12. Herr, *Dispatches,* 54-55.

13. O'Brien, *If I Die,* 84.
14. Ibid., 41-42.
15. Ibid., 95-96.
16. *Anything Can Happen* 263.
17. Edmund Wilson, "The Emergence of Ernest Hemingway," *The Shores of Light: A Literary Chronicle of the Twenties and Thirties* (1952; New York: Vintage, 1961) 120-121.
18. O'Brien, *If I Die,* 139.
19. Ibid., 32.
20. Ibid., 68.
21. Ibid., 66.
22. George Orwell, *Homage to Catalonia* (1938; San Diego: Harcourt, 1980) 149.
23. Ibid., 232.
24. O'Brien, *If I Die,* 205.
25. Ibid., 30.
26. Ibid., 22-23.
27. Ibid., 40-41.
28. Rorty, *Achieving Our Country,* 100.
29. Orwell, *Homage to Catalonia,* 3.
30. O'Brien, *If I Die,* 91.
31. Ibid., 147.
32. Herr, *Dispatches,* 16.
33. Ibid., 28.
34. Daniel Zins, "Imagining the Real: The Fiction of Tim O'Brien," *The Hollins Critic* 23 (1986) 3.
35. Herr, *Dispatches,* 20.
36. Tim O'Brien, *Northern Lights* (New York: Delacorte, 1975) 189.
37. Ibid., 4.
38. Ibid., 3.
39. Ibid., 8.
40. Ibid., 4.
41. Ibid., 7.
42. Ibid., 210.
43. Ibid., 248.
44. Ibid., 181.
45. Ibid., 21.
46. Ibid., 134.
47. Ibid., 345.
48. Milton J. Bates, "Tim O'Brien's Myth of Courage," *Modern Fiction Studies* 3 (1987): 268.
49. O'Brien, *Northern Lights,* 300.
50. Ibid., 301.

51. Ibid., 70.
52. Elias Lonnrot, *The Kalevala, or Poems of the Kalevala District, trans. Francis Peabody Mangoun, Jr.* (Cambridge: Harvard UP, 1975) Poem One.
53. O'Brien, *Northern Lights,* 144.
54. Ibid., 347.
55. Ibid., 60.
56. Ibid., 117.
57. Ibid., 87.
58. Ibid., 347.
59. Ibid., 200.
60. Ibid., 222.
61. "Two Interviews," 138
62. Tim O'Brien, *Going after Cacciato* (New York: Delacorte, 1979; New York: Delta Trade, 1989) 179. Citations are to the Delta edition.
63. Ibid., 27.
64. Ibid., 13.
65. Ibid., 209.
66. *Anything Can Happen* 267.
67. Dennis Vannatta, "Theme and Structure in Tim O'Brien's Going after Cacciato," *Modern Fiction Studies* 28 (1992): 246.
68. John Updike, "Layers of Ambiguity," *The New Yorker* 27 March 1978: 128.
69. "Ibid., 130.
70. O'Brien, *Going after Cacciato,* 4.
71. Tobey C. Herzog, "Going after Cacciato: The Soldier-Author-Character Seeking Control," *Critique* 24 (1983): 89.
72. O'Brien, *Going after Cacciato,* 25.
73. Ibid., 44.
74. Michael M. Raymond, "Imagined Responses to Vietnam: Tim O'Brien's Going after Cacciato," *Critique* 24 (1983): 100.
75. O'Brien, *Going after Cacciato* 300.
76. Ibid., 25.
77. *Anything Can Happen* 269.
78. "An Interview with Tim O'Brien," by Martin Naparsteck, *Contemporary Literature* 32 (1991): 4.
79. O'Brien, *Going after Cacciato,* 9.
80. Ibid., 188.
81. Ibid., 247.
82. Ibid., 181.
83. Ibid., 124.
84. Ibid., 125.
85. Ibid., 125.
86. Ibid., 70.
87. Ibid., 226.

88. Ibid., 127.
89. Ibid., 136.
90. Ibid., 100.
91. Ibid., 166.
92. Ibid., 286.
93. Arthur Saltzman, "The Betrayal of the Imagination: Paul Brodeur's The Stunt Man and Tim O'Brien's Going after Cacciato," *Critique* 22 (1980): 36.
94. O'Brien, *Going after Cacciato,* 63.
95. Ibid., 141.
96. Thomas Pynchon, V (1961; New York: Perennial, 1986) 35.
97. Tim O'Brien, *The Nuclear Age* (New York: Alfred Knopf, 1979; New York: Laurel, 1979) 284. Citations are to the Laurel edition.
98. Ibid., 287.
99. Ibid., 144.
100. Ibid., 149.
101. *Anything Can Happen* 271.
102. O'Brien, *Nuclear Age,* 67.
103. Ibid., 151.
104. Ibid., 23.
105. Ibid., 191.
106. Ibid., 101.
107. *Anything Can Happen* 270-271.
108. O'Brien, *Nuclear Age,* 122.
109. Ibid., 231.
110. Ibid., 233.
111. Ibid., 330.
112. Ibid., 22.
113. Philip Roth, *Zuckerman Unbound* (New York: Farrar, Straus and Giroux, 1981) 219.
114. O'Brien, *Nuclear Age,* 35.
115. Ibid., 343.
116. Ibid., 271.
117. Ibid., 40.
118. Ibid., 77.
119. Ibid., 180.
120. Ibid., 135.
121. Ibid., 35.
122. Ibid., 17.
123. Ibid., 136.
124. Ibid., 9.
125. Ibid., 79.
126. Ibid., 359.

NOTES TO CHAPTER EIGHT

1. Joanne S. Frye, *Living Stories, Telling Lives: Women and the Novel in Contemporary Experience* (Ann Arbor: U of Michigan P, 1986): 17-18.
2. DeLillo, *The Names,* 151.
3. Henry Roth, *Call It Sleep* (1934; New York: Noonday, 1991) 213.
4. James Baldwin, *Go Tell It On The Mountain* (New York: Grosset, 1953) 263.
5. Ibid., 272.
6. Ibid., 273.
7. William R. Nash also discusses the relationship of Faith and the Good Thing, Go Tell It on the Mountain and Call It Sleep in some detail. William R. Nash, Charles Johnson's Fiction (Urbana, University of Illinois Press, 2003) 156-161.
8. Charles Johnson, *Faith and the Good Thing* (Atheneum, 1974; New York: Plume, 1991) 8. Citations are to the Plume edition.
9. Ibid., 12.
10. Ibid., 69.
11. Stanley Crouch, "Charles Johnson: Free at Last," *Notes of A Hanging Judge: Essays and Reviews 1979-1989* (New York: Oxford Press, 1990) 143.
12. Charles Johnson, *Being and Race: Black Writing Since 1970* (1970; Bloomington: Indiana UP, 1988) 3.
13. "Interview with Jonathan Little," *Contemporary Literature* 34 (1993) 169.
14. "Cyrus Colter Speaking With Charles Johnson and Reginald Gibbons On January 19, 1991," *Callaloo* 14 (1991): 890.
15. Johnson, *Faith and the Good Thing,* 34.
16. Henry Louis Gates, Jr., *The Signifying Monkey: A Theory of African -American Literary Criticism* (1988; New York: Oxford UP, 1989) 6.
17. Jennifer Hayward, "Something to Serve: Constructs Of The Feminine In Charles Johnson's Oxherding Tale," *Black American Literature Forum* 25 (1991): 694.
18. Johnson, *Faith and the Good Thing,* 30.
19. Ishmael Reed, *Mumbo Jumbo* (New York: Atheneum 1972):4.
20. Charles Johnson, *The Sorceror's Apprentice: Tales and Conjurations* (New Yor: Atheneum, 1986; New York: Plume, 1994) 5-6. Citations are to the Plume edition.
21. Ibid., 16.
22. Ibid., 3-4.
23. Ibid., 21.
24. Ibid., 55.
25. Ibid., 46.
26. Ibid., 53.
27. Ibid., 54.
28. Ibid., 45.
29. Ibid., 50.

30. Gary Storhoff, "The Artist as Universal Mind: Berkeley's Influence on Charles Johnson," *African American Review* 30 (1995): 541.
31. Johnson, *Faith and the Good Thing,* 24.
32. Ibid., 112-113.
33. Ibid., 100.
34. Ibid., 6.
35. Graff, *Literature Against Itself,* 12.
36. Johnson, *Faith and the Good Thing,* 115.
37. Johnson, *Being and Race,* 171.
38. Johnson, *Faith and the Good Thing,* 78.
39. Ibid., 153.
40. Ibid., 158-159.
41. Ibid., 160.
42. Ibid., 149.
43. Ibid., 165.
44. Johnson, *Sorceror's Apprentice,* 84.
45. Ibid., 92.
46. Johnson, *Faith and the Good Thing,* 66.
47. Ibid., 66.
48. Hayward, "Something to Serve," 690.
49. Johnson, *Faith and the Good Thing,* 180.
50. "Interview with Jonathan Little," 161.
51. "Interview with Jonathan Little," 161.
52. David Hall, *Richard Rorty: Prophet and Poet of the New Pragmatism* (Albany: State U of New York P, 1994) 97.
53. Johnson, *Oxherding Tale,* 152.
54. Ibid., 109.
55. Ibid., 61.
56. Ibid., 67.
57. Ibid., 121.
58. Ibid., 152.
59. Ibid., 125.
60. Ibid., 130.
61. Jane Tompkins, *Sensational Designs: The Cultural Work of American Fiction 1770-1860* (New York: Oxford UP, 1985) xiv.
62. Johnson, *Oxherding Tale,* 132.
63. Ashraf Rushdy, "The Phenomenology of the Allmuseri: Charles Johnson and the Subject of the Narrative of Slavery," *African American Review* 26 (1992) 383.
64. Johnson, *Sorceror's Apprentice,* 156.
65. Ibid., 164-165.
66. Ibid., 167.
67. Ibid., 149.

68. Bloom, *The Western Canon,* 58-59.
69. Johnson, *Oxherding Tale,* 143.
70. Ibid., 118.
71. Ibid., 28-29.
72. Ibid., 50.
73. Johnson, *Faith and the Good Thing,* 192.
74. Ibid., 89.
75. Johnson, *Sorceror's Apprentice,* 103.
76. Ibid., 6.
77. Johnson, *Oxherding Tale,* 11.
78. Ibid., 44.
79. Ibid., 55.
80. Ibid., 18.
81. Johnson, *Faith and the Good Thing,* 92.
82. Johnson, *Oxherding Tale,* 107-108.
83. Ibid., 92.
84. Ibid., 115.
85. Ibid., 13.
86. Ibid., 141.
87. Ibid., 176.
88. Jonathan Little, "Charles Johnson's Revolutionary Oxherding Tale," *Studies in American Fiction* 19 (1991): 143.
89. Johnson, *Oxherding Tale* 8.
90. Ibid., 7.
91. Ibid., 85.
92. Ibid., 79.
93. Ibid., 43.
94. Ibid., 32.
95. Ibid., 124.
96. Ibid., 176.
97. Ibid., 120.
98. Ibid., xvii.
99. Charles Johnson, *Middle Passage* (New York: Atheneum, 1990; New York: Plume, 1991) 25. Citations are to the Plume edition.

NOTES TO CHAPTER NINE

1. Paul Auster, *Mr. Vertigo* (New York: Viking Penguin, 1994; New York: Penguin, 1995) 47. Citations are to the Penguin edition.
2. Auster, *Leviathan,* 13
3. Ibid., 137.
4. Ibid., 250.
5. Don DeLillo, *Libra* (New York: Viking Penguin, 1988) 293-294.

6. Margaret Scanlan, "The Writer among Terrorists: Don DeLillo's Mao II and The Rushdie Affair," *Modern Fiction Studies* 40 (1994): 242.
7. Christian Moraru, "Consuming Narratives: Don DeLillo and the "Lethal" Reading." Don Delillo 90.
8. DeLillo, *Mao II,* 19.
9. Auster, *The Art of Hunger,* 140.
10. Auster, *Leviathan,* 59.
11. DeLillo, *Mao II,* 20.
12. Auster, *Leviathan,* 117.
13. Ibid., 10.
14. Auster, *Mr. Vertigo,* 49.
15. DeLillo, *Mao II,* 28.
16. Ibid., 37.
17. DeLillo, *White Noise,* 21.
18. Ibid., 30.
19. O'Brien, *The Things They Carried,* 38.
20. Ibid., 86-87.
21. Ibid., 38-39.
22. Johnson, *Middle Passage,* 1.
23. Melville, *Moby Dick* (1851; New York, Signet, 1980) 507-508.
24. Ibid., 450.
25. Johnson, *Middle Passage,* 23.
26. Melville, *Moby Dick,* 398.
27. Richard Chase, "Melville and Moby Dick," *Melville: A Collection of Critical Essays, ed. Richard Chase* (Englewood Cliffs: Prentice, 1962) 57.
28. Johnson, *Middle Passage,* 41.
29. Ibid., 30.
30. Brian Fagel, "Passages from the Middle: Coloniality And Post-Coloniality in Charles Johnson's Middle Passage," *African American Review* 20 (1996): 625.
31. Homi K. Bhabha, "Signs Taken for Wonders: Questions of Ambivalence and Authority under a Tree outside Delhi, May 1817," "Race," *Writing and Difference* 173.
32. Johnson, *Middle Passage* 124.
33. Johnson, *Middle Passage* 179.
34. Herman Melville, "Benito Cereno," *The Norton Anthology of American Literature* 2227–8.
35. Johnson, *Middle Passage,* 129.
36. "Interview with Jonathan Little," 166.
37. DeLillo, *White Noise,* 189.
38. Ibid., 51.
39. Detailed in Ralph Gardner Jr., "Writing That Can Strengthen The Fraying Threads Of Memory," *New York Times* 30 January (1997): C:1,8.
40. "An Outsider in this Society," 47.

41. Godfrey Hodgson, *America in Our Time: From World War II to Nixon, What Happened and Why* (New York: Vintage, 1976) 75.
42. DeLillo, *White Noise,* 22.
43. Jameson, *Postmodernism,* 19.
44. Hodgson, *America in Our Time,* 4.
45. JFK, directed by Oliver Stone, box notes.
46. DeLillo, *Libra,* author's note.
47. O'Brien, *The Things They Carried,* 49-50.
48. DeLillo, *Libra,* 16
49. Ibid., 77.
50. Ibid., 125.
51. Ibid., 70.
52. Ibid., 221.
53. Don DeLillo, *Underworld* (New York: Scribner, 1997) 24.
54. Ibid., 467.
55. Ibid., 290.
56. Ibid., 82.
57. Auster, *Leviathan,* 27
58. Ibid., 100.
59. Ibid., 41.
60. Auster, *Hand to Mouth,* 35.
61. Auster, *Leviathan,* 43.
62. Johnson, *Dreamer,* 61.
63. Arthur Saltzman, "Leviathan: Post Hoc Harmonies," Beyond the Red Notebook 165.
64. Auster, *Leviathan,* 116.
65. Ibid., 44.
66. Ibid., 42.
67. Auster, *Mr. Vertigo,* 1.
68. Ibid., 155.
69. Ibid., 15.
70. Ibid., 7.
71. Ibid., 10.
72. Ibid., 121.
73. DeLillo, *White Noise,* 64.
74. Auster, *Mr. Vertigo,* 129.
75. Ibid., 196.
76. Ibid., 127.
77. Ibid., 277.
78. Ibid., 278-279.
79. Ibid., 165.
80. Ibid., 191.
81. Ibid., 121.

82. Ibid., 236.
83. O'Brien, *The Things They Carried,* 72.
84. Ibid., 181.
85. Ibid., ix.
86. Ibid., 78.
87. Ibid., 79.
88. Ibid., 122.
89. O'Brien, *In the Lake of the Woods,* 266.
90. Ibid., 107.
91. Ibid., 273.
92. Ibid., 299.

NOTES TO CHAPTER TEN

1. O'Brien, *The Things They Carried,* 227.
2. Auster, *Leviathan,* 44.
3. DeLillo, *White Noise,* 13.
4. Ibid., 139.
5. Ibid., 38.
6. Ibid., 46.
7. Ibid., 119.
8. Joan Didion, *Play It As It Lays* (1970; New York: Noonday. 1990) 77.
9. DeLillo, *White Noise,* 19.
10. Auster, *Leviathan,* 242.
11. Ibid., 245.
12. Ibid., 37.
13. Paul Auster, "The City and the Country," *The New York Times* (September 9, 2002) A-23.
14. Don DeLillo, "In the Ruins of the Future," *The Guardian,* December 22, 2001, http://www.guardian.co.uk/saturday_review/story/0,3605,623666,00.html.
15. DeLillo, *Libra,* 144.
16. Ibid., 145.
17. Jameson, *Postmodernism,* 23.
18. Frank Lentricchia, "Libra as Postmodern Critique," *Introducing Don DeLillo* (Durham: Duke UP, 1991) 198.
19. Thoreau, Walden, 153.
20. Frank Norris, *The Octopus* (1901; New York: Penguin, 1986) 51.
21. DeLillo, *Libra,* 3
22. Ibid., 13.
23. Ibid., 104.
24. Primo Levi, *Survival in Auschwitz,* trans. Stuart Woolf (1958; New York: Collier, 1960) 29.

25. DeLillo, *Libra,* 11.
26. Ibid., 10.
27. Ibid., 355.
28. Ibid., 100.
29. Ibid., 450.
30. Magali Cornier Michael, "The Political Paradox within Don DeLillo's Libra," *Critique* 35-3 (1994): 147.
31. Auster, *Mr. Vertigo,* 14.
32. Ibid., 96.
33. Ibid., 95.
34. O'Brien, *In the Lake of the Woods,* 107.
35. Ibid., 214-215.
36. Johnson, *Middle Passage,* 66.
37. O'Brien, *In the Lake of the Woods,* 73.
38. DeLillo, *White Noise,* 64.
39. Vincent A. O'Keefe, "Reading Rigor Mortis: Offstage Violence and Excluded Middles in Johnson's Middle Passage and Morrison's Beloved," *African American Review* 30 (96): 641.
40. Auster, *Leviathan,* 265.
41. DeLillo, *Underworld,* 239.
42. Johnson, *Dreamer,* 62.
43. Johnson, *Dreamer,* 108.
44. Johnson, *Middle Passage,* 145.
45. Ibid., 130.
46. Ibid., 137.
47. Ibid., 13.
48. Ibid., 13.
49. O'Brien, *The Things They Carried,* 105.
50. O'Brien, *In the Lake of the Woods,* 21.
51. O'Brien, *The Things They Carried,* 106.
52. Auster, *Leviathan,* 97-98.
53. O'Brien, *The Things They Carried,* 90.
54. Mark Heberle, *A Trauma Artist: Tim O'Brien and the Fiction of Vietnam* (Iowa City: University of Iowa Press, 2001) 191.
55. O'Brien, *The Things They Carried,* 88.
56. Ibid., 117.
57. DeLillo, *Underworld,* 78.
58. Ibid., 748.
59. DeLillo, "In the Ruins of the Future."
60. O'Brien, *In the Lake of the Woods,* 169.
61. Ibid., 227.
62. Ibid., 210.
63. O'Brien, *The Things They Carried,* 113.

64. Don DeLillo, "Pafko at the Wall," *Harper's* (October 1992): 37.
65. Ibid., 68.
66. DeLillo, *Underworld,* 11.
67. Ibid., 614.
68. Ibid., 610.
69. Auster, *Leviathan,* 270.
70. Lorrie Smith, "'The Things Men Do:' The Gendered Subject in Tim O'Brien's Esquire Stories," *Critique* 36 (1994): 23.
71. O'Brien, *The Things They Carried,* 142.
72. Ibid., 139.
73. Johnson, *Middle Passage,* 123.
74. DeLillo, *Mao II,* 159.
75. Ibid., 214.
76. DeLillo, *Underworld,* 560.
77. DeLillo, *Mao II,* 7.
78. O'Brien, *In the Lake of the Woods,* 151.
79. DeLillo, *Underworld,* 63.
80. Ibid., 416.
81. Ibid., 237.
82. DeLillo, "In the Ruins of the Future."
83. DeLillo, *White Noise,* 82.
84. DeLillo, *Libra,* 22.
85. Ibid., 366.
86. Thomas J. Ferraro, "Whole Families Shopping at Night," *New Essays on White Noise* 35.
87. DeLillo, *White Noise,* 79.
88. DeLillo, *Libra,* 25.
89. Ibid., 16.
90. Ibid., 1.
91. Ibid., 390.
92. Johnson, *Dreamer,* 90.
93. DeLillo, *Libra,* 447.
94. Hantke, *Conspiracy and Paranoia,* 156
95. DeLillo, *Libra,* 446.
96. "Outsider in this Society," 49.
97. Auster, *Leviathan,* 109.
98. Auster, *Mr. Vertigo,* 40.
99. Ibid., 37.
100. Ibid., 282.
101. Johnson, *Middle Passage,* 168.
102. Ibid., 102.
103. Ibid., 162.
104. Ibid., 181.

105. Auster, *Leviathan,* 132.
106. DeLillo, *White Noise,* 63.
107. Ibid., 88.
108. Paul Cantor, "Adolf, We Hardly Knew You," New Essays On White Noise 48.
109. DeLillo, *White Noise,* 230.
110. DeLillo, *White Noise,* 254.
111. DeLillo, *White Noise,* 290.
112. DeLillo, "In the Ruins of the Future."
113. Katherine Hayles, "Postmodern Parataxis: Embodied Texts, Weightless Information," *American Literary History* 2 (1990) 412.
114. DeLillo, *White Noise,* 313.
115. DeLillo, *Mao II,* 149.
116. Ibid., 180.
117. Ibid., 173.
118. O'Brien, *In the Lake of the Woods,* 92.
119. Ibid., 244.
120. O'Brien, *The Things They Carried,* 51.
121. Ibid., 54.
122. *Entertainment Weekly* 17 October 1997: 69.
123. Tom De Haven, "High Anxiety," *Entertainment Weekly* 3 October (1997): 74.
124. Tony Tanner, "Afterthoughts on Don DeLillo's Underworld," Don Delillo 136.
125. John LeClair, "An Underhistory of Mid-Century America," *Atlantic Monthly,* October 1997: 113.
126. Ibid., 116.
127. DeLillo, *Underworld,* 827.
128. LeClair, "An Underhistory of Mid-Century America," 116.
129. De Haven, "High Anxiety," 75.
130. DeLillo, *Underworld,* 70.
131. Ibid., 827

NOTES TO THE AFTERWORD

1. Paul Auster, *Timbuktu* (New York: Henry Holt, 1999; New York: Picador, 2000) 9. Citations are to the Picador edition.
2. Paul Auster, *The Book of Illusions* (New York: Henry Holt, 2002) 17.
3. Tim O'Brien, July, July (New York: Houghton Mifflin, 2002; New York: Penguin 2002) 244. Citations are to the Penguin edition.
4. Ibid., 250.
5. Ibid., 133.
6. Auster, *Timbuktu,* 158.
7. Auster, *The Book of Illusions,* 205.

8. Charles Johnson, *Soulcatcher and Other Stories* (San Diego: Harvest/ Harcourt, 2001) xxi.
9. Ibid., 28.
10. Ibid., 30.
11. Ibid., 19.
12. Ibid., 2.
13. Ibid., 53.
14. Nash, *Charles Johnson's Fictions,* 192.
15. Johnson, *Soulcatcher,* 11.
16. Ibid., 73.
17. Ibid., 67.
18. Ibid., 44.
19. Ibid., 45.
20. Ibid., 109.
21. Ibid., 110.
22. Ibid., xv.
23. Ibid., 36.
24. Auster, *Timbuktu,* 4.
25. Ibid., 109.
26. Ibid., 35.
27. Ibid., 56.
28. Ibid., 97.
29. Ibid., 161.
30. Peter S. Temes, "Review ofThe Book of Illusions," San Francisco Chronicle, Sunday, September 8, 2002.
31. Interview, Failbetter.com.www.failbetter.com/2002–2004/Austerinterview.htm
32. Interview with Dan Epstein, *3 AM Magazine,* 2001.
33. Auster, *The Book of Illusions,* 183.
34. Ibid.
35. Ibid., 3.
36. Ibid., 14.
37. Interview with Robert McCrum, "Letters from America," from *The Guardian Unlimited,* Dec 16, 2001.
38. Auster, *The Book of Illusions,* 39.
39. Ibid., 89.
40. Ibid., 179.
41. Ibid., 183.
42. Ibid., 207.
43. Don DeLillo, *The Body Artist* (New York: Scriber, 2001) 29.
44. Auster, *The Book of Illusions,* 15.
45. DeLillo, *The Body Artist,* 100.
46. Ibid., 65

47. David Cowart, *Don DeLillo and the Physics of Language* (Athens: University of Georgia Press, 2002) 205.
48. Auster, *The Book of Illusions,* 243.
49. Ibid., 117.
50. DeLillo, *The Body Artist,* 31.
51. Auster, *The Book of Illusions,* 255.
52. Interview, Failbetter.com.
53. Mark Heberle, *A Trauma Artist: Tim O'Brien and the Fiction of Vietnam* (Iowa City: University of Iowa Press, 2001).
54. O'Brien, *July,* July, 4.
55. Ibid., 33.
56. Ibid., 42.
57. Heberle, *A Trauma Artist,* 291.
58. O'Brien, *July,* July, 199.
59. Ibid., 149.
60. Ibid., 269.
61. Auster, *The Book of Illusions,* 318.
62. Paul Auster, "Random Notes-September 11, 2001, 4:00 PM; Underground," 110 Stories: New York Writes after September 11, Ulrich Baer, ed. (New York: New York University Press, 2002) 34.
63. Ibid., 36.
64. Interview, National Public Radio: "All Things Considered," September 8, 2002.
65. Auster, *The Book of Illusions,* 200.
66. Interview, National Public Radio: "Fresh Air," September 9, 2002.
67. Ryan Simmons, "What is a Terrorist? Contemporary Authorship, the Unabomber, and Mao II." *Modern Fiction Studies* 45-3, Fall 1999: 676.
68. Interview with Todd Leopold, "Tim O'Brien's Reunion from Hell," CNN.com, Wednesday, October 9, 2002.
69. O'Brien, *July,* July, 281.
70. Ibid., 302.
71. Ibid., 306.
72. Richard Rorty, "Fighting Terrorism with Democracy," *The Nation,* October 3, 2002.
73. DeLillo, "In the Ruins of the Future."
74. Marco Abel, :Don DeLillo's 'In The Ruins of the Future': Literature, Images, and the Rhetoric of Seeing 9/11," *PMLA,* October 2003, vol 118, no 5, pages 1236-1250.
75. Don DeLillo, *Cosmopolis* (New York: Scribner, 2003) 5.
76. Ibid., 8.
77. Tom Wolfe, "One Way Street," *The New Yorker,* March 31, 2003.
78. DeLillo, ſn the Ruins of the Future."
79. DeLillo, *Cosmopolis,* 91.

80. Ibid., 8.
81. Ibid., 36.
82. Ibid., 96.
83. Ibid., 90.
84. Ibid., 22.
85. Auster, *Book of Illusions,* 108.
86. DeLillo, *Cosmopolis,* 206.
87. Ibid., 183.
88. DeLillo, *The Body Artist,* 36.
89. Johnson, *Soulcatcher,* xiv.
90. DeLillo, *Cosmopolis,* 174.
91. Ibid., 177.
92. Jeremy Green, "Disaster Footage: Spectacles of Violence in DeLillo's Fiction," *Modern Fiction Studies* 45-3, Fall 1999: 575.
93. DeLillo, "In the Ruins of the Future."
94. DeLillo, *Cosmopolis,* 60.
95. Ibid., 100.
96. DeLillo, "In the Ruins of the Future."
97. DeLillo, *Cosmopolis,* 193.
98. DeLillo, "In the Ruins of the Future."
99. DeLillo, *Cosmopolis,* 208.
100. Ibid., 191.
101. Ibid., 191.
102. DeLillo, "In the Ruins of the Future."
103. Johnson, *Soulcatcher,* 110.

Bibliography

Abel, Marco. "Don DeLillo's 'In the Ruins of the Future': Literature, Images, and the Rhetoric of *Seeing* 9/11." *PMLA* 118 (2003): 1236–1250.

Aeimone, Joseph Oran, et al. "Teaching Literature in the Academy Today: A Roundtable." *PMLA* 112 (1997): 104–112.

Aldridge, John. *The American Novel and the Way We Live Now.* New York: Oxford UP, 1983.

Alford, Steven. "Spaced Out: Signification and Space in Paul Auster's *New York Trilogy.*" *Contemporary Literature* 34 (1995): 613–632.

Auster, Paul. *The Art of Hunger: Essays, Prefaces, Interviews, and the Red Notebook.* New York: Penguin, 1993.

_____. *The Book of Illusions.* New York: Henry Holt, 2002.

_____. "The City and the Country." *The New York Times,* Monday, September 9, 2002, Sec A, p. 23.

_____. *Hand to Mouth: A Chronicle of Early Failure.* New York: Henry Holt, 1997.

_____. *In the Country of Last Things.* New York: Viking Penguin, 1987.

_____. *The Invention of Solitude.* New York: Sun Press, 1982.

_____. *Leviathan.* New York: Viking Penguin, 1992.

_____. *Moon Palace.* New York: Viking Penguin, 1989.

_____. *Mr. Vertigo.* New York: Viking Penguin, 1994.

_____. *The Music of Chance.* New York: Viking Penguin, 1990.

_____. *The New York Trilogy.* New York: Penguin, 1990.

_____. "Random Notes—September 11, 2001, 4:00 PM; Underground." *110 Stories: New York Writes after September 11.* Ulrich Baer, ed. New York: New York UP, 2002) 34–36.

_____. *Smoke & Blue in the Face: Two Films.* New York: Hyperion, 1995.

_____. *Timbuktu.* New York: Picador, 2000.

_____. "Why Write?" *New Yorker,* 25 Dec. 1996: 86–89.

_____. "Interview with Dan Epstein." *3 AM Magazine.* http://www.3ammagazine.com/litarchives/nov2001/paul_auster_interview.html

_____. "Interview with Failbetter.com. http://www.failbetter.com/2002–4/austerinterview.htm.

_____. "Interview with Joseph Mallia." *The Art of Hunger* 264–276.

_____. "Interview with Larry McCaffery and Sinda Gregory." *The Art of Hunger* 277–320.

_____. Interview, National Public Radio: "All Things Considered," September 8, 2002.

_____. Interview, National Public Radio: "Fresh Air," September 9, 2002.

_____. "Interview with Robert McCrum. *Guardian Unlimited,* Dec 16, 2001. http://books.guardian.co.uk/departments/generalfiction/story/0,6000,619258,00.html

_____. Interview. "Memory's Escape: Inventing the Music of Chance, a Conversation with Paul Auster." By Mark Irwin. *Denver Quarterly* 28 (1994): 111–122.

Bakhtin, M.M. *The Dialogic Imagination: Four Essays.* 1981. Ed. Michael Holmquist. Trans. Caryl Emerson and Michael Holmquist. Austin: U of Texas P, 1996.

Baldwin, James. *Go Tell It on the Mountain.* New York: Grosset, 1953.

Barone, Dennis, ed. *Beyond the Red Notebook: Essays on Paul Auster.* Philadelphia: U of Pennsylvania P, 1995.

_____. Review of *Leviathan. Review of Contemporary Fiction* 12 (1992): 193–194.

Barth, John. *Chimera.* 1972. Fawcett, 1989.

_____. *The Floating Opera and the End of the Road.* 1956. New York: Doubleday, 1988.

_____. *The Friday Book: Essays and Other Nonfiction.* New York: Putnam's, 1984.

_____. *Further Fridays: Essays, Lectures, and Other Nonfiction 1984–1994.* Boston: Little, 1995.

_____. *Lost in the Funhouse.* New York: Bantam, 1968.

_____. "The Literature of Replenishment: Postmodernism and the Rebirth of the Novel." *Atlantic,* June (1980): 65–71.

Barthelme, Donald. *City Life.* New York: Farrar, 1970.

_____. *The Dead Father.* 1975. New York: Penguin, 1986.

Barthes, Roland. *The Pleasure of the Text.* 1973. Trans. Richard Miller. New York: Hill & Wang, 1975.

Bates, Milton J. . "Tim O'Brien's Myth of Courage." *Modern Fiction Studies* 30 (1997): 263–280.

Baudrillard, Jean. *The Revenge of the Crystal: Selected Writings on the Modern Object and Its Destiny.* Trans. and ed. Paul Foss and Julian Pefanis. London: Pluto 1990.

Bawer, Bruce. *Diminishing Fictions: Essays on the American Novel and its Critics,* St. Paul: Graywolf, 1988.

Beidler, Philip. *American Literature and the Experience of Vietnam.* Athens: U of Georgia P, 1982.

Bell, Madison Smartt. *All Soul's Rising.* New York: Pantheon, 1995.

Bellow, Saul. *The Adventures of Augie March.* 1949. Greenwich: Fawcett, 1953.

_____. *Sieze the Day.* 1956. New York: Fawcett, 1965.

Berger, Thomas. *Who is Teddy Villanova?* 1977. New York: Dell, 1978.

Berman, Neil David. *Playful Fictions and Fictional Players: Game, Sport and Survival in Contemporary American Fiction.* Port Washington: National University Publishing, 1981.

Bhabha, Homi K. "Signs Taken for Wonders: Questions of Ambivalence and Authority Under a Tree Outside Delhi, May 1817." Gates 163–184.

Berthoff, Warner. *The Ferment of Realism: American Literature 1884–1919.* New York: Free, 1965.

Birkerts, Sven. *American Energies: Essays on Fiction.* New York: Morrow, 1992.

_____. "Reality, Fiction, and *In the Country of Last Things.*" *Review of Contemporary Fiction* 14.1 (1991): 66–69.

Bloom, Harold. *The Anxiety of Influence.* 1973. London: Oxford UP, 1975.

_____, ed. *Don DeLillo: Bloom's Modern Critical Views.* Philadelphia: Chelsea House, 2003.

_____. *The Western Canon: The Books and Schools of the Ages.* New York: Harcourt, 1994.

Bonn, Marie. "Can Stories Save Us? Tim O'Brien and the Efficacy of the Text." *Critique* 36 (1994): 2–15.

Boyle, T. Coraghasen. Rev. of *Mason & Dixon,* by Thomas Pynchon. *New York Times Book Review,* 18 March 1997.

Brooks, Van Wyck. *The Confident Years: 1885–1915.* New York: Dutton, 1995.

Bryant, Paula. "Discussing the Untellable: Don DeLillo's *The Names.*" *Critique* 29 (1987): 16–29.

Bryson, Norman. "City of Dis: The Fiction of Don DeLillo." *Granta* 1.2 (1980) 145–157.

Bull, Jeaffrey S. "What about a Problem that Doesn't Have a Solution? Stone's *Flag for Sunrise,* DeLillo's *Mao II,* and the Politics of Political Fiction." *Don DeLillo: Bloom's Critical Views* 149–163.

Burroughs, William. *Naked Lunch.* 1959. New York: Grove Weidenfeld, 1990.

Byrd, Rudolph P. "Oxherding Tale and Siddhartha: Philosophy, Fiction, and the Emergence of a Hidden Tradition." *African American Review* 30 (1996): 549–558.

Campbell, Joseph. *The Hero with a Thousand Faces.* 1949. New York: Pantheon, 1961.

_____. ed. *Myth, Dreams, and Religion.* New York: Dutton, 1970.

Cantor, Paul. "Adolf, We Hardly Knew You." *New Essays on* White Noise" 39–62.

Caramello, Charles. *Silverless Mirrors: Book, Self and Postmodern American Fiction.* Talahassee: U of Florida P, 1983.

Carmichael, Thomas. "Lee Harvey Oswald and the Postmodern Subject: History and Intertextuality in Don DeLillo's *Libra, The Names,* and *Mao II.*" *Contemporary Literature* 34 (1994): 204–218.

Carter, Everett. *Howells and the Age of Realism.* 1950. Hambden: Archon, 1966.

Chase, Richard. *Herman Melville: A Critical Study.* New York: Hafner, 1971.

_____. *Quest for Myth.* 1949. New York: Greenwood, 1969.
_____, ed. *Melville: A Collection of Critical Essays.* Englewood Cliffs: Prentice, 1962.
Civello, Paul. *Literary Naturalism and Its Transformations: Frank Norris, Ernest Hemingway, Don DeLillo.* Athens: U of Georgia P, 1994.
Conroy, Mark. "From Tombstones to Tabloid: Authority Figured in *White Noise.*" *Critique* 35 (1993): 96–110.
Conway, Daniel W. and John E. Seery, eds. *The Politics of Irony: Essays of Self-Betrayal.* New York: St.Martin's, 1992.
Coover, Robert. *The Public Burning.* 1977. New York: Bantam, 1978.
Couser, G. Thomas. "Going After Cacciato: The Romance and the Real War." *The Journal of Narrative Technique* 13 (1983): 1–10.
Cowart, David. *Don DeLillo and the Physics of Language.* Athens: University of Georgia Press, 2002.
Crouch, Stanley. "Charles Johnson: Free at Last!" *Notes of a Hanging Judge: Essays and Reviews 1979–1989.* New York: Oxford UP, 1990. 136–143.
Crowther, Hal. "Clinging to the Rock: A Novelist's Choices in the New Mediocracy." *Introducing Don DeLillo* 83–98.
Culler, Jonathan. "Prolegomena to a Theory of Reading." *The Reader in the Text* 46–66.
De Haven, Tom. "High Anxiety." Rev. of *Underworld,* by Don DeLillo. *Entertainment Weekly* 3 Oct. 1997: 74–75.
DeLillo, Don. *Americana.* Boston: Houghton Mifflin, 1971.
_____. *The Body Artist.* New York: Scribner, 2001.
_____. *Cosmopolis.* New York: Scribner, 2003.
_____. *End Zone.* Boston: Houghton Mifflin, 1972.
_____. *Great Jones Street.* Boston: Houghton Mifflin, 1973.
_____. "In the Ruins of the Future." *The Guardian,* Saturday, December 22, 2001. http://www.guardian.co.uk/saturday_review/story/0.3605,623666,00.html.
_____. *Libra.* New York: Viking Penguin, 1988.
_____. *Mao II.* 1991. New York: Viking Penguin, 1991.
_____. *The Names.* New York: Alfred Knopf, 1982.
_____. "Pafko at the Wall." *Harper's* October 1992: 35–70.
_____. *Players.* New York: Alfred Knopf, 1977.
_____. *Ratner's Star.* New York: Alfred A. Knopf, 1976.
_____. *Running Dog.* New York: Alfred Knopf, 1978.
_____. *Underworld.* New York: Scribner, 1997.
_____. *White Noise.* New York: Viking Penguin, 1985.
_____. "The Art of Fiction CXXXV." By Adam Begley. *Paris Review* Fall 1993: 275–306.
_____. Interview. *Anything Can Happen* 79–91.
_____. "An Outsider in this Society: An Interview with Don DeLillo." By Anthony DeCurtis. *Introducing Don DeLillo* 43–66.
Derrida, Jacques. "Some Statements and Truisms about Neologisms, Newisms, Postisms, and Other Small Seismisms." *Modern Literary Theory: A Reader.*

3rd Ed. Eds. Philip Rice and Patricia Waugh. London: Arnold, 1996. 368–378.

Didion, Joan. *Play It as It Lays.* 1970. New York: Noonday, 1990.

Doctorow, E.L. *Ragtime.* 1974. New York: Fawcett, 1991.

Duvall, John N. "Baseball as Aesthetic Ideology: Cold War History, Race, and DeLillo's 'Pafko at the Wall.'" *Modern Fiction Studies* 41 (1995): 285–314.

Eco, Umberto. *The Role of the Reader: Explorations in the Semiotics of Texts.* Bloomington: Indiana UP, 1979.

Ehshtain, Jean Bethke. "Don't Be Cruel: Reflections on Rortyian Liberalism." *The Politics of Irony* 199–217.

Eliade, Mircea. *Myth and Reality.* 1968. New York: Harper, 1968.

Fagel, Brian. "Passages from the Middle: Coloniality and Postcoloniality in Charles Johnson's *Middle Passage.*" *African American Review* 30 (1996): 625–634.

Farrel, Frank B. *Subjectivity, Realism, and Postmodernism: The Recovery of the World.* Cambridge: Cambridge UP, 1994.

Faulkner, William. *Absalom, Absalom!* 1936. New York: Vintage, 1990.

Ferraro, Thomas, J. "Whole Families Shopping at Night." *New Essays on* White Noise 15–38.

Fiedler, Leslie. *Love and Death in the American Novel.* 1966. Normal: Dalkey, 1997.

Fish, Stanley. *Is There A Text In This Class? The Authority of Interpretive Communities.* Cambridge: Harvard UP, 1980.

Flores, Mark. Review: *The Book of Illusions.*" *USA Today* http://www.usatoday.com/life/books/reviews/2002–09–16-auster-lusions_x.htm.

Forster, E.M. . *Aspects of the Novel.* 1927. London: Arnold, 1963.

Foucault, Michel. *Discipline and Punish: The Birth of the Prison.* 1975. New York: Vintage, 1979.

Frazier, Charles. *Cold Mountain.* New York: Atlantic Monthly, 1997.

Fredman, Stephen. "How to Get Out of the Room that is the Book? Paul Auster and the Consequences of Confinement." *Postmodern Culture* May 1960.

Freud, Sigmund. *Group Psychology and the Analysis of the Ego.* 1921. Trans. James Strachey. New York: Norton, 1959.

Frye. Joanne S. *Living Stories, Telling Lives: Women and the Novel in Contemporary Experience.* Ann Arbor: U of Michigan P, 1986.

Gaddis, William. *A Frolic of His Own.* 1994. New York: Scribner, 1995.

_____. *JR.* 1971. New York: Penguin, 1993.

_____. *The Recognitions.* 1952. New York: Penguin, 1983.

Gardner, John. *On Moral Fiction.* New York: Basic, 1978.

Gardner, Ralph Jr. "Writing that Can Strengthen the Fraying Threads of Memory." *New York Times* 30 January 1997: C:1,8.

Garret, George. "'Once More into the Breach, Dear Friends, Once More:' The Publishing Scene and American Literary Art." *Review of Contemporary Literature* 8.3 (1988): 7–15.

Gass, William H. *Fiction and the Figures of Life.* New York: Knopf, 1970.

_____. "A Revised and Expanded Preface." *In the Heart of the Heart of the Country.* 1968. Boston: NonPareil, 1989.

Gates, Henry Louis. *The Signifying Monkey: A Theory of African-American Literary Criticism.* 1988. New York: Oxford UP, 1989.

_____. ed. *"Race," Writing, and Difference.* Chicago: U of Chicago P, 1986.

Gleason, William. "The Literature of Perception: Charles Johnson's *Oxherding Tale.*" *Black American Literature Forum* 25 (1991): 705–728.

Graff, Gerald. *Literature Against Itself: Literary Ideas in Modern Society.* Chicago: U of Chicago P, 1979.

Green, Jeremy. "Disaster Footage: Spectacles of Violence in DeLillo's Fiction." *Modern Fiction Studies* 45 (1999): 571–599.

Griffin, Bryan F. "Panic Among the Phillistines." *Harper's* August 1981: 37–53. "Part II." *Harper's* September 1981: 41–56.

Griffiths, Frederick T. "Sorcery is Dialectical: Plato and Jean Toomer in Charles Johnson's *The Sorcerer's Apprentice.*" *African American Review* 30 (1996): 527–538.

Haber, Honi Ferm. *Beyond Postmodern Politics: Lyotard, Rorty, Foucault.* New York: Routledge, 1994.

Hall, David L. *Richard Rorty: Prophet and Poet of the New Pragmatism.* Albany: State U of New York P, 1994.

Hantke, Steffen. *Conspiracy and Paranoia in Contemporary American Fiction: The Works of Don DeLillo and Joseph McElroy.* Frankfort Au Main: Lang, 1994.

Hartshorne, Charles. "Rorty's Pragmatism and Farewell to the Age of Faith and Enlightenment." *Rorty and Pragmatism* 16–28.

Hassan, Ihab. *Paracriticisms: Seven Speculations of the Times.* Urbana: U of Illinois P, 1975.

_____, *The Postmodern Turn: Essays in Postmodern Theory and Culture.* Ohio: Ohio State University, 1975.

Haugaard, Kay. "Suspending Moral Judgment: Students Who Refuse to Condemn the Unthinkable—a Result of Too Much Tolerance?" *Chronicle of Higher Education* 27 June, 1997: B5.

Hayles, N. Katherine. "Postmodern Parataxis: Embodied Text, Weightless Information." *American Literary History* 2 (1990) 394–422.

Hayward, Jennifer. "Something to Serve: Constructs of the Feminine in Charles Johnson's *Oxherding Tale.*" *Black American Literature Forum* 25 (1991): 689–704.

Heberle, Mark. *A Trauma Artist: Tim O'Brien and the Fiction of Vietnam.* Iowa City: U of Iowa, 2001.

Heller, Joseph. *Something Happened.* New York: Knopf, 1974.

Hemingway, Ernest. *In Our Time.* 1925. New York: Collier, 1986.

Hendin, Josephine. *Vulnerable People: A View of American Fiction Since 1945.* New York: Oxford UP, 1978.

Herr, Michael. *Dispatches.* 1977. New York: Vintage, 1991.

Herzog, Tobey. "*Going After Cacciato:* The Soldier-Author-Writer Seeking Control." *Critique* 24 (1983): 88–96.

Herzogenrath, Bernd. *An Art of Desire: Reading Paul Auster.* Amsterdam: Rudopi, 1999.

Hoffman, Eva. *Lost in Translation: A Life in a New Language.* 1989. New York: Penguin, 1990.

Hodgson, Godfrey. *America in Our Time: From WWII to Nixon, What Happened and Why.* 1976. New York: Vintage, 1978.

Howard, June. *Form and History in American Literary Naturalism.* Chapel Hill: U of North Carolina P, 1985.

Howe, Irving. *Politics and the Novel.* 1957. New York: Columbia UP, 1992.

Howells, William D. *A Hazard of New Fortunes.* 1890. New York: Signet, 1983.

_____. *Life in Letters of William Dean Howells.* Ed. Mildred Howells. New York: Doubleday, 1928.

Iser, Wolfgang. *The Act of Reading: A Theory of Aesthetic Response.* Baltimore: Johns Hopkins UP, 1978.

Jameson, Fredric. *The Political Unconscious: Narrative as a Socially Symbolic Act.* Ithaca: Cornell UP, 1981.

_____. *Postmodernism, or the Cultural Logic of Late Capitalism.* Durham: Duke UP, 1993.

Jauss, Hans Robert. *Toward an Aesthetic of Reception.* Trans. Timothy Bahti. 1982. Minneapolis: U of Minnesota P, 1989.

Johnson, Charles. *Being and Race: Black Writing Since 1970.* Bloomington: Indiana UP, 1988.

_____. *Dreamer.* New York: Scribner, 1998.

_____. *Faith and the Good Thing.* New York: Atheneum, 1974.

_____. *Middle Passage.* New York: Atheneum, 1990.

_____. *Oxherding Tale.* Bloomington: Indiana UP, 1982.

_____. "Philosophy and Black Fiction." *Obsidian* 6 (1980): 55–61.

_____. *The Sorcerer's Apprentice: Tales and Conjurations.* New York: Atheneum, 1986.

_____. *Soulcatcher and Other Stories.* San Diego: Harvest/Harcourt, 2001.

_____. Interview. By Jonathan Little. *Contemporary Literature* 34 (1993): 159–181.

_____. "Cyrus Colter Speaking with Charles Johnson and Reginald Gibbons on January 19, 1991." By Cyrus Colter. *Callaloo* 14 (1991): 887–897.

_____. "Interview with Charles Johnson." By Michael Boccia. *African American Review* 30 (1996): 611–618.

Johnson, Diane. *Terrorists and Novelists.* New York: Knopf, 1982.

Johnson, John. "Superlinear Fiction or Historical Diagram: Don DeLillo's *Libra.*" *Modern Fiction Studies* 40 (1994): 319–342.

Joyce, James. *Portrait of the Artist as a Young Man.* 1916. New York: Penguin, 1916.

Kaplan, Steven. *Understanding Tim O'Brien.* Columbia: U of South Carolina P, 1995.

Karl, Frederick R. *American Fictions 1940/1980: A Comprehensive History and Critical Evaluation.* New York: Harper, 1983.

Keesey, Douglas. *Don DeLillo.* New York: Twayne, 1993.

Kermode, Frank. *The Sense of an Ending: Studies in the Theory of Fiction.* London: Oxford UP, 1967.

Klinkowitz, Jerome. *Literary Disruptions: The Making of a Post-Contemporary American Fiction.* Urbana: U of Illinois P, 1975.

Kronich, Joseph. "*Libra* and the Assassination of JFK: A Textbook Operation." *Arizona Quarterly* 50 (1994): 109–132.

Kucich, John. "Postmodern Politics: Don DeLillo and the Plight of the White Male Writer." *Michigan Qurterly Review* 27 (1988): 328–341.

Kuehl, John. *Alternate Worlds: A Study of Postmodern Antirealistic American Fiction.* New York: New York UP, 1989.

Kundera, Milan. *The Art of the Novel.* New York: Grove, 1986.

Lavender, John. "The Novel of Critical Engagement: Paul Auster's 'City of Glass.'" *Contemporary Literature* 34 (1993): 219–239.

LeClair, Thomas. *The Art of Excess: Mastery in Contemporary American Fiction.* Urbana: U of Illinois P, 1983.

_____. *In the Loop: Don DeLillo and the Systems Novel.* Urbana: U of Illinois P, 1987.

_____. "An Underhistory of Mid-Century America." *Atlantic Monthly* October 1997: 116–118.

LeClair, Thomas and Larry McCaffery, eds. *Anything Can Happen: Interviews with Contemporary American Novelists.* Urbana: U of Illinois P, 1983.

Lemon, Lee. "John Barth and the Common Reader." *Review of Contemporary Fiction* 10.2 (1990): 42–49.

Lentrecchia, Frank, ed. *Introducing Don DeLillo.* Durham: Duke UP, 1991.

_____, *New Essays on* White Noise. Cambridge: Cambridge UP, 1991.

Levi, Primo. *Survival at Auschwitz.* Trans. Stuart Wolf. 1958. New York: Collier, 1960.

Little, Jonathan. "Charles Johnson's Revolutionary *Oxherding Tale.*" *Studies in American Fiction* 19 (1991): 141–152.

Lonnrot, Elias. *The Kaleva, or Poems of the Kaleva District.* Trans. Francis Peabody Magoun Jr. . 1963. Cambridge: Harvard UP, 1975.

Lyotard, Jean Francois. *The Postmodern Condition: A Report on Knowledge.* Trans. Geoff Bennington and Brian Massumi. Foreward by Frederic Jameson. Minneapolis, U of Minnesota P, 1984.

Mailer, Norman. *Advertisements for Myself.* New York: Putnam, 1959.

_____. *Armies of the Night: History as a Novel/ The Novel as History.* New York: NAL, 1968.

_____. *The Naked and the Dead.* 1948. New York: Holt, 1981.

_____. *Why Are We in Vietnam?* New York: Putnam's, 1967.

McCaffery, Larry. *The Metafictional Muse: The Works of Robert Coover, Donald Barthelme, and William H. Gass.* Pittsburgh: U of Pittsburgh P, 1982.

McClure, John. "Postmodern Romance: Don DeLillo in the Age of Conspiracy." *Introducing Don DeLillo* 99–116.

McHale, Brian. *Postmodernist Fiction.* New York and London: Methuen, 1987.

McInerney, Jay. *Bright Lights, Big City.* New York: Vintage, 1984.

McKay, Janet. *Narration and Discourse in American Realistic Fiction.* Philadelphia: U of Pennsylvania P, 1982.

McLuhan, Marshall. *Understanding Media: The Extensions of Man.* New York: McGraw, 1964.

McPherson, William. "Remaking Narrative." *Poetics Journal* September 1987: 140–150.

McWilliams, Dean. "Time in Tim O'Brien's *Going After Cacciato.*" *Critique* 29 (1988): 245–256.

Melville, Herman. *Moby Dick, or the White Whale.* 1851. New York: Signet, 1980.

_____. *Benito Cereno. Norton Anthology of American Literature.* Third Ed. Ed. Nina Baym, Ronald Gottesman, et al. New York: Norton, 1989. 2224–2278.

Michael, Magali Cornier. "The Political Paradox of Don DeLillo's *Libra.*" *Critique* 35 (1994): 146–156.

Miller, Henry. *Tropic of Cancer.* New York: Grove, 1961.

Miller, J. Hillis. Letter. "Today, Tomorrow: The Intellectual in the Academic Society." *PMLA* 12 (1997): 1138.

Moller, Mary Elkins. *Thoreau and the Human Community.* Amherst: U of Massachusetts P, 1980.

Moraru, Christian. "Consuming Narratives: Don DeLillo and the "Lethal" Reading. *Don DeLillo: Bloom's Modern Critical Views* 89–105.

Mott, Christopher. "*Libra* and the Subject of History." *Critique* 35 (1994): 131–145.

Muther, Elizabeth. "Isadora at Sea: Misogyny as Comic Capital in Charles Johnson's *Middle Passage.*" *African American Review* 30 (1996): 649–658.

Nabokov, Vladimir. *Speak, Memory.* 1942. New York: Vintage, 1966.

Nash, William R. *Charles Johnson's Fiction.* Urbana: U of Illinois P, 2003.

Nealon, Jeffrey T. "Work of the Detective, Work of the Writer: Paul Auster's 'City of Glass.'" *Modern Fiction Studies* (1996): 91–110.

Nelson, Marie. "Two Consciences: A Reading of Tim O'Brien's Vietnam Trilogy." *Third Force Psychology and the Study of Literature.* Ed. Bernard J. Paris. Rutherford: Farleigh Dickinson UP, 1990. 262–279.

Newman, Charles. *The Postmodern Aura: The Act of Fiction in an Age of Inflation.* Evanston: Northwestern UP, 1985.

Nietzsche, Friedrich. *On the Geneology of Morals and Ecce Homo.* Ed. Walter Kaufmann. Trans. Walter Kaufman and R.J. Hollingdale. New York: Vintage, 1966.

Norris, Frank. *The Octopus.* 1901. New York: Penguin, 1986.

Oates, Joyce Carol. *them.* Greenwich: Fawcett, 1969.

O'Brien, Tim. *Going After Cacciato.* New York: Delacorte, 1978.

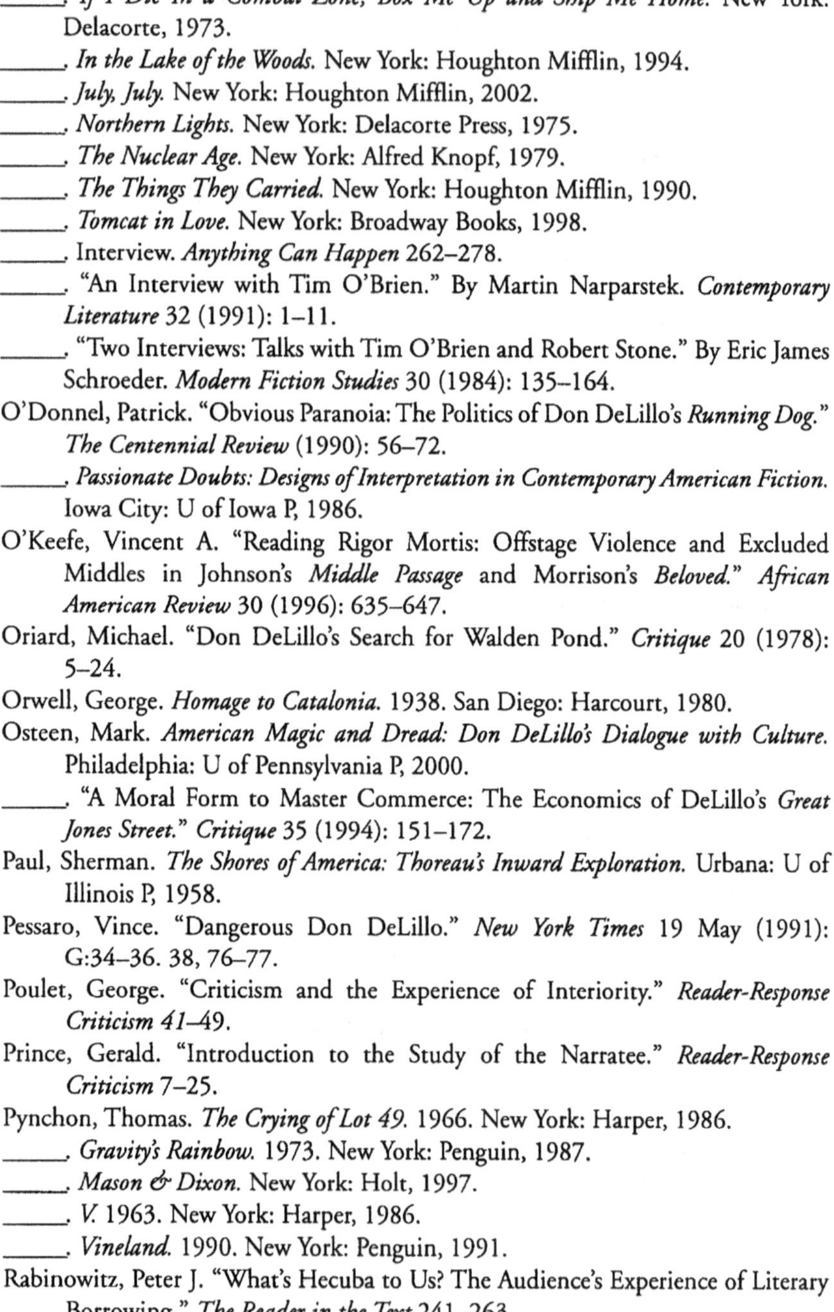

_____. *If I Die In a Combat Zone, Box Me Up and Ship Me Home.* New York: Delacorte, 1973.

_____. *In the Lake of the Woods.* New York: Houghton Mifflin, 1994.

_____. *July, July.* New York: Houghton Mifflin, 2002.

_____. *Northern Lights.* New York: Delacorte Press, 1975.

_____. *The Nuclear Age.* New York: Alfred Knopf, 1979.

_____. *The Things They Carried.* New York: Houghton Mifflin, 1990.

_____. *Tomcat in Love.* New York: Broadway Books, 1998.

_____. Interview. *Anything Can Happen* 262–278.

_____. "An Interview with Tim O'Brien." By Martin Narparstek. *Contemporary Literature* 32 (1991): 1–11.

_____. "Two Interviews: Talks with Tim O'Brien and Robert Stone." By Eric James Schroeder. *Modern Fiction Studies* 30 (1984): 135–164.

O'Donnel, Patrick. "Obvious Paranoia: The Politics of Don DeLillo's *Running Dog.*" *The Centennial Review* (1990): 56–72.

_____. *Passionate Doubts: Designs of Interpretation in Contemporary American Fiction.* Iowa City: U of Iowa P, 1986.

O'Keefe, Vincent A. "Reading Rigor Mortis: Offstage Violence and Excluded Middles in Johnson's *Middle Passage* and Morrison's *Beloved.*" *African American Review* 30 (1996): 635–647.

Oriard, Michael. "Don DeLillo's Search for Walden Pond." *Critique* 20 (1978): 5–24.

Orwell, George. *Homage to Catalonia.* 1938. San Diego: Harcourt, 1980.

Osteen, Mark. *American Magic and Dread: Don DeLillo's Dialogue with Culture.* Philadelphia: U of Pennsylvania P, 2000.

_____. "A Moral Form to Master Commerce: The Economics of DeLillo's *Great Jones Street.*" *Critique* 35 (1994): 151–172.

Paul, Sherman. *The Shores of America: Thoreau's Inward Exploration.* Urbana: U of Illinois P, 1958.

Pessaro, Vince. "Dangerous Don DeLillo." *New York Times* 19 May (1991): G:34–36. 38, 76–77.

Poulet, George. "Criticism and the Experience of Interiority." *Reader-Response Criticism* 41–49.

Prince, Gerald. "Introduction to the Study of the Narratee." *Reader-Response Criticism* 7–25.

Pynchon, Thomas. *The Crying of Lot 49.* 1966. New York: Harper, 1986.

_____. *Gravity's Rainbow.* 1973. New York: Penguin, 1987.

_____. *Mason & Dixon.* New York: Holt, 1997.

_____. *V.* 1963. New York: Harper, 1986.

_____. *Vineland.* 1990. New York: Penguin, 1991.

Rabinowitz, Peter J. "What's Hecuba to Us? The Audience's Experience of Literary Borrowing." *The Reader in the Text* 241–263.

Rafferty, Terrence. Rev. of *Vineland,* by Thomas Pynchon. *New Yorker* 19 February (1991): 108.

Raymond, Michael M. "Imagined Responses to Vietnam: Tim O'Brien's *Going After Cacciato.*" *Critique* 34 (1983): 97–104.

Reed, Ishmael. *Mumbo Jumbo.* New York: Atheneum, 1972.

Rorty, Richard. *Achieving Our Country: Leftist Thought in Twentieth Century America.* Cambridge: Harvard UP, 1997.

_____. *Contingency, Irony, and Solidarity.* Cambridge: Cambridge UP, 1993.

_____. "The Inspirational Value of Great Works of Literature." *Raritan* 16.1 (1996): 8–17.

_____. "Fighting Terrorism with Democracy," *The Nation,* October 3, 2002. http://www.thenation.com/doc.mhtml?i=20021021&s=rorty.

_____. *Philosophy and Social Hope.* New York: Penguin, 1999.

_____. "Robustness: A Reply to Jean Bethke Elshtain." *The Politics of Irony* 219–223.

_____. *Rorty and Pragmatism: A Philosopher Responds to His Critics.* Ed. Herman J. Saatkamp Jr. Nashville: Vanderbilt UP, 1995.

_____. "Tales of Two Disciplines." *Callaloo* 17 (1994): 575–585.

Roth, Henry. *Call It Sleep.* 1934. New York: Noonday, 1991.

Roth, Philip. *Operation Shylock: A Confession.* 1993. New York: Vintage, 1994.

_____. *Zuckerman Unbound.* New York: Farrar, 1981.

Rowen, Norma. "The Detective in Search of the Lost Tongue of Adam: Paul Auster's 'City of Glass.'" *Critique* (1991): 224–234.

Rushdy, Ashraf H.A. "The Phenomenology of the Almusseri: Charles Johnson and the Subject of the Narrative of Slavery." *African American Review* 26 (1992): 373–394.

_____. "The Prospects of Desire: Forms of Slave Identity in Charles Johnson's *Middle Passage.*" *Arizona Quarterly* 50 (1994): 73–108.

Russel, Allison. "Deconstructing *The New York Trilogy:* Paul Auster's Anti-Detective Fiction." *Critique* 31 (1990): 71–84.

Saltzman, Arthur. "The Betrayal of the Imagination: Paul Brodeur's *The Stunt Man* and Tim O'Brien's *Going after Cacciato.*" *Critique* 22 (1980): 32–38.

_____. *Designs of Darkness in Contemporary American Fiction.* Philadelphia: U of Pennsylvania P, 1990.

_____. "The Figure in the Static: *White Noise.*" *Modern Fiction Studies* 40 (1994): 805–826.

_____. "*Leviathan:* Post Hoc Harmonies." Barone 162–170.

Scanlan, Margaret. "The Writer among Terrorists: Don DeLillo's *Mao II* and the Rushdie Affair." *Modern Fiction Studies* 40 (1994): 229–252.

Scholes, Robert. *Fabulation and Metafiction.* Urbana: U of Illinois P, 1979.

Simmons, Ryan. "What is a Terrorist? Contemporary Authorship, the Unabomber, and DeLillo's *Mao II.*" *Modern Fiction Studies* 45 (1999): 675–695.

Slotkin, Richard. *Gunslinger Nation: The Myth of the Frontier in Twentieth Century America.* New York: Atheneum, 1992.

_____. *Regeneration through Violence: The Myth of the American Frontier 1600–1860.* Middleton: Wesleyan UP, 1973.

Smith, Lorrie N. "'The Things Men Do:' The Gendered Subject in Tim O'Brien's *Esquire* Stories." *Critique* 36 (1994): 16–40.

Springer, Carsten. *Crises: The Works of Paul Auster.* Frankfurt am Main: Peter Lang, 2000.

Sontag, Susan. *Against Interpretation.* 1961. New York: Dell, 1966.

Sorrentino, Gilbert. *Mulligan Stew.* New York: Grove Press, 1979.

Steinbeck, John. *East of Eden.* 1952. New York: Penguin, 1986.

Stevick, Philip. *Alternative Pleasures: Postrealist Fiction and the Tradition.* Urbana: U of Illinois P, 1980.

Storhoff, Gary. "The Artist as Universal Mind: Berkeley's Influence on Charles Johnson." *African American Review* 30 (1996): 539–548.

Streitfeld, David. "Don DeLillo's Gloomy Muse: The PEN/Faulkner Winner and His Novels of Conspiracy." *Washington Post* 14 May 1997: C:1,4.

Suleiman, Susan and Inge Crossman, eds. *The Reader in the Text: Essays on Audience and Interpretation.* New Jersey: Princeton UP, 1980.

Tabbi, Joseph. *Postmodern Sublime: Technology and American Writing from Mailer to Cyberpunk.* Ithaca: Cornell UP, 1985.

Tanner, Tony. "Afterthoughts on Don DeLillo's *Underworld.*" *Don DeLillo: Bloom's Modern Critical Views* 129–148.

_____. *City of Words: American Fiction 1950–1970.* New York: Harper, 1971.

Temes, Peter S. "Review: *The Book of Illusions.*" *San Francisco Chronicle,* September 8, 2002. http://www.sfgate.com/cgi-bin/article.cgi?f=/chronicle/archive/2002/09/08/RV72609.DTL

Thomas, Brook. *American Literary Realism and the Failed Promise of Contract.* Berkeley: U of California P, 1997.

Thoreau, Henry David. *Walden, or Life in the Woods. Norton Anthology of American Literature.* Third Ed. Ed. Nina Baym, et al. New York: Norton, 1989. 1635–1807.

Todorov, Tzevetan. "Reading as Construction." *The Reader in the Text* 67–82.

Tompkins, Jane P. *Sensational Designs: The Cultural Work of American Fiction 1770–1860.* New York: Oxford UP, 1985.

_____, ed. *Reader-Response Criticism: From Formalism to Post-Structuralism.* Baltimore: Johns Hopkins UP, 1980.

Trilling, Lionel. *Beyond Culture: Essays on Literature and Learning.* New York: Vintage, 1965.

Updike, John. "Layers of Ambiguity." *New Yorker* 27 March 1978: 127–33.

_____. "One-Way Street." *The New Yorker,* March 21, 2003. http://www.newyorker.com/critics/books/?030331crbo_books1

_____. *Rabbit Redux.* 1971. New York: Fawcett, 1991.

_____, *Rabbit, Run.* 1960. New York: Fawcett, 1991.

Venatta, Dennis. "Theme and Structure in Tim O'Brien's *Going after Cacciato.*" *Modern Fiction Studies* 28 (1992): 242–246.

Warren, Robert Penn. *All the King's Men.* 1946. San Diego: Harcourt, 1982.

Washburn, Katherine. "A Book at the End of the World: Paul Auster's *In the Country of Lost Things.*" *Review of Contemporary Fiction* 14 (1994): 62–65.

Watt, Ian. *The Rise of the Novel: Studies in Defoe, Richardson, and Fielding.* 1957. Berkeley: U of California P, 1974.

Weisenburger, Steven. *A* Gravity's Rainbow *Companion.* Athens: U of Georgia P, 1988.

Werner, Craig Hanson. *Paradoxical Resolutions: American Fiction Since James Joyce.* Urbana: U of Illinois P, 1982.

Wilde, Alan. *Middle Grounds: Studies in Contemorary American Fiction.* Philadelphia: U of Pennsylvania P, 1987.

Wilcox, Leonard. "Baudrillard, DeLillo's *White Noise,* and the End of the Heroic Narrative." *Contemporary Literature* 32 (1991): 346–366.

Wilson, Edmund. *The Shores of Light: A Literary Chronicle of the Twenties and Thirties.* 1952. New York: Vintage, 1961.

Wolfe, Tom. *The Bonfire of the Vanities.* 1987. New York: Bantam, 1988.

_____. "Stalking the Million-Footed Beast: A Literary Manifesto for the New Social Novel." *Harper's* November 1989: 45–56.

_____. "The Worship of Art: Notes on the New God." *Harper's* October 1984: 61–66.

Woods, Tim. "Looking for Signs in the Air: Urban Space and the Postmodern in *In the Country of Last Things.*" *Beyond the Red Notebook* 107–128.

_____. "*The Music of Chance:* Aleatorical (Dis)harmonies within 'The City of the World.' " *Beyond the Red Notebook* 143–161.

Wright, Richard. *Black Boy.* 1944. New York: Harper, 1993.

Wynne-Davies, Marion, ed. *The Bloomsbury Guide to English Literature.* New York: Prentice, 1990.

Zins, Daniel L. "Imagining the Rain: The Fiction of Tim O'Brien." *Hollins Critic* 23 (1986): 1–12.

Index

K

L

M

R

S

W

X

Z

For Product Safety Concerns and Information please contact our EU representative GPSR@taylorandfrancis.com
Taylor & Francis Verlag GmbH, Kaufingerstraße 24, 80331 München, Germany

www.ingramcontent.com/pod-product-compliance
Lightning Source LLC
Chambersburg PA
CBHW071512110726
47908CB00003B/808

* 9 7 8 0 4 1 5 8 0 3 4 4 1 *